The Green of the Spring

The Green of the Spring

Jane Gurney

BANTAM BOOKS

TORONTO · NEW YORK · LONDON · SYDNEY · AUCKLAND

THE GREEN OF THE SPRING

A BANTAM BOOK   0 553 40407 5

Originally published in Great Britain by Bantam Press,
a division of Transworld Publishers Ltd

PRINTING HISTORY
Bantam Press edition published 1992
Bantam edition published 1992

This book is set in 10/11¼pt Times by
Kestrel Data, Exeter

Bantam Books are published by Transworld Publishers Ltd,
61-63 Uxbridge Road, Ealing, London W5 5SA, in Australia by
Transworld Publishers (Australia) Pty. Ltd, 15-23 Helles Avenue,
Moorebank, NSW 2170, and in New Zealand by Transworld Publishers
(NZ) Ltd, 3 William Pickering Drive, Albany, Auckland.

Printed and bound in Great Britain by
Cox & Wyman Ltd, Reading, Berks.

Acknowledgements

Grateful thanks to the patient and helpful staff at:

The Imperial War Museum
The Imperial War Museum Sound archives,
   Photographic archives, Film archives
The British Newspaper Library, Colindale
Greenwich Local History Library
Greenwich Borough Museum
Stratford Local History Library
Guildford Local History Library
Guildford Institute Library
Farnborough Library
Farnham Library
Aldershot Library
The Prince Consort Library, Aldershot
Le Musée de la Guerre, La ʾargette, Neuville St Vaast
Le Musée de la Guerre, Ypres
Sanctuary Wood Trench Museum, Ypres
Clandon Park (National Trust)
The Royal Air Force Museum, Hendon
The Royal Artillery Museum, Woolwich

and especially to Vic Waller at the Aldershot Military
Museum, for being so encouraging and tolerant of my military
ignorance, and to Sandy Polak for driving me round the
battlefields and for crying when he read the manuscript!

1

'Mr Ferry, do *you* think there's going to be a war?'

Ferry twitched. He should have been ironing *The Times* to get the worst of the printer's ink off the pages before laying it, crisply folded, beside his employer's plate at the breakfast table. Instead, he had been caught poring over the editorial on page three.

'Lord, Daisy.' He glowered irritably at the girl in a housemaid's neat uniform who was hovering in the doorway of his pantry. 'You made me jump, creeping around like that. How would I know if there's going to be a war? The government doesn't confide in me. Haven't you anything better to do at this time of the morning than ask me stupid questions?'

'Sorry, Mr Ferry.' The housemaid's tone was meek, but she stood her ground. As butler to the Brownlowe family, Ferry was supposed to rule the servants' hall with a rod of iron, but Daisy knew from past experience that he barked in a vain attempt to disguise an innate reluctance to bite. Ferry spent sleepless nights agonizing over his responsibility to impose discipline, though on the whole Maple Grange ran very well despite the lack of it.

'I just thought . . . as you'd got the paper there. . . . Mother's been a bit worried, you see, because my brother's an army reservist,' Daisy wheedled.

'*And* her young man,' Cook said, appearing behind her in the doorway.

'He's not exactly my young man, Mrs Driver.' Too late, Daisy wished she had been more reticent when Joan, the senior housemaid, had quizzed her about her 'follower'. Clearly Joan, though sworn to secrecy, had not kept those shyly-confessed confidences to herself.

'Oh, go on with you. *We've* seen him hanging about in the lane waiting for you, on your days off,' Mrs Driver said. 'And if he's not your young man, what about that kiss he gave you last Saturday night?'

Daisy could feel the heat spreading across the fair, freckled skin of her cheeks. It was one of the trials of her life that she blushed so easily and that blushing clashed so horribly with the bright copper-red of her hair. She wondered fleetingly how she could get even with perfidious Joan.

'So what does it say in the paper, Mr Ferry?' Cook craned forward, and the housemaid moved aside to let her by. There wasn't room for two in the doorway, especially when one of them had the comfortable bulk of Mrs Driver.

'Well. . . .' The butler smoothed his hand absent-mindedly over the sparse grey strands of hair arranged to hide his bald patch as he scanned the printed columns. 'Let's see . . . yesterday's Bank Holiday is extended to Wednesday on account of the gravity of the situation. . . . The naval reservists have been asked to make their way to their depots and the mobilization of the army is in hand. That socialist fellow Mr Keir Hardie's made an anti-war speech in the House of Commons. He says if we join in, we'll ask ourselves one day why he did it. Seems to think we should let old Kaiser Wilhelm carry on however he likes on the Continent and turn a blind eye. An attitude like that's a disgrace to the nation, if you ask me. Oh, and it says here that there's likely to be more problems on the railways today. Possible cancellations of some excursion services because of the unpredictability of national events. "Travellers cannot be assured that they will reach their destinations", it says. That'll be a disappointment for Miss Laura and Mr Oliver, if they have to cancel their outing.'

'Miss Laura. Oh!' Daisy's hand covered her mouth, momentarily. 'I was supposed to take her hot water in at twenty past seven.'

'Well, you're late,' said Ferry. As if to underline his words, the carriage clock on the drawing room mantelpiece could be

8

heard distantly chiming the two bells of the half hour. 'Scatterbrained, that's what you are. I swear you'd forget your head if it wasn't screwed on,' the butler scolded, but it was difficult to be angry with Daisy. He'd tried often enough to nag her into efficiency. She'd stand there chewing her lower lip, eyes downcast, the very picture of dejection, but underneath it all he knew that her spirit was as cheeky and resilient as a sparrow's.

'Well, get on with you, girl,' he said, severely.

Daisy dodged around the stout figure of Mrs Driver and fled down the flagstone passage. In the scullery, she filled a brass water-can from the hot tap at the sink and lugged it towards the back stairs, stiff-armed to keep the heat of it clear of her legs.

She had already climbed the stairs twice in the last half hour with tea trays for the two ladies of the house, Miss Laura and Miss Jessie, and she'd promised to come back with Miss Laura's hot water earlier than usual because the young mistress wanted extra time to get dressed ready for her expedition today. Instead, because Daisy had forgotten, she would have to hurry to be in time for breakfast.

But it was bad news about the war. . . . The house-maid's brow creased as she toiled up the steep flight of steps. Just two weeks ago, everyone around Guildford had been more concerned with the hot weather and the harvest and the Primrose League's Bank Holiday Fête arrangements. If there were any clouds on the horizon, they had stemmed from the troublesome Irish situation. Now, suddenly the German army was sitting threateningly on the borders of Belgium and practically the whole of Europe was up in arms.

Not that Daisy understood what it was all about. Just trying to follow the discussions on the subject which Mr Ferry and Mrs Driver conducted over their late-evening cocoa was apt to give her a headache. But she gathered that everyone was sick of the way the Germans and the Austrians were throwing their weight about and the Government had made a promise to stick up for the Belgians, so it looked increasingly as though Great Britain might be sucked into the war as well.

Daisy had been five years old, back in 1899 when the last war was declared. Then it had been far away in South Africa, and one of her uncles had marched away in a stiff khaki uniform and never come back. He'd been a big man, smiling and lively, apparently indestructible until a Boer rifleman had proved otherwise. Her mother and her grandmother had cried for days after the telegram came. Even now she could still feel the ache of fear and bewilderment that the sight of her mother's grief had aroused. It had been Daisy's first experience of bereavement, for she had no recollection of the father who had died of meningitis while she was still in her pram.

'I've lost a husband and a brother, must I lose my only son as well?' Mrs Colindale had protested bitterly, seven years later, when Daisy's brother Robert announced his intention of enlisting with the Queen's Royal West Surrey Regiment. But Robert had stuck to his decision, despite her resistance.

'I don't fancy being a farm labourer,' he'd said, stubbornly. 'Or an apprentice to some tradesman, not just yet, anyway. I want to see the world a bit first.'

When Daisy saw him parading, peacock-proud in his uniform, she'd understood his choice, though her mother had been convinced that Robert would come to a sticky end in some hot and humid outpost of the Empire. But Private Colindale had emerged cheerfully unscathed from his soldiering experiences in India and Aden, and finding that seven years in the army had quenched his wanderlust, he had recently married and settled down to a good job assembling motor vans at the big Dennis works in Guildford. The fact that as an ex-soldier he was still on the army's reserve list, liable to be called up immediately to meet any national crisis, had seemed unimportant at the time.

But last weekend, on Daisy's day off, her mother had brought out the photographs of Robert in his old uniform and they had talked about the possibility of a new war. Mrs Colindale hadn't cried, but the strain had been there in her face . . . and watching her, Daisy, who was trying to make up her mind whether or not she might be in love with Robert's workmate and fellow-reservist, Arthur Bright, had felt a cold shiver of foreboding.

She had reached the thick brown carpet of the landing now. Outside the green bedroom, she drew a deep breath to dispel her nervousness before knocking at the panelled door. Not that she expected to be met with anger, Miss Laura was too much of a lady to lose her temper with a servant, but that was precisely why Daisy felt bad about letting her down over the late arrival of the hot water.

The early morning tea was cold in its pot and the thinly cut bread and butter on the delicate china plate was untouched when Daisy came into the room. Laura Brownlowe was sitting on the low east windowsill that looked out over the stable yard, watching Griffin bring out the horses. Daisy heaved an inner sigh of relief. Judging by her mistress's dreamy expression, she hadn't even noticed the time.

From where Daisy was standing, the view through the open window was obscured by the thin muslin net and the looped-back floral brocade of the curtains, but she could hear the scrape of iron-shod hooves in the cobbled yard, and Griffin's quiet voice talking to the animals.

Everyone said Griffin was good with the horses, even Nichols, the dour head groom, who wasn't normally given to praising anybody. When Daisy had time, which wasn't often, she would sometimes pause between duties to watch Griffin at work – though taking care that he wouldn't see her doing so, in case he should misunderstand her interest. It was satisfying to observe the skill with which he buffed the smooth coats of the hunters to a more perfect sheen, hissing under his breath to keep the dust out of his lungs, or tacked up the carriage horses ready for a drive, his fingers flying expertly over the supple leather and shining buckles of the harness. The rumour ran in the servants' hall that other establishments

11

in the area had tried to poach Griffin, but he said he liked his place at Maple Grange too much to shift.

Sometimes Daisy got the impression that she was one of the reasons for his preference. She hoped that wasn't true, flattering though it might be, because she was walking out with Arthur and she didn't want any complications. Anyway, Griffin was strange. In ways that it was difficult to put your finger on, he held himself aloof from his fellow-servants and though he didn't say much, there were times when his crooked smile seemed to be at odds with what he did say, as if he were secretly mocking his listener.

But now was no time to be thinking about Griffin, or even about Arthur Bright, though the memory of the way he'd kissed her in the lane the other night would keep surfacing in her mind. Daisy deposited her burden safely inside the china basin on the washstand, then came to stand by her mistress at the window.

'Going to be cooler today, Miss Laura, by the look of it.'

Behind the gables of the stable block, the sky was dappled over with streaks of cumulus cloud. Unusually, after the heatwave conditions of July, there was a breeze spinning the cockerel weather-vane mounted on the chimney behind the tallest gable. Laura Brownlowe rose from the windowsill, stretching her arms above her head so that the wide sleeves of her silk dressing gown slipped back from her wrists, baring the pale skin of her arms to the elbows.

'Yes . . . just my luck,' she agreed, ruefully. 'We've all been complaining about the hot weather for so long and now it's going to turn on me, just because I've an outing planned. I only hope it won't rain.'

'It's Oxford you're going to, isn't it, Miss? Cook was packing the hamper earlier.'

'That's right. Mr Oliver's going to show me his college, where he and Mr Allingham will be studying in October. And Mr Allingham's brother is coming along as well, because he was at Oxford too, a few years ago. Don't go for a moment, Daisy, I'd like your advice.'

12

Laura crossed the room and extracted two dresses from behind the panelled double doors of the wardrobe. She held first one, then the other against her slim figure.

'If you were going for a day on the river and you wanted to look your very best, which would you wear?'

Daisy considered the question seriously, her head to one side. Either of the dresses was pretty beyond anything she could ever hope to afford. One was in fine blue-and-white striped cotton, the high neck and deep cuffs trimmed with broderie anglaise. The other was more elaborate, of white muslin overlaid with lace and embroidered silk net, with tiny pearl buttons all down the front of the bodice. It had probably cost the equivalent of at least a year's wages for an under-housemaid, but she felt no jealousy. Rich girls like Miss Laura wore lace by the yard. For someone like Daisy the collar of Honiton that Arthur had given her for her birthday last month was something to be worked and saved for. That was the way of the world.

'Well, Miss Laura . . . the white lace is the prettiest and I'd say it suits you the best, but I'd be afraid of spoiling it in a boat. And there'll be the train first, won't there, with smuts and things? The striped one is more suitable, I suppose.'

'Thank you, Daisy. I expect you're right.'

But as she was leaving the room, Daisy saw out of the corner of her eye that it was the striped cotton dress which was being replaced in the wardrobe. Well, what of it? There was no reason why her opinion should be taken seriously. It was more surprising, these days, that it had been asked for in the first place.

There had been a time when Daisy was on easier terms with her young mistress. She had come to Maple Grange as a shy fifteen-year-old, nervous about her dizzying promotion from maid-of-all-work in a small house to under-housemaid in a large one. She had been all thumbs, petrified of making mistakes that would send her plummeting back to her old, lowly status, and the daughter of the house had been kind; probably, Daisy recognized, because she herself was lonely.

13

In the intervening years, however, the young girl had come out of the schoolroom and had been sent to Paris to be 'finished'. The polishing effect of Paris on Miss Laura had been very noticeable indeed and now Daisy was too much in awe of her to try to recapture the familiarity of their old exchanges.

Halfway down the narrow back staircase leading to the servants' quarters, there was a bend in the stair and a small landing with an uncurtained window which, like the one in the green bedroom, overlooked the stable yard. Daisy hovered by the window for a moment. Griffin was currying the muscled shoulder of Blackie, the elderly cob who pulled the governess cart which was still the main mode of transport for the younger Brownlowes. The groom glanced upwards as he worked and his dark eyes seemed to be looking directly at Daisy, though he didn't smile. Confused, she hastily stepped back and continued on her way downstairs. It seemed that encounters with Griffin, however distant, always had an uncomfortable effect.

'A dress is easily come by and easily replaced,' Laura thought, tucking the blue-and-white cotton dress back among the clothes hanging in her wardrobe, 'but a whole, precious day in the company of Edward Allingham . . . now *that* is an opportunity to be seized with both hands and every advantage that you can muster!'

It was almost a year, she calculated, since she had last seen Edward. She had changed. Finishing school in Paris, where she had painstakingly transformed her atrocious schoolgirl-French into a fluent grasp of the language, had produced other more gratifying improvements. The childish plumpness had been honed away from her figure, the clumsiness of long legs and sharp elbows brought under control. The young woman who had stepped off the ferry at Folkestone a week ago was as poised, graceful and ornamental a companion as any man could wish for.

She had learned how to dress and how to smile in a way

14

that combined allure with aloofness, even how to modulate her eager, impetuous speech. Nowadays her voice was low and husky, 'so that a gentleman has to lean forward to hear you', as Miss Sharp, the elocution tutor, had reminded her over and over again until it became a matter of habit. And – most painful lesson of all – she had become a 'good listener'. It was a pity that in moments of stress or high excitement the old, opinionated, scatty Laura still burst through the veneer of charming Miss Brownlowe. But that isn't going to happen today, she resolved. Not in front of Edward, for whose sake she had undertaken the whole transformation.

Six years of loving him . . . she could remember every detail of their first meeting: that summer speech day at her twin brother Oliver's school. The gravelled drive in front of the old grey building had been crammed with the carriages of visiting families; sunlight glinted on the slate cladding of the turrets and the glass in the mullioned windows. Twelve-year-old Oliver and his friend James were fooling around over a picnic tea on the edge of the cricket field. Out in the centre, a donkey patiently pulled the roller to and fro, its small hooves cased in leather boots to protect the lovingly maintained surface on which, after lunch, the boys were threatening to thrash the masters' Eleven. The sweet scent of crushed grass drifted towards the visitors as they sat on rugs, eating cucumber sandwiches and strawberry tartlets in fragile pastry cases.

Rupert Brownlowe, Laura's father, was some distance away, chatting with an old friend remembered from his own long-ago days at the school. Freed from Pa's sobering influence, Oliver, who was no respecter of his sister's feminine dignity, had got hold of her straw hat and he and James tossed it tantalizingly over her head while she made ineffectual snatches. Aunt Jessie, languid from the heat, was protesting faintly about the disturbance and the threat to the champagne glasses caused by the boys' boisterous activities. A shadow fell across the blanket and a brown hand scooped the hat up in mid-parabola and restored it to its owner.

Laura looked up, blinking into the bright sun. A tall young man towered over her. As she became accustomed to the glare, she saw lean, strong features, eyes that were almost black under arched eyebrows and hair with the blue-black glint of a raven's wing. Her heart seemed to lurch down into the area under the curve of her ribs and then bounce back, thudding. She became agonizingly aware of the cream and pastry crumbs on her chin.

'My brother Edward,' said James, casually. James, mousy-haired, skinny and resoundingly ordinary, was hard to equate with this godlike being in a cricket blazer. 'He's won all the prizes. Isn't it sickening?'

Later, seated on the scarred wooden chairs in the Great Hall, Laura had watched Edward climb the steps to the dais time after time – to accept the Form Prize, the Horace Prize, the Essay Prize, the Best Innings of the Season Prize. . . .

'Your brother's a very talented young man,' Rupert Brownlowe said to James. 'What will he do next?'

'Oh, Balliol this autumn and after Oxford he'll join my father's law firm, I suppose.'

Edward Allingham had been eighteen that year. Apart from the casual gesture that had retrieved her hat, he had seemed distant and unattainable, but Laura had worshipped him. Then and ever since. It was an emotion that gave a focus to sensations which had been vaguely stirring inside her for some months. At twelve she was newly aware of boys, not just as noisy or ridiculous pests of the brotherly kind but as males, and for the first time she was confronted with one who might even be worthy of the mastery over women which Edwardian society accorded him. Sometimes, indulging in furtive day-dreams about the object of her adoration, she imagined him standing close to her, his lean face intense with passion, asking her . . . no, *demanding* that she should be his. Whatever that meant.

She gleaned news of his successes at Oxford from his brother on holiday visits to the Brownlowes' house near Guildford. At intervals she held her breath and lived with mentally crossed fingers over reports of romances, which blessedly fizzled out. The opportunities for meetings were rare, but occasionally Edward transported James over to Guildford from their home at Hindhead. Impressively, he had acquired a motor: a sleek navy-blue Riley Tourer with shining brass accessories and plumply upholstered black leather seats.

'He bought it second-hand,' James reported, 'from a friend of Father's who decided to try this motoring lark and then got browned off at the way it kept breaking down and getting punctures by the roadside. Don't let that nonchalant air of my brother's fool you, he's as pleased as Punch with it. You should see him giving little lectures to the local schoolboys about the way it works.'

I wish he would do the same for me, Laura thought wistfully. Her father had lately invested in a family car, a Rover Landaulette, but Aldridge, the chauffeur, was the only one who understood the mysteries of its functioning, and he was not disposed to share his knowledge with Laura. He had been known to let Oliver polish the lamps and even look under the bonnet occasionally, but it seemed that girls were not supposed to be mechanically minded.

Edward could at least have offered her a ride in his motor. But he didn't. Each eagerly anticipated encounter left Laura depressed for weeks, because her hero obviously still saw her as a child, regardless of the embarrassing new curves of her figure, the pinned-up hair and the long skirts that proclaimed her womanly status. He had even, shamingly, called her by Oliver's nickname for her. Brat.

Not any more. Last autumn, collecting James and his battered brown leather schoolboy luggage at the end of a half-term visit, Edward had unexpectedly been invited to stay for some hunting.

'Why not come over for a few days in November and try out one of my novices?' Rupert Brownlowe had suggested over lunch.

'Well, sir, that's a very tempting idea. . . .'

Rupert bred hunters that regularly won prizes at the county

show and the offer of one of his mounts was a flattering gesture, so Edward had taken leave from his father's London law firm and, to Laura's delight, had become part of the household for a whole glorious week – proving himself to be a fearless, efficient rider who outstripped his host's expectations of his performance.

Laura was secretly sympathetic to foxes. Although she enjoyed the breathless, breakneck dash of the chase, she hated the outcome and usually found a way to be absent from the kill. But for Edward's sake, during that week she had put her mare at every fence, plunged through every stream, and after one particularly hectic pursuit had been 'blooded' by the Master of Foxhounds. The smell of blood as he stroked the hacked-off brush across her cheek had almost made her sick, but it had been worth it for the look of admiration in Edward's eyes.

'Well done, Miss Brownlowe,' he'd said, as they turned for home. His use of her surname had brought a surge of hope. 'Brat' was growing up – and at last he knew it.

But he had departed without any further demonstration that he appreciated her new maturity, and Laura, having absorbed all that the limited curriculum of the local academy for young ladies could offer, was to be sent abroad to finishing school. Leaving for Paris had been agony, but she'd schemed and rehearsed for the day when she would see him again, determined that when it came, she would be equipped to make his admiration permanent.

Today. . . . She revolved slowly in front of the cheval mirror beside the washstand, examining herself critically from every angle. The mahogany frame of the mirror enclosed the reflection of a bright-eyed girl with a clear, healthy complexion under the thickly piled and pinned crown of golden-brown hair. The pearl-buttoned collar of her muslin dress ended in a ruffle of lace just under the throat. The top and its hobble skirt were expensively overlaid with a fine Brussels lace jacket, open-fronted, with sleeves that were cropped at the elbow, beneath which the full muslin sleeves of the dress

18

were gathered into deep tucked-and-ruffled cuffs at the wrist. The only colour came from the blue satin sash, the silk knitted purse on its silver frame and the echoing blue-and-silver of the enamelled watch pinned to the front of the jacket. Laura had chosen her accessories with care in Paris, and knew that the blue was no more intense than that of her eyes.

Edward *had* to love her. He must.

As Laura descended the stairs with the care that her fashionable hobble skirt demanded, the gong in the hall could be heard, announcing breakfast. The sound of it vied with the eight clear chimes of the long case clock. At Maple Grange the gong, struck with absolute punctuality by Mr Ferry, always coincided with the clock. Eight o'clock: breakfast; one o'clock: lunch; eight o'clock: supper. It was a routine that Laura had absorbed in her earliest days, even before she and Oliver were old enough to join the adults in the large, shadowy dining room, and instead had peered between the turned oak rails of the bannisters to spy on their parents and guests filing down the hall towards countless formal dinner parties.

Then, the reflection of many candles in the long gilt mirrors and the glowing mahogany surface of the dining table, the flowers, the silver and the delicate china, had seemed to be the symbols of a mysterious adult ritual that contrasted excitingly with the comfortable oilcloth-and-rice-pudding ambience of the nursery. It had been the summit of Laura's ambitions to glide downstairs and parade into the dining room behind her elegant mother, Sylvia Brownlowe, whose French scent, couture clothes and the creamy double rope of pearls which were her favourite jewels, had seemed to her daughter to epitomize sartorial perfection.

Nowadays Laura took the splendours of the dining room for granted and since her return from Paris she had been entitled to wear the rope of pearls, but her dream of adult status had lost something in coming true. There were few formal supper parties on the grand scale now at Maple Grange, because the lovely mother whose portrait smiled down from the chimney breast in the drawing room had died in the year

19

before Laura met Edward. It still hurt, illogically, that Sylvia – a distant, adored figure – had slipped away from her daughter at just the stage when they might have had something to say to one another.

In the wake of the funeral, Rupert Brownlowe's younger unmarried sister Jessica had arrived to supervise the household. Typically, Aunt Jessie was not among the Brownlowes assembled in the dining room when Laura arrived. She preferred to take breakfast in her room, postponing the trials of the day. Rupert, however, was already installed at the table. He never waited for the gong, but had his letters and his newspaper brought to him ten minutes early. Now he was frowning over *The Times*.

'Good morning, Pa.'

Her father looked tired and worried. Some business problem would have kept him awake as usual, Laura thought, and as she passed his chair she leaned over to give him a quick, affectionate kiss on his clean-shaven cheek. As she had expected, the gesture embarrassed him as much as it pleased him and he pretended to ignore it, creasing the edge of the newspaper between his forefinger and thumb.

'You're looking very grand today, Brat. But aren't you afraid of falling out of a punt in that dashing outfit?'

Trust Oliver to try to puncture his sister's confidence with the use of the old nickname. Laura, in her turn, ignored him, turning her attention to the row of covered dishes ranged on a heated tray on the sideboard. As she did so she noted from beneath her lowered eyelashes that James Allingham, at any rate, was not immune to the impact of her appearance. He had just dropped his fork.

She had found James and Oliver, released from their final term at school, already installed at Maple Grange on her return from Paris. Since then, James had been blushing and stammering in her presence. It was a rather satisfying affirmation of her newfound power. She hoped his brother would be similarly impressed, though it was difficult to imagine the stylish and athletic Edward disconcerted by anything.

'I suggest it might be wise to cancel your outing, Oliver.'

Rupert Brownlowe registered, in passing, the effect of his words on his daughter. Laura, who for some reason was dressed up today like a dog's dinner, in a garment more suitable for a garden party at Buckingham Palace than a railway journey, was sitting with a forkful of kedgeree arrested in mid-air and her mouth unbecomingly open. Had she learned nothing at that overpriced establishment in Paris?

'Pa, that would be rather difficult!' Oliver protested. 'It's been arranged for ages.'

'It's hardly vital, though, that you should show your sister the college and the town today. Surely any other day before the Michaelmas term begins in October would be equally suitable?'

'But sir, Edward Allingham's supposed to be meeting us in Oxford. He's the one that knows his way about. And today's one of the few days he's free.'

'If he can get there from London.' Rupert tapped his newspaper with his forefinger. 'Yesterday there were considerable problems on the railways – excursion trains cancelled, crowds of Bank Holiday travellers stranded.'

'We haven't bought excursion tickets, though. They won't refuse to honour regular tickets, surely? And now that the Bank Holiday's over—' said Oliver.

'It isn't.' It was probably unfair of Rupert to be irritated by his children's ignorance of national events, in view of the fact that he hogged the newspapers for most of the day. 'It has been extended to Wednesday because of the crisis in Europe. So I really don't think that a pleasure trip to Oxford warrants the attention—'

'Excuse me, sir, but what exactly *is* the current situation in Europe? I missed seeing yesterday's paper.'

Someone, Rupert thought with annoyance, should have taught young James Allingham not to interrupt his elders. 'The Germans are poised to march through Belgium,' he said irritably. 'France has mobilized her troops. The mobilization of our own army is in hand and the navy has already been alerted to guard the Channel ports against the threat of an attack by the German navy, should we become embroiled in this war.'

'But surely we aren't seriously going to war?' Oliver said, his eyes fixed on his father's face. 'I know that archduke fellow got shot in Sarajevo back in June, we heard about it at school. And then our German teacher went home in a hurry. But I don't see what an Austrian archduke has got to do with us?'

'I agree that the events which triggered the current confrontation may seem remote,' Rupert replied heavily. 'But England has made certain international undertakings and I am afraid that if we are to honour our promises, our involvement is probably unavoidable.'

Oh, the war! the whole subject bored Laura indescribably. There had been a swelling tide of concern and speculation during her last weeks in Paris, with very little concrete information to base it on, about how the Germans, the Austrians, the French and the Russians were about to become embroiled in some monumental armed squabble over a tinpot little country called Serbia. At school, there had been heated arguments in the dormitory between the English and French pupils and the German and Austrian girls. She had mostly tried to ignore them. It would have been too bad if that distant, unregarded event had had the effect of delaying her long-awaited encounter with Edward! Fortunately, despite the dampening effect of the news at breakfast, Rupert Brownlowe's advice that the expedition to Oxford should be abandoned had been retracted – since James had pointed out that it was already too late to telegraph Edward to prevent him from setting out to meet them as arranged.

'I'm not even sure he's coming from London. I think Mother said he'd be staying for the weekend with some friends of his in Iffley, which isn't far from Oxford.'

The journey had been almost unbearably tedious for Laura, keyed up as she was with anticipation. Inwardly seething with nervous tension, she had survived the hour it took for the train to travel from Guildford to Reading, the long wait at Reading station for a connection and now at last the countryside was merging into the grey suburbs of Oxford of the dreaming spires.

'We'll be there in a minute. Edward said he'd meet us at the station.'

James uncoiled himself from his seat and reached into the overhead luggage rack for the wicker hamper which had been stowed there. A year or two ago he would have had to stand on tiptoe, but in the time that Laura had been away he had grown like a weed and now he was as tall as his brother had been at eighteen. But he was still too thin, the mousy brown hair flopped untidily on his brow and the sunshine that had given Oliver a healthy tan had turned James's skin pink and caused his beak of a nose to peel. Laura had heard him describe himself cheerfully as the ugly duckling of his good-looking family. It had to be admitted that he would never be as handsome as Edward, she thought, and then averted her eyes hastily as, swinging the hamper down from the rack, he gave her his usual lopsided grin. The hamper was packed tightly with what Mrs Driver regarded as the minimum provisions for a party of four healthy young people to take on a picnic lunch – and would probably have fed a family of ten for a fortnight.

As the train coasted the last few yards into the station, Laura occupied herself in hooking the silver chain of her purse over her wrist and examining her snowy skirt for specks of smut from the engine.

Oliver stuck his head out of the window and surveyed the platform. 'There's Edward,' he said, and then, on a surprised note, 'Oh!'

'What's the matter?' James said.

'There's someone with him.'

The train had stopped, with a squeal of brakes and a hiss of released steam. James slid back the door lever and as the heavy door swung back, he jumped down to the platform.

Oliver handed the hamper out after him. Lastly, Laura stepped cautiously forward, wishing that the French designer Poiret, who had popularized hobble skirts, had taken more account of the difficulties occasioned to their wearers in getting out of trains.

The step of the railway carriage was high above the platform and the constricting hem of the skirt, stretched to its limit, impeded her even more than she had expected. She over-balanced slightly on reaching the ground and stumbled forward with a few short, running steps. Edward's hands steadied her and she looked up, mortified but grateful. The lovingly remembered face was as handsome as ever, the quizzical dark eyes under those arched brows sent her pulse rate soaring. But behind him, politely hovering, was a girl, or rather a woman. As dark-haired as Edward, with something like the same straight-backed stance and slightly arrogant lift of the chin, the superficial resemblance between them suggested that she might have been a cousin or even a sister. But as Edward released Laura's shoulders and turned to the dark girl, Laura recognized with a sickening stab of dismay that this stranger was no relation, but someone infinitely more threatening to all her long-nourished plans.

'I'd like you to meet Miss Margaret Churchill,' said Edward, with an air of pride which was like the twisting of a knife inside Laura's cold body. 'We are engaged to be married.'

24

2

Margaret Churchill caught the expression on Laura's face in the few seconds before it was erased, and recognized with wry amusement that the Brownlowe girl was in love with Edward. Wasn't everyone? Margaret had known him for too long to feel greatly threatened by an encounter with yet another intense young lady who worshipped the ground on which her undeniably picturesque fiancé trod. After two days of being his publicly acknowledged wife-to-be, she was already getting used to the surprise in people's eyes on hearing the news, which she correctly interpreted as meaning: 'How did a plain girl like her manage to hook herself a man like him?'

She had found it bewildering herself when Edward first began to show a taste for her company. She had no illusions about her claims to beauty – she would have been the first to admit that Laura Brownlowe, for instance, knocked spots off her in the appearance stakes. And as the daughter of a hard-up country vicar, her financial prospects were so small as to be virtually invisible to the eyes of any fortune-hunter. But gradually she had come to understand his interest.

Edward was an intellectual snob. She didn't blame him, in fact it was a tendency she probably shared and, even if she didn't, she was prepared to forgive him this minor fault. She was simply the cleverest girl he had met, the only one with whom he could carry on a prolonged, intelligent conversation about the political and social issues which were beginning to absorb him. Whilst she didn't always share his opinions, he told her approvingly, at least she contested them on a well-informed basis.

At twenty-four, Edward was formulating vague ambitions to be a Member of Parliament. Margaret thought he had probably decided that he merited a clever wife, and that she would do. But if the decision to propose had been that cold-blooded, his behaviour since her guarded acceptance had become surprisingly ardent. She could almost believe that he was seriously in love with her.

'Poor Laura Brownlowe,' Margaret thought, as Edward hooked her hand tenderly and possessively over his arm, and made the introductions. 'This is plainly going to ruin her day.'

'Daisy. Miss Jessie wants to see you in the morning room.' Ferry loomed in the doorway of the green room, where Daisy and Joan were in the middle of making the bed.

'Now? Right away?'

It jarred the two girls to be interrupted. Years of working as a team had given their activities a synchronized rhythm like the long-rehearsed movements of a dance and they could have predicted almost to a second how much time the routine would occupy. Every morning, through all the main bedrooms of Maple Grange, they faced each other across the beds, wordlessly stripping back covers, stretching, tucking and folding bedclothes, plumping pillows and smoothing counter-panes before swinging on to the next room leaving immaculate tidyness behind them in place of rumpled disorder. Today there were still three bedrooms left to attend to, but Mr Ferry only heaved a sigh at Daisy's temerity in questioning a summons from below, and stalked away.

She pulled an apologetic face at Joan. 'I dunno what it's all about. Can you manage on your own for a bit?'

The morning room was cool and dark, with a heavily patterned wallpaper of stylized flowers on a midnight-blue background. Long muslin curtains over the windows kept the sunlight from fading the furniture, so efficiently that Jessica Brownlowe, seated at the tall secretaire desk where she wrote her letters, had a lamp switched on beside her. The shaded light threw upward shadows across her thin face, accentuating its weariness. Jessie was a small, deadly serious woman of thirty-five, who gave the impression of being permanently braced to meet some new unpleasantness in her life. Even her smile was tired.

'Ah, Daisy. I understand you know this young man?'

Daisy had come in from the brightness of the hall, where sunlight streamed through the stained glass panels inset in the windows, spilling patterns of colour over the white walls and polished parquet floor. It was a moment before her eyes adjusted enough to enable her to identify Miss Jessie's visitor, hovering uneasily beside the library table. He moved towards her and she gave a gasp of recognition, which was followed by a twinge of apprehension. Was it all right to 'know' Arthur? What on earth was he doing here, when he should have been at work . . . and was Miss Jessie about to hold her responsible for his intrusion on the premises? She nodded nervously.

'Mr Bright has asked for special permission to speak to you today,' said Jessie in her clipped, unemotional voice. 'As you know, you are normally expected to ensure that your personal life does not intrude upon your duties, but in the circumstances I am prepared to make an exception.'

What, wondered Daisy, were 'the circumstances'? Arthur touched her arm, his voice husky with excitement.

'The Queen's are on Emergency Mobilization, Daisy. The first battalion was ordered back to Bordon barracks from the training camp at Rushmoor several days ago. There's a strong rumour that they'll be going to the war. Nothing official yet, but an old mate of mine in the regiment has tipped me that mobilization papers are expected to go out to reservists later today. And there's something I wanted to get settled with you, before I go.'

Daisy stared at him, open-mouthed. It was one thing to have scared herself with the thought of Arthur being involved in the war. It was another thing to find her worst fears so suddenly confirmed like this. Her legs seemed to have turned to jelly.

'I think it would be best if I gave you some time off, Daisy,' Jessie broke in. 'You may take the rest of today.'

'Thank you very much, ma'am,' said Arthur, smiling broadly. Almost a whole day! It was better than he'd hoped.

Daisy was strictly entitled to one day per month, and he knew she'd already used up this month's allocation. He himself was AWOL from work – but after this morning's news from his friend in the Queen's, his job no longer seemed important.

'Well, run along,' said Jessie, briskly. 'Don't waste it!'

She watched the stocky young man and the housemaid leave the room and for a moment she felt cold and utterly depressed. How old was Daisy? Nineteen or twenty? And Arthur Bright couldn't be so very many years older. And he was planning to go off to the war, to kill or be killed, before he'd even had a proper taste of life.

'Oh, don't be so mawkish,' she told herself. 'You're probably ten years older – and what difference has it made to how much life you've tasted? Besides it's only the Government playing safe, mobilizing the troops just in case they should be needed. That young man will probably hang around barracks for a week or two, passing the time with drill and kit inspections, and then be told the panic is over. And if so, I dare say he'll be disappointed that there wasn't more action!'

The phrase he had used: *something I wanted to get settled with you, before I go.* . . . . Had the looming prospect of active service stampeded him into making rash declarations of devotion to Daisy Colindale?

'Men are such prevaricators,' Jessie thought. 'Sometimes it takes a good scare to make them acknowledge their feelings.' Take Tom Carlisle at the bank, for instance. For almost five years he had courted Jessie, but so shyly and cautiously that she had never dared to let herself count on a proposal. It was only when he discovered that he was seriously ill that he had got around to telling her that he loved her. And by then, of course, it was too late.

She remembered with sharp clarity the damp corner of the churchyard where he was buried. The pale flowers, the mourners in black and her own feeling of hollow, hopeless finality as they'd lowered his coffin into the ground. She had known then that her chance was gone, that there would never be anyone else for her, and the ten years that had passed since the funeral had proved her right.

Well, good luck to Daisy Colindale, even if it took the threat of a war to make her young man speak up! Jessie fumbled in her pocket for a handkerchief and dabbed quickly at her eyes. Then she pushed the memory of Tom Carlisle into the back of her mind, as resolutely as she had buried his photograph in the depths of her closet, and applied herself to the tedious business of answering her morning's post.

Edward Allingham's Riley was parked outside Oxford station.

'I brought the motor,' Edward called back over his shoulder, leading the way. 'We've been staying with Margaret's family for the Bank Holiday weekend and we thought it might be nice to have a runabout with us. I'm afraid it's only a two-seater, though. If we go ahead slowly and meet you in Broad Street outside Balliol, you can follow in a cab, can't you?' He had signalled towards the waiting line of vehicles in the cab rank, and a horse was already trotting towards them.

Margaret Churchill walked confidently round the car to the seat beside the driver's. Well after all, it was her right, Laura reminded herself, fighting against the demeaning tears which seemed to be building up behind some kind of dam in her throat.

She hadn't even the consolation, she reflected bitterly, as the car bowled ahead of the cab between the elegant buildings of Beaumont Street, of losing the man of her dreams to a woman of superior beauty. Admittedly, Margaret was vivid in colouring and those eyes, as darkly intense as her fiancé's, looked directly at you in a way that demanded attention; but her black hair was coarse, her features bony and to Laura's critical, Paris-trained eyes, she had no dress sense whatsoever. The beige two-piece linen costume she wore was ostentatiously plain, totally unfashionable . . . and cheap. There was no other way to describe it.

'Look, Brat, that's the Ashmolean Museum.' Oliver nudged her helpfully as they passed a grandiose neo-classical building behind a stone balustrade. The whole point of this expedition, in his view, was for his sister Laura to appreciate the architectural and historic glories of his future place of study, but disappointingly she didn't even turn her head to admire the stately columns, the moulded wreaths or the ornate portico of the famous edifice.

Oliver had preceded Laura into the world by just a few minutes. Sharing the same birthday, they also shared the same fine bone-structure, the same soft, golden-brown hair and blue eyes, but the supposed psychic sympathy of twins was lacking. He was clumsily, unthinkingly fond of his sister, but he was as dense as any other boy when it came to plumbing the depths of female emotion. By now, however, even he could tell there was something the matter.

'Are you all right, Sis?'

No answer. Laura stared ahead of her, her lips pressed tightly together. Uncomfortably, Oliver searched his mind for something to engage her attention. He cleared his throat and turned to James. 'You didn't tell us Edward was engaged.'

'It's news to me. I've been away at school. And Edward's never been the most forthcoming of brothers.' James turned an anxious, placatory glance towards Laura's rigid face. 'I honestly didn't know. I'm sorry.'

That sideways look told Laura what she least wanted to know in the circumstances – that James, the bystander, understood her feelings and pitied her disappointment.

'Why sorry?' she snapped, hating him for understanding. 'She seems like a perfectly splendid girl to me. And heaven knows, it's high time Edward found himself a wife. He must be getting quite old now, isn't he?'

Edward waited with the Riley just beyond the graveyard that fronted the squat, square tower of St Mary Magdalene church. Carts and carriages skirted the machine gingerly, while the usual gaggle of small boys hovered a discreet distance from the glossy dark-blue perfection of its bodywork. Down the road in Cowley, William Morris had recently converted his bicycle workshop to the manufacture of cars, but a motor was still enough of a novelty among the horse-drawn traffic of Oxford's busy streets to attract an audience of admiring urchins.

'This is Balliol College on our left,' Edward announced, as the three cab-passengers walked up, having paid off their driver. He gestured at the cream-coloured stone building with something like the same proprietorial pride that he had displayed on introducing his fiancée. 'Oliver and James will be studying here in October. They've both been awarded exhibitions,' he explained to Margaret.

'Well done!' Margaret said. 'Your families must be so proud of you.'

'Oliver's were expecting it, he's always done well in exams. But mine were stunned,' James said. 'I'm supposed to be the family dunce, you see.'

There was a faint, ironic edge to this prosaic statement. Laura caught it, even in her present dispirited state, and it occurred to her for the first time that James might actually have minded all those years of living in the shadow of Edward's dazzling achievements. The sharp little comment from the good-natured fool was as disconcerting as if a favourite puppy had suddenly snapped at a caressing hand.

'I think we'd better come back for a tour of the college later,' Edward said after an uncomfortable pause, 'and have our river trip and picnic now, in case it rains in the afternoon. *The Times* weather forecast said we might get showers later.' He and Margaret began to debate the rival merits of taking a punt on the Isis from Salters at Folly Bridge, or on the Cherwell towards Marston from Magdalen Bridge. From their conversation Laura could tell that they had already shared Oxford punts in a past of which she, mooning over Edward in far-away Paris, had been humiliatingly ignorant.

'When are you two planning to get married?' Oliver asked, as the punt glided away from the boating hut under the bridge by Magdalen tower. 'Or is it too early to ask? When did you become engaged?'

'At the weekend, officially, though it's been in the air for some time I suppose,' Edward said. 'We've known each other for years.'

He and Margaret were seated side by side on one of the cushioned bench seats with Oliver and Laura facing them. James, after a short struggle with Oliver, had agreed to be the first to propel the punt and was standing in the stern, manipulating the long pole.

'As for a wedding date, we haven't had a chance to discuss that,' Edward continued. 'Of course this threat of war may well affect our plans.'

'You're going to rush off and volunteer for the army, are you, Edward?' Oliver asked, leaning over the low side of the boat to dabble his hand in the water.

'It did occur to me that I might have to,' Edward said.

Laura had been surveying the far bank of the river, where well-kept gardens sloped down to the water, lined by drooping willows and laburnums. She had seemed to be detached from the conversation, but now she switched her gaze abruptly to Edward's face.

'Or I might,' said Margaret gently. Edward's eyebrows climbed.

'You?'

'If there's a war in Europe, nurses will be needed.'

'Oh, but surely—' Edward began, but Laura broke in on a note of incredulity.

'You're a *nurse*? A *paid* nurse?'

'Certainly I am paid. A pittance, considering the nature of the work and the training, but a salary. Why, don't you approve of nurses?'

Laura flushed. 'It isn't exactly that I don't approve. Not of nurses, as such. I mean, I'm sure there's a need for such people. But do you think that women of our social standing ought to be working for money? Surely to do so is to deprive the less fortunate members of society of the opportunities for

32

an employment that they genuinely need?' She was quoting the often-expressed views of the various Guildford ladies who took tea with Aunt Jessie, and she realized even as she said it that she was being pompous, but it was too late.

'My dear girl.' Margaret sounded amused. 'I don't know much about your social standing, but as far as mine is concerned I need the money! I don't have a large private income and I certainly don't wish to live like a parasite off my father or any other man, now that I'm of an age to make my own way in the world. I take it, from what you say, that you *don't* work?'

'No. Of course not,' Laura said coldly. Was Margaret suggesting that she was a parasite, merely because she followed what were the normal activities for a well-reared young woman of the middle classes?

'What on earth do you find to do with your time?'

'I have plenty to do.' Laura found herself defending a position which she felt should have needed no defending. 'I help my aunt of course, with running the household. And arranging things. And entertaining guests. And I'm thinking of taking up some voluntary work soon, helping the poor of our parish in some way.'

'Oh. I see.' But it was mortifyingly plain that Margaret didn't see, and that she regarded Laura's 'busy' existence as mere time-filling. Behind the calm phrases, her tone was unmistakably sarcastic. 'Well, I know many girls enjoy such things but I'm afraid that to sit at home arranging the flowers and playing the pianoforte and planning bridge parties or fund-raising bazaars would bore me to tears.'

'You see,' Edward put in hastily, 'Margaret has studied at Somerville College. So she would feel the need to occupy her mind more than some other girls might.'

He had meant to restore the peace, but he was not the most tactful of young men and his comment sounded to Laura like: 'She is more clever than you, so what will do for *you* will not do for *her*.' Her colour deepened. She opened her mouth to dispute the implication hotly, then bit the words back as a fragment of teacherly wisdom from her Paris education slipped into her mind. *Simply because someone else chooses to be offensive or controversial, that does not mean that a lady need pay attention to it.* Let Margaret flatter herself that her selfish attitude was justified, or even praiseworthy. Let Edward delude himself that the insufferable Miss Churchill was something special when she was merely ill-mannered and pushy. It had nothing to do with Laura Brownlowe. . . . But it did. It did. It stung unbearably.

'Oliver. It really is your turn to do some work!'

James's intervention cut through the increasingly hostile atmosphere. By the time he and Oliver had changed places, the boat's occupants had remembered their manners and were all determined to find something more impersonal to discuss. They settled with relief on the subject of lunch, and the most pleasant surroundings for it.

The breeze had blown away the clouds that had threatened showers earlier in the day. It ruffled the surface of the water, stirred the leaf-heavy branches of the trees along the bank and breathed gently against their faces. They found a meadow with a convenient overhanging willow whose branches offered a tethering post for the punt and a handhold for the disembarking passengers. Laura hung back as the others scrambled up the riverbank. Her wretched skirt again . . . the beautiful, unsuitable clothes she'd worn to impress Edward were going to make it extremely difficult to get out of the boat.

Behind her, James waited patiently. She grasped hold of a low branch, placed a tentative foot on the bank, hauled herself grimly up until she felt safe, then gasped as the released branch sprang back, catching at the front of her lace jacket and flipping her enamelled watch from its pin. It arched through the air and into the water.

Instinctively, James lunged for it. Not for nothing had he been the best slip fielder in the school cricket team. The watch was already slipping down among the fronds of water weeds, a foot below the surface, as he grasped it, dropping to his knees in the rocking punt. Laura uttered a stifled scream as for a moment it looked as though he would be tipped over the side. But he regained his balance and clambered to his feet, holding the watch out to her. His right arm was soaked to the shoulder.

'Oh! Your clothes . . . but it was silly, you should have let the watch go. It really didn't matter,' Laura said.

James would have preferred simple gratitude. He stood there, the water streaming down over his fingers, shirt and striped blazer clinging clammily to his arm, and felt like a fool. It was a familiar sensation in the history of his acquaintance with Laura Brownlowe.

'You ought to have given your mother some warning I was coming. And you might have warned me!'

Daisy spoke in a reproachful undertone. She and Arthur sat stiffly side-by-side in the small, square front parlour of Mrs Bright's terraced house in Guildford. The horsehair sofa on which they perched was upholstered in a slippery chintz and the hard doming of its seat precluded relaxation. Judging by the chilly atmosphere, the overpowering smell of polish and the regimented orderliness of the ornaments, the room was seldom used.

Daisy was acutely aware of the noises Arthur's mother was making out in the kitchen on the other side of the hall. Mrs Bright had insisted on making them a cup of tea and a bite to eat, but there was something about the energy with which she clashed the kettle down on to the range and clattered the crockery which suggested that she was not best pleased with the way a visitor had been thrust upon her. When Daisy had offered to help, she had been directed very firmly into the parlour.

'I only heard about the mobilization this morning,' Arthur defended himself. 'There wasn't time to beat about the bush. Anyway, she already knew about you, or at least she knew that I had somebody. She's been chivvying me for ages to bring you home to be introduced.'

35

Daisy could imagine the circumstances in which Mrs Bright would have expected to meet a prospective daughter-in-law: Sunday tea, best china, best clothes and everyone on their best behaviour. As it was, Arthur had carted Daisy off to Guildford without revealing what he had in mind and then, as they strolled along a residential back street near the station, he had hauled her unexpectedly through a doorway, to be confronted by an elderly woman on her knees scrubbing the floor, up to her elbows in soapsuds.

'Ma, this is Daisy. We're going to get married.'

And he hasn't even proposed! Daisy thought, torn between outrage at being taken for granted and flattery that he wanted her. She watched the woman scramble up from the floor with an almost comically appalled expression on her weatherbeaten face and said to her, 'Pleased to meet you, Mrs Bright.'

'Did you say *married*?'

Daisy sympathized with this stunned reaction. Of course she'd thought idly from time to time about the possibility of being engaged to Arthur. Since the day that Robert had brought him home from the factory for supper and he and Daisy had 'hit it off', they'd walked together, picnicked together, been to the pictures together, as often as her days off and his free time would permit – though Arthur's free time was taken up by activities with 'the lads at the works' rather more than some girls would have thought acceptable at this supposedly most ardent stage of courting. It was a bit of a damper Daisy had found, to be told that your 'best boy' wasn't available on the one day that you were, because he'd agreed to take part in a cricket match.

In spite of this, she'd allowed herself to think about being married to him one day, but only in a vague, far-distant future. Her imaginings went no further than conjuring a picture of them strolling hand-in-hand through fields deep with buttercups towards a little cottage of their own. Arthur was handsome and nice and the look in his grey-blue eyes sometimes made her feel warm and shivery at once, trembly with excitement. But he'd only kissed her the one time, and while it had been thrilling and all that, she hadn't properly decided yet whether she wanted the reality of marriage. Her mother had dropped dark hints about what men expected from a wife and Daisy wasn't sure she liked the sound of what had been outlined.

'I don't think your mother approves of me,' she whispered, as she and Arthur waited in the parlour for the promised refreshments to materialize.

'Oh, I shouldn't worry. She's always a bit cool with strangers. And I suppose she might be a bit disappointed, just at first,' said Arthur unwisely. 'There's an old girlfriend of mine she was rather hoping I'd get hitched to, a girl called Adelaide who's the daughter of a crony of hers. I've kept telling her I don't fancy Adelaide that much, but Ma's a funny old thing. When she gets an idea into her head it takes some shifting.'

'Oh. I see.' The news that Arthur had an ex-girlfriend came as an unpleasant shock to Daisy. 'This Adelaide,' she inquired carefully, 'have you ever . . . I mean, did you ever *kiss* her?'

Arthur shot her a startled glance. His ears, Daisy noticed suspiciously, were going red.

'Once or twice,' he mumbled, 'but not seriously.'

'Once or twice', Daisy recognized, must be interpreted as at least twice. Which meant that the unknown Adelaide, Mrs Bright's candidate, had been on the receiving end of more kisses from Arthur than the girl to whom he had just proposed. It didn't seem right. Daisy had never so much as held hands with another man before she started seeing Arthur. True, he was five or six years older than her, and men were supposed to be different, but she couldn't help wishing that she'd been the first girl he'd courted.

'Maybe you shouldn't have brought me here today. Maybe you should have given your mother a bit of a chance to get used to the idea before you introduced us,' she said, feeling depressed.

'But it was the only way I could think of,' Arthur said, 'to make sure you always knew what was happening to me. I'll write to you, of course, if we get sent overseas, but there might be situations when we're only allowed to write to next-of-kin. And if anything happens to me, it's my parents they'll notify.'

Horrified by the bleakness of his words, Daisy forgot to be offended by his revelation of a past entanglement. Timidly, she touched his arm. 'Arthur, you will be careful, won't you? Don't go being too heroic and getting yourself killed.'

'Course I'll be careful.' He smiled down at her, squeezing her hand. 'I've got something to be careful for, now, haven't I? It'll all be over by Christmas and then you and I can talk about wedding plans.'

'I hope you like ham sandwiches and plum cake,' Mrs Bright said, shouldering her way through the doorway with a loaded tray. Arthur hastily dropped Daisy's hand and sprang up to take the tray.

'There was no need to go to all that trouble, Ma,' he said.

'It's no trouble,' said Mrs Bright, but her eyes were cold. 'It's not every day that my son tells me out of the blue that he's planning to get married to a total stranger. What exactly brought on this announcement by the way?'

There was a short silence. Daisy and Arthur exchanged glances.

'Ma,' said Arthur, at last. 'You know all this talk about a war . . . ?'

Margaret was feeling guilty. In letting herself get involved in a near-argument with Edward's friend on the subject of women and employment she had let herself down. Laura Brownlowe was very young and rather provincial, and it wasn't her fault that she shared the conventional attitudes. There was, moreover, the likelihood that her hostility had been at least partly motivated by jealousy, whereas Margaret was older and ought to have known better than to bicker. The fact that she had encountered the same attitude to her work in scores of other girls and was heartily sick of it was no excuse on this occasion.

'I wish I hadn't been so sharp with Miss Brownlowe earlier,' she told Edward. The picnic over, they were touring Balliol under the guidance of a helpful porter. Knowing the building and the porter's patter of old, Margaret and Edward had wandered ahead of the rest of the party among the cloistered corridors and had emerged through a doorway into an enclosed garden. The well-kept borders edging the trim lawn were vividly ablaze with roses, the scent of them heavy in the air, and with the sunlight sparkling on the new diamond-and-sapphire ring on her finger, Margaret wanted to be on good terms with the world.

'Don't worry about it, darling.' Edward had not yet recovered from the novelty of being able to call her by that name. He smiled at her, his hand brushing against her fingers. 'Laura won't, I'm sure. She was just being a bit young and thoughtless and I'm not surprised she irritated you.'

'Have you known her long? I thought she seemed to have rather a crush on you.'

'Laura? Good lord, I hope not. I've known her for years I suppose, but she's just a baby.'

'She's Oliver's twin, isn't she? Eighteen or nineteen.'

'That's right. Much too young for me. I think my brother is quite keen on her, though. It might even be mutual, which would be nice. She should suit him very well in a few years.'

Margaret was sure that Edward was wrong. Whatever James might feel for Laura, it was obvious that the girl hadn't the slightest interest in him. But having heard what she wanted to hear, namely that her fiancé was not attracted to the pretty Miss Brownlowe, she did not feel inclined to put him right.

'Wasn't it sweet,' she murmured, 'the way James rescued her watch? A real knight-errant gesture. Would you do something like that for me?' she added, tilting her head back to look into his eyes.

'Like a shot.' Recognizing what was expected of him, Edward bent his face towards her. Neither of them was used to flirting and their noses bumped together awkwardly as they kissed.

James, standing in the shadow of the doorway, unseen by the couple in the garden, heard a sharp intake of breath behind him and found that Laura was at his elbow. Her face was flushed and he wondered how long she had been there and whether he felt more bothered on her behalf or his own. Given that she blatantly adored Edward, it must have been distressing to hear herself described as a baby and fobbed off, as it were, with a little brother. On the other hand, it wasn't actually true that he was keen on her and the suggestion embarrassed him. He couldn't help being aware of her prettiness which always seemed to turn him into a clumsy, inarticulate ass, but until today what he had mostly felt was exasperation at her naivety, coupled with dislike of the effect her presence had on him. This new feeling of pity was a nuisance and he didn't know what to do with it. He hesitated, trying to make up his mind whether he ought to say something and if so, what. But Laura's averted expression was too forbidding. He felt as though he were an intruder, not only on Margaret and Edward's intimacy, but on Laura's witnessing of it. He found himself retreating from the scene without a word, leaving her standing there, her cheeks stained with colour, her watchful eyes bleak.

As Edward emerged, satisfied, from exchanging a long and tender kiss with his fiancée, he remembered something that he had been meaning to broach with her.

'By the way, darling, I assume that you didn't really mean what you said earlier about going off to the war as a nurse?'

'Why should you assume that?' Margaret said, in what a more experienced man than Edward would have recognized as a dangerously quiet voice.

'Well, after all, if we're going to be married . . . ? You'll be giving up this nursing business, surely?'

'I hadn't planned to. Particularly in the present situation.'

'Oh, come on, Margaret. . . .' Suddenly, Edward was rattled. 'I don't want to have a wife of mine loitering about by any other man's bedside, war or no war. When we're married, I'll expect you to be at home in the normal way.'

'I see,' said Margaret. She looked at him calmly, and braced herself for their first real clash of wills. 'Then I suppose we had better reconsider the engagement, hadn't we?'

'You don't mean that?'

Edward's face was so stricken that for a moment Margaret was tempted to tell him that of course she hadn't meant it, that simply being married to him would guarantee her undying happiness and that she was prepared to give up anything that he asked. But it wasn't true. However much she loved him, she knew that she needed her independence, her salary, her work. Perhaps in time, if she became a mother, she might feel different . . . but merely to settle down into a dutiful little housewife, dependent for her survival on the largesse of a man? She couldn't do it. Besides, having followed the course of events in Europe over the past few months, she suspected that nurses were about to become needed as never before.

'Margaret?' said Edward.

'Dear Edward . . . please try to understand. . . .'

'Oh, there you are,' said Oliver, wandering past his eaves-dropping sister into the garden, blissfully unaware of having interrupted anything. 'I wondered where everyone had got to. That porter chap could talk the hind leg off a donkey.'

For various reasons it was a subdued little group that left Balliol a few minutes later. Only Oliver was still smiling, his good-looking features smug. The porter had been masterly in implying that his captive audience was the most promising prospective undergraduate that he had yet encountered. It was this piece of duplicity, rather than his rambling account of the college's history, that had earned him the generous tip he had just received. The party came out through the porter's lodge to find a sizeable mob gathered around a handcart in the street.

'The evening paper's out,' Edward said. 'And something's up, by the look of it.'

He pushed his way through the crowd surrounding the news vendor's cart and emerged after some struggle with a copy of the paper.

'My God!' he said, staring down at the pages. 'This is it.'

'What's happened?' James said, craning to read over his shoulder.

'We've sent an ultimatum to the Germans, demanding that they withdraw their forces from Belgium by midnight tonight. That's eleven o'clock our time, it says. Only another five hours or so.'

'And if they don't?'

'Then we'll be at war.'

'Germany won't back down,' said Margaret, her face pale.

'I know,' said Edward, grimly. 'So it's war.'

The lane which led past the big double iron gates of Maple Grange was bounded on one side by a high stone wall surrounding the garden, and on the other by the fields of the Home Farm which provided meat, dairy produce and vegetables for the household as well as grazing for the horses. Behind the garden wall was planted the line of tall maples which had given the house its name. In the bright moonlight the trees cast long bars of shadow across the lane as Daisy and Arthur strolled towards the Grange, fingers entwined.

All day, Daisy had had a sensation that things were moving too fast. Her brain hadn't yet come to grips with the notion that the war was real and imminent, not just a scare in the papers or a subject for gossip in the post office. The revelation that Arthur might be going away into danger had shaken her. At the back of her mind, too, was the realization that if the first battalion of the Queen's, including its reservists, was going to be shipped abroad to fight the Germans, her brother Robert would probably be going too, so that her mother and sister-in-law Louella must be at least as worried as she was now.

But for the moment, Arthur was here and she was here, and there was a small ring on her finger which they had spent a happy hour choosing from a jeweller's shop in Guildford. It had a narrow gold shank and a circle of seed pearls surrounding a tourmaline, which Arthur had told her was like a daisy. The tenderness in his voice when he said it had been quite different from his normal bantering manner. She felt warm and weak with emotion and she didn't want the day to come to an end.

They were passing the dark bulk of the farm's hay barn at the side of the road and the lights of Maple Grange could already be seen through the trees when Arthur stopped dead, listening intently.

'There's a horse coming down the drive from the house. And wheels. A cart or a trap or something.'

Daisy, too, could hear the horse's hooves and the crunching of wheels on gravel. Peering towards the dim outline of the gate piers, they saw the wavering light of a carriage lamp moving between the bushes that fringed the drive.

'It'll be Griffin, going to the station,' Daisy whispered. 'He was supposed to meet Mr Oliver and Miss Laura from the train.'

'Come in here, then, quick.'

Arthur tugged Daisy off the hard surface of the road and through a gap in the fence beside the hay barn. There was no logical reason why they should hide, since Daisy had permission from Miss Jessie to be out, but she found that she did not want Griffin to see her with Arthur. She followed, obediently.

The horse's hooves came nearer. They shrank back against the wood planking of the barn, shoulders touching, as the trap bowled past them in the lane. Daisy's heart thumped under her constricted ribs. She was tensely aware of the nearness of Arthur's body. As the sound of the hooves receded, his hands groped towards her, crept around her waist and slid up her back.

'Daisy. . . .' he said softly.

His breath was warm against her cheek. With one hand he turned her face so that he could kiss her properly. As excitement took hold of him, the kiss became urgent, bruising her mouth, and she began to feel a little frightened by this new intensity of Arthur's.

'Please, Daisy . . . I love you. . . .'

His hands brushed against her breasts now, fumbling with the fastenings of her blouse. Swamped by unfamiliar feelings, Daisy gasped and trembled. Her upbringing instructed her to push him away, but at the same time there was no denying that the sensations produced by his caresses were pleasant, if fraught with danger.

'Don't . . . you. shouldn't . . . stop that, Arthur,' she said, unconvincingly.

'Christ, I want you, Daisy. Please. . . .'

Arthur's voice shook. He was crowding her against the planking of the barn now, his body pressed against hers. His knee forced itself between her legs. Suddenly panicking, she struggled in real earnest against the grip of his hands.

'Stop it, Arthur! It's not right. Not till we're married.'

'But Daisy, what if I never came back? What if I got killed, and we'd never known . . . I want to know, don't you? I don't want to die without ever knowing what it's like to hold you, to love you . . . like this. . . .'

The hurried, coaxing words seemed to flow over her, blanketing her reactions. *What if I never came back? What if I got killed, and we'd never known . . . ?* No man had ever held her like this, on the edge of all the dark mysteries of sex, and like Arthur, she too wanted to 'know'.

Sensing victory, his grip on her arms relaxed. 'It's all right, Daisy,' he said softly and soothingly, as if to a frightened horse. 'It's all right. I'll be careful. Ah, Daisy, I love you. . . .'

Her blouse was unbuttoned, the thin fabric spread open. The straps of her camisole slipped sideways and Arthur's mouth wandered over her bare shoulder and down, his hands cupping and lifting her breasts, his thumbs stroking her flesh with gentle, insistent pressure. 'Come inside the barn,' he whispered.

Groping with one hand, he had found the door and dragged it open. Inside was warm velvet darkness and the scent of hay. Daisy passed through the gap, moving in a daze of excitement. Arthur followed her in, bumping against her back, his hands already peeling her blouse back over her shoulders.

'We shouldn't . . .' Daisy murmured again. But it was only a last, token protest. She sank down on the hay bales, yielding to the weight of his body pressing against hers.

Then I suppose we had better reconsider the engagement. . . .

The words ran round in Laura's brain. Edward Allingham was engaged to be married. That was a disaster. Edward's intended wife was already quarrelling with him about the conditions of their future together. That, for Laura, was hope.

Suppose that they could not agree, suppose that Edward came to realize that Margaret was selfish and wilful, that she was all wrong for him . . . ?

Laura? She's just a baby. . . .

Oh, it was no use. It had been a terrible, terrible day.

As Griffin brought Blackie to a halt in the stable yard, Laura climbed quickly down out of the trap and headed for the house. She hardly noticed whose hands had helped her out, or even that her expensive skirt had torn at the back seam, making her descent easier.

'Good night, Laura,' said James, who had provided the hands.

Unhearing, Laura stalked into the house to be met in the hall by Aunt Jessie.

'Did you have a good day?' Jessie inquired automatically, before she registered her niece's expression.

'Yes, thank you.' Laura's response was dully unconvincing.

'Have you heard the news? About the ultimatum to Germany?'

'Oh. That. Yes,' said Laura. 'I'm utterly exhausted. Where's Daisy?'

It was part of Daisy's duties to provide maid service to the younger Miss Brownlowe when required. At this moment Laura's bruised spirit wanted only the peace of her own bedroom, the comforting familiarity of Daisy's hands helping her to undress, and the solace of her own bed.

'I gave her some time off,' said Jessie, worried by Laura's white face but not knowing how to question without prying.

'Time off?' Laura echoed wearily.

'Her young man's in the army reserve, and they're being mobilized. So I thought I'd give them a chance to say their goodbyes. I'm glad I did – Mrs Driver tells me that the butcher's boy saw a notice going up outside the school, instructing army reservists to report for duty tomorrow. I didn't think you'd mind doing without her, just this once.'

Laura decided she was past caring. In her room, she peeled the lace dress off anyhow and let it fall to the floor. Then she climbed into her bed and, finally, allowed herself to cry. It was past eleven o'clock and by now, the country was officially at war, but there was no room in Laura's private tragedy for national events.

3

Will Griffin, under-groom at Maple Grange, was cleaning tack. It was a job that he could have done in his sleep, which was fortunate, since his mind was elsewhere. Why was it, he asked himself savagely, scrubbing at the dismantled sections of a double bridle with a dampened sponge, that of all the girls in the world one particular female, nothing special, could twist herself round your heart without even trying and throttle all your common sense?

Before he came to Maple Grange, Griffin hadn't had much to do with women, nor had he wanted to. A boy from the Doctor Barnardo's home, the abandoned child of gipsy parents, he had found it enough of a struggle to make his way in the world without adding romantic involvements to his problems. The job at the Grange was his fifth since leaving the orphanage, and he had meant it to be a brief interlude, merely another tread on his stairway to success.

He had started out modestly as the stable lad in a coal-heaver's yard, but he was a hard worker, with a special knack of bringing out the best in highly-strung or stubborn horses, and he had moved steadily upwards. He knew when he accepted Rupert Brownlowe's offer of a job that the cachet of working with Rupert's show hunters would give him the entrée to the larger stables of the district. He fully expected his next position to be that of head groom to some minor member of the aristocracy, and he expected to attain it soon.

Then he met Daisy.

On his first morning at the Grange, wandering into the kitchen to inquire about the arrangements for his dinner, he had come face to face with an enormous heap of folded linen sheets advancing from the doorway which led through to the laundry. Two small-boned hands, one at the top and one at the bottom, precariously supported the heap, while beneath it could be seen a long grey worsted skirt and a pair of neat black boots. The weight of the linen was causing the boots to stagger across the quarry-tiled expanse of the kitchen floor, and it was obvious that the carrier could not see where she was going.

'Allow me,' said Griffin politely, and removed the top half of the stack of sheets.

The girl thus revealed had a mop of ginger hair, wisps of which were drifting free from an ineffectively pinned chignon to dangle around her pale, freckled face. What he noticed first was the lively sparkle of her green eyes. What he noticed next was the unaccustomed rapid thumping of his own heart as she gave him a sunny smile.

'Oh, thanks,' she gasped. 'They were heavier than I thought and then I couldn't find the table to put 'em down!'

'Can I carry them anywhere for you?'

'Thank you very much for the offer but I don't think you'd better, or they might whiff a bit of horse.'

Too late, Griffin realized that his most recent task had been the forking of manure into the midden and that the aroma still clung to his clothes. He hastily dumped the sheets on to the scrubbed surface of the kitchen table.

'Sorry,' he muttered, his face reddening. 'I wasn't thinking.'

The girl treated him to a repeat of the first grin. Its effect on Griffin the second time round was even more pronounced.

'Actually,' she told him kindly, '*I* think it's a nice smell, but I have a feeling the Brownlowes go more for lavender.'

That was all it took to breach the defences that Griffin had hitherto deluded himself he had erected around his heart. By the time he discovered that Daisy was already 'spoken for' by a regular admirer, it was too late. She was in there and he was stuck with this helpless, baffled longing.

It had never occurred to Griffin, who spent the minimum of time in the vicinity of mirrors, that he might compete with the unknown Arthur Bright for Daisy's affections. He had no idea that his lean, hard-muscled figure, his dark, sallow features and even his reticence might be attractive to a woman. In the months that followed, he had mostly avoided close contact with the object of his thwarted affections and contented himself with watching her sometimes from a distance. That Daisy was aware of his scrutiny, and unnerved by it, was another thing that Griffin did not realize.

The expected job offers came and he found he could not take them. He was addicted to his daily glimpses of Daisy. He had spotted her last night in the lane with her young man, when he was driving Blackie to pick up the three youngsters from the station. To be strictly accurate all he'd seen was a couple of figures in the moonlight, melting rapidly into the shadow of the hay barn over the road. But he'd known it was her, he had a kind of sixth sense where Daisy was concerned, and all night his imagination had been torturing him with vivid depictions of a red-headed girl in the arms of her lover. . . . Hating Arthur Bright for his luck, Griffin worked his way through the contents of the harness room with saddle soap and unusual ferocity.

Rupert Brownlowe had been expecting the declaration of war, but when it came he was unsure what to do about it. He was slightly impatient with the reasons behind the Government's action; he realized that the country had a duty to its allies, but it was only fifteen or sixteen years since Britain had been offering alliance to Germany and had been on the verge of war with France over territorial disputes in Africa. Now the French, everybody's old enemy, were supposed to be whiter than white and the Germans were being lambasted as a bunch of power-crazy despots, although the Kaiser was related to the English royal family when all was said and done.

Once the die had been cast, however, Rupert experienced a rush of patriotic emotion and longed to offer his services in the defence of his country. The question was, what services could he offer? He was in his fifties, with no particular skills other than that of knowing how to live as a gentleman should. He was shrewd at conserving his inherited money by investment, and at making the executive decisions at the light engineering works which he owned. He was a valued director of several other companies in the city. He could ride and shoot and until the recent onset of arthritis he had played a passable game of tennis. But when it came to waging war he acknowledged sadly that he would be nothing but a liability. War was a young man's business.

The letter that arrived by first post on Wednesday, August the fifth, gave him one answer to his frustrated urge for action. It informed him that as a result of the present crisis the army had an urgent need to requisition large numbers of remounts. All horse-owning gentry and farmers were instructed to take a proportion of their animals to the nearest designated inspection centre to enable the army to make its choice of suitable animals.

It was not an easy order for Rupert to comply with. Every horse in his stables was an old and faithful friend or a highly valued part of his careful breeding and training programme. Nor could the Home Farm's horses be easily spared, with the harvest still to come. But he derived a certain dogged satisfaction from the idea of giving up all that he had cherished. It was the first of his many gestures of atonement for being too old to fight.

'Mr Brownlowe says you've to take all the hunters down to Guildford this morning, for the army.' Nichols, the head groom, looked in over the half door of the harness room with his usual dour expression.

'Army?' said Griffin, hanging up the last of the cleaned bridles on its peg.

'Looking for hunters, hacks, draught horses. Anything that's going spare.'

'Ours aren't going spare.'

'Mr Brownlowe says they are. Take the lot, he says, all but Blackie and Plumbago, and let 'em take their pick. They'll most likely only want half, but we've to part with any they fancy.'

'Even Starbright?' Griffin couldn't believe it. Starbright was the pride of the stables, the shining five-year-old chestnut mare that Rupert had bred from his own stallion and his wife Sylvia's thoroughbred. With Miss Laura in the saddle, Griffin had been told, she'd swept the board at last year's hunter trials and only Laura's absence in Paris this summer had postponed her confidently anticipated triumph in the Ladies' Hunter class at the county show.

'Even Starbright,' Nichols confirmed, tight-lipped.

'But surely there's no need . . . ? The army doesn't need that good a horse?' the groom protested.

'That's not up to me,' said Nichols. '*When my country is at war, the least I can do is to offer the best that I have*, that's what the guv'nor said. Mr Oliver and that Allingham lad'll help you to take the horses into town.'

Griffin shrugged. It was not his place to question his employer's orders, but that didn't prevent him from feeling sick at heart over the prospect of parting with half the animals he'd cared for so devotedly over the last few months. In the back of his mind, too, was the realization that halving the stables would mean halving the need for grooms. Nichols, the old hand, would probably be secure, but what about Will Griffin, the Johnny-come-lately on the staff? Always in the past he had chosen his own time for moving on from a job. He didn't relish being pitchforked into unemployment.

Well, if he had to transport the horses to Guildford and stay while they were assessed, he had better warn Mrs Driver that he would be absent for the midday meal. As he came into the kitchen, she and Joan and Susie the scullery maid were clustered around Daisy. Joan was teasing the young house-maid about something, her insistent nasal voice vying with Daisy's laughing protests.

'Yes, you did, girl, don't you try to deny it. *I* heard you creeping in at midnight, for all I was so exhausted from doing the work of the two of us all day.'

'Go on, it was never midnight.'

'Yes it was, I heard the clock. Lucky Mr Ferry didn't catch you at it, before you had a chance to brush the hay seeds out of your hair. Swept 'em up quick enough this morning, didn't you?'

Griffin tried not to think of the meaning behind Joan's words as he looked at Daisy in her blue summer uniform with the white apron tied about her small waist. As usual, the sight of her made him feel obscurely happy.

'Hullo, Griffin. Come and take a look at Daisy's ring,' invited Joan, oblivious of the effect of her words.

'Ring?' said Griffin, and the happiness drained out of him.

'Yes, her Arthur popped the question last night, on account of him being called up. Isn't it pretty?' Joan grabbed Daisy's resisting hand and flourished the seed-pearl daisy in front of Griffin's nose.

'Very nice,' he mumbled. And, discovering a desperate need to be alone to absorb the news, he turned on his heel and walked away.

'I wonder what he wanted?' Mrs Driver said, as the kitchen door closed behind him. 'He looked proper blue in the face about something, didn't he?'

Daisy had been feeling pleasantly exhilarated by the excitement of showing off her ring, but suddenly all her elation evaporated. She remembered that Arthur, even now, would be reporting for duty with his old regiment, that in all probability he would soon be sent overseas to fight the Germans. . . . And she couldn't help remembering, too, that last night in the hay barn, with Arthur lying spent and contented beside her, his promise to be 'careful' long forgotten, she'd heard the governess cart coming back along the lane from Guildford Station. She'd pictured Griffin sitting up there in the trap, with the reins resting lightly between his brown fingers as he drove, and she'd had a strange, forlorn feeling that maybe, just maybe, she'd made a terrible mistake.

But it was too late now, wasn't it?

Griffin rode Starbright into Guildford. He had an idea that

it would be his last chance. How could the army resist the offer of such a horse? Especially since Rupert, stubbornly exposing himself to patriotic loss, had set an unrealistically low price on her, should she be chosen.

The mare paced sensibly, ignoring the more skittish starts and sidesteppings of the two other horses that her rider controlled on leading reins. But then, thought Griffin sadly, her top-quality breeding had made her sensible from birth. A horse in a thousand, a ladies' mount, far too good to be ridden into the ground by some insensitive lout of a cavalry officer.

Behind him, Oliver and James clattered, each leading a further two horses on reins. Griffin could hear them talking cheerfully as they rode and he knew they were indifferent to the fact that with this journey, ten seasons of careful breeding policy were being destroyed. All those patient hours of breaking and schooling, all that hard work – some of it Griffin's – would be gone for nothing. Behind them at Maple Grange the stalls were almost empty. Only Rupert's own regular mount, Plumbago, and Blackie, manifestly too old to be of use to the army, had been exempted from the selection process.

'I thought it was rather splendid of Pa to say he'd be willing to part with Starbright,' Oliver said to James, as they dismounted outside the offices of the Capital and County Bank in Guildford Market and joined the queue waiting for the judgement of Colonel Anderson, the army buyer.

'He didn't have to, then?' James said.

'Oh, no, they just want a proportion of horses from every owner. But Pa wanted them to take their pick of the best in his stables, as it's for the war. Pretty fine don't you think, Griffin?'

Griffin leaned his back against the wall of the building, stroking his hand gently down over the white blaze on Starbright's velvet nose. He turned a reflective gaze on Oliver's face and did not reply. The sideways twist of his mouth, however, gave warning that he didn't share the boy's opinion. Oliver felt a surge of irritation. When he spoke to a groom, one of his father's servants, he expected a prompt and civil response.

'Griffin?' he repeated, unwisely.

The groom straightened up and the look in his dark eyes made Oliver feel distinctly uncomfortable.

'No,' he said flatly. 'Since you ask, I think it's a pointless gesture and likely to result in the criminal waste of a good horse.'

'Give them an inch and they'll take a mile' was a saying that summed up Jessie's mother's attitude to servants. And she was probably right, Jessie thought with an inward sigh as she listened to Daisy Colindale's latest appeal for time off. Coming so soon after yesterday's special concession, Mother would probably have sent her packing back to her work, and with a flea in her ear. But then, Jessie wasn't Mother and she couldn't shut her ears to the appeal in Daisy's voice as she pleaded for just an hour or two to see her fiancé and her brother off at the station in Guildford. It was true that for the moment the reservists who had been mobilized were only being sent to join the Queen's at nearby Bordon, but the crack first battalion were prime candidates to form part of the British Expeditionary Force. Today's goodbyes could well be for a long time . . . even for ever, Jessie recognized, with a shiver.

'All right, Daisy. Just be back as soon as you can. . . . That's a very pretty ring by the way,' Jessie said, as the girl turned away.

'Yes, ma'am. It's my engagement ring,' Daisy told her with shy pride. 'Arthur chose it, he said it was like a daisy.'

So Arthur Bright had indeed been prompted to declare himself to his sweetheart and in due course, God and the fortunes of war permitting, the little housemaid would be married and the mother of a family. Jessie made an effort to feel benevolent and pleased for Daisy, but she was ashamed of the wave of pure envy that washed over her without warning, leaving her shaken. Why, she thought disconsolately, when so many girls found happiness and the fulfilment of motherhood, was she condemned to be lonely? What deficiencies of personality or appearance had made her a reject?

Jessie had come to Maple Grange with relief and gratitude. At the time, the task of taking over her widowed brother's household had offered a lifeline out of the limbo of spinsterhood. She'd had such good intentions, wanting to make Rupert comfortable, wanting to be a consolation to those poor, motherless children . . . but Rupert seemed to need so little from her and she'd forgotten how quickly children grow up. Her nephew Oliver was a gruff young stranger who'd obviously found her clumsy expressions of sympathy embarrassing. He had returned to his boarding school after the funeral with evident relief and she had failed equally to establish any deep relationship with Laura. She was afraid that in the eyes of her niece, and indeed of the entire household, she was a very poor substitute for Sylvia.

Since then she had gone through the motions of running the house with a painstaking attention to detail which she suspected was totally redundant. Everyone already knew their business. Rupert decided on the social events, if any, that he wished to host. Mr Ferry supervised the staff and dealt with any repairs that were necessary, Mrs Driver made up the menus, Laura did the flowers, everyone followed their usual routines. All she had to do was approve things. If she disappeared, would anyone miss her, in spite of all her exertions? And yet they were real. Tasks that other women apparently found easy demanded such an effort of concentration from Jessie. She felt constantly dragged down by a lethargy which she was too modest to recognize as sheer boredom. She did sometimes wonder whether she might have other talents as yet undiscovered . . . but if so, they were a long time revealing themselves. She couldn't even play bridge.

At times she half hoped that Rupert would marry again, though that would make her an incumbrance at the Grange, neither use nor ornament. But Ralph, with swan-like devotion to the memory of his dead wife, had shown no interest in a second marriage. So Jessie soldiered on despondently, making her lists, interfering where she need not interfere, and being far too soft, she was sure, with the servants.

All down the streets to the station the crowds were gathering. The Territorials had been assembling at the Drill Hall since ten o'clock that morning, their numbers periodically augmented by companies arriving by train from other districts. Throngs of men in uniform queued patiently for kit inspections, medical inspections and the issuing of orders.

Despite the tedium of waiting, there was a current of excitement and eagerness among the soldiers. This, after all, was what they had been rehearsing for through all the weekend drills and summer training camps they'd attended despite the scepticism of wives and sweethearts or employers. Citizens who until lately might have jeered them as tin soldiers were now clamouring to be admitted to their ranks. A few of their number who had failed their medicals slunk away with shame and disappointment rather than relief. For them there would be no march to the station through the cheering populace.

'Ruddy amateurs, those Territorials,' Arthur Bright said under his breath to his mate Robert Colindale, as they donned their newly re-issued uniforms at the regimental depot on the other side of the town. 'I reckon they'd wilt under fire like a bunch of violets.'

The reservists had been instructed to report for duty at the depot in Stoughton Barracks, but it had proved difficult for Arthur and Robert, still in their civvies, to shoulder their way through the tidal wave of humanity in the town centre. Groups of khaki-clad Territorials had kept getting in their way. Arthur felt a smug contempt for the spare-time soldiering experience of the Territorials; he'd resented the way they'd strutted today, lapping up public adulation on account of their uniforms while he, an accredited ex-regular, went unrecognized in the crowd.

'Mmm,' said Robert, not really listening. He had other things on his mind. For one thing he was feeling distinctly uncomfortable in his uniform. It was so hot and prickly and

56

tight round the waistband. More than a year since he'd worn one, of course. He'd been issued with something in his old size, in accordance with the Quartermaster's records, but he'd put on a bit of weight in the meantime. That was down to Louella's good cooking.

He was trying not to feel too bad at the prospect of saying goodbye all over again to Louella. He wished that she hadn't insisted on coming to the station with the crowds to see him off. He would rather have had that last kiss at home, those few tears, and left it at that. They'd only been married for five months. 'I hope she'll be all right,' he said.

'Who?'

'Louella.'

'Oh, she'll be all right. She's got her family, and your ma and Daisy to keep her company,' Arthur said cheerfully. 'And your separation allowance'll come through nice and regular, no worries there, now you've signed that form to arrange it.'

'I suppose so. It's not much though, is it? A lot less than I was earning at the works.'

'She'll manage. She's a good manager, your Lou. And it won't be for long. We'll be back in a month or two, plastered with medals.'

Robert didn't answer. For the umpteenth time that day he put his hand into the breast pocket of his uniform to check that he hadn't lost the silver Vesta case Louella had given him as a farewell gift this morning, wrapped in a piece of tissue paper.

'Think of me when you light a match,' she'd said, trying to be brave, though her mouth was quivering. It made him feel hot and soft to remember her like that. Women were the devil, they got under your skin and weakened you. If it weren't for having to leave Louella, he thought ruefully, he'd be really looking forward to this jamboree. As it was . . . well, he hoped Arthur was right about it being over quickly.

Men and horses waited patiently in a line along the side of the market square, reins tethered to the top rails of the cattle pens which filled the area. At the head of the line the army's inspector ran his hands expertly over each animal before deciding on its potential as a cavalry mount or draught horse for the gun-teams and supply wagons.

Without warning, in amongst the waiting animals and their attendants catapulted two snarling, yapping curs, oblivious of everything except a desire to rip each other's throats out. Locked together, the two whirling bodies, one black, one yellow, cannoned against Starbright's legs, sending her cavorting sideways with a jerk that snapped her reins. In a moment Griffin was in front of her, one hand hooked into the cheekpiece of her bridle, the other laid flat and calm against her shoulder as she kicked out at the scrapping animals – her small, oiled hooves beating a frenzied tattoo on the ground.

'Steady, girl. All right. Steady. Don't get yourself in a fret.'

Responding through her panic to the familiar, soothing voice, Starbright dropped her head and stood with her four legs braced, trembling, the sweat rising in a sticky scum on her coat. As the dogs' momentum carried them on to wreak similar havoc in another part of the yard, someone rushed by with a bucket of water, cursing, and flung it in the general direction of the troublemakers. Out of the corner of his eye, Griffin could see that one of the other Brownlowe horses had broken loose and was now careering wildly round the square, broken reins flapping against its knees. Behind it ran Oliver, caught unawares and clearly too rattled to remember that the last way to recapture a frightened horse is to chase after it waving your arms about. James Allingham was moving sensibly to check the tethering of his own charges.

'Well done,' said a voice close by Griffin's shoulder. 'I thought your mare would be off as well, but you controlled her very efficiently.'

Griffin turned to see a young man in army uniform watching him from the open window of the office where the selection panel had been conducting the paperwork of the requisitioning process.

'She's used to me,' Griffin responded drily.

58

'She's a very fine-looking animal. I dare say you'll be sorry to see her go, if she's picked,' the soldier said, emerging a moment later from the doorway of his office to study Starbright more closely. He was a subaltern, Griffin recognized by the insignia on his sleeve, and probably not much older than Oliver Brownlowe though he was trying hard to disguise his youth by the growth of a tentative moustache.

'She's not mine,' Griffin said. 'I'm just the groom.'

'Are you in charge of all of these horses?' The subaltern waved a hand towards the eight remaining animals from the Grange. The ninth was still cantering aimlessly round the square, just clear of a breathless Oliver, while the men who might have been asked to help looked on, too amused by the spectacle to step forward and intercept the horse.

'That's right. They belong to Mr Brownlowe at Maple Grange.'

'Nine horses, eh? He must run quite a sizeable stables, if this is half his stock.'

'He sent the lot,' said Griffin. 'If they're wanted. He thought it was his duty.'

'That was generous of him,' the young officer said. Then he looked again at Griffin and Starbright. 'But not so good for you, presumably, if we take them all?'

'Maybe not.'

'What will you do in that event?'

'I hadn't thought about it.'

'If you should consider volunteering,' said the subaltern, 'spare a thought for the Artillery. We could use a good man who can handle horses.'

'I'll bear that in mind,' said Griffin.

Daisy and her mother and Louella had debated for a long time about whether to wait with the throng in the town centre or whether to go straight to the station. In the end they had opted for the station as the safer bet – because of the way the crowd was building up between the Drill Hall and the railway line, they might be unable to force their way through it to say their final goodbyes.

By midday they had elbowed themselves a place near the station's main entrance and settled down to wait. The first detachment of reservists had left the Stoughton Barracks a little after ten, but the second, including Arthur and Robert, was not expected to depart until the afternoon. Daisy and Louella had put on their best print dresses and straw hats trimmed with flowers in an effort to lift the heaviness of their hearts. Mrs Colindale had dashed this attempt by wearing black.

'I thought we might have a long wait,' Louella said. She had brought pasties and lemonade in a basket.

'Oh, you angel, I'm starving,' said Daisy. Louella's pasties were delicious, light and crumbly pastry packed with minced meat and vegetables, dripping with good gravy juices, but when they were unwrapped Daisy found that her appetite had faded. Remembering why she was here in this holiday-crowd, instead of dusting and polishing at the Grange, her stomach seemed tight and cramped and chewing was a chore. She was half-aware, too, of other vague aches and upheavals inside her body, the aftermath of last night's rough handling by Arthur.

'I don't feel very hungry just now, after all,' she muttered, putting her half-eaten pasty back into its wrapping.

'Neither do I.' Louella, too, replaced her dinner in the basket. Her mother-in-law munched on stolidly, because her hard life as a widow with two children to support had taught her never to waste good food, but plainly her heart wasn't in it.

The day wore on. Daisy tried not to think of Joan's likely reaction to a second day of double duty in her absence. The crowd gossiped, argued, stirred itself for false rumours of movement at the Drill Hall and resettled, grumbling, to wait. At four o'clock, as rain-clouds gathered over the town, they heard the distant waves of cheering that announced the departure of the troops from the Drill Hall. The cheering went on and on as each fresh section of the crowd welcomed the sight of seven hundred newly mobilized officers and men of the Territorial battalion of the Queen's marching proudly through the cleared streets. They were men who had volunteered for overseas service, even though the Territorials were officially only committed to home defence duties, and their courage was getting the recognition it deserved. But despite the warmth of the crowd's response to the troops, Daisy was shivering. The wind was chilly now, blowing her thin dress against her legs, and the first drops of rain fell on her best straw hat.

It was under a cloudburst that the khaki-clad ranks at last arrived to be loaded, together with horses, baggage and bicycles, into a special train for Chatham. With them went two field guns, the sight of which sent a murmur of approval through the crowd. *Our boys mean business.* . . .

The soldiers had been singing as they marched. But as a child Daisy had seen the Queen's Regiment on parade, and there was something missing.

'Why aren't there any bandsmen?' she whispered to Louella.

'Because they're going to war, love.'

The old man who had answered her question wore campaign medals on faded ribbons pinned incongruously to the front of his damp and shabby suit. The raindrops glistened on the moulded bronze discs that proclaimed his involvement in long-ago battles. 'In wartime the band does double duty as stretcher-bearers for casualties, you see. That'll be their rôle now.'

'I see. Thank you,' said Daisy politely, trying to smile. But she wished he hadn't told her. She didn't want to be reminded of the possibility of casualties at this moment. She averted her eyes from the sight of the men who carried the folding stretchers against their shoulders the way other troops carried their guns. But then above the cheering, her ears caught the thin piping of a fife and the beat of a drum.

'They're playing "Braganza".' Louella nudged Daisy as

she recognized the regimental march. '*They* wouldn't go without their music.' And now the little detachment of reservists swung into sight in the distance, behind the larger body of the Territorials.

Daisy had never seen Arthur in uniform. He wasn't particularly tall but the battledress suited his stocky figure. Her throat constricted with pride. He looked so handsome, marching straight-backed and serious through the rain to fight for his country. She *did* love him, she thought, ashamed of the moments of doubt she'd had last night and this morning. She'd wait for him to come back and then they'd be married and they'd be happy. Beside her, her mother was sobbing loudly into her handkerchief and Louella cheered madly, waving towards her husband who was striding along next to Arthur Bright. The people around the station were friends and relations of the troops, permitted on to the platform to say goodbye, and already Daisy's party was being swept along by the impetus of the crowd. She lost Louella and her mother in the rush. Craning her neck, she saw that the reservists were being shepherded towards a different train. Crushed and jostled, she struggled after Arthur's receding back, suddenly terrified that she wouldn't get near enough to talk to him. She wasn't even sure he had seen her in the mob.

'Arthur!' she called desperately.

He climbed into one of the maroon carriages and disappeared. Her heart sank, but to her relief he reappeared a moment later at a window of the carriage and slid it down, looking eagerly out over the shifting sea of faces on the platform. With a last push and shove, Daisy arrived panting at the window. When she stood on tiptoe his face was still a foot above hers.

Suddenly there seemed to be nothing to say. She felt self-conscious, aware of spectators, of her clammy dress sticking to her back and of the wet tendrils of hair drooping round her face. She racked her brain for suitable parting phrases.

'What's that you've got there?'

He was carrying a small, red-covered book. He glanced

down at it, vaguely surprised to discover that he was holding anything at all.

'Oh, this? Gospels,' he said. 'They were doling them out at the entrance. Present from the King I think. I dare say he thought we ought to have something to improve our minds on the journey.'

'I wanted to get you a present,' Daisy said, remembering Louella and the Vesta case. 'But I didn't have time. At least I did, I suppose, while we were waiting for you to come, but I was afraid of missing you.'

'I don't need anything.' Arthur reached down and touched a forefinger to her cheek. 'Just the memory of your pretty face'll do me.'

There was another silence.

'Daisy. I wanted to tell you. Last night . . . it meant a lot to me,' Arthur said softly. Daisy drew in her breath sharply and her insides seemed to melt. Then a voice from inside the carriage said on an accusing note, 'Hey, mate, when can I have a turn at the window? My girl's waiting, same as yours.'

'Sorry.' Arthur grimaced apologetically at Daisy. *He's going* . . . she thought, agonized. Someone behind her dug a sharp elbow into her back and she stumbled against the side of the train, her hat slipping sideways. As she straightened it, Arthur leaned out, his voice suddenly urgent.

'Give me one of those flowers off your hat. To bring me luck.'

Daisy snatched off the hat, shaking the raindrops from its brim and handed it up to Arthur. He wrenched one of the artificial flowers free from the ribbon band around the crown. As he passed the hat back, she realized that he'd chosen a Michaelmas daisy. His other hand closed around her wrist, tugging her nearer. His head bent low and for a moment his mouth pressed against hers.

''Bye love. I'll be seeing you.'

Then he was gone; and another head and shoulders filled the gap.

Daisy stood alone, wedged and pummelled by the crowd.

Out of the corner of her eye she glimpsed a face she knew from somewhere. She turned her head. Mrs Bright was standing on the edge of the crush looking grimly towards the window where Arthur had been. If she had seen Daisy, she gave no sign of it. Tearless, she stared on until the train pulled away. Only the last surge of the crowd, waving and cheering, obliterated her small, stiff figure from Daisy's sight.

Oliver and James had a problem: the army having accepted Rupert Brownlowe's generous offer of all his horses, they had nothing left on which to ride home.

'I suppose we'd better find a cab in the town. Or hire a couple of hacks from The Angel in the High Street,' Oliver said, stuffing a folded wad of banknotes, cash payment for the horses, into his pocket. 'Where's Griffin by the way?'

'I don't know,' James said. 'He was talking to that army fellow the last time I saw him. Should we go looking for him?'

'No, I don't think so. He might have cut off home already. Though there won't be much for him to do when he gets there.' The wider implications of the day's activity began to dawn on Oliver. 'I wonder if Pa's thought about that?'

If Rupert Brownlowe was anything like his son, James thought wryly, the impact of his decisions on his staff would be the least of his concerns. Increasingly these days, aspects of Oliver's attitudes and behaviour provoked exasperation in his old schoolfriend; but liking each other was a long-established habit and the alliance still survived despite the recognition by James that Brownlowe was a typical insensitive scion of the gentry and by Oliver that Allingham Minor had shocking socialist tendencies.

There were, predictably, no horses left at The Angel.

'Oh, this is ridiculous. I suppose we'll just have to walk,' grumbled Oliver.

'How far is it?'

'About five miles. I wonder where Griffin is?'

As they trudged towards the Farnham road, the groom drew level with them on a hired bicycle.

'I never thought of that.' Oliver was impressed. 'Where've you been, Griffin?'

'Enlisting,' said Griffin laconically.

'*Enlisting?*' Oliver echoed, startled. 'What, already?'

Griffin shrugged.

'I thought I might as well. I'll be getting back now.'

He pedalled on and with one accord Oliver and James turned back towards the bicycle hire shop. Later, as they cycled tranquilly home, Oliver began to feel ashamed that his father's groom had beaten him, a former star of his school's Officer Training Corps, into joining the war effort.

'Perhaps that's what we ought to have been doing,' he said to James.

'What is?'

'Enlisting.'

'You're not serious?' James said, after a pause.

'Absolutely, old chap.'

'But that's crazy.' James braked his bicycle to a halt and stood there, legs propped apart, regarding his friend with troubled eyes. 'What about Oxford?'

'Oxford can wait. They'd have us back afterwards. How about it, James? It'd be fun. I rather fancy a cavalry regiment, don't you?'

'No,' said James starkly. 'I don't. That may be your version of fun, but it isn't mine. I don't relish the idea of dashing about on an over-excited charger, trying to swipe people's heads off with a sabre. And I'm even less interested in letting them lop off *my* head. I'd rather stick to reading History at Balliol thanks very much, and leave the killing to those who like that sort of thing.'

'Oh.' Oliver digested this statement for a while, and his face took on a mulish look. He wanted to enlist. He saw himself in the photographs, chin up, shoulders back, expression suitably serious, in a well-cut uniform from Burberry's; they did a decent, comfortable khaki woollen material, not like those awful stiff, scratchy Standard Issue tunics worn by the troops he'd seen today. He could imagine the captions on the photos which would be ranged in silver frames on the top of the piano in the drawing room at Maple Grange: Second Lieutenant Oliver Brownlowe, one of the first to volunteer . . . First Lieutenant Brownlowe, an inspiration to his men . . . Captain Brownlowe, awarded the Military Medal for his courageous conduct in battle. . . .

But he didn't want to do it alone. He wanted James to keep him company. And James, infuriatingly, didn't want to play the game.

Griffin leaned his hired bicycle against the wall of the stable yard and climbed the stone outer stairs to the grooms' quarters over the tack room and corn store. He packed his things quickly and methodically into the scuffed leather suitcase they'd given him when he left the orphanage ten years ago.

There wasn't much to pack. He'd never been one for accumulating possessions. The only items that weren't purely functional pieces of clothing or equipment were the certificate stating the details of his origins as a foundling – since his birth was presumed not to have been registered by his delinquent parents – and a photograph in a sleeve of tissue paper.

Rupert had gone through a phase of being interested in photography and earlier in the summer he'd taken a picture of the staff, lined up self-consciously in the stable yard in their working clothes. Afterwards, proud of the clarity of the resultant print, he'd distributed a copy to each of the subjects.

Griffin was in the back row, his dark eyes glowering towards the lens. Nichols was on his right and beside him in his black suit, chest thrown out like a self-important penguin, Ferry the butler. Aldridge, immaculate in chauffeur's uniform, propped one glossy boot on the bottom step of a mounting block. The gardeners, flanking Mrs Driver and Joan, made up the second row. The front row consisted of the gardener's boy, the boot boy, the scullery maid . . . and Daisy.

Griffin looked at the photograph for an extended moment

before he laid it down carefully on top of the folded clothes and shut the case.

He had just enough time to see his employer before the dinner gong. He waylaid Rupert emerging in evening dress from sherry in the drawing room.

'I want to give notice, sir, immediately. You won't be needing me now the horses have gone.'

'No, I suppose not.' Rupert looked worried. 'But look here, Griffin, there's no need to rush off like this, you know. I don't want you to lose out. I'm perfectly prepared to keep you on till you find another place.'

'It'll be the same all over, now, grooms out of work,' said Griffin flatly. 'Anyway, I've got my next place fixed up.'

'Ah,' said Rupert. 'Jolly good. Where are you going?'

'France, I should think, or Belgium.'

'Sorry?' Rupert said, puzzled.

'I've joined up, sir. Volunteered.'

'Oh, well *done*, Griffin!'

Rupert's enthusiasm took the groom by surprise. He recoiled as his employer thumped him on the shoulder.

'I think that's absolutely splendid of you. The war'll be over in no time if the young chaps like you come forward like this. Well done,' Rupert said again.

The reaction in the servants' hall was more muted.

'I'm sure I'm sorry to see you go,' said Mrs Driver. 'You're a quiet one, but still. . . . Write and tell us how you get on, won't you?'

'Why did you do it?' said Joan, curiously.

Griffin looked at Daisy, newly back from Guildford with her pretty print dress bedraggled and her eyes pink and puffy with weeping.

'I thought I might as well,' he said, as he had said to Oliver earlier. 'There's nothing here for me now.'

4

In 1893 when Rupert Brownlowe proposed marriage to Sylvia
Cathcart, he had already had a house built to suit his
requirements, in the pleasant countryside south of the Hog's
Back ridge between Guildford and Farnham. The workmen
he engaged had been the best of their trade and he was proud
of the results.

Admittedly, the Grange was of comparatively modest size,
with only eight main bedrooms and four reception rooms if
you discounted the staff quarters, but 'It's got all the modern
conveniences,' Rupert pointed out, leading his wife-to-be
through a succession of sparsely furnished rooms which Sylvia
found depressingly soulless. 'Electricity, run by a generator –
no groping about with oil lamps or guttering candles for you,
my love. And a bathroom. And the kitchen suite is on the
ground floor, not in the basement, so you won't have to run
up and downstairs when you want to consult with your cook.'

With an effort, Sylvia managed to mask her reaction to the
house which she knew Rupert had planned in conjunction
with his architect. How could she tell him she didn't like it?
She had no choice but to like it. She was committed to the
match with Rupert, of whom her parents thoroughly approved,
and with whom she expected to fall in love in the proper way
once they were married. Modern houses did not appeal to her
at all; she would have preferred an eighteenth-century home
of mellow stone, with long, shuttered windows and an
established garden, like the dearly loved one in which she had
grown up. The brickwork of Rupert's house was still raw and
red, the mock-Tudor half-timbering of the upper storeys
garish, and the new plants in the herbaceous borders were
only tentatively taking root, leaving large patches of hoed soil

visible between their apologetic clumps. But she had to agree that properties like her family home were rarely available and often highly inconvenient, however beautiful. Her mother, after all, had been making the same point for years.

After her marriage, Sylvia became quite fond of the Grange. It was a challenge to make it attractive, and challenges overcome can be very satisfying. The harsh red brick of the façade was gradually mellowed and softened by climbing roses, Virginia creeper and wisteria; the aggressive orange of the parquet floors acquired a glowing patina through years of assiduous polishing, providing a flattering background for the eastern rugs she placed upon them; and the garden became one of the most admired in the district. In the rooms she mixed her own inherited pieces of good Georgian furniture with other antiques which she chose on the tours of the countryside which she and her husband made every summer. She had a gift for interior design and Rupert, proud of her artistic sense, happily bought her anything she wanted.

'And at least,' Sylvia's mother remarked on her visits, with a touch of envy, 'you can run the place on a shoestring staff.'

Getting servants was becoming a problem as the Victorian era gave way to the Edwardian. It was all very well for the gentry in remote rural areas where the working classes had few alternatives to agricultural labouring or going into service, but in the Guildford area the men had the army or the blossoming industries to tempt them away and the girls could opt for shop or factory work, or even, if their families could afford the training fees, acquire the new office skills of shorthand and typing.

What Mrs Cathcart regarded as a shoestring staff consisted at first of fifteen full-time employees plus a charwoman and a laundress who came in from the village. To cope, with such a limited amount of help, the rigid old definitions of who did what had to go and the housemaids had to be prepared to turn their hands to a little light laundry, for instance, or even to scrub the occasional floor in an emergency. On the plus side for the servants, Rupert was ready to invest in such labour-saving devices as the newest vacuum cleaner, though unexpectedly for a man who supported progress, he had refused to have a telephone installed, regarding it as a fiendish device which would mean the ruin of all privacy.

By the time Daisy Colindale joined the staff, its number was reduced to twelve. Sylvia, tragically, had died of a severe bout of food poisoning on an Italian holiday. Rupert no longer had the heart to entertain as she had done, and the ambitious French cook and his assistant had soon been replaced by down-to-earth Mrs Driver as cook-housekeeper. The nursery nurse had been dispensed with as soon as Oliver was old enough to go to boarding school and Sylvia's own personal maid had gone too. Jessie said she certainly didn't need a maid and the new girl, Daisy, could do whatever was needed for Laura.

Daisy had been interviewed for the post of under-housemaid by a diffident Jessie, newly arrived and inwardly quaking at having to play Mistress of the House. Remembering her own mother's larger staff and all their sternly-adhered-to divisions of labour, Jessie was somewhat apologetic in outlining how flexible Daisy's duties would be. But to her relief the girl had expressed herself perfectly ready to tackle anything that came along, and no, she didn't consider it the least bit infra dig for a housemaid to do the odd bit of laundering.

In comparison with Daisy's previous post in which her duties might have been roughly defined as doing everything, single-handed, and looking sharp about it, she found the workload at Maple Grange positively restful and Jessie Brownlowe a very easy-going mistress. So on the afternoon of 25 August, 1914, when directed by Mrs Driver to wash out a bundle of teacloths, Daisy complied cheerfully.

It wasn't worth lighting the fire under the copper in the laundry for such a small load, so she boiled them up in a pan on the range and then rinsed them in the scullery.

'I'll just peg these out, Mrs Driver.'

Half an hour later, though, she hadn't reappeared and there was work to do. Exasperated, the cook stuck her head round

70

the door of the servants' hall but the room was empty except for Joan, who was engaged in darning a torn sheet through which Mr Oliver had managed to stick his foot the week before.

'Joan, go and fetch Daisy in from the laundry, will you? I've the pastry to make and Susie's got the vegetables to deal with and there's company expected for tea any minute.'

Joan wandered out into the back regions – it was too hot to hurry, even if Mrs Driver was getting rattled – and came upon her fellow housemaid by the washing line in the yard outside the laundry. Daisy stood with her back propped against the warm brickwork of the wall, her hands clasped over her apron and a faraway expression on her freckled face. On the line a couple of linen teacloths had been pegged out to dry, while on the ground beside her, unregarded, lay most of the basinful of washing which should by now have been bleaching in the hot afternoon sun.

It was not hard to guess what she had on her mind. All the staff knew that a postcard from the British Expeditionary Force in France had been delivered for Miss Daisy Colindale by first post that morning and Joan had no intention of letting her escape without having a sight of it first.

'Mrs D's been asking for you,' she said. Daisy came to awareness again with a guilty start, reaching hastily for another teacloth.

'Here, Daisy, let's have a look at that postcard of yours.'

'Why? It's not addressed to you,' Daisy said. Her tone was bantering but she put her hand protectively over the pocket in the front of her apron, through the thin linen of which the outline of the card could be seen.

'Oh, come on. I only want to know how our lads are getting on out there. Don't be so mean. Mrs Driver'd skin you alive if I told her how you'd been slacking about instead of getting on,' Joan added by way of persuasion.

Skinning alive was an exaggeration, but the cook had a rough side to her tongue which Daisy preferred not to experience if she could help it. And she *had* been slacking she realized, though she hadn't meant to. One minute she'd been pegging out the cloths, same as usual . . . and it seemed like only the next that Joan had come through the arched doorway in the wall and jolted her out of her daydreaming – in which memories of her last evening with Arthur, the farewell at the station and, disturbingly, the look in Will Griffin's dark eyes as he'd said he was leaving, had been inextricably mixed together.

It seemed disloyal to have allowed the thought of Griffin to intrude on her recollections of Arthur and as a gesture of atonement to her absent fiancé she touched a forefinger briefly to the ring she wore, before she reluctantly dug the card out of her pocket. It had no stamp, just the words 'On Active Service' in capitals at the top, which had ensured its free transportation via the BEF's own postal system.

Joan scanned it eagerly, glancing first at the sepia-tinted photograph of an unidentified French town and then, more closely, at the densely packed lines of handwriting on the back. Scattered along the lines were patches of black where the army censors had inked out anything they thought might compromise security.

Joan's lips moved as she deciphered the message. Daisy waited impatiently. She could have recited every word – she'd read it often enough since its arrival.

Dear Daisy, we landed at (blank) on (blank), but the Powers That Be decided that we ought to be in (blank) instead, holding hands with the French army to keep out the Boche. After going some of the way by train, we are now footslogging towards the fighting. It's mostly on cobbled roads which play merry hell with your ankles, and some of the lads are out of condition so it's very hot work, but the locals along the way are welcoming and turn out to cheer us on. They say we're heading for (blank). Hope it isn't all over before we get there. We can hear the guns. Be seeing you soon, Arthur.

72

The words had left their recipient with a deflated feeling. If only Arthur could have said something a bit more romantic in this, his first eagerly awaited communication since he'd gone off to the war – something that would acknowledge the intimacy of those hours in the hay barn. Admittedly, it was difficult to be lover-like on a postcard that nosey people like Joan and the postman, to say nothing of the censor, would be bound to read. But if that was the problem, why couldn't he have sent a letter instead? Louella, she'd heard via her mother, had had at least two letters from Robert since he went away, both of them full of love and nostalgia.

We can hear the guns . . . it sounded so ominous. Gave her butterflies in her stomach even to think about it.

Arthur, writing his postcard to Daisy, had mentioned the welcoming French crowds who had been giving the incoming forces an enthusiastic reception ever since they'd landed at Le Havre on 13 August. He had thought it wiser not to include the fact that most of them were women – and that included some very pretty girls, avid to demonstrate their approval of the Brave English Tommies in a practical way.

They'd clamoured for 'Souvenirs' and this had become a nuisance eventually – some of the lads had parted with rather too many of their uniform buttons and badges before the novelty wore off, and no doubt they'd cop it next time there was a formal parade. But Arthur had enjoyed the cheering, the flowers and gifts of sweets and chocolate that had been pressed on the troops, and especially the impassioned kiss he'd received on the outskirts of Le Nouvion from a vivacious blonde girl with bold blue eyes. He wouldn't have been human if he hadn't relished that. He'd felt a slight qualm that the embrace had been handed out in full view of his prospective brother-in-law, Robert Colindale, but fortunately the girl had gone on to kiss Robert as well.

'So if he says anything to Daisy, I'll just have to get my own back by spilling the beans to Louella,' Arthur reflected.

Remembering the French girl brought an appreciative smile to his lips as he trudged along the road. She'd smelled warmly of some scent or other – was it lily of the valley? And as she'd pressed her body deliberately against his, a shock of arousal had gone through him and he'd hardly known where to look for a few moments. Afterwards he'd wished he'd had the presence of mind to take full advantage of the opportunity and kiss her back. After all, who could tell when he'd next get a chance to cuddle up to a pretty girl?

Arthur's heel skidded sideways on the slippery surface of the pavé, ricking his ankle painfully, and he swore softly under his breath. On the long train journey from Le Havre to Le Nouvion, packed forty to a cattle truck in the sweltering heat, he and his mates had been uncomfortable enough, but you couldn't expect luxury when you were going to war. Funnily enough the officers had been transported in first-class carriages, but that, too, was only to be expected – they were a different breed. And in retrospect the cattle trucks had been a comparatively cushy mode of transport. After that it was Shank's Pony all the way for the Infantry.

Yesterday the battalion had marched fourteen miles on these infernal cobbles from Le Sart to Les Bodelez, and this morning they'd set out at five o'clock towards Maubeuge, a few miles south of the Belgian border below Mons. The straight road ran on and on, probably some old Roman route, through unspectacular countryside. The first meal of the day hadn't come until one o'clock in the afternoon, adding growling stomachs to protesting muscles. It was tough on the reservists, still struggling to get back to fitness after the soft life they'd led in civvy street.

At first Arthur had marched with a light heart, despite the weight of the pack on his back and the overheated, prickly discomfort of his uniform. The scenery was uninspiring but the edges of the wheatfields were bright with poppies and charlock and camomile-scented mayweed and this was an adventure. Something to beat building motor vans any day, he'd told himself while roaring out the words of music-hall songs like 'Tipperary' or the new one, 'Belgium Put The Kibosh On The Kaiser', and joining with gusto in the flippant catechisms.

'Are we downhearted? NO-O-O-O!'

'Are we going to win? YES!'

But the light-heartedness had given way to stoicism, and finally to grim endurance. His legs ached, his blisters swelled and burst inside the stiff-leathered boots. The distant sound of artillery fire, heard at mid-afternoon as the troops snatched a rest at Bettignies before they crossed the border, had been a chilling reminder of what they were heading for. Reliving the kiss from a pretty French girl was one way to lift a man's flagging spirits and take his mind off the state of his feet. No harm in that. All the same, wiser not to mention the incident in the postcard he'd sent to Daisy today to quieten his conscience.

Had he been just a little bit hasty in asking Daisy to marry him? She was a smashing girl, he wasn't denying it, but he'd let himself get carried away with all the excitement of the mobilization news and now he wasn't so sure if he wanted to spend the rest of his life with her. She'd been sweet and warm, that night in the barn . . . but just a bit, well, *passive*, which had disappointed him at the time and still bothered him in retrospect. The French girl, now, she wasn't the passive kind at all. . . . She'd reminded him of Adelaide, his old girlfriend. He and Adelaide had quarrelled a lot in their courting days and he'd thought he was glad to be shot of her, but she'd certainly been exciting to kiss.

Daisy . . . Adelaide . . . ?

He'd sort out his feelings when he got home.

'We can hear the guns,' Joan read aloud, peering at the smudged writing on Arthur's card. 'So they'll be in the thick of it by now, I dare say.'

'Put that away you two,' scolded Mrs Driver, bustling through the archway. 'Joan, I sent you out to fetch Daisy in, not to stand about gossiping. Aren't those cloths pegged out yet? You'd better finish them off then, and no more dawdling. Daisy, you come with me. And tuck that blessed hair of yours in tidily, girl. I want you to take the tea trolley into the drawing room. I've got it laid out ready, since I couldn't find anyone to help me.'

Daisy retrieved the postcard from Joan and gripped it temporarily between her teeth as she repinned the errant strands of hair which were escaping, as usual, from their chignon. Mrs Driver had already stomped off towards the kitchen and Daisy, her coiffure under control again, ran to catch up.

'Sorry I was so long with the washing . . .' she began.

'Oh, never mind.' Unexpectedly, Mrs Driver didn't scold. Instead, she held out her hand for the postcard which the housemaid was in the act of returning to her apron pocket. 'What does he say, then, your young man?'

'Not a lot. And what he did say, they've painted bits out of.' Resignedly, Daisy parted with her private mail for the second time that day. Then her eyebrows lifted as she saw the tea trolley.

Afternoon tea at Maple Grange was always a formal affair, but this was something special. Jessie and Laura, who had small appetites, would normally have been satisfied with bread-and-butter thinly sliced, but today there were fancy biscuits, fruitcake and small, crustless triangles of sandwiches. The crowded plates jostled against the gleaming silver tea-service and the cups and saucers of the best Crown Derby porcelain.

'Who's the visitor?' she asked.

'Miss Alice Delamere – Mr Rupert's married sister's girl,' Mrs Driver said. 'Come over from Dorking way. Mr Ferry had to let her in while you and Joan were wasting time outside.'

On the board over the door, the bell from the drawing room jangled and Cook glanced towards it, clicking her tongue against her teeth. 'Hurry up, Daisy, they'll be wondering what's become of their tea. And mind you come straight back.

Miss Delamere's chauffeur is in the servants' hall now and he'll be needing tea as well.'

As she wheeled the trolley through the swing door and down the polished parquet of the corridor, Daisy eyed the sugar bowl longingly. It was piled high with lump sugar, the tongs balanced precariously on top. There had been a shortage of sugar in the shops since the war broke out, thanks partly to what Rupert described as 'irresponsible panic buying of essential foodstuffs' among the local householders. He had forbidden Mrs Driver to participate. Consequently, since such stocks of sugar as could still be found in the Guildford grocers had almost quadrupled in price, the staff had been told to cut down on their consumption. You wouldn't have known there was any such shortage from the generous provision in the bowl. Daisy surreptitiously removed a lump and slipped it into the capacious pocket of her apron before she knocked on the drawing-room door.

Alice Delamere sat on the linen-covered sofa in front of the fireplace. Jessie and Laura faced her from flanking armchairs, a degree of strain apparent in their upright postures.

'. . . And of course, Laura,' Alice was saying eagerly, her hands clasped around her plump, silk-enveloped knees, 'Hugh and I would like you—'

She broke off as Daisy brought in the trolley and waited while the maid positioned it beside Jessie's elbow. Aware of three pairs of eyes on her, Daisy stooped over the oil burner sitting in the tiled hearth of the fireplace. Having struck a match from the enamelled box on the mantelpiece to light the burner, she set down the little silver kettle on its trivet to simmer, ready for topping up the teapot.

'Thank you, Daisy,' Jessie said. 'That's all.'

Whatever the purpose of Miss Delamere's visit, Daisy told herself as she made her way back to the kitchen, popping the purloined sugar lump into her mouth as she went, it had given Miss Laura an expression that would curdle milk.

It was certainly no consolation to Laura, still smarting over the blight of her own ambitions, that her cousin should be revealing her wedding plans – and with what in normal circumstances would have been unseemly haste, a mere month after the engagement had been announced in *The Times*.

'We'd like you to be a bridesmaid, Laura,' Alice resumed, as the door closed behind Daisy. 'The ceremony is to take place on Saturday, at Saint Martha's church.'

'What exciting news,' Jessie said brightly. She always found conversation with this particular niece hard going and today she wasn't getting much help from Laura. Usually the two girls got on well enough, gossiping away about parties and fashions, subjects on which Jessie felt she had nothing to contribute. But so far this afternoon, Laura had said practically nothing.

'Tea, Alice?' Jessie poured Earl Grey into a wide-bowled cup patterned with roses and passed it to the girl on the sofa. Alice helped herself generously to sugar with the silver tongs and selected a sandwich before continuing.

'We're sorry that it's such short notice, but Hugh expects to be sent overseas very soon, so it's a case of now or never, really. Or rather,' she corrected herself, 'now or waiting for ages until this silly war's been sorted out.'

Her round face and large, pale-blue eyes were glowing with pride, Laura noted waspishly. She had been introduced to Second Lieutenant Hugh Molloy and, from what she could remember, he was an utter ninny. Still, as such he should suit Alice very well.

'But aren't you worried that he might get himself killed?' she asked unkindly, ignoring Jessie's frown and the little shake of her aunt's head that was supposed to warn her off the subject. 'Wouldn't it be better to wait and see? I mean, it'd be a bit of a waste if your parents spent a fortune on the wedding and then Hugh bit the dust, wouldn't it?'

'Well . . . I . . . I don't think. . . .' Well-mannered Alice was clearly confounded by her cousin's frank observation. She bit into her sandwich, her eyes lowered.

Jessie hurried to the rescue. 'I expect your mother's very busy with all the arrangements. So many things to think about!

78

You will let us know if there's anything at all we can do, won't you? More tea, Alice? Cake?'

As she dispensed hospitality, Jessie was wondering, with half her mind, what on earth had got into Laura lately. Ever since that Oxford trip she'd been like a bear with a sore head. Was it something to do with that young man, James Allingham's brother, whom Laura had shown signs of being keen on in the past? Questioned about the trip she'd been very monosyllabic, saying only that they'd been on the river and that Edward had brought his new fiancée along. Of course it could be the war, which had shaken everyone up to some extent, but Laura didn't seem much interested in that, outwardly at any rate. Whatever the reasons for her behaviour, there was no excuse for raising the possibility of early widowhood at what ought to have been one of the happiest times of poor Alice's life.

Jessie made a mental note to tackle Laura on the subject once their guest had gone. In the meantime she launched determinedly on to the safe topic of Alice's trousseau. The detailed description of the various garments, and the attendant difficulties of obtaining them in a hurry, successfully smoothed over the uncomfortable moment.

'. . . And ivory-white satin for the wedding gown, embroidered with pearls, and a court train of satin lined with tulle . . .' prattled Alice, happily, 'and for going away, a pale-pink net costume with a cream satin sash, and the most divine Leghorn hat which Mother found me in Bentalls in Kingston, trimmed with cream silk roses and swathes of brown tulle. And we want the bridesmaids to wear dresses of rose-pink ninon covered with ivory embroidered net. I've brought the fabric with me, and a sketch from *Vogue* for your dressmaker to follow, Laura. I do hope she won't be too rushed to do a good job.'

Laura stared silently into her teacup, biting her lower lip. Jessie was thankful that there were no more cutting remarks, but if her normally rather clothes-conscious niece was too preoccupied with private problems to show an interest in what she was to wear on such a significant occasion as a family wedding, there must be something seriously wrong indeed.

'Laura,' Jessie said tentatively as they stood on the gravelled sweep by the sundial, watching the Delameres' emerald-green De Dion Bouton bowling away down the drive, 'I hope you won't think I'm being intrusive . . . ?'

She hesitated. Laura's expression was distinctly discouraging. But Jessie's sense of duty impelled her to continue. 'I couldn't help noticing how sharp you were with Alice.'

'Well, she gets on my nerves. She's so smug and pleased with herself and her precious Hugh and her ivory-white satin.' Laura mimicked her cousin's round-eyed expression and breathless voice with wicked precision.

'Wouldn't you be if you were going to get married?' Jessie suggested, mildly.

'Well I'm not, so I don't see any point in speculating about how much better or worse than Alice I'd be if I was.'

Laura marched towards the house, her face averted. Behind her, Jessie spread her hands helplessly. She didn't know how to deal with Laura at the best of times but this new aggressiveness was even harder to handle than the reticence she'd been used to.

'I can see that something's upsetting you,' she persisted forlornly as they came into the hall. 'I just wondered if there was anything I could do to help?'

'No thank you,' said Laura, with finality.

There was nothing anyone could do, she was thinking bitterly, as she headed for the privacy of her own room. Much less anyone like Aunt Jessie! For heaven's sake, what was the point in pouring out your emotional secrets to someone so hopelessly ineffectual?

She means well, said a small voice in the back of Laura's mind. *She's only trying to help. She does care about you.*

But it was Edward's caring that Laura pined for and Edward was lost to her. He'd got himself engaged to that clever-clever, self-opinionated nobody, Margaret Churchill. You tried and tried, you made yourself as pretty and elegant and well-mannered as you possibly could. You read the books he'd talked about, studied the subjects you knew he liked to discuss, wore the colours he was supposed to favour . . . and in the end, where did it get you? Men were a bunch of fools Laura decided, scowling as she climbed the stairs, and if being sweet and attentive didn't work, you might as well give up the whole effort and indulge yourself by behaving thoroughly badly. If men like Edward wanted a girl to be as arrogant and outspoken as Margaret, well then, they could have it!

The small, nagging voice in the back of her mind told her she was being childish. She ignored it.

'What about Laura?' said James.

'No, better leave her out of it. She's in a foul mood. She's *always* in a foul mood these days,' said Oliver. 'Heaven knows why.'

James thought he knew why, but it wasn't up to him to interpret the behaviour of his friend's sister and he wasn't particularly anxious to press for her inclusion in their trip to Farnborough to see the aeroplanes at the Flying School. He didn't think aircraft engineering was likely to interest her and he would be inhibited by her boredom. He shrugged his shoulders. 'All right. Are we riding, or using those bikes we hired?'

'Bikes, I suppose. It wouldn't be much of an outing with Plumbago and Blackie. I'd have sore wrists from holding Plum in all the way, and you'd wear your legs out kicking Blackie on.'

It would not occur to Oliver to offer his guest the better mount, James recognized with resignation. And having recently experienced the frustration of trying to get Blackie to move at anything faster than a desultory trot, he agreed wholeheartedly with Oliver's choice of transport.

'I wish Pa'd thought a bit more about his family's needs before he handed over all the decent horses to the army,' Oliver grumbled as they pumped up the tyres of their bicycles in the stable yard. Nowadays the yard seemed depressingly

81

quiet and poor old Nichols wandered disconsolately round the empty stalls like a ghost. Pride in his father's patriotic gesture had been rapidly displaced for Oliver by irritation over the limitations it had been imposing on his mobility ever since. The fact that Rupert, with a car and a chauffeur at his own disposal, had apparently not noticed the inconvenience caused to his family was a further cause for exasperation.

'I wonder where your horses are now?' James said. 'I expect Starbright's a cavalry remount, the pride and joy of some young Hussar. And that groom of yours who volunteered, I wonder which regiment he's ended up in?'

Oliver didn't reply. Volunteering was another sore subject. He was still aggrieved that James had been such a wet blanket about joining in the fun of the war, though in the end it probably wouldn't matter all that much. He'd decided to go it alone, but his first attempts to find a regiment that would commission him had met with some disappointing rebuffs. All that had come of his applications to various cavalry regiments had been a series of terse notes informing him that at present they were up to strength so far as officers were concerned. He'd sent a telegram to his old Officers' Training Corps commander asking for advice, and there had come back the briefest of telegrams advising him to try the recruitment office of his local regiment.

The Queen's might be a 'Royal' regiment, but it was still infantry and Oliver saw himself as a cavalry man. That was where the action was. That was where the battles were won in breathtaking, glorious charges across open countryside, your lance or your sword in your hand. Not in chivvying some straggling battalion of foot-soldiers about in the mud.

He was getting discouraged when he saw the advertisement in *The Times* on 10 August. Lord Kitchener, the recently appointed Secretary of State for War, was looking for two thousand young men aged between seventeen and thirty, to be temporarily commissioned as officers in the 'New Army' he was raising for the war effort. Oliver had applied at once, making his preference for a cavalry posting clear, and had been interviewed at the War Office in London by a brisk recruitment officer who seemed totally unimpressed by his OTC experience or his position as rifle-shooting champion of the school team. He had been bracing himself for another rejection when the man told him that he could expect his appointment to be gazetted within a fortnight. Since then he had been avidly scanning the lists in the daily paper. So far the army, swamped with volunteers, had not managed to allocate him to any regiment. But any day now. . . .

*

'Daisy, Daisy, give me your answer do.
I'm half crazy, all for the love of you. . . .'

The song, drifting back down the road from the head of the column, dredged up persistent memories inside the head of a driver of a battery of the Royal Horse Artillery, in support of the fifth cavalry brigade, on the road to Mons.

Daisy. . . . When last seen, her expression had been utterly woebegone. Griffin wished he could fool himself that it was because she was sorry to see him go, and not because of saying goodbye to her fiancé earlier that day. Even without closing his eyes he could still summon up with ease the image of her face.

Her lashes, he remembered, were surprisingly dark and thick in contrast to the soft, drifting clouds of her hair, that was as bright as fine strands of copper wire under the sun, redder by candlelight. Sometimes at supper, at the long kitchen table at Maple Grange, he'd watched her for whole minutes at a time just for the pleasure of seeing those thick lashes drop, highlighting her pale cheeks with their dusting of ginger-gold freckles. It made his guts contract, even now, to visualize the curve of her cheek in profile. And all the other soft curves of her, too. . . .

No good dwelling on what you've lost, let alone what you never had. He dragged his mind back to the present – not that it was inspiring. The long column of guns and ammunition wagons, of which Griffin's gun team was a part, trailed wearily along the road, the wheels throwing up a drift of fine white dust that settled like powdered snow on the faces of the men and their uniforms and the horses' backs. Another hour before they stopped to water the horses.

Griffin had been slightly stunned by the speed with which the army, having persuaded him to take the King's shilling, had catapulted him towards the active defence of King and Country. He'd expected weeks, perhaps months of training. But on reporting for duty with the Artillery at Aldershot, he had been recognized by the young subaltern who'd spoken to him during the remount requisitions at Guildford Market.

'We've met, haven't we? Aren't you that chap I saw at Guildford the other day, who was so good with horses?'

'Yes, sir, we've met,' said Griffin cautiously. He'd already gathered three things about the army: firstly, that officers on the whole expected to be treated by rankers with more respect than he'd been accustomed to giving even to the gentlemen who were his previous employers; secondly, that rankers were entitled to no respect at all; and thirdly, that if you annoyed an officer, he had considerably more power to make his displeasure felt than, for instance, a young sprig like Oliver Brownlowe.

But the subaltern seemed to be an exception. His grin was unaffectedly friendly. 'Glad you acted on my advice,' he said. 'We'll make good use of you. Been allocated to any particular battery yet?'

'No, sir.'

'Good. Then you can come on to mine. Normally you'd have to go through the whole rigmarole of assessments and training but I think we can dispense with most of that. I'm one driver short – he managed to break a leg in field manoeuvres two days ago and I suspect we'll be off to France within a few days. You can ride, I take it?'

'Yes, sir.'

'You'll have to prove it to my sergeant, but that'll be no problem.'

Proving his horsemanship, Griffin discovered, meant taking

a bad-tempered grey gelding around the arena of the big indoor riding school at the rear of the barracks – to the bellowed commands of a sergeant who seemed to be regarding Second Lieutenant Forsythe's commendation of the new recruit as a personal insult.

'Right, let's see what you can do. Drop reins! Cross stirrups! Fold arms! T-r-rot! Canter! Circle right . . . circle left. . . .'

Cantering the grey in steady figures of eight, using only the weight of his balanced body and the relentless pressure of his legs to drive the uncooperative animal on in the direction indicated, Griffin could tell that the sergeant wanted him to get it wrong. Well, he didn't feel like obliging.

'All right,' the NCO said tersely, at last. 'You can take back your stirrups. See those jumps? Twice round. Off you go.'

There was something about the clenching of the man's fist on the crop he carried that gave Griffin a warning. Passing the sergeant for the second time, he was ready for the wild kick and twist that his mount made in mid-air as the crop came down sharply across its rump, just as it rose to meet a barrier of crossed poles and tin cans.

The aim, of course, had been to unseat the rider and leave him humbled amid the debris of the jump. Instead he sat the buck with ease and finished his two rounds of the grid with the obstacles left intact. If the sergeant's little ploy was routine, Griffin reflected, he couldn't blame the gelding for being bad-tempered.

'Good show,' said Forsythe, coming forward from the side of the arena. 'I don't think we can fault that, can we, Sergeant?'

'No, sir.' The sergeant turned to Griffin, unsmiling. 'A lot of 'em *say* they can ride,' he said, with grudging approval. 'But you're not bad. What's your driving experience? Handled any teams?'

'I've driven four-in-hand in my last place,' Griffin said.

'That'll do. At least you'll know to keep the traces taut.'

So Griffin found himself appointed a driver in the Royal Horse Artillery in the battery subsection overseen by Forsythe, who, anxious to ensure that his unit was battle-ready when the call came, took the new recruit to Laffan's Plain where his section was drilling, and gave him a rapid course of instruction on his duties.

'Right, there are six guns to a battery. Two guns to a subsection. Six horses to draw each gun and limber.'

'Limber?' said Griffin. 'Sir,' he remembered to add.

'That metal box on two wheels. It contains two dozen rounds of ammunition. The gun hooks on behind. Then we have the supporting ammunition wagons. Six horses for each gun and each ammunition wagon. As you can see, the horses are harnessed in pairs on either side of the draught pole leading from the limber. We call them leaders, centre and wheelers, depending on their position. The leader points the way, the wheeler has to do the braking, the centre just has to keep his distance. Otherwise we get what is known as a "leg over" situation, in which the whole outfit is apt to come to a grinding halt. I'm starting you off as a Centre man, to keep it simple for the time being.

'The whole point of the Horse Artillery is to get to where we're going like bats out of hell – our objective is to support the cavalry. That's why we have a lighter gun, a thirteen-pounder instead of an eighteen-pounder like the Field Artillery. We don't slow down for little humps in the ground. I'll get the team to demonstrate.'

Griffin watched while the three drivers of the gun team, mounted on the nearside horse of each pair, kicked their mounts into a gallop almost from a standing start and careered across the rough grass – the limber and gun bucketing after them. As Forsythe had said, they made no concessions to the state of the ground, hitting one particularly vicious ridge at a speed which sent the gun flying into the air before it crashed back to earth in a way which would have meant disaster for the wooden-wheeled vehicles of Griffin's previous experience. But the breakneck progress of the team did not slacken. They continued to race round the field, the grinning faces of the drivers showing how exhilarating they found the exercise, before finally skidding to a flourishing halt, forelegs braced, in front of their subaltern.

'Think you can do that?' said Forsythe.

'I think so, sir.' Griffin was itching to try.

'Fine. Carry on.'

The other drivers on his new team at first greeted him with the same suspicion that he had encountered from the sergeant instructor. But his skill with the horses overcame his 'new boy' status very quickly. All they wanted was someone who could handle the job and ensure that they wouldn't be left behind when the battery was ordered overseas.

'You certainly fell on your feet, though, when you got sent to us,' said Dawson, the lead driver of the team. 'Forsythe's is the best subsection in the whole blinking Horse Artillery and The Horse Artillery's the élite of the Regiment. You should see us in the full dress uniform! A sight to gladden a young girl's heart that is, and no mistake. The girls I've kissed on the strength of my uniform . . .' he added, reminiscently.

Griffin did not doubt that Dawson would prove a very efficient ruffler of maidenly tranquillity when clad in a close-fitting black tunic plastered with frogging, a broad scarlet stripe on the leg of his tight black trousers, his head adorned by a shako with a scarlet trim and his swaggering confidence buffed for conquest. 'But you won't get a look-in there,' the heartbreaker added cheerfully, eyeing Griffin in his civilian clothes. 'In fact you'll be blinking lucky to get any uniform at all.'

The army was indeed hard pushed to supply its tidal wave of volunteers with the most basic combat kit. Griffin passed them on the barrack square, the new recruits drilling glumly with broomsticks instead of guns, their dreams of glory temporarily punctured. But within a day Forsythe, tireless in his pursuit of a flawless subsection, had hounded a weary quartermaster into unearthing a full set of khaki combat kit for his replacement driver.

Griffin spent the days that followed in learning new routines at an unaccustomed rate. He loved the gallops with the gun team. They challenged all his skill as a rider and answered a need for extreme physical exertion and risk that he had long suppressed as Rupert Brownlowe's calm and orderly groom. He had always been a loner. Now he discovered how satisfying it could be to operate as part of a team. In other ways his duties were not so very different from those he had carried out at Maple Grange. He helped to care for the battery's horses, housed in stalls in the huge, two-storeyed Artillery barracks. He slept in a communal barrack room above the stables, where he was allotted a metal-framed bed with a shelf above it, a bedroll, a tin trunk for his possessions and an issue of sheets and blankets. The bed frame extended for sleeping and was contracted in the daytime to make room for a long trestle table and benches to be set up in the centre of the room, at which the men ate the food fetched in tin pails and dixies from the kitchen. They were never away from the smell of horse.

Through watching the gunners at work, Griffin began to understand the ways in which the gun was loaded and aimed and with his usual thoroughness he mentally filed the information for future reference.

'Morning sarn't. How's our new man shaping up?'

'See for yourself, sir.'

It was a week after Griffin's arrival at the barracks. He was aware of Forsythe's eyes on him as his team carried out a speed drill. A sharp blast on the whistle from the sergeant sent the horses galloping towards the designated firing point. Griffin leaned forward in the saddle, kicking his own mount on while keeping a weather eye on the 'hand' horse galloping alongside; he used the whip in his right hand to urge the horse on or to hold it back with a warning touch on the collar pad of its harness if it threatened to get out of step. At the firing point the team came to a collective halt and as the drivers moved to detach the traces from the limber, the mounted gunners, having tossed their horses' reins to a waiting horse holder, were already unhooking the big gun and setting it up for firing.

Moving in unison, the drivers remounted and galloped back to the 'wagon line', reaching it as the gunners furiously spun height-adjustment wheels and snapped open the shell chamber to prepare for loading and firing at the preordained range. Meanwhile the limber gunners had the limber propped forward on its pole, lid raised, and were passing out the long gleaming shells. Even as the drivers dismounted, the arm of the leading gunner went up to show that the gun was ready to fire.

Griffin stood panting at his horse's shoulder, awaiting the subaltern's verdict.

'I think he'll do,' said Forsythe, with satisfaction. 'A very polished performance by the whole team, Sergeant.' He raised his voice.

'Right men, here's the news you've been waiting for. Brigade to be ready to move at six hours' notice.'

Hats flew into the air as they raised a ragged cheer.

There had followed a tiring succession of journeys by boat, train and road, across the channel and through Normandy and Picardy towards the Belgian border. They'd had to transfer the horses on board ship by slings, a process to which the animals did not take kindly, and afterwards had come the agonizingly slow progress of the trains, with eight horses coaxed and bullied into every crammed wagon and the only break in the monotony the four-hourly stop for watering. Now there was this road trek, for mile after dusty mile . . . but at least it was a relief to be in the saddle again.

Looking back over his shoulder and across the top of the limber, Griffin could see the gleaming bulk of the gun they were pulling. It looked reassuringly solid and powerful, a lethal machine maintained at the highest level of efficiency. How the French had cheered the guns as they'd passed among the crowds at the port! The Boche wouldn't argue for long with those, they'd exulted. *Les Boches finis . . . Guillaume fini . . .* And the small children had drawn their fingers across their throats with grinning relish, miming the impending fate of the Kaiser and his hated troops.

Nobody had raised the point that the advancing Germans had guns of their own . . . and many more of them.

Griffin had signed on 'for three years or the duration of the war, whichever is the longer'. Lord Kitchener had stipulated that those should be the terms for the new recruits, but his estimate was widely viewed as being over-cautious. 'It'll all be over by Christmas', that's what everyone else reckoned. They'd wipe the floor with the Germans and show Kaiser Wilhelm that what he'd reportedly called their 'contemptible little army' was worth ten of his rabble. And then they'd go home.

The trouble was, Griffin didn't have a home any more, or anything much to go home for.

5

Cycling along the high east-west ridge of the Hog's Back, James and Oliver paused to scan the green-and-gold chequered landscape of fields and woodland spread out to the North. Farnborough, their destination, was lost in a haze of sunlight on the horizon. They turned off the long ridge and freewheeled downhill into Ash Green, the breeze against their hot bodies a relief from the blistering heat of the afternoon.

At the foot of the slope they came up behind an old man ambling along the narrow lane with a large wicker basket clutched under his arm. Despite the dazzling sunshine he was wearing a shabby brown woollen coat, shabby at the elbows and cuffs and distinctly dirty. Oliver rang his bell to give warning of their coming, but the man continued to plod doggedly along and as the cyclists drew abreast of him he meandered into their path, forcing Oliver to swerve violently to one side, the unplanned manoeuvre almost throwing him into the road. He caught a glimpse of a startled face as he shot by.

'Daft old coot,' he said furiously, as James came up alongside. 'Weaving about like that. Nearly had me over. D'you think he was drunk or something?'

'Just old and tired, I'd say. And deaf as well,' said James. 'He obviously hadn't heard us.'

'What's he doing now?'

'He's gone down that footpath towards the railway line. I suppose it's a short cut.'

'Good riddance. He's a menace on the roads,' said Oliver, watching over his shoulder as the pedestrian made his unsteady way along the narrow footpath which dropped down the side of the embankment. Oliver's front tyre wobbled as it hit a rut and he hastily returned his attention to the road. In the centre of the humpback bridge ahead, where the road crossed the railway line, stood a soldier with a Lee Enfield rifle slung over his shoulder. As the two cyclists approached, he unhooked the gun and raised the stock deliberately to his shoulder.

'Halt. Who goes there?' he called, squinting along the barrel. Oliver and James exchanged glances of amusement as they slowed to a halt.

'One of the Territorials,' Oliver whispered. 'I heard they'd been posted to guard railway bridges in case some German spy decides to blow 'em up to inconvenience the army.'

The sentry was young and twitchy. They heard a distinct click of the trigger going back as he cocked the gun. Abruptly the situation ceased to be funny.

'Stop and identify yourselves. Show your hands.'

'My name's Brownlowe, from Maple Grange, the other side of Seale.' Oliver bestrode his bike, hands raised, palms forward. 'And this is my friend Allingham. He's from Hindhead.'

'Dismount. Come forward. Slowly.'

They wheeled their bicycles forward obediently.

'What's in the saddlebags?' the sentry said. His skinny figure and ferret-sharp features were stiff with self-importance. Everything about him irritated Oliver. *Wonderful what a uniform and a gun will do for his type*, he was thinking, his resentment sharpened by the knowledge that this youth had an official rôle in the war, however trivial, and as yet he, Oliver, didn't.

'It's only food,' James said.

'Oh yes? Show me.' And the boy gestured peremptorily with his rifle butt.

'For heaven's sake. This is ridiculous. Do we look like German saboteurs?' Oliver demanded.

'I couldn't say. I don't know what a German saboteur looks like, do I?' the young soldier replied stolidly.

'That's fair comment, Oliver,' said James, straight-faced. 'You wouldn't expect a spy to carry a big notice around his neck saying *Ich bin von Heidelberg*, would you? So this gentleman has to be on the safe side. I think we should cooperate, don't you?' And he unbuckled the straps on his saddlebag to reveal packed sandwiches and a lemonade bottle. Reluctantly, Oliver followed suit and, having satisfied himself that there were no explosives hidden in the picnic lunch, the soldier waved them on.

'Officious little blighter,' muttered Oliver.

'Just doing his job,' said James soothingly.

They were thirty yards on down the road when they heard the sentry's voice again.

'Halt. Who goes there? Stop and identify yourself. Stop, I said!' And a moment later, with increasing agitation, 'Here, you! Halt, or I'll fire!'

'That old man . . . ?' James said, braking hard. A shot rang out.

'Christ!' said Oliver.

'Come on!' James slewed his bike round in a scatter of grit and dust. When they rejoined the young soldier below the bridge, he was standing in the long grass by the footpath, looking down at a sprawl of shabby brown coat and splayed limbs, with a wicker basket half-obscured beneath.

'He wouldn't stop when I called,' said the soldier, white-faced and appalled at what he'd done. 'And he had something suspicious in that basket.'

'He was deaf, you idiot,' said James. From out of the basket a small puppy struggled, whimpering with fright. Oliver scooped it up and stroked his hand absent-mindedly over its head, staring curiously down at the motionless body.

'Is he dead?' he asked.

'I dunno,' the soldier responded, barely audible.

'Hadn't we better check?'

It was James who turned the body over carefully. The old man's eyes stared up into the sun, unblinking. There was no doubt, even without the spreading red stain on his shirt, beneath the opened front of his coat, that the soldier's aim had been better than his judgement.

'It weren't my fault,' the lad said. He was on the verge of tears. His hands, clenched around the stock and barrel of his gun, were trembling.

Oliver couldn't take his eyes off the body. It was the first time he had seen anybody dead. He was rather pleased with the way he was taking it. Good practice for the war. 'I suppose we'd better go and get some help sent back,' he suggested.

'I'll go, if you'll stay here.' The soldier was pathetically eager to get away from the body of his victim.

'No, you can't. That'd be deserting your post,' Oliver told him firmly. 'Come on, James. Looks like we'll have to postpone the Farnborough trip for now.'

As an afterthought he dropped the shivering puppy into the carrier basket at the front of his bicycle. Somebody had to look after the poor little brute, after all.

Mr Oliver's rescued puppy was a black-and-brown mix of labrador and border collie, of no value as a gun dog or anything else, as Rupert commented dismissively when it first got underfoot.

'Probably on its way to be drowned when you came across it,' he added. 'Hand it over to Nichols and tell him to see to it. Humanely, of course.'

'Do I have to, Pa?'

Oliver had never owned a dog. There had been dogs on the premises from time to time, puppies that Rupert and Laura 'walked' for the local hunt. They came, were taught rudimentary manners and went, changing from one school holidays to the next, so he had never bothered to get attached to them. The mongrel puppy was different. So far, it had followed its new master about with dumb devotion, became suitably chastened when shouted at and was ready to retrieve sticks for as long as Oliver could be bothered to throw them – thumping its stubby tail in pathetic gratitude for any attention he could be bothered to bestow. Best of all, it was selective in its affections and had been heard to growl at Ferry.

'Do you want to keep it? I can't imagine why.'

'If it's all right with you, Pa, I would.'

Rupert shrugged his shoulders. 'Well, just make sure it's not a nuisance for the staff, that's all.'

Oliver gave the animal a name, and 'it' became 'he'.

'Magnus?' said Laura dubiously. 'Why Magnus?'

'Magnus the Magnificent. To give him something to live up to.'

As far as the staff were concerned, Magnus's nuisance value was unmitigated. He howled plaintively through the night from his kennel in a corner of the stable yard and left puddles everywhere he shouldn't when permitted indoors by his new master.

'As if we haven't got enough to cope with, what with the war and everything,' muttered Joan, wrinkling her nose as she took a mop to the latest misdemeanour.

The war was beginning to make itself felt in Surrey. The local paper reflected the changing preoccupations of its reader. Accounts of cricket matches or the prices fetched for beef cattle at farm auctions had been replaced by lists of Surrey men who had already volunteered for the armed forces, and reports of spy scares or the harrowing experiences of tourists who'd managed to struggle home from ill-timed Continental holidays.

'I see the Red Cross is appealing for the loan of beds and bedding to equip emergency hospitals for wounded troops,' Rupert said at breakfast on the day after his son introduced Magnus into the household. 'Jessica, you had better look something out for them.'

'Yes, Rupert.' Since the war began, Jessie had felt obliged to put in an appearance at the breakfast table each morning. It was up to the entire population, Rupert said, to play its part cheerfully and energetically, accepting whatever hardships were in store; and giving up her peaceful private breakfasts was one of Jessie's hardships. Her brother wanted her to be available for his daily news bulletins about the war, and his

95

reviews of his family's contribution to the waging of it. Now, in response to his instruction, she made a rapid mental assessment of the contents of her store cupboards.

She didn't think there was a decent spare bed in the house suitable for donation. In fact, it was high time that the maids' old iron bedsteads were replaced, and Mrs Driver had been bemoaning the shortage of good sheets only yesterday – Joan spent far too much time, she claimed, repairing linen that had worn so thin as to tear at the slightest mishandling. But it was no good going into detail about such matters with Rupert; he would only become tetchy.

'And they've asked for volunteers to carry out various duties,' he continued. 'What do you propose to do? Jessica? Laura?'

'What duties?' Laura asked, from the end of the table.

'Let's see . . . nursing, cooking, scrubbing, laundering, clerical and typing duties. There must be something among that list that you can usefully undertake,' her father said genially.

Laura pulled a face. 'I suppose I might try some nursing training,' she decided, at last. Jessica was silent. She was thinking that none of the activities that Rupert had just outlined were of the kind that he would deign to undertake himself. Why was it that women always got shunted into the menial activities while men got the action and the glory? Then she felt ashamed of her flash of rebelliousness.

That's the sort of thing the suffragettes would say . . . she rebuked herself. And even the suffragettes had now voted to suspend their campaigning for votes for women, in the face of the common peril. . . . She became aware of Rupert waiting, eyebrows raised, for the answer to his question about what she proposed to do for the war effort. 'Oh . . . I've been invited by Mrs Cardew at The Laurels to join a working party,' she said hastily. 'Making hospital supplies I think she said. Bandages and slings and things, and pyjamas for the wounded. And Mrs Grey is getting up another group to make baby clothes for the families of soldiers and sailors who are away at the war . . . though I'm not sure why they should need any more baby clothes just at this moment. One would have thought, if their husbands were away. . . .'

Her voice trailed away. Rupert was giving her an odd look and Oliver had just suppressed a snort of laughter. '. . . And one of the army wives is organizing parcels of comforts for the Queen's regiment on active service,' she added, 'so I've said I'll help to collect and pack items for those—'

'Good, good,' said Rupert impatiently. He hadn't wanted details, he'd just needed to assure himself that his womenfolk were properly organized. 'Laura, you'll enrol for Red Cross training promptly I hope? It could tie in rather well, because I'm considering offering this house as a hospital for wounded officers.'

Jessie spluttered into her tea.

'Is something the matter, Jessica?'

'N-no. It's just a little unexpected.' In fact, Jessie was appalled by the suggestion. Where did Rupert propose to put these wounded officers, to say nothing of all the nurses and doctors and surgeons who would presumably be needed to tend to them? How did he intend to dispose of his family while the Grange became a hospital? And what would the staff say? She dabbed at her mouth with her napkin and told herself to keep calm.

'Well, there's a meeting of the Red Cross committee this afternoon,' Rupert continued. 'You'd better go along and make the offer.'

'Very well. But I'm sure it would come better from you,' Jessie said doubtfully. She had encountered some of the ladies who ran the committee and found them intimidatingly efficient.

'I don't have time,' said Rupert. 'I have business in London. And I'll be taking Aldridge and the motor by the way – assuming, that is, that he can get hold of any petrol. This shortage and the price rise is nothing short of scandalous. It's all the fault of the panic-buyers. Anyway Nichols can take you in the governess cart.'

Jessie slotted the instruction into what was already a crowded day. The food shortages had become alarming in the last few days, showing no signs of improving, and she was under pressure from Mrs Driver to do a little panic-buying of groceries herself. Moreover she had planned to spend the afternoon at the Home Farm in an attempt to charm Mr Inglis, the farmer, out of the bad humour occasioned by Rupert's regular and vociferous complaining about the quality of the food supplied to the house.

'Don't he know there's a war on?' Mrs Inglis had said yesterday with ominous insolence, when instructed to convey a message to her husband about the unacceptability of yesterday's basket of vegetables for the house. 'We're having enough trouble managing, what with half the regular harvest helpers going off to enlist, without having to worry about the odd slug on Mr Brownlowe's lettuces.'

It was a comment that Jessie would not dare to repeat to her brother, but it indicated that some smoothing down of the disgruntled couple was long overdue. Well, it will simply have to wait till tomorrow, she reflected, momentarily relieved at the postponement of what had promised to be an embarrassing exercise. Then she imagined herself relaying Rupert's hospital proposal to the daunting ladies of the Red Cross Committee and her spirits drooped again.

Rupert, having skimmed through the contents of the local paper, had turned his attention to a new publication – a weekly magazine that he had recently ordered from the newsagents, which promised him a detailed, fully illustrated account of the progress of the war.

'Good heavens! Listen to this.'

Jessie, Laura and Oliver duly concentrated. They were getting used to Rupert's new habit of relaying war news over the remains of the kedgeree and recognized that they were expected to take it seriously. James Allingham, however, reached for another piece of toast from the silver rack and began to spread it with butter and marmalade.

'It is reliably reported,' Rupert read, suppressing his

irritation at the bad manners exhibited by his son's guest, 'that an elderly Belgian priest has been strung up in his own bell tower by jeering Prussian troops and his body used as the clapper for his bell, his crime being the keeping of carrier pigeons to supplement his meagre diet. This made him, to the crazed eyes of the jackbooted invaders, an undoubted spy.'

The story, graphically illustrated by the magazine's artists in a manner that closely imitated photography, had horrified Rupert – in his book the elderly and the clergy were traditionally sacrosanct sections of the community. He was taken aback when James, having swallowed a mouthful of toast, remarked thoughtfully, 'I wonder what that means, when they say *It is reliably reported*?'

'Well, of course it means that the facts have been gathered from reliable sources.'

'But what makes them reliable? Being anti-German? There aren't any photographs of the enemy actually doing all these terrible things, just those rather sensational drawings.'

'It can hardly be expected that they would pose for the photographers while executing a priest,' Rupert said sarcastically. 'Though they seem ready enough to do so when feeding Belgian refugee children.' He turned another page disgustedly. A sepia-tinted shot of a 'jackbooted invader' with a child on his knee leered up at him. 'Like this rubbish. Taken for propaganda purposes of course, in an attempt to cover up what they are actually doing in Belgium. No . . . as this magazine makes clear – maiming, raping and pillaging is more the invader's style!'

He caught sight of Jessie's startled expression and frowned. Now this wretched Allingham boy had got him discussing unmentionable subjects like rape in front of the ladies. Not that Jessica herself had shown much taste, he recalled, in referring so indelicately to the effects on baby-production of absentee service-husbands.

'But that "Berlin Butchers" style of reporting is so one-sided,' James persisted. 'I'd be much more convinced the incidents are genuine if the reports were more objective. A German soldier can't even salute a passing funeral without it being "an ironic gesture". If the Belgian priest with the carrier pigeons was innocent, assuming the whole story isn't trumped up, then I agree it's a horrific act. But in Guildford our lot are arresting German waiters as potential spies with no grounds for proof. The last issue of that same magazine included news that our troops in Belgium are summarily executing German "spies" and there's no outcry about that. And if a Frenchman in civilian clothes takes pot shots at the Germans he's a brave "*franc-tireur*" but when the other side resorts to disguise it's "dastardly subterfuge".'

'But we're fighting a war!' Rupert put down the magazine beside his plate and leaned forward across the table, the knuckles of his clenched hands white with the effort of keeping his temper.

'So are they, sir. That's the point. But the war-history publications are puffing our side's actions as noble and heroic and lending credence to every wild rumour about the enemy purely in order to stoke up public feeling. It's a recruitment aid,' James said – not noticing, because he was so engrossed in a subject that interested him, how badly he was trespassing on his host's areas of conviction.

To say that Rupert was appalled, to be challenged like this at his own table, was an understatement. He was used to deference in his household. Until now, his conversations with James had been the polite exchanges about the weather and the cricket results, benign on Rupert's side and respectful on James', that convention demanded. He was torn between the urge to demolish the boy's ridiculous arguments and an awareness that to descend to debate on the subject with someone who had only just ceased to be a schoolboy would be beneath his dignity.

It was no use, he couldn't stay silent. 'What further need do we have to *stoke up feeling*, as you put it?' Rupert exploded. 'Haven't they been the aggressors? Haven't they invaded neutral Belgium and sent millions of refugees fleeing for their lives? Isn't it clear that they're operating a calculated campaign of terror against the refugees? Look at the disgusting behaviour of their troops at Herstal, turning on those poor women in the way they did.'

The women in question, workers at the National Arms Factory in Belgium, had reportedly poured boiling water on a troop of Uhlans – who had reacted with what James felt was predictable savagery in the circumstances.

'But don't you agree, sir, that it would have been a bit difficult for a scalded Uhlan to remember that munitions workers armed with pans of boiling water were innocent, helpless victims, even if they *were* women?'

Belatedly it dawned on James that Rupert emphatically did not agree. The expression on his face suggested that if he had had access to a pan of boiling water at that moment he would not have hesitated to pour it over James.

'I am disgusted by your attitude young man,' Rupert said at last. His voice shook with emotion. Of course, he was telling himself, it was all down to background. The Allinghams were known dabblers in socialism – members of the Fabian Society who were, in Rupert's estimation, a group of misguided so-called intellectuals, peddling a lot of unrealistic nonsense about changing society by non-aggressive confrontation and about men being born equal – as if you could expect a man like Rupert to go through the pantomime of behaving like the equal of his blacksmith or his chauffeur. Rupert had sometimes been concerned by Oliver's choice of companion. If he had realized what such ideas could lead to, he would have forbidden the association long ago. In his opinion, the views James had just voiced amounted to treason and he said so.

'Oh, come on, sir. That's ridiculous. I'm just playing Devil's Advocate,' James protested, genuinely startled by the response that his attempts to be rational had provoked.

'This war is not a game,' said Rupert, and left the table and the room.

There was an uncomfortable silence.

'I seem to have upset your father,' James apologized to

Oliver. 'I'm sorry. I never realized he was swallowing all that stuff in the magazine.' Now that the little confrontation was over he was embarrassed by his own uncharacteristic outspokenness.

'It's not stuff,' Oliver said, breathing hard. 'It's genuine reports of genuine suffering and there are troops of ours, even now, who are risking their lives to avenge it. I agree with Pa. I think your remarks were pretty well beyond the pale for an Englishman.'

James laughed, out of pure nervous tension, and then regretted it when he saw the flush of fury it had brought to Oliver's good-looking features.

'Sorry,' he said. 'But you're being awfully pompous.'

Oliver abruptly pushed back his chair and followed his father out of the room. James was left with the Brownlowe women. Jessica, tight-lipped, toyed with her napkin ring, plainly wishing herself elsewhere. But Laura, he discovered, was studying him with unusual interest. He cleared his throat.

'Well . . . I'll go and pack my things, I suppose. I seem to have outstayed my welcome.'

'Oh, they'll calm down,' Laura said. 'I expect Oliver'll come back and make things up in a while. It's normally him that has the rows with Pa, only he doesn't usually get to say quite so much before Pa blows him up.' She reached for the magazine her father had dropped beside his plate, and studied the relevant report for a moment.

'It is a bit sensational, the way it's told,' she said. 'But it could still be true . . . though naturally no one wants to believe even the Germans could behave so brutishly.'

'Yes, that's right. It could be true. The only point I was trying to make is that we ought to exercise caution and not assume that it always *has* to be true,' James said quickly, eager to have someone understand his attitude. 'And though you say that no one wants to believe those reports, it seems to me that most people do want to. They're eagerly reading anything they can lay their hands on that will reinforce their belief that the war's a just cause. But *is* it a just cause? Do we get told what's going on – or only what our leaders want us to know? I've heard that Kitchener wouldn't let war correspondents go with the troops. Told 'em to supply themselves with horses and then promptly made sure that the army requisitioned the horses. So the Press is dependent on what the War Office chooses to tell them. And the people in charge of this war, on both sides . . . well, they've so much tied up in it. It wouldn't be beyond them to manipulate public opinion, would it? For all we know, the Germans are telling their people that our lot are the bullies and the butchers, and publishing illustrations that are supposed to prove it, like the ones in that magazine.'

'But with our troops, it wouldn't be true,' Laura said simply. 'The British always fight fair, don't we?'

James gave it up. The Brownlowes were all in the same mould, he told himself sadly. Bone-headed patriots, as unquestioningly loyal to their leaders as the dog Magnus was to his owner. He wished he could sort out his own feelings so clearly – it would be a great relief to know exactly where one's sympathies lay. He found the flavour of Rupert's magazine repellent, and the war-fervour in the streets seemed all wrong to him. War wasn't a game. On that point, at least, he agreed wholeheartedly with his host. It was a grim exercise in human destruction and James, who had never hated anyone enough to want him dead, shied away from the thought of getting involved in armed slaughter. But at the same time he had to admit the illegality of the German invasion of Belgium. And if a crime is committed and supported by arms, how do you punish it except by the use of arms?

He postponed the resolving of this moral dilemma and went upstairs to pack.

As Laura had predicted, Oliver had calmed down within an hour. 'Let's not quarrel,' he said. 'It's only a difference of opinion, and what's that between friends?' But the words came out stiffly and he couldn't put much warmth into his invitation to continue the visit, partly because it had to be recognized that Pa was very annoyed indeed about the incident, and Pa annoyed was a fearsome thing to behold. Besides, the difference of opinion had at the time seemed more like a chasm than a rift. So although James's departure was achieved with civility, it was with obvious relief that Oliver saw him go. And Laura, James was sure, had never cared much for his company.

Ironically, though he did not know it, this morning was the first time that Laura had seen any resemblance between colourless James and his resplendent brother. Just for a moment, as the words tumbled out, his animated face had held her attention and she'd thought, *there is someone worth knowing better* . . . but then he'd gone and she kicked herself for having such a stupid notion.

'One more thing, Jessie,' said Rupert, as he prepared to set off on the trip to London that he had described briefly as 'business'. 'The army's billeting officer has been here and I have told him we'll take as many of his men as he wishes.'

Jessie closed her eyes for a moment. So she was to part with all their spare bedding, of which they hadn't any. She was to convert the house into a hospital, at which point they'd need all that bedding and more. She was to expect the imminent arrival of an unspecified number of soldiers. She wished wanly that Rupert would make up his mind where exactly she was supposed to allocate his resources.

She was so exasperated by the events of the morning that she allowed herself the luxury of telling James Allingham, as he shared her transport into Guildford, that she agreed with him entirely about the tone of Rupert's magazine, and especially with his comment to Laura about how avid the nation seemed to be for news of German atrocities.

'I do wish people wouldn't take such a *delight* in this war,' she said, with unaccustomed vigour. James, who hadn't previously noticed Oliver's downtrodden-looking aunt having an opinion about anything, was too startled to reply.

The Red Cross Committee was as ruthlessly efficient as Jessie had feared, and as condescending. Rupert's offer of his home as a hospital, when she was finally able to voice it, was turned down after the barest consideration, as 'unsuitable'. The suitability of a home, Jessie suspected ruefully, was in direct proportion to the social importance of its owners and there were other members of local society whose claims to the distinction of offering hospitality to wounded heroes far outweighed those of Rupert Brownlowe.

Jessie came home dreading the prospect of conveying the rejection to her brother – to find that twenty cheerful recruits to Kitchener's New Army, on their way to intensive training on Salisbury Plain, had been billeted for the weekend in the rooms over the stable block. They were nice enough lads and properly respectful Joan told her, but of course feeding them and dealing with their laundry would mean extra work for the staff. And Nichols, complaining bitterly, had had to move his belongings over to the farm for the duration of their stay.

'. . . And I don't know how we're supposed to manage for food, with that lot eating us out of house and home,' said Mrs Driver as Joan gave her a hand with making a gigantic casserole for supper. She was cross and agitated at the prospect of catering for so many, at such short notice.

'They're paying, aren't they?' said Joan. 'The requisitioning billet says two-and-six per day for each soldier's food and accommodation, so Mr Rupert won't be out of pocket! There's plenty round here that would've been glad to give them lodgings for that, *and* better lodgings than a few old mattresses just thrown down on the floor over the stables.'

'That's all very well,' retorted Mrs Driver, slapping down a chunk of braising steak on to her chopping board and slicing into it with venom. 'But who is it that has to worry about the stocks in the larder and the dairy? And who's going to have to scold that lazy old trout Inglis into sending up more beef and vegetables for tomorrow? Miss Jessie won't manage it, she's far too meek and mild. And will you look at this?' She gestured with a blood-smeared knife towards the diet sheet which had been provided as guidance to the correct nourishment for the visitors. 'As if I don't know how to feed a working man, and me a cook to gentlemen's households for thirty years!'

Mr Rupert's patriotic profit from the billeting rates wasn't going to come to much thought Joan, as the cook, sniffing indignantly, proceeded to toss considerably more beef than the prescribed amount into the casserole dish at her elbow. 'Still, we all have to do our bit to help beat the Germans,' the housemaid told herself philosophically. For Joan, doing her bit seemed likely to prove personally as well as morally satisfying. One of the soldiers was showing flattering signs of interest.

The First Battalion of the Queen's was also trying to do its bit, but with growing frustration.

'What I want to know is,' said Arthur Bright, 'when the hell are we going to get a crack at Jerry? All this bloody marching. *Hurry-up-lads-or-you'll-miss-the-war.* And when we get there, nothing to do all day but sit about and wait for supper time.'

'And digging,' Robert Colindale reminded him dourly.

'And digging,' Arthur agreed with bitter recollection. 'Christ, if I'd wanted to play at moles I'd have joined the sappers, not the infantry.' He groped in the breast pocket of his tunic for a packet of Woodbines and offered one to his companion. Robert silently produced Louella's Vesta case and their heads bent together over the flame.

It was almost six o'clock on the afternoon of 23 August. Last night they had reached Le Croix Rouveroy, a few miles south of Mons, at the end of a gruelling day's marching, and had collapsed thankfully into exhausted sleep in a range of farm outbuildings on the edge of the village. At half past three in the morning they had been unceremoniously roused from the hay, presented with entrenching tools and told to dig trenches in the bone-hard ground among the cabbages, and then they had sat in them under a hot sun, awaiting their baptism of fire.

Hour followed hour. Away to the North-west they could

hear the constant crackle of rifle fire and the boom of detonating artillery shells.

'Someone's catching it hot,' Robert said, dragging nervously at his cigarette.

'Let's hope it's Jerry. About time Herr General von Kluck got what's coming to him.' Arthur began to hum a tune under his breath and the soldier next to him took it up with the words. Soon a whole group of them were softly singing the mocking song, leaning their backs against the soil wall of the trench, legs splayed out in front of them.

> '. . . Kaiser Bill, he's feeling ill,
> The Crown Prince he's gone barmy.
> We don't give a—
> For old von Kluck
> And all his bleedin' army. . . .'

'Right lads, on your feet! We're going forward. Reinforcing the Second Infantry Brigade.'

The subaltern who brought the order arrived at a run from a nearby wireless post. Hastily Robert stubbed his cigarette out in the dirt and scrambled upright, reaching for the loaded rifle propped beside him. His mouth was dry, the palms of his hands suddenly damp with sweat. He surreptitiously rubbed first one hand, then the other, against his khaki-clad thighs. Shooting a sideways glance at his friend he caught Arthur in the act of moistening his lips nervously with his tongue. It was comforting, Robert thought, to know that your mates were as scared witless as you were. They filed forward.

False alarm. After further hours of aching tension, lying about in an open field with every sense straining for signs of an attack, at dusk they were ordered back to their trenches.

Rupert came back from London smiling broadly, his bad mood of the morning completely dissipated by the events of the day. Even Jessica's timid revelation that his generous offer to provide hospital accommodation had been snubbed by the

Red Cross Committee could not puncture his high good humour.

'No matter, no matter. There's more ways than one of contributing to the war effort. Mine shall be in the field of manufacture. I signed a contract this afternoon with the War Office.'

'Do the army need lawn mowers?' Jessie said blankly. Rupert's little engineering works had been operating in this area with steady, if not spectacular success until the war began, but lately she had gathered from her brother's gloomy comments that the national obsession with trim lawns had been somewhat reduced.

'Don't be so frivolous, Jessica. We shall be making shells. Artillery shells.'

And the beauty of it was, he thought jubilantly, it would kill two birds with one stone. What was good for the War Office would also be the saving of Rupert's flagging business. Virtue's Just Rewards indeed.

'A pretty wedding,' was how Alice Delamere's marriage to Hugh Molloy was described by those attending. It was generally agreed that Alice's parents had done wonders in providing such a picturesque occasion at such short notice. Of course, it helped that the groom and many of the male guests were in uniform. The sight of so many fine young men demonstrating their readiness to take up arms in the cause of their country was apt to bring a lump to the throat of every right-thinking Englishman.

Laura, self-conscious in rose-pink ninon, a colour and a fabric she hated, stood behind her cousin's small, plump figure at the head of the aisle with the frothing lace of Alice's court train spread carefully over the chequered quarry tiles at her feet. She wondered idly what would happen if she trod on it. She was hot and bored. Her chaplet of flowers seemed to trap the heat on her forehead. She'd decided that she didn't like Alice and she'd never wanted to be a bridesmaid anyway – though the gold locket which Hugh had presented to each of the four bridesmaids had shown surprising good taste. He certainly did look better in the full dress uniform of the Royal Horse Guards, she had to admit. Amazing what all that gold braid and aiguillettes could do for sloping shoulders and a weak chin.

His best man, on the other hand, had all the advantages of the uniform and a much better profile. His face looked vaguely familiar to Laura, but she couldn't put a name to it. She'd have to find out at the reception.

Robert sucked in his breath. As he peered over the top of his trench, squinting along the barrel of his rifle, a small party of cavalry emerged from a belt of trees in the distance and by the blue-grey uniforms and distinctive spiked helmets he could tell that they were Prussian Uhlans.

'Sir . . . ?' he whispered warningly to the man on his right, the young first lieutenant who was at that moment in charge of their company.

'I see 'em,' the lieutenant said under his breath. 'Scouts. And being careless about it. Let 'em get well in range.'

All along the line of the shallow trench the men crouched unmoving, holding their fire until the riders, cantering unsuspectingly forward, were within four hundred yards.

'Now!'

There was a brief, murderous burst of rifle fire. The British Expeditionary Force had rehearsed its riflemen to the point where they could deliver sixteen accurate rounds per minute and when the fusillade was over, three of the riders lay spreadeagled in the dust amid their threshing horses. As the percussion smoke cleared, the fourth rider could be seen bolting back the way he had come, lying low on his terrified horse and pursued by the last hopeful bullets of the infantrymen.

'Damn. Missed one,' said the lieutenant unemotionally. 'You'll have to do better next time. Reload.'

The three Uhlans were emphatically dead. It took a little longer to finish off the wounded horses. Seemed a bit of a shame, Robert thought. A horse couldn't choose which side it was on, after all. The incident had been a relief, dispelling the tension like the scoring of a first run after a slow opening to a cricket match against unknown adversaries. But the brief surge of jubilation evaporated a few minutes later, giving way to dismay when 'B' company was ordered to withdraw and not told why.

'It's not just us. Everybody's doing it,' the young subaltern said wearily, as he organized his men into a resentful approximation of marching order.

'But we haven't had a proper crack at Jerry yet, sir.'

'Well, that's not my fault is it? Any complaints, make 'em to Field-Marshal French. *He's* in charge, not me.'

'But why are we retiring, sir?'

'I don't know, do I. Orders from Top Brass.'

'I wish Top Brass'd make up their tiny minds,' Arthur said sourly as the First Queen's retraced its steps towards Bettignies. Shells exploded in the village behind them as they filed down the road, but the German guns were aimed at someone else. They were still the disgruntled spectators in this war.

Robert trudged sullenly along the road. He wouldn't be sorry to leave these grimy coal mining towns and the scruffy villages among the slag heaps, which to a Surrey man's eyes looked stark and unappealing. But it was no fun to be heading back the way you'd come so soon with an unbeaten German army following hotly on your tail, to judge by the nearness of some of those shells. He didn't understand why the BEF was retreating when the Queen's hadn't even had a chance to show what they could do, and it got harder when they caught up with the struggling tail of a stream of panic-stricken refugees trundling hand-carts and prams piled high with what was left of their possessions. They were grey-faced with terror and seemed to hate the British soldiers they saw as abandoning them to their fate, almost as much as they hated the Germans who constituted it.

He shrugged his shoulders in a vain attempt to relieve the pressure of his pack harness. He'd stripped down to the waist two days ago while trench digging under a blazing sun, and now his burnt back was giving him hell where the straps chafed against it. Chaos again. Orders without explanations again. Seventy-seven pounds of kit to be lugged about on your back again and nobody'd so much as mentioned dinner. He was beginning to remember why he'd been so glad to leave the bloody army.

6

Hymns. Prayers. More hymns. Vows. 'Do you, Hugh, take this woman to be your lawful wedded wife . . . ?'

Laura shifted her weight to the other leg. The ceremony seemed interminable. A small black insect emerged from one of the roses in her bouquet and crawled across her hand. She flicked it away.

'Do you, Alice, take this man to be your lawful wedded husband?' The usual promises. For better or for worse, for richer or for poorer, in sickness and in health, till death did them part. Alice, simple and silly and vain, turned her head to look up at the man beside her.

'I do,' she said softly. Suddenly, without warning, Laura felt tears pricking at her eyes. Against her will she owned that she was in the presence of something important, that Alice and Hugh really did care for each other and that it was she, Laura, who had been silly and vain when she mocked their emotion. She blinked furiously.

It was over. Beside her, the chief bridesmaid, Alice's schoolfriend, stooped to pick up the lace train and Laura automatically stooped beside her. They filed into the vestry. As Alice, with her veil folded back from her face, signed her name, shoulder to shoulder with Hugh, the organist could be heard striking up the introductory chords of Mendelssohn's Wedding March. In the congregation there was a sharp collective intake of breath. *Mendelssohn? How unpatriotic!*

The Delameres had agonized long and hard over the suitability of including the march in the music for the ceremony. It was unfortunate that the composer of the most suitable, popular and generally uplifting piece of music

112

associated with weddings should be a German. All over the country, orchestras were banning Teutonic pieces from their repertoires and there had even been an attempt to remove Wagner and Beethoven from the Promenade Concert season, until Sir Henry Wood put his foot down and insisted that the choice of programme was a matter of culture and not patriotism. But Alice had set her heart on Mendelssohn. She couldn't imagine leaving church to any other music she'd stated firmly. She'd been dreaming of her wedding day long before the war was declared, and after all, he was a long-dead German rather than a modern bullier of Belgians. So it was decided that, following Sir Henry's example, cultural considerations might be permitted to overrule warlike ones in this instance.

The procession moved off sedately down the aisle; but it was hard to keep one's step slow and stately with such a joyous tune urging one on. Laura, concentrating on staying an appropriate distance behind her cousin, suddenly caught sight of a familiar face amongst the congregation and missed her step. In doing so she caused the bridesmaid behind her, one of Hugh's clutch of sisters, to stumble and bump against her back. Scarlet-cheeked, Laura fell into step again, hoping furiously that *he* hadn't noticed.

Edward Allingham was in uniform.

She hadn't expected him to be here. She hadn't seen him since the day at Oxford. She noted the uniform, a painfully new and immaculate khaki. He'd said he might be volunteering for the army on the day the war began. So he would be going away. Where? How soon?

And did she care?

Yes.

'I was at prep school with Hugh,' Edward explained later in the marquee which had been erected on the tennis lawn of Mr and Mrs Delameres' home. He handed Laura a glass of champagne. 'And we've kept in touch. Also, my father and his father do business together I believe. Alice looks very charming, doesn't she?' he added as the bride floated past

113

them on Hugh's arm, her wreath slightly askew and her face glowing with happiness.

'So do you, Edward, so do you.' Oliver had annexed an entire bottle of champagne from a passing manservant and already some of the effervescence had transferred itself from the bottle to his manner. He poured himself a refill, splashily. 'The uniform is very impressive. Subaltern, I take it? Which regiment have you honoured?'

'Oh the Queen's, of course.'

'Really?' Oliver's eyebrows climbed. He took an extended sip from his glass. 'What made you go for an *infantry* regiment, may I ask?'

'Basically, theirs was the nearest recruiting office,' Edward responded drily. 'Besides, such sentiment as I feel is for the local regiment. And I've got a sort of cousin who's ADC to the brigadier, which speeded up the process of getting me gazetted.'

'Oh. I see,' said Oliver, and a small shaft of jealousy shot through him. Other men had influential relations pulling strings to help them to their commissions. He, Oliver, had not. 'Seems a pity though,' he said carelessly.

'Why? What's wrong with the Queen's?' Edward's quiet tone didn't change but his lips tightened with annoyance.

'Well, the infantry are rather second-rate aren't they?'

'The infantry are the ones who'll fight this war,' Edward responded quickly.

'How d'you make that out?'

'I've been reading the predictions of a man called Ivan Bloch. Back in 1900 he said that in the next war everybody would be entrenched – and that the spade would be as indispensable to a soldier as his rifle. The cavalry is outdated as a fighting force. From what I've gathered about the equipment and strengths of the armies involved in this war, I think his reasoning was very sound.'

'Oh, well,' said Oliver. 'If you want to take the word of a Fritz. . . .'

'As it happens, Bloch was a Pole.'

Oliver shrugged. 'Same thing. Foreign. Anyway, I reckon you and Mr Bloch were wrong and the place to be is with the caval-ree.'

'I'm afraid you're mistaken.' Charles McKay, Hugh's best man, had been listening to the conversation. 'I hate to say it, because I'm a cavalryman myself, but I do believe it's the artillery who'll do the damage. Napoleon said it himself, after the horse artillery broke his cavalry at Waterloo. *C'est avec l'artillerie qu'on fait la guerre.*'

'If you think that, why did you join the Blues?' Oliver demanded.

'Oh . . . probably because I don't have the brains to be a gunner,' Charles admitted. 'All those calculations of trajectory and so on . . . much simpler just to gallop flat out and swing your sword. And the plumed helmet was a big inducement,' he added, with a smile.

'What d'you think, James?' Oliver said. James had appeared a few moments before and was hovering diffidently on the edge of the group. 'Who's going to win this war for us? The cavalry, the artillery or the infantry?'

'The Royal Flying Corps, I should think,' James said. He smiled at Laura. 'Hullo. You look awfully hot.'

Laura gave him a long, withering look and was pleased to see that his eyes dropped and his cheeks reddened. *Cheeky beast!* she thought furiously.

'Oh, we all know you're crazy about planes,' Oliver said to his friend. 'Personally you wouldn't get me anywhere near one of those bits of string and canvas. Suicide traps, the lot of them.'

Laura expelled a sigh of impatience and finished the champagne in her glass. Put any group of young men together these days, she had discovered, and they would drone on and on about how to win the war. She longed for Edward to notice her. He'd handed her the champagne glass absent-mindedly, not really seeing her, the way he always behaved in his dealings with Laura. She wished she could detest him, as she'd been trying to do for weeks, but he looked so handsome in his uniform that it hurt her to look at him.

'And how is Miss Churchill?' she asked him brightly, taking advantage of a gap in the conversation. 'How does she feel about your commission?'

'You'd better ask her yourself. Margaret . . .' Edward called. The dark-haired girl detached herself from a group of guests and came to stand by Edward. *So she is already so acknowledged as his partner that she must be included in wedding invitations*, Laura thought with dismay.

'Miss Brownlowe's been asking after you. And also how you feel about my new rôle,' Edward explained. His voice was noncommittal, but Laura sensed that she'd stumbled on a sore spot.

'I'm very well, thank you,' Margaret said. 'Though rather tired. I've become involved with training VAD nurses to go out to the fighting. As far as your second question is concerned, I naturally regret that Edward has felt it necessary to join the army but of course it's up to him to decide what he must do. I hope and expect that he'll accord me the same freedom.'

It was obvious, from the pinprick pointedness of her words, that the subject was one on which she and Edward had lately clashed. Laura remembered the garden at Balliol and the discussion that Oliver had interrupted. Clearly the question of whether or not Margaret should offer her services to nurse the wounded had not yet been resolved. Laura resented being dragged into a private quarrel . . . but all the same she couldn't resist stirring the disagreement a little more.

'But aren't you awfully proud of Edward?' she asked.

'No more than I was,' said Margaret. 'Do you think I should be, just because he's declared himself prepared to kill people?'

Laura's eyes widened. All the girls she knew thought it was simply splendid to volunteer. 'Prepared to defend his country, surely? And its moral standards? Don't you think they're worth fighting for?'

'There are other ways to defend one's moral standards than

by blowing people to pieces because they don't agree with them.'

'Margaret,' said Edward gently, 'you are shocking Miss Brownlowe.'

Margaret looked up at him slantwise through her lashes, and without warning her rather gaunt features broke into a smile.

'Oh, that would never do,' she said and took his hand, and Laura became aware of some underlying vibration of understanding between them which transcended their quarrel and by which she was utterly excluded. She had a horrid feeling she was being laughed at.

'Miss Brownlowe. Your glass is empty. Allow me to fetch you a refill.'

Laura turned her head, grateful for the interruption. Charles McKay stood at her elbow. She remembered now where she had seen him before – at a hunt ball, two years ago. He'd asked her for a dance and she'd been obliged to tell him that her card was full – about which he had been rather flatteringly regretful she recalled. She'd had no idea he was in the army . . . but then in those days she'd had no interest in the local boys. All her romantic inclinations had been towards Edward. And a terrible waste of her time that had proved to be, she reminded herself bitterly.

She summoned up her most winsome smile for Charles. He, at least, wasn't mesmerized by the clever Miss Churchill. He showed an inclination, which was very soothing in the circumstances, to be mesmerized by Laura instead. On the spur of the moment she decided to try her hand at flirtation. With any luck Edward would at least register that *someone* didn't think she was 'just a baby'.

'Actually, I believe I'll come with you and inspect the buffet. I simply must try one of those vol-au-vents,' she said, and tucked her hand inside the crook of Charles' arm. 'The Delameres' cook is famous for them.' Her voice sounded artificially bright to her own ears, but the young soldier looked delighted.

'Ah, Brownlowe. Has your lad joined up yet?'

The words addressed to Rupert by an acquaintance came clearly to Oliver's ears, as did his father's reply.

'No, not yet. So far as I can make out, he's trying, but nobody will have him.'

Oliver had been ashamed of his lack of success. He had not been aware until now that his father knew of his efforts to obtain a commission and was also embarrassed by his apparent failure. Rupert's joking tone had not concealed a certain dry exasperation.

Scowling, Oliver tilted the almost empty champagne bottle over his glass. Somehow Rupert always did notice his failures, picking up on his occasional low-scoring innings or the one bad exam result in an otherwise glowing report. The colour flamed in Oliver's cheeks. He *must* get into a regiment soon . . . or this damned war would be over without him.

His friend James was watching Laura getting on famously with the best man and wondering why he had bothered to feel sorry for her on that Oxford trip. It was obvious from her current behaviour that she hadn't cared so very much about Edward after all. But then something about her diamond-hard smile and the over-animated chatter that she was directing at her companion made him realize that the glittering performance was just that. An act, for Edward's benefit . . . of which its target, talking quietly to his fiancée, was quite oblivious.

Blast. If only he didn't keep noticing these things. It was a damned nuisance, James thought ruefully, being so aware of another person's pain.

Griffin looked down at his horse. It was a sturdy little bay gelding, fifteen hands two inches and lion-hearted, generous in all its responses. In the weeks since he'd joined the battery, he'd grown attached to the bay. Now it lay on its side, flank heaving, and he saw the glistening white of exposed bone running from knee to fetlock – where a chunk of exploding shrapnel shell had sliced away skin and flesh leaving the nearside foreleg splintered and useless.

All around him horses lay sprawled and shattered. So this was how it ended, Griffin thought: the glorious gallop with the guns.

He'd lost count of the days they'd been on the move in a nightmare of noise and heat, dust and debris, fighting a running battle with the German cavalry divisions which were harrying their retreating army. Everywhere their own cavalry scurried to fend off another attack on the grimly enduring infantry battalions, the horse artillery went too – to fling round after pulverizing round at the enemy . . . who sent it back with interest. Now, after the latest dawn dash to the rescue of another battery, (blown to bits, one gun left firing and that with only two men, the frantic messenger had told them,) Griffin's companions and the 4th Cavalry Brigade they were supporting seemed to have silenced the enemy guns.

For the time being. And not without cost. The German guns, as a last furious gesture from the men dying among them, had sent a shell tearing into the lines where Griffin and his fellow drivers were hanging on to their plunging, terrified team against the moment when they'd be called on to harness up yet again and drag the overheated gun into another battle station. But some of them wouldn't be dragging anything anywhere, ever again.

'May I borrow your revolver, sir?' Griffin said as Forsythe rode up to survey the carnage. The young subaltern handed the revolver over without comment and Griffin bent over the bay, laying his hand on its shoulder. The animal snorted and tried to rise, its poor peeled foreleg thrusting at the air, its head jerking with the vain effort. Griffin looked sadly into the bloodshot dark eye that stared up sideways at him. 'Poor old thing,' he said softly. 'Poor old thing. Time to make an end of it.'

Shifting his position, he managed to get the gun's muzzle to the vulnerable place between the animal's eyes. After a moment's hesitation he squeezed the trigger and as the gun kicked in his hand, the heavy head jerked once more. When it fell back, there was no longer any light in the staring eye.

Forsythe had moved on down what was left of the line. Looking about for him, Griffin saw Dawson instead, half-reclining with his back propped against a tree. The weird thing about the driver's appearance was that his body ended at the thighs, where shreds of tattered khaki trouser clung to two bloody stumps.

Somewhere there was still the steady crack of rifle fire, and screaming, and the thunder of hooves as the 11th Hussars saw off the remnants of the German division. But the remorseless rain of artillery fire seemed to have stopped, as Griffin stumbled over to Dawson and sank down beside him. Dawson's face was pallid with shock, but he was conscious and rational despite the stained grass that bore testimony to his loss of blood.

'Got a cigarette?' he said. Griffin, cold-handed, fumbled in various pockets before remembering that he didn't smoke and had given away his ration. He shook his head.

'My pocket, you idiot,' said Dawson, with the ghost of his usual vigour. Griffin located the pack and a packet of Vestas in the indicated place and lit a cigarette before passing it over to Dawson.

'Well, we're well and truly blooded,' Dawson said, dragging at the cigarette.

'Yes.'

'I've had it, haven't I?'

'No,' said Griffin, because it was unthinkable to say 'yes'.

'Course I have.'

'Does it hurt? I might be able to get some morphine. Forsythe's got a medical pack.'

'No. It's all right. Numb.'

'The RAMC boys'll be here any minute and take you down to a clearing station. Get you fixed up.'

'They'll be too bloody late. Write to my girl will you, Griffin? Tell her I died grinning. Letter with an address in my top pocket.'

120

Dawson finished his cigarette and Griffin stamped out the stub beside him as he died.

'Better get that arm seen to,' said Forsythe when the driver returned his revolver. He looked ten years older.

'Arm?' Griffin stared at him uncomprehendingly before he became aware that the dull throbbing in his left arm and the stickiness in his hand, which until now had seemed like separate sensations belonging to someone else, were caused by a shard of shrapnel that had ploughed upward along the length of his forearm. He groped in one of the many canvas pouches of his kit for his field dressing and pressed it into place, but the blood continued to seep through and under the pad. He sat down again on the grass. Sooner or later, he supposed a medical orderly or a stretcher-bearer would notice his condition and deal with him. But for the moment everyone was fully occupied in the grim task of picking up the pieces – literally – of the other battery.

'Is there something wrong with me?' Laura wondered. Every-one else seemed to be so relentlessly fervent about the war – everyone except James Allingham, who was now acknow-ledged to be weird even by Oliver, and except the insufferable Margaret Churchill. Laura would hate to be bracketed with either of them, but to her the events in Belgium and France were still unreal, a distant vortex towards which so many of the young men who made up her social sphere were now being sucked – leaving behind them a drab society in which it seemed to be a crime to enjoy oneself.

Even the boys who had not yet been posted to the Front were absorbed by its drama, agonizing over the question of should-they-shouldn't-they-go? Well they should, Laura reckoned, and get the whole wretched business over and done with as soon as possible. Then everyone could get back to normal.

The tennis parties and dances that would have been her usual summer diversions had been suspended in the face of the crisis. Apart from Aunt Jessie's War Work and this nursing business, there wasn't a thing to do. To add to her depression she deliberately had to dress as plainly as possible these days, because to look pretty and smart was considered, like everything else that made life worth living, to be unpatriotic. Though how throwing one's dressmaker out of work was supposed to help the war effort, no one had yet explained to Laura. Instead of going on lazy summer picnics, she was expected to help Aunt Jessie pack up endless parcels of tobacco, chocolate and knitted goods as 'comforts' for the troops, whose reaction to being deluged by woolly mufflers in August could only be imagined. As for the nursing training which she had undertaken at Rupert's insistence, it seemed better suited to equipping her for domestic service than for giving succour to the wounded and it was for this that Laura reserved the hate that she couldn't yet seem to feel for the Germans.

She loathed the cold school hall in which the training took place: the beastly splintered wooden floor and the smelly waterproof sheets that she was required to scrub; the miles of bandage that she had to wind and the insolent schoolboys, sons of the training instructress, on whom she was expected to practise the art of applying slings and dressings. It seemed to her that the instructress took a sadistic delight in humiliating her in a way that had nothing to do with helping the war effort.

'That awful Snelling woman!' she exploded, coming in exhausted and seething from a particularly uncomfortable training session to find Jessie in the drawing room, stitching conscientiously at a baby's nightgown for the Soldiers and Sailors Families' Relief Association. 'I could strangle her! The way she looked me up and down and told me that my work was "below standard", as if I'd been a hired skivvy straight from the Board School instead of a lady! I don't see the point of this obsession with *cleaning* everything all the time anyway. I'm sure she does it just to give us horrible red hands and chipped fingernails like hers!'

'Hygiene is very important to prevent wound infection,' Jessie said unhelpfully.

'All right. So when we actually get some wounded soldiers to nurse, *then* I'll scrub! Meanwhile it's just a waste of time.'

Jessie, who read the casualty lists, thought that the time was rapidly approaching when the newly set-up voluntary hospitals would be called upon to play their part. Privately she felt apprehension for the safety of any soldier that her niece might be called upon to nurse. It was a demanding profession and Laura had never been particularly methodical or patient, preferring to get through life by inspiration rather than by diligence. But perhaps she was being unfair? The volunteers were only supposed to be auxiliaries after all, and conceivably the sight of a pretty face like Laura's would be a healing factor in itself for a wounded soldier, an antidote to the horrors of war. But not if she scowled like that!

Laura plumped herself down on the sofa beside her aunt, jogging Jessie's elbow and causing her to prick her finger, which Laura failed to notice.

'Aunt Jessie, I had a letter from Alice this morning.'

'Oh yes?' Jessie sucked a pinprick of blood and stitched stolidly on, keeping the finger carefully clear of the flannel fabric.

'Hugh's back in barracks now and she's feeling a bit low about it, left twiddling her thumbs in that flat they've taken in London. She's written inviting me to pay a visit and I think I ought to go. Do you think you could have a word with Pa about it and convince him it's a good idea?'

'Why don't you ask him?' Jessie said, finishing her seam and breaking off the thread. Laura grimaced.

'I did. This morning. But you know how keen he was for me to do this nursing training and I'd have to miss some of it. He wouldn't listen when I told him how much Alice needed me. But he'd listen to you.'

Jessie doubted it. And she didn't think Alice's needs would have achieved such priority in Laura's mind if they hadn't coincided so neatly with her own wishes. But she could imagine that Alice must be desperate for company if she was willing to invite even her acidic cousin Laura, and she sympathized a little with Laura's urge to escape from the awful Mrs Snelling. So she said she would see what she could do.

It wasn't easy to persuade Rupert to agree to the London visit, but as Jessie persisted with her mild remarks about how sad it must be for the new bride to be parted from her husband so soon, how close the cousins were (which wasn't strictly true), how pale and peaky Laura was looking due to overwork on her training course (for which statement Jessie felt obliged to cross her fingers behind her back), gradually Rupert weakened and eventually sanctioned the trip. Rather surprised by her own success, Jessie relayed the news to Laura.

'Oh, thank you Aunt Jessie! You're a marvel! I'd given up hope . . . but what about the train fare? And I'll need some spending money. . . .'

It was eternally irritating to Laura that she had no proper allowance like Oliver, so that although her father had always paid her dressmaker's bills without demur, financing anything out of her ordinary routine meant going cap in hand to Rupert.

'It's all right. I've arranged all that.'

'Darling Aunt, you're amazing!' And the normally distant Laura actually gave Jessie a hug before running upstairs to sort out her clothes for the trip. 'We'll go and see Hugh at his barracks if you come,' Alice had written in her invitation. 'And Charles McKay says he's very much looking forward to meeting you again. I think you've made quite a conquest there. . . .'

Rupert felt it was rather noble of him to agree to the London visit in the circumstances. He didn't like to acknowledge the importance of his daughter's presence in his life but the truth was he'd be lonely without her. Oliver was also flying the nest, but that was different. He'd always had problems achieving a comfortable relationship with Oliver – somehow he couldn't stop picking holes in everything the boy did, though he was a good enough lad really and deserved more encouragement than Rupert could bring himself to give. Perhaps there was an element of jealousy in his reactions?

Both the children had inherited Sylvia's good looks but what in Laura was a pleasing reminder of her beauty somehow seemed to jar when Rupert glimpsed his dead wife in his son's features. And when Oliver got his Oxford place it had reminded Rupert of an old disappointment when his own parents had dismissed him as 'non-academic' and denied him the chance of going to university.

Still, Oliver was in uniform now, which was a great source of pride. At the beginning of September his commission had been gazetted in *The Times*.

For weeks Oliver himself had got up at dawn to waylay the paper boy and sneak a first glance at the newspaper. As he'd turned the pages eagerly and caught sight of his own name, his spirits had soared. Then plummeted.

First Lieutenant Oliver Brownlowe, to the Royal Regiment of Artillery.

They'd made him a damned gunner.

Too later, Oliver remembered – and regretted – the way he'd puffed up his scientific skills in his interview at the War Office, his proficiency with a rifle and knowledge of the properties of explosives. He'd desperately wanted them to think what a fine fellow he was and how useful he could be to the war effort. But in the cavalry, for heaven's sake, not the artillery!

He tried to cheer himself with the memory of what Charles McKay had said at Cousin Alice's wedding, that line about how Napoleon had reckoned it was with the artillery that you made war. But it wasn't the least consolation. What did Napoleon know anyway? He was just a Frog, and a beaten Frog at that.

Rupert received the news of his son's commission with gruff congratulations through which his satisfaction was clearly visible, and a handsome advance on his allowance to cover the cost of the uniform.

'The army'll pay for it in due course. Theoretically. But it's bound to take them some time to get around to it, given their mountains of paperwork. And there's no sense in stinting on your kit, my boy,' he said, with more paternal warmth in his manner than Oliver could remember for a long time. 'You'll go to Burberrys' of course,' he went on. 'I gather that their entire tailoring department has been turned over to the making of officers' uniforms and they can provide a complete kit within four days.'

He'd failed entirely to notice that Oliver was sulking about the posting.

'Well, I never,' said Mrs Driver, pleased. 'A postcard from Griffin. I told him to write but I thought he'd forget.'

'What does he say?' Joan said, standing on tiptoe to read over her shoulder. Daisy went on laying the long pine kitchen table for staff breakfast, apparently not interested by the news.

'Well, he's over there. With the artillery. Fancy that, same as Mr Oliver. He says he's seen a bit of action, but I suppose he can't say where on account of the censors. Says he helped to see off a load of Jerries that had blown up all the guns of another battery. Oh, and he's wounded.'

'Badly?' said Daisy sharply, all her indifference gone, as keen-eyed Joan noticed, though Mrs Driver did not.

'No, just a scratch he says. They get a wound stripe to wear on their sleeve, don't they? That'll be nice for him. Fancy our Griffin turning out a hero.'

Griffin waited at a base hospital, fretful with boredom, for his stitched-up arm to heal. 'A minor wound,' they'd told him cheerfully, though by then it was hurting like hell. 'Soon have you fit for action again.' Probably it was the sight of the other soldiers despatching words of reassurance to their loved ones that had prompted in him a sudden and surprisingly intense longing to have someone, somewhere, care about how he was getting on.

Forsythe, thank heaven, had taken over the task of writing to Dawson's girlfriend. 'It's my job as his officer,' he'd said tight-lipped, as he strapped up the driver's arm ready for transportation to the casualty clearing station, and Griffin had thankfully relinquished the task. He couldn't imagine what to say in a letter to a stranger whose feelings for the dead man could only be guessed. Something about what a good mate he'd proved in the few short weeks you'd known him?

It was hard enough composing a brief message to Mrs Driver. If the nurses hadn't been hovering helpfully, offering to take letters to the post, he'd have given it up. But Mrs Driver was the nearest thing to motherly he'd experienced in his lonely life; and besides he had a vague, barely acknowledged hope that other members of the staff at Maple Grange might care just a little bit, too.

'Mr Rupert was pleased to hear about Griffin's postcard, wasn't he?' said Joan, as she and Daisy went through the bed-making routine upstairs. 'You'd have thought it was all down to him that Griffin joined up.'

'I suppose it was in a way,' said Daisy. 'If he hadn't sent off all the horses. . . .'

'Well, Mr Rupert reckoned that the fighting Griffin was talking about must have been at Néry, quite a big engagement he said, so Griffin really is a hero. You didn't get any mail from your Arthur, then?' Joan added slyly.

Blast Joan! Daisy thought as the usual furious blush suffused her cheeks. She knew perfectly well there hadn't been any more mail – as if you could receive anything in this nosy household without the news being broadcast to all and sundry.

Was he still 'her Arthur'? The ring on her finger said so. But only one little miserable postcard to your fiancée, when everyone else in the BEF seemed to be writing stacks and stacks of letters from the Front . . . it was humiliating. She'd have been worried sick about him if it hadn't been for the occasional understated card from Robert, saying laconically that he and Arthur were fine, tired, bored or whatever the current mood might be. She detected his embarrassment at his friend's continued silence. It wasn't fair of Arthur to treat her like this, Daisy thought miserably. What on earth was he trying to do to her?

'I used to think,' Joan mentioned, watching Daisy sideways as she plumped up pillows, 'that you were a bit soft on Griffin.'

'Don't be daft, Joan!' But it came out, Daisy realized with chagrin, far too quick and breathless to be convincing.

'And that he was a bit soft on you. Only he didn't like to say so, what with Arthur being your young man.'

'Daisy! Miss Jessie wants to see you.' The merciful interruption was from Mrs Driver, puffed after climbing the stairs. 'Morning room,' she added unnecessarily since it was Jessie's invariable location at this time of the day. The housemaid hurried down the stairs.

'Ah. Daisy.' Jessie's face was troubled as the girl came into the room. 'I . . . there's a telegram arrived for you.'

'Telegram?' Daisy's heart stood still. Wasn't that how they – the War Office – broke bad news about casualties to the next of kin? Her hands clenched and unclenched at her sides.

'It's local,' Jessie said gently, understanding her terror. 'I don't think it can be – well, you'd better open it.'

The telegram was from Louella and sparsely worded for economy's sake.

'Your mother's ill. Please come if you can.'

Mrs Colindale was never ill. She was as tough as old boots, she'd had to be to bring up two children while working all the hours God sent, making artificial flowers for hat-trimming – hers had been the daisy which Arthur Bright had carried away with him to the war. Finally she'd saved enough to buy herself a sewing machine and begun to turn out ladies' blouses which she sold to a store in Guildford. Louella was a big help there. After she'd married Robert, she'd started sketching out new designs for the blouses, and since she had a talent for dreaming up trimmings and drapings that looked complicated but were quick and easy to achieve, the little business had become a success. The profits were modest, but it was a big step forward for Mrs Colindale who'd existed on the meagre earnings from piecework. But now she was ill. . . .

With the telegram still clutched in her hand, Daisy ran straight from Miss Jessie in the morning room to her attic bedroom to stuff nightclothes into a travelling bag, and then to the stable yard to scrounge a lift from Nichols, who was about to set off with the governess cart to take Miss Laura to her nursing class.

Nichols was in a bad mood and so was Miss Laura, who had to be dropped off first. Daisy hadn't the nerve to ask for her mission to be given priority and Miss Laura didn't ask why Daisy wanted to go into Guildford, merely moved aside to make room for her on the bench seat in the back of the trap. Stoically, Daisy suffered Nichols' moans all the way from Mrs Snelling's house to the other side of Guildford about how much of a nuisance the war was proving in his life. She'd hoped to persuade him to deliver her to her own front door, but he was too surly to oblige and she had to hurry uphill all the way from the end of the street. As she reached the familiar brown-painted front door in the terrace of cottages where she'd been brought up, Daisy stopped to catch her breath before turning the handle.

She'd been feeling a bit queasy herself lately, and today she'd done no more than pick at her breakfast with the result that now she was starving. Still, Louella would have something good simmering on the kitchen stove. Louella was a great cook who sometimes said, laughingly, that Robert had only married her for her dumplings.

The front door opened directly into the sitting room, where normally on a summer's day Mrs Colindale and Louella would have been working together: Louella snipping out blouses at one side of the table in the centre of the room and Mrs Colindale sewing away steadily at the Singer on the other. But when Daisy walked into the room the sewing machine was covered and the swatches of fabric were packed away into the pine trunk under the window. Increasingly uneasy, she crossed the narrow square hall to the kitchen. There was no cooking pot on the blackleaded range to give off the delicious aroma she'd anticipated. And the fire in the range was out, though normally it should have been kept burning all through the summer for boiling up hot water if not for cooking.

'Daisy! I wasn't expecting you. At least, not so soon.'
Louella stood in the doorway leading to the stairs and Daisy
was shocked by the change in her sister-in-law's appearance.
She'd last seen Louella on the day the battalion went from
Guildford. Then she'd been rosy-cheeked and pretty, her figure
straying towards a plumpness that Robert called 'bonny', her
dark hair shining in its neatly pinned roll on the back of her
head. Now she looked considerably thinner and there was no
colour in her cheeks. Her cotton dress was crumpled and her
apron, shockingly for fastidious Louella, was dirty.

'Miss Jessie said I could come right away. She's good is
Miss Jessie. But what is it, Lou? What's up with Mother? And
what's up with you, come to that?'

Louella brushed her hands self-consciously over the grubby
apron.

'Nothing a good meal couldn't cure, I reckon,' she said
wryly. 'She's just weak and dizzy, but it's hardly surprising
on what she's eaten in the last month.'

'But why? What's made her lose her appetite?'

'Nothing. There just hasn't been the money to satisfy it.
Since Robert went there's been no wages coming in. And the
price of food's gone up and up. And the store won't take any
more blouses – they say the bottom's fallen out of the market
because all the posh ladies are making economies to help the
war effort.'

Daisy remembered that Miss Laura had recently cancelled
a commission for a party gown from her own dressmaker, and
that the ladies who visited Miss Jessie were all adopting an
austere style of clothing these days in place of their former
frills and finery. She swallowed, conscience-stricken. She
should have realized.

'I wish you'd told me, Lou. I'd have helped. I've got a bit
put by.'

'Your mother wouldn't let me,' said Louella. 'She said she
didn't want to go worrying you, and Robert's Separation
Allowance would be coming through soon and we'd be all
right. But we've waited and waited, and it hasn't. We went

130

to see a lady at the Soldiers' Friends Committee the day before yesterday – she helped us fill in all the forms weeks ago – and she said a lot of allowances have been delayed coming through and there's a good deal of hardship because of it. She asked if things were really desperate. Well, you know Mother. She wouldn't admit they were. Said we'd manage and came home. Only when she came in through the door, she fainted and she's been listless and ill ever since. Her face looks like it's all fallen in . . . and I'm at my wits end to know what to do, Daisy. I just took her up her dinner and all we'd got was a bit of bread and cheese and the bread was stale and the cheese was that dry, she could hardly eat it. So I thought it was best to let you know. I owe the woman at the Post Office the money for the telegram,' she added drearily.

Daisy thought rapidly. She had a few coins in her purse, enough money to pay for a good dinner for now, and later she'd think about sending to the Grange for more from Miss Jessie who acted as 'bank' for her savings.

'I'll run round to the shop, Lou, and get a bit of beef and some new bread and butter and greens. If you could light the stove while I'm gone . . . ?'

'I can't,' said Louella starkly. 'There's no coal.' She rubbed her hands distractedly over her hollowed cheeks. 'You'd think,' she said with bitterness, 'that when they took our men off to fight their wars, they'd see the women that depended on them didn't go short, wouldn't you? *Your country needs you*, that's what they say, and *Think of the poor Belgian refugees*. . . . Well, why doesn't someone think about us? What are we supposed to do? We need them too!' Her hands came together over her shaking mouth and her eyes were bright with tears.

Next morning in the small back bedroom at Mrs Colindale's house, the early light filtered through the closed curtains over the window. Louella, huddled under the blankets of the double bed she'd shared with Robert, was wakened by an unfamiliar sound – not the usual chirping and scrabbling of sparrows in the eaves but a spasmodic gasping. At the same time she realized that Daisy, who should have been lying beside her, was no longer there. She struggled into a sitting position and peered between the black iron railings at the foot of the bed.

Daisy was doubled up over the china basin on the painted pine washstand, her shoulders heaving. A sour, acid smell reached Louella's nostrils as she swung her legs to the floor, feeling for her slippers.

'For heaven's sake, what's up with you?' she said. But when Daisy's indistinct response was followed by another bout of retching, understanding dawned on Louella. 'Oh, Daisy. You haven't . . . ? You aren't . . . ?'

But she had and she was, Daisy thought bleakly as she straightened up, pushing a sweat-damp strand of hair away from her forehead. Dear God, let Arthur come home soon. . . .

7

From Mons to Rozoy, it is 136 miles as the crow flies. As the men of the British Expeditionary Force retreated for thirteen days under a sweltering sun, it was 200, with von Kluck's army snapping at their heels. At Le Cateau a section of the exhausted force paused to fight a bloody fending-off engagement which they could regard as a victory of sorts despite the heavy casualties, before continuing the long retreat that their generals preferred to describe as a 'strategic retirement'. At last, thirty miles from the walls of Paris as the city braced itself for a siege, the hunted rallied and turned on the hunters. Now it was the German army's turn to fall back across the flat countryside cut across by deep-flowing rivers whose bridges they were often too hard-pressed to destroy behind them.

For the British public at home, the revival of the Allied fortunes was cause for celebration and exultation. For the infantry the reality was autumnal rain and flooded trenches, skirmishes, shelling and inevitably, as the enemy turned its attention towards the Channel ports, more marching.

'Where are we going *now*, Sarn't?'

'Some place called Wipers.'

Into the newly established hospitals poured the wounded of the battles at Mons and Le Cateau, the Marne and the Aisne.

'Oh, Laura, it's wonderful to see you!'

Alice flung her arms round her cousin's neck. Laura, surprised, took a step back. She wasn't much given to embracing in the street. But then she reminded herself how thankful she'd been to be rescued by Alice's invitation from the moil and toil of nursing training and she returned the hug gingerly.

'How's London life?' she said as the cab driver carried her luggage up the flight of steps to the front door of the house in a Regency square where Alice and Hugh had leased a flat. The act had surprised both sets of parents, who had assumed that in a war situation Alice's place would be with her family until the Conquering Hero's return. But Laura, however little she normally sympathized with Alice's emotions, could understand her wish to get away from the Delamere household in the circumstances. It wasn't worth getting married unless you left home after all, and it must have been delightful to be alone with one's husband, playing at house, even if the husband was Chinless Hugh and the idyll lasted only for the pitifully brief honeymoon.

'London life?' Alice said in response to Laura's question. 'Much more lively than in Guildford I should think.'

'It could hardly be *less* lively! No fun at all to be had. All the young men are going off to fight and the girls think about nothing but War Work. Aunt Jessie's knitting woolly garments for the soldiers' and sailors' wives and serving teas for troops at the YMCA and Pa's turning his factory over to munitions work and Oliver's gone to Woolwich to train for the artillery, so life has been very, very dreary.'

'Never mind. Now you're here, I'll find plenty for us to do,' Alice said soothingly. 'Come upstairs, I'll tell the girl to make us some tea.'

'You have a *girl*?' Laura tried to imagine ingenuous Alice as the mistress of servants.

'Yes of course. Just a "general" help. Not very bright, but she'll do. It's only a tiny flat.'

The flat was, indeed, tiny. 'Like a doll's house,' pronounced Laura after a guided tour of the small, square rooms, over-filled with cheap furniture, ugly chintz and unremarkable pictures. 'But very sweet,' she added kindly.

'Oh, well, it'll do for now. I expect we'll move again soon,' said Alice. 'Once the war's over.'

Later, as they finished their tea (marriage and the pangs of separation hadn't altered her cousin's appetite for pastry, Laura noticed), Alice laid her plate down on the mahogany surface of the table at her elbow and looked thoughtfully, even critically, at her cousin.

'I thought we might go somewhere after tea,' she said, 'but you may wish to change your clothes first.'

Laura had celebrated the trip to London by daring to look pretty again and was wearing a deep blue silk jersey blouse, swathed and draped from a high collar, and a matching blue linen skirt with a velvet cummerbund. But her cousin's expression, she realized with mortification, was more dubious than envious. Surely Alice hadn't joined the ranks of bores and bigots who thought one should play one's part by playing down one's assets?

'Why?' Laura demanded. 'Don't you like what I've got on?'

'Oh, yes, it's very smart. But perhaps something a bit plainer might be more appropriate.'

Laura mentally reviewed the contents of her luggage, packed with a view to reinforcing the impression she was supposed to have made on Charles McKay. Nothing 'plain' had been included.

'Why?' she repeated. 'What are we going to do?'

'Go to a talk on the Voluntary Aid Detachments. I'm planning to volunteer and I'd rather not miss it, if you don't mind.'

It hardly seemed worth coming to London to get away from the dreary subject of nursing if one was going to be dragged off to a lecture on the subject. Out of the frying pan into the fire. . . .

'Are you really going to be a VAD, Alice?' Laura said.

'Oh yes. Only for home of course, not for overseas, so as to be here whenever Hugh comes home on leave. But I want to do my bit you know. In case Hugh is wounded or anything.' Alice tried to make a joke of it, but the mere contemplation of such a horrible eventuality hurt her.

135

'What is the situation with Hugh? I know some of the Horse Guards went out with the British Expeditionary Force,' said Laura.

'Yes. He was awfully upset that his squadron got left behind. Well, I expect they couldn't send the entire Household Cavalry out at once, their duties here are so important,' said Alice with a touch of pride. 'And in a way it was a good thing for us, or we couldn't have got married. But now it looks as though the remaining Blues are going to be used to help form an extra cavalry brigade for reinforcements. I don't really know much about it. But Hugh thinks they'll be going very soon now.' She fidgeted with a button on one of her cuffs for a moment, then her head jerked up and Laura saw that she was fighting back the tears. 'I know it's happening to lots of girls. I know the men have to go and their country needs them and we have to support them. I know he's a wonderful soldier and he'll be all right and he'll come back to me soon. But oh, Laura . . . I *wish* he didn't have to go. I'm so scared.'

'Poor old Alice,' said Laura. *Help!* she thought. What *do I say*? She leaned forward and patted her cousin's hand awkwardly. 'Look, cheer up. Maybe the war'll be over by the time he gets there?'

'Maybe.' Alice drew a long breath. 'Anyway I thought the best thing is to keep busy and not worry, so I started going to the VAD classes a few days ago. We've got a wonderful teacher, Laura, she's giving the talk this afternoon. Actually I believe you've met her. She was at my wedding.'

'Oh, yes?' said Laura, her mind racing to meet the inevitable.

'Margaret Churchill. She's engaged to Edward Allingham, you know.'

'Yes. I know,' said Laura.

'Today at 4.30 p.m. – talk on VAD service by Sister Margaret Churchill of the London Hospital' announced the notice pinned up on the board outside the school hall. A thin drizzle was falling and the first dead leaves from the chestnut trees that lined the road were slippery underfoot as the two girls hurried from the cab into the building, clutching the lapels of their coats together to keep the spots of rain from their clothes.

The hall where the audience was assembling was chilly, the long, gothic windows uncurtained and the antiquated boiler in the corner unlit. As a concession to the gloom of late afternoon, the old-fashioned oil lamps hanging on long chains from the vaulted ceiling had been lit, but the recesses of the large room remained in shadow. As usual everyone had avoided sitting at the front and the latecomers were forced to take their places under the eye of the lecturer, who was already in position behind a table on the dais at one end of the room. The wooden benches were hard and scuffed, too low to seat an adult in comfort and prone to splinters, Laura discovered with distaste as she and Alice settled themselves in the front row. She caught Margaret's eye and raised a hand in greeting, but there was no answering flicker of recognition from the girl on the platform.

In her nurse's uniform Margaret looked even plainer than she had on that day in Oxford. Her starched white headsquare, tied at the back of her neck, was too severe for her thin face; the stiff apron with its large red cross rendered her shapeless and there were dark rings of tiredness under her eyes. She was, however, a lucid and authoritative speaker, her low voice carrying effortlessly to all the corners of the room as she explained the selection process, the details of the uniform and equipment needed and the conditions under which these would-be nurses would find themselves serving.

'I don't know what you expect,' said Margaret as she gathered her notes together to signal that she was approaching the end of her lecture. 'Maybe some of you see yourselves holding the hands of wounded heroes, gently mopping their fevered brows and earning their undying gratitude. The reality is far less glamorous, I'm afraid – not least because a significant proportion of those heroes will die, however hard their doctors and nurses try to save them.

'It is only fair to warn you that the majority of the work

attached to VAD nursing will consist of grim, basic drudgery. A VAD's rôle is to serve as an extra pair of hands to the trained nurses. So she'll be dealing with bedpans, bedsores and if she happens to end up on field service, bedbugs. She'll be carting about innumerable meals on trays and applying dressings to the less aesthetic parts of the male anatomy and swabbing down the doctors' tables and making the matron's tea. Or, if she's considered good enough, she may well find herself dealing with the most horrific injuries. Already I've heard from girls I know, working at hospitals in France, who are having to feed amputated limbs into furnaces, or pack a gauze wick into an abdominal wound that stinks to high heaven, or insert a feeding straw into a face that's a mass of bandages.'

'Heavens. It sounds absolutely irresistible,' Laura whispered sarcastically to Alice. Her cousin's admiration for Margaret, relayed to Laura in the cab all the way to the hall, had stirred up the simmering resentment she still felt towards the girl who had annexed Edward. And the fact that Margaret had, in her view, snubbed her just now had added fuel to the flames. She had not expected her voice to carry, but there was a small titter of embarrassed amusement from the girls in the row behind her and Margaret paused, letting her eyes dwell on the source of the disturbance. Alice, cringing, sent back an agonized grimace of apology. Laura brushed a speck of dust from her blue skirt and told herself defiantly that she didn't care if Margaret *had* heard her.

'Those girls, I believe, are proud of the job they are doing,' Margaret continued, 'but again, I would stress that there is nothing glamorous about the work. Our doctors find that they are having to deal with a new type of wound complication, a bacterial infection. It has been labelled gas gangrene. Perhaps the agricultural land where the fighting's taking place is to blame – it's heavily manured which may explain the particular virulence of this bacteria. Anyway, it breeds very rapidly. A few days' delay between the injury and the hospital treatment can mean that an infected limb, for instance, is past saving. Once it sets in, our medics don't yet know how to treat it.

The area round the wound swells up like a balloon and is full of a particularly vile, putrid-smelling gas – hence the name. Often the patient dies of what may initially have been a superficial wound. Please understand that I'm not saying this to create a sensation or to put you off the idea of volunteering,' Margaret said, looking over Laura's head at the rest of her audience. 'Heaven knows, volunteers are needed. I just want you to know what you're letting yourselves in for. Before you sign on the dotted line you have to ask yourselves some searching questions about whether you can cope with this kind of thing. Once you're in the thick of it, you'll have no choice. There will be people relying on you. That's all. Any questions?'

'Yes. I have a question.'

It was Laura who had raised her hand first. The bald facts that Margaret had laid before the audience had confronted her with grim realities that were far outside her experience. She didn't even want to *think* about such horrid subjects; and she resented Margaret even more for making her feel inadequate than she had resented her for the snubbing of a wave of greeting.

'Yes?' Margaret said, unsmiling.

'Is there any particularly therapeutic effect attached to the choice of uniform? I mean it's clearly designed to be as unflattering as possible to the wearer, so I assume there must be some hidden benefit to the patient.'

Again Laura's comment provoked a reaction from the audience: a gasp of horror at her flippancy from the more serious potential volunteers, a snort of suppressed laughter from those who, like herself, had registered the extreme plainness of the garb worn by the lecturer.

'The uniform,' said Margaret, with cutting control, 'is intended to be warm, practical, economical and easily cleaned. I can assure you that if you ever find yourself nursing in a field hospital, the degree to which it enhances your feminine charms will be the very least of your concerns.'

There had been a distinct emphasis on the word 'if', which

implied that she very much doubted whether this particular female would ever find herself in such a situation. This time the suppressed laughter from the audience was against the questioner and Laura, reddening, had to concede that for the time being at least, Margaret had got the better of her.

It was still drizzling as they left the hall.

'Surely you don't still want to be a VAD, Alice?' Laura asked as they hurried towards the junction with the main road, where a cab might be found.

'Yes, I think so.'

'Even after those horror stories about amputated limbs and gangrenous wounds?'

'Somebody has to deal with them,' said Alice seriously.

'Well, sooner you than me!'

'I just hope I can do it, Laura. It would be so awful to find that one couldn't, and let people down.'

Alice was very quiet in the cab on the way back to the flat, but she cheered up when they were back in her small bedroom and preparing for the evening's entertainment. Hugh Malloy and his friend Charles were to join them for dinner, though unfortunately they would have to depart promptly at the end of the evening. Hugh was not permitted to spend the night away from the cavalry barracks, Alice revealed, blushing, except when officially on leave.

'We'll go to McKinley's. Do you know McKinley's, Laura?'

'Mmm? No,' said Laura, slightly distracted by the sight of her cousin's silk crepe dinner gown. Inevitably it was in Alice's favourite shell pink, but the bodice was cut low enough to suggest that Mrs Delamere had had no hand in the choosing of it. Now that she was a married woman, Alice was certainly shedding some of her demureness Laura thought. She watched her cousin applying powder with a swansdown puff to the extensive areas of her bosom that were on display.

'They have a band for dancing. Oh, we'll have such fun. Hugh says he wants to show me off to the other officers,' Alice said happily.

140

'Hasn't he done that yet?'

'No, not really.' Alice's cheeks, neck and powdered décolletage turned a deeper shade of rose. 'We've rather tended to do things just with each other, till now.'

'What sort of things?' Laura realized too late that it was an intimate question and that she and Alice, despite their kinship, were not really on such terms.

Alice reached hastily for her pearl-drop earrings. 'Oh . . . you know . . . getting to know each other,' she mumbled as she hooked them into her lobes.

Laura would have liked to ask Alice about sex. She knew that the late Queen Victoria had advised closing one's eyes and thinking of England. Was it really so awful as this phrase implied, or was it the ecstatic and sensual experience that novelists like Elinor Glyn suggested? Laura had read *Three Weeks*, condemned as risqué and passed round furtively in a brown paper cover in the dormitory at finishing school, and her own sensations when in the vicinity of Edward Allingham inclined her to believe in ecstasy. But how could she *know*, without having to commit herself by getting married?

'Are you glad you married Hugh?' she asked.

Her cousin raised a luminous face. 'Oh yes,' she said softly with a reminiscent smile. Laura mentally chalked up a vote for Elinor Glyn. But Alice was not about to expand on the delights of being a wedded wife. Briskly, she changed the subject.

'Of course, we've seen a bit of Charles McKay. Charles is simply dying to see you again, Laura. He thinks you're the most wonderful girl he's ever met.'

Lieutenant McKay must be easily impressed Laura decided, if he could elevate her to such status on the strength of two brief encounters: during one of which, as she recalled with a spasm of shame, she had been slightly the worse for champagne and far more flirtatious than a well brought-up girl had any business to be. All the same, it was rather gratifying. If only it could have been Edward. If only she could stop thinking about Edward. She wondered where he was at this moment and if he ever thought about her.

Fortunately for Laura's peace of mind she had no idea that Edward was in London and that earlier in the afternoon they had been within a hundred yards of each other. He had been waiting for his fiancée in a teashop near the school hall; but there were other concerns on Edward's mind than Oliver Brownlowe's young sister. He was trying not to lose his temper at the discovery that although he had forty-eight hours leave and had come to London expressly to see Margaret, she could only spare him a bare half-hour between her talk and her next spell on duty.

'I'm sorry, Edward.'

'But I wrote and told you I was coming.'

'I know. But I can't just drop everything, can I?'

Edward scowled, fiddling with a teaspoon. He looked, Margaret thought, like a sulky schoolboy – with his lower lip jutting and his handsome face stiff with disappointment. She would have liked to reach out and take his hand, but years of habitual restraint kept her from touching him.

They were the only occupants of the teashop and it was with obvious reluctance and a meaningful glance at the clock on the wall behind the counter that the waitress had taken their order. Having brought their tray, she returned to the stacking of crockery and sorting of cutlery, the sound of her activities faintly distracting. Margaret poured out tea for herself and Edward, but when she pushed his cup and saucer towards him he ignored it, staring instead at the steamed-up window and the rain dribbling down the pane outside.

Margaret sighed and straightened her back. It had been a difficult day. She felt tired and rumpled and half her mind was still preoccupied with churning out phrases which, had they been produced at the right time, might more effectively have demolished Laura Brownlowe's gibe about her uniform. Not that she could disagree, really. Even she, who made no concessions to vanity, had pulled a rueful face when she had first confronted her drab, uniformed reflection in a mirror. In a less harried state of mind she probably would have conceded with a laugh that it had been designed to keep sex out of the wards. Today she wasn't in the mood for dealing with shafts of misplaced wit from trivial chits like Laura.

For the past week she had been on nights at the hospital. This morning after coming off duty she had had six hours' sleep, which her weary frame kept reminding her was not enough, followed by a hurried lunch and two hours' intensive reading of a report on the pathetically inadequate strategems for coping with the new gas gangrene. She had left her lodgings, faced a mile's walk through the rain to the school hall, and had found Edward waiting in the street – already simmering with outrage because the landlady wouldn't let him go up to her room. He had not reacted well on hearing that she would be back on duty again at six o'clock and meanwhile had to give a lecture.

Anyone would have thought that she had planned the whole thing to inconvenience him, whereas she had had to wrestle with her conscience to honour her promise of delivering the lecture. Arriving at the school, still distracted by the rival claims on her time, she had recognized Laura before the start of her talk, had seen the wave of greeting and knew she should have returned it. But somehow the sight of that shining golden head and that elegant blue ensemble had brought out her meanest impulses. Laura, she knew, would not have hesitated to cancel any and every arrangement for the sake of Edward's company. Margaret, who had a wardful of patients awaiting her, and who appreciated the desperate need for nursing volunteers, could not afford the luxury of such a gesture. But then Laura would need only to tear herself away from – what was it she did? – flower arranging, bridge parties and piano practice? She had probably scarcely noticed, immersed in her cosy little middle-class world, that there was a war on.

Margaret sipped her tea, her eyes straying to the clock. Edward turned back from the window just in time to spot the direction of her gaze.

'I'd better come straight to the point, hadn't I?' he said, 'since time is so short,' he added bitterly. 'I've got forty-eight hours' leave, of which a little under four hours is now gone. I don't know when I'll get another one. I could get sent overseas at any time. I want us to get married before I go.'

The tea in Margaret's cup slopped dangerously close to the rim. She put the cup down and stared at Edward.

'Well?' he said. 'What do you think? It's not impossible. We could do it by special licence. I've got one, as a matter of fact. And I've contacted a cleric who knows my father, who says he'll oblige.'

Margaret cleared her throat. 'This is a bit sudden, isn't it?' she said.

'The timing wasn't my choice. I'm sorry,' he said. 'I thought it was a good idea. You don't seem to think so.'

'It's taken me by surprise, that's all.' Margaret studied his face. 'I don't understand,' she said slowly, 'why you suddenly want to get married *now*. I thought we'd more or less decided to wait until the war was over?'

'Had we? Maybe you had. We didn't discuss it much, did we?'

'No, because you went off and got yourself a commission,' Margaret pointed out.

'And you had to rush back to work,' he countered. 'Like you always do. Look here Margaret, it was just that I started thinking about the war and . . . I've got a feeling it could go on for a long time. And it seemed to me that such a lot of things are uncertain at the moment, so maybe we should confirm the things we can be sure of. Before it's too late. Unless of course you had your heart set on a big, formal ceremony?' he added with a touch of sarcasm. 'I didn't think that sort of thing mattered to you.'

'Of course it doesn't,' said Margaret quickly.

'Then will you?'

'I don't think I can. You see it's possible that nurses who have a husband at the Front may not be allowed to serve overseas.'

'So give up nursing.' Edward leaned forward eagerly then saw her expression and hastily changed tack. 'I'm not trying to belittle the importance of what you're doing, please don't think that – but surely if you want to stick at it for now, you could stay at home in your present place? There must be stacks of useful work for you to do here.'

'Is there? I felt such a fraud today Edward, preaching to those girls about the stark realities of nursing the war-wounded when I'm in a civilian hospital.'

'They'll probably have to take military casualties soon enough if the war goes on.'

'I suppose so.' Absent-mindedly, Margaret twisted the engagement ring on her finger. 'But the really vital work – for the more experienced ones like me – must be at the field hospitals behind the lines, coping with the wounded at the earliest stages.'

'That doesn't mean you have to do it.'

'It does. To me it does, Edward. I've wanted to put my name forward for weeks. I've only hung back because I felt I should discuss it with you first.'

'That was considerate of you.' Edward's tone was scathing. 'Do you mean *discuss* it? Or do you mean, inform me of your decision?'

'I suppose that's what I do mean,' Margaret admitted.

'Don't I count for anything?' he said fiercely.

'You do. Of course you do.'

'But this is more important?'

'Yes,' said Margaret, quietly. 'For now I think it is. Edward, why can't you see this from my point of view? You volunteered—'

'That's different.'

'Is it? Why? Suppose someone were to say to you, "All right, Allingham, you're a smart chap, we could do with you on the staff. You won't have to go out with your regiment, you can stay here and organize things at home. Plenty of important administrative work going." As a matter of fact,' she added, 'I have a godfather on Kitchener's staff. I

145

could probably get that arranged for you. Would you like me to?'

'Of course not. I couldn't skulk about at home while the others went off to do the fighting. What kind of a soldier do you think I am?' demanded Edward.

'And what kind of a nurse do you think I am?' Margaret parried, gentle but inexorable. There was a pause.

'So you won't marry me now?'

'I wish I could,' she said. 'I really do wish it, Edward.'

'So do I.' He gave her a twisted smile. 'Still, if you won't, you won't and that's that.' Abruptly he stood up, pushing back his chair. 'I suppose you'd better be getting back, then.'

'I suppose so.'

He gave her his arm, walking down the street, but he kept it as stiff and rigid as a ramrod, holding her away from his side. Margaret glanced up briefly at his set profile. She wished that she could afford to turn him towards her, to kiss that stubborn, scowling mouth and smooth open those clenched fists. But in their reserved, cautious relationship there had been no room for such gestures, and now was not the time to begin when she was already so sorely tempted from the path of duty by what he asked.

Outside the cast-iron gates of the hospital entrance she waited uncertainly for him to kiss her goodbye.

'Meggie . . .' he said. It was the nickname of her nursery days, the name her parents called her and until now, nobody else. Edward's arms went round her, his hands in the small of her back pressed her against him. There were small droplets of rain on the shoulders of his uniform, damp under her cheek as his mouth brushed gently against her eyebrow and then her ear.

'Is it so impossible to marry me?' he said, his voice so low that she could barely hear it. 'That was what you promised me just a few weeks ago, wasn't it? I want so much to be able to think of you as my wife when I'm away. I want to be able to remember us together.'

There was an unmistakable hint of passion in the difficult

sentence and just for a moment all Margaret's defences threatened to come crashing down. She knew she wasn't beautiful; she had always doubted her ability to stir Edward deeply in a physical sense, and in all the time she had known him, she had instinctively kept disguised the extent to which he succeeded in stirring her. When he'd first proposed marriage with a dry and formal suggestion that they should suit each other pretty well, she had replied with equal urbanity that it seemed like a good idea. But under the calm façade, her treacherous heart would keep yearning for love – however inappropriate that might be for plain, sensible Margaret.

'I don't know,' she whispered uncertainly. *Please*, she thought, *make me do what you want. Convince me it's all right.* But already Edward was in retreat from the unwonted exporute of his feelings.

'I suppose you'll want to think it over. I did rather spring it on you. When do you come off duty?' he said, his hands dropping to his sides. His voice had steadied and sounded merely polite.

'About six o'clock tomorrow morning.'

'All right. I'll be waiting for you outside the hospital. You can tell me then what you've decided. We'd still have time, just.' He kissed her, finally, with a restraint that left her aching for the restoration of that hunger she had glimpsed a moment before. 'Till tomorrow then.'

He walked away into the evening drizzle and Margaret, squaring her shoulders, became Sister Churchill again.

The building which housed McKinley's restaurant dated from the Regency period, and its interior fixtures still included the old hinged window shutters. From the street the restaurant presented a closed and cheerless appearance, but inside it was all opulence and blazing light from the many crystal chandeliers which dangled from the high, moulded ceiling. Their glitter was reflected and magnified by the tall gilt mirrors that lined the walls. The carpet underfoot was thick and soft and in the four corners of the room, helmeted and armoured statues of the gods glowered from their Corinthian pedestals over the diners. The tables were dispersed around a parquet dance floor beside which a small orchestra played waltzes and foxtrots, the music almost drowned by the constant buzz of conversation.

'I expect Charles will be here in a moment. We were just leaving when he got a message to report to the CO so he told me to come on ahead,' said Hugh, passing leather-bound menu books to Alice and Laura.

'I hope the service has improved since we were last here,' Alice said. 'They lost most of their waiters when the war was declared – Germans who rushed home, or were interned,' she explained to Laura. 'A lot of the restaurants were relying on German waiters.'

'I know. In Guildford, too. A few of them stayed on, pretending they were Swiss or something, but you could tell they weren't – they looked so worried,' said Laura. 'Pa asked one of them to prove his nationality and the poor chap couldn't. I felt quite sorry for him even though he *was* a German.'

A waiter brought dry sherry in cut crystal glasses.

'We're waiting for one of our party,' Hugh told him. 'We won't order till he arrives.'

Laura sipped her sherry, watching Hugh and Alice gazing into each other's eyes and feeling that she was in the way. Under the table, she was sure they were holding hands.

'Would you mind awfully if Alice and I had a dance while we're waiting for Charles?' Hugh asked. The question was for form's sake – he was already standing up to lead his wife to the dance floor.

Chinless Hugh was improved by marriage. Already, after only a few weeks, he appeared older, more confident and more mature. He and Alice seemed very *together*, Laura thought with a flicker of envy as they walked away. It was the same togetherness that she had sensed between Edward and Margaret at the reception. Would she ever share that intangible link with a man?

'Hullo Miss Brownlowe, how nice to see you again.'

Charles McKay pulled out the chair opposite hers and sat down. The uniform that he and Hugh wore today was not the dark blue striped with scarlet and trimmed with gold that they had worn at Hugh's wedding, but a serviceable khaki battledress. It had, nevertheless, an indefinable glamour. Like Hugh, he seemed older somehow. Perhaps it was the war that was turning these boys into men? Laura, returning his smile, felt a flutter of excitement in the pit of her stomach. It wasn't that swooping sensation that Edward always managed to induce in her, but still it was something.

'I'm sorry I'm late,' Charles said. 'Summons from the CO.'

'Yes, Hugh told us. Nothing bad, I hope.'

'No, far from it! Well, depends how you look at it I suppose. Good news, in that we've been waiting for it. Not so good for Alice. We're off to Ludgershall tomorrow to form part of the new Seventh Cavalry Brigade. After that it's just a matter of days before we go to war.'

There was a kind of suppressed glow about him, as if a light were burning somewhere deep under his skin. Laura had noticed that same electric glow in other young men of her acquaintance who were on the verge of going into action. It seemed completely alien to her that anyone should actually look forward to battle, with all its attendant danger and discomfort. But men seemed to be like that. She felt mildly offended that Charles, who reportedly thought her the most wonderful girl in the world, should now be so pleased at the prospect of having to go away. She resolved to remind him of what he was leaving behind.

'It seems a shame to waste this music,' she said.

'Would you like to dance?' he offered with alacrity.

During the waltz Charles rediscovered the degree to which he had been attracted to her. Laura could have pinpointed the exact moment when his eager, excited mood was replaced by an unsureness, a look of longing which reminded her vaguely of Oliver's dog Magnus.

'I say, Miss Brownlowe, would you be awfully offended if I wrote to you when we're over there?'

'I'd be more offended if you didn't,' said Laura, and let him hold her a little closer. She felt pleasantly thrilled, but totally in control of the situation.

In the middle of the night an elderly man in Margaret's ward suffered a heart attack. There was hurried activity, the summoning of doctors, the soothing of other patients to be dealt with. At dawn the man died. His family had been sent for but came too late, and cried, and needed consolation. Margaret took the distraught widow and daughters and the bewildered, sleepy-eyed grandchildren into an anteroom to let them talk out their grief. Embroiled in the dispensing of sympathy and practical information about registering the death, she failed to notice that the nurse who was to relieve her had arrived and when she remembered to look at the watch pinned to her apron, it was ten past seven.

Snatching up her cloak she almost ran down to the gate, but there was no sign of Edward.

'Sister Churchill! A chap left a note for you,' called the porter, tapping on the glazed window of his office. 'Army officer, he was. Hung around for over an hour. Seemed a bit fed up about something.' He handed over a folded sheet of paper.

'I gather I have your answer. I'll write. Yours, Edward.'

In the darkened ward, sometime around midnight, Margaret had resolved to marry Edward now and let someone else with less to lose do the front-line nursing. It seemed her decision had been overturned.

8

Daisy had a feeling something was wrong. It had started when Miss Jessie, who had gone off this morning for her regular stint at Stoughton Barracks to pack comfort parcels for the troops, had come home earlier than expected with a very odd expression on her face – close to tears Daisy would have said. Ferry had been summoned to the drawing room for a conference, and now he was locked in earnest discussion in the pantry with Mrs Driver. Instinct told Daisy that their conversation was not about the day's menus or the ordering of more coal. She hovered near the closed door, wishing that she had the nerve to use an inverted glass against the wood to help her overhear. So far all she'd managed to catch was one comment when Mrs Driver, voice raised in agitation, had cried, 'But she has a right to know, doesn't she?' before being hushed by the butler.

It was no good, the murmur of voices behind the door was too muffled for her to make any sense of it. She shrugged her shoulders and returned to the kitchen. No doubt if it was something important that concerned her in any way, she'd hear about it in due course, and meanwhile she might as well get on with her work or there'd be no cake for the staff's afternoon tea.

Until the mysterious new development had interrupted them, she'd been turning her hand to cake-making under Mrs Driver's supervision, while on the other side of the big table the cook prepared pastry for the steak-and-kidney pie that was to be the Brownlowes' lunch. Daisy knew that it wasn't wise to meddle with the pie – Mrs Driver wouldn't brook any encroachment on her patch – but the cake was ready in its tin for the oven. She ran a finger round the rim of the mixing bowl to scrape up the last of the concoction of eggs and flour, milk, sugar and raisins. It wasn't often that the Colindale budget had run to cakes when she was a child, but whenever she'd had the chance to taste it, she'd always preferred the uncooked cake mix to the finished product. She probably still did she decided, licking her finger appreciatively before she opened a drawer in the painted pine sideboard on the far side of the kitchen. Extracting a sheet of paper from the stack which the cook kept there, she crossed to the range. The heat buffeted against her cheeks as she opened the heavy door and dropped the paper on the oven floor.

'If it burns,' she recited to herself, 'the oven is too hot. When the paper becomes dark brown, it is suitable for pastry. When light brown it does for pies. Dark yellow for cakes.' Or was it the other way round? She concentrated, mentally picturing the guide in the copy of *Mr Black's Household Cookery* that Mrs Driver kept on a shelf in the servants' hall. No, that was right, if the paper turned a dark yellow it would indicate that the oven was at the correct heat for cake-baking.

'There she is,' said Mrs Driver, coming heavy-footed into the kitchen with Ferry behind her. 'Oh Daisy, love, what a world it is!'

The unexpected endearment shook the little maid almost as much as Mrs Driver's agitated expression. And Ferry, Daisy thought with her heartbeat accelerating uncomfortably, looked like a man at a funeral. He cleared his throat.

'We thought perhaps it was best you should know,' he began. 'Though there isn't that much to actually *know*, I suppose, not at this minute. But it doesn't look too good, does it? Oh dear, we'll just have to hope for the best won't we? They may be prisoners.'

There was a pause. Daisy tried to fathom what lay behind the butler's garbled phrases and his companion's pink-rimmed eyes.

'Is it Arthur?' she said at last.

'We don't know,' Ferry said. 'It could be. The chances are

152

. . . well, the fact is it seems like there's been a bit of a disaster with the Queen's.'

'Miss Jessie was at the barracks this morning,' Mrs Driver broke in, her jowls quivering with emotion. 'And Mrs Morgan who's in charge of the parcels, she said there'd been a message received from the boys of the battalion at the Front, and it said. . . .' She took a deep breath to steady her voice, '. . . it said, "Thank you very much for the parcels, but don't send us any more for now. We have plenty as there's only about fifty of us left."'

'Fifty?' Daisy repeated, her mind unable to make sense of the number. The four companies of the first battalion that left Bordon had been up to strength. Almost a thousand officers and men. There'd been news filtering through about casualties from time to time, but nothing on this scale. The skin on her back seemed to contract, making her shiver.

'We'll just have to wait for the lists,' said Mrs Driver. 'And the telegrams. That poor Mrs Morgan . . . her husband's with the battalion, you know.'

Arthur and Robert. In her mind's eye Daisy saw them again as she had seen them in August, marching in their khaki uniforms through the streets of Guildford; and then she heard the stutter of guns and imagined the orderly ranks toppling over like ninepins. Dazed, she turned towards the oven. The paper she had laid inside was burned black and disintegrating.

'I think we should give Daisy Colindale a little holiday,' said Jessie. The Brownlowes, minus Oliver, were assembled in the drawing room after supper. Jessie was occupied in piecing together yet another matinée jacket for the temporarily fatherless children of soldiers and sailors. Rupert wrote his daily entry, which nowadays seemed to consist of endless lists of the outlay necessary for converting the factory to shell production. And Laura played the piano softly in the background.

'Daisy? A holiday? Why?' said Laura, still playing. The

153

Chopin *Nocturne* was a favourite which she knew by heart, but the gentle cadences were at odds with her irritation at Jessie's suggestion.

Laura had at last returned from London that afternoon, less in response to her father's gruff comments in his occasional short letters that he missed having her about the place, than because the attractions of the visit had palled. Charles McKay and Hugh Malloy had departed with the Seventh Cavalry Brigade in late September, perhaps to participate in the defence of Antwerp they said, though as usual it was impossible to tell even the soldiers' nearest and dearest exactly what they were up to. After they went, Alice had become preoccupied with her nursing training and leaving Laura to her own devices, she'd spent whole days at a time at the London Hospital where she had obtained a place through the influence of the hateful Margaret Churchill. When she was at home she alternated between worrying about Hugh's safety and pestering her cousin to test her for her forthcoming examination.

There were still concerts and shopping and the sights of London to keep Laura amused, but the parks were full of men practising the digging of trenches and the streets at night were so dark and cheerless. The Government had ordered the dimming of streetlamps at the beginning of October as a precaution against possible air raids, since the enemy's Zeppelins were known to be capable of reaching London. The prospect of bombs raining from the sky on to a furtively darkened city was a sobering thought. Laura would have pushed it aside; she had a well-honed capacity for ignoring unpleasant facts that she could not change. But she found that trying to get Alice to enthuse about any proposed entertainment instead of pining for Hugh or rehearsing the correct way to arrest a haemorrhage was like trying to get a lump of lead to bounce. It got worse when the hospital received an influx of wounded Belgian soldiers, evacuated after the fall of Antwerp. This event plunged Alice into a frenzy of anxiety about Hugh's possible fate and even when he sent a letter assuring her that he had not been involved at Antwerp, it was of small consolation.

When Laura skimmed through the letter which Alice had passed over to her, she had at first assumed that, clumsy endearments aside, it was merely a banal catalogue of Hugh's encounters with old school chums. *Thought we would meet up with Albert, but instead we nearly ran into Yorick and now we are staying pretty close to Maurice. A few of us got lost last week, beastly show.*

'It's code,' Alice explained. 'We worked one out before he left, so he could tell me more or less where he was without the censor blacking it out.' She was cleaning Hugh's dress sword, which he had left behind because it was an expensive engraved one from Wilkinson's and too good for the waging of war. Instead he had drawn a standard issue sword from the stores and Alice had promised to take care of the original for him in the meantime, a task which in Laura's opinion she fulfilled to excess. She polished assiduously at the already gleaming blade.

'*Albert* is Antwerp. *Yorick* is Ypres. I think *Maurice* is Messines, and *a few of us got lost* means. . . .'

'I can guess,' said Laura.

The little doll's-house flat had become positively claustrophobic in the long autumn evenings. The shortcomings of Alice's 'girl' were the last straw; she was too young and untrained to deal effectively with the guest's wardrobe. After weeks of anxiety about the damage liable to be caused by an over-hot pressing, after struggling with her own buttons and even in desperation goffering her own frills, Laura had abandoned Alice to her loneliness and come home to the calm, elegant surroundings of Maple Grange and the efficiency of Daisy's ministrations. It was too bad that Aunt Jessie was now proposing to let the girl disappear.

'She's had some bad news about her fiancé and her brother,' Jessie explained, 'and I think it might help her to be with her family.'

'Oh.' The *Nocturne* broke off on a discord and the performer

155

gazed at her aunt in dismay. Laura might have grown away from her old friendship with the young housemaid, but a residue of affection remained and it was awful to think of poor good-natured little Daisy on the receiving end of bad news from the Front.

'What sort of bad news?' Rupert closed his diary. Unencumbered by sentimental considerations for his staff, he had registered only that Jessie seemed about to set an unwise precedent. 'Dead? Missing? Wounded? Prisoner?' he barked.

'I'm not sure. It hasn't been confirmed. But it seems that his battalion has suffered very heavy losses and naturally she's under some stress waiting to hear.'

'If it isn't confirmed,' Rupert pronounced briskly, 'then there's no need for her to assume the worst and start demanding holidays, is there?'

'Oh, she isn't *demanding* anything.'

'I'm glad to hear it. We must all soldier on in the face of adversity,' said Rupert. 'Like the troops at the Front, you know.'

Laura, accepting with some relief her father's judgement that feeling bad for Daisy would be premature, shifted through some music manuscripts and embarked on 'Rose Among the Heather', singing softly in her clear contralto.

'Oh by the way, Jessie,' Rupert remembered, 'I've given Aldridge the sack.'

Hiring and firing of servants was supposed to be Jessie's province – delegated, when it came to the male staff, to Ferry. But Rupert meddled without compunction.

'I thought it might induce him to volunteer. He's young and fit, he's just the type that Kitchener's after for the New Army. And he won't find another chauffeur's job in a hurry,' Rupert added with satisfaction. 'Not with the petrol shortage and so many cars being requisitioned for military use.'

'Do you think it was quite fair,' Jessie said, laying her sewing in her lap and fixing her timid brown eyes on her brother, 'to *force* him to make such a decision?'

'I'm not forcing him. I'm merely encouraging him to consider that option by removing one of his other options. Of course I mentioned what I hoped the outcome would be and I think he took it on board.'

'But who's going to drive the Landaulette?' Jessie knew that Rupert had successfully resisted the requisitioning of his vehicle on the grounds that it was essential to his work for the war effort.

'Aha,' said Rupert triumphantly. 'Laura can do that.'

'*Laura?*'

'Yes. She tells me she took a course with a school of motoring while she was up in London and staying with Alice. Very smart of her,' said Rupert, and he beamed approvingly in the direction of his daughter, though three months ago he would have regarded the idea of a young lady undertaking any such practical activity as disgracefully unfeminine. Laura, recognizing with satisfaction that her new skill was likely to absolve her from her father's previous ambitions for her as a VAD nurse, returned his smile as she sang.

> 'Rose, thou pretty rose so-o red,
> Blooming in the he-e-ath-er. . . .'

'Oh. I see,' said Jessie dubiously. If Laura was as dashing behind the wheel of the Landaulette as she was on the back of a horse, her aunt anticipated some disturbing journeys. She took up the matinée jacket again and began to set a tiny sleeve into place. 'It will save on his wages anyway, I suppose,' she said.

'That is immaterial,' said Rupert irritably, though the thought had crossed his mind. The factory was currently expected to be a bottomless pit so far as expenditure was concerned, and even retrenchment on the scale of a chauffeur's salary would help. But he didn't like his sister's implication that parting with Aldridge might have been prompted by economic considerations. 'If it were not for the fact that his King and country need him, of course I would not be dispensing with my chauffeur's services,' he said. 'Or at the very least, I would be inviting him to transfer to the factory. But I recognize where my duty lies.'

Jessie, snipping off a length of wool and threading it into a darning needle, was silent. She wondered if Aldridge would appreciate being an instrument of his employer's fulfilment of duty. Reading between the jingoistic lines of Rupert's war-news magazine as it proclaimed the achievements of 'Our heroes at the Front' and the fun they were having trouncing the Hun, she thought that the chauffeur might have had his reasons for having held back from volunteering. That awful rumour about the Queen's . . . and the groom who had gone . . . Griffin? Wounded once already in the earliest weeks. She must remember to ask Mrs Driver if they'd heard any further news about him.

Now that the war was three months old, Griffin was getting used to snatching his sleep by daylight between the routine demands of horse-care. And to spending his nights transporting ammunition and supplies to the gun position four or five miles from the wagon lines – along roads and tracks which the German artillery methodically shelled throughout the hours of darkness with a view to discouraging such activity.

The guns of Griffin's battery were installed in pits scooped out of the ground, roofed over with corrugated-iron sheeting and camouflaged by foliage to keep the enemy's spotter planes from reporting their position to their opposite numbers on the German side of the trench lines. The German gunners, who knew that they must be out there somewhere, bombarded the area at random and the surrounding countryside was pock-marked with the results. Occasionally a shell found its target and there'd be a sombre funeral service over the victims. Forsythe's battery hoped, as they shoved the gleaming shells into the breeches of their guns, that their own fire was creating equal inconvenience among the German lines.

At least they were now firing eighteen-pounders. In a way

this represented a demotion: the horse gunners were supposed, at least by their own reckoning, to be a cut above the field gunners, but the facts had to be faced. Thirteen-pounders were fine for keeping up with the cavalry but in this semi-static war of trenches, the greater range of a field artillery gun or, better still, the lobbing power of a howitzer, was what was needed. Gradually the lighter guns were being sent back to store and their teams switched to operating the more effective eighteen-pounders.

As the rainy season wore on, the shell craters filled with water and the churned mud of the tracks became lethally slippery. By night, bringing up the wagon loads of replacement ammunition from the depots, the drivers had to keep a sharp look out for the gleam of moonlight on water. A lapse of concentration could send horses and wagon slithering sideways into a flooded pit, which meant hazardous and exhausting hours lost in dragging them out again.

These days Griffin was adept at scouring the neighbourhood for fodder for the horses that were his responsibility; he had become hard-hearted about anyone else's animals. He could scrounge and barter with the best of the drivers and had developed a new talent for stealing from other units the items of harness and equipment that were needed to replace those destroyed or lost by his own battery, an activity known euphemistically as 'winning'. He could lie about his crimes with a straight face and an untroubled conscience. He had become inured to the monotony of the daily diet of tea and bully beef, bread and jam, or the tins of pork-and-beans in which the pork was a greasy, half-inch square of something vaguely fibrous lurking at the bottom of the tin. If he remembered Mrs Driver's pot roast with a certain wistfulness, he didn't join in the complaints of his fellow soldiers as he chewed resignedly on whatever was dished into his dixie by the much-abused cook operating the field kitchen. One of his most useful new skills was an ability to estimate the approximate nearness of a descending shell and the right direction in which to travel to avoid it. What he had not yet managed to get accustomed to was the utter silliness of some of the orders emanating from high command.

'We've been told to clip out the horses,' said Forsythe on a mid-November day when the rain had been coming down in a steady slant since before dawn. In the horse lines the animals stood meek in their misery, coats streaked, heads down and tails tucked in, up to their fetlocks in mud.

'But that's ludicrous, sir,' Griffin said, aghast. As a groom back in England, he'd been accustomed to clipping out the Brownlowe horses in November. Unclipped, a hunter or a carriage horse working hard would have to struggle and sweat, and the long, thick pelt of a winter coat made grooming more difficult. But out here, in campaign conditions? 'There'd be some sense in it if they were being kept in barracks. But tethered out day and night through the winter, on the rations they're getting . . . ? It'll do for them, sir, they'll catch any ailment that's going.'

'I know,' said Forsythe and his shoulders slumped. He had just finished a stint as Forward Observation Officer with the infantry in the front-line trenches. It had culminated in four hours in a Forward Observation Post, a term which glorified the muddy sap running out from the trenches and from which it had been Forsythe's task to radio back instructions about the targeting of his guns for maximum effect. He and the signaller who accompanied him had made a number of nerve-racking forays on their stomachs through the mire to mend the communications wire where it had been broken by enemy artillery fire. Forsythe was still getting over his surprise at the fact that he had survived the experience and he didn't feel up to justifying the latest insanity emanating from headquarters. 'But what else can we do? Orders are orders.'

'Pity we remembered to bring the clippers if you ask me, sir,' muttered Griffin bitterly.

'Mmm,' Forsythe said on a speculative note. 'I wonder . . . ?' and later he reported to his commanding officer that alas, his section could not carry out the instruction to clip the horses because their clippers had mysteriously gone missing.

Griffin and the other drivers made the statement true that night with a borrowed entrenching tool in the mud among the horse lines. Word spread even as they were digging and before the earth was shovelled back, the rest of the battery's clippers had gone into the hole.

'Thank God,' said Griffin, as he stamped the disturbed ground flat again over the buried articles, 'for a subaltern with sense.' And he started to whistle softly as he tacked up a team, ready for the nightly chore of restocking the shell piles.

'You're in a good mood,' said Lockett, the driver who had replaced Dawson. 'Heard from your girl today, did you?'

Griffin didn't answer, but he stopped whistling. His torn arm had mended, leaving only the long, magenta ridge of the scar, but the small, aching wound inside him that was his memory of Daisy refused to heal. The occasional letters from Mrs Driver mentioned her briefly. *Our Daisy's worried about her young man in the Queen's*, the last one had said, weeks ago now. *She's gone very quiet*. Griffin had heard rumours about the Queen's. Back at the ammunition dump he'd got talking with one of the field artillery drivers who'd been at Gheluvelt when the broken remnants of a battalion had staggered by. Asked who they were, one of their number had said starkly, 'We're the First Queen's. What's left of it.'

Daisy's young man in the Queen's. The one she cared about, the one she missed and fretted for. Griffin kept waiting for the hurt to go away but stubbornly, it didn't.

Lockett failed to notice the lack of a response to his question. He, at any rate, had heard from *his* girl and with the tactlessness of a happy man, he was preparing to tell Griffin all about her.

Early in August 1914, prior to their embarkation with the British Expeditionary Force, the first battalion, the Queen's Royal West Surrey Regiment, had paraded on the barrack square at Bordon camp. Someone had taken a photograph for the battalion records. On 9 November, having been pulled out of the front line, the First Queen's paraded again, and again a photographer recorded the scene.

The farmyard was considerably smaller than the barrack square at Bordon, but in the circumstances that hardly mattered. The warrant officer who had written home to Guildford that no more comfort parcels were needed had overestimated the number of the survivors. If you counted the cooks and the transport men, thirty-two other ranks and one officer remained of the élite fighting force that had been the first battalion. The rest were being shunted towards Germany as prisoners of war, or lay sprawled in the trench-scarred fields near Gheluvelt, or had been shovelled hastily into their makeshift graves. If they were among the luckier ones, they lay patiently waiting for attention from the overworked surgeons and nurses at the base hospitals. For days the roads running back from Ypres had crawled with ambulances and wagons, requisitioned London buses and stretchers on wheeled handcarts – anything that could be pressed into service to transport the casualties of the German army's latest push.

The front line, as defined by the trenches occupied by the Allies and their enemy, was now the shape of a rough arrowhead east of Ypres, with the BEF and the French army apparently pushing out into German-occupied territory. In reality the arrowhead was all that they had been able to hang on to in the face of the enemy's frenzied assault. It looked good, it sounded good: 'the Ypres salient'. It provided its holders with the worst of all possible worlds, an exposed position which could be attacked on both flanks.

At home in England, the editor of Rupert's illustrated magazine of war news was busy redefining the carnage around Ypres for the benefit of the British public – as a stirring victory for the brigades in khaki.

Among the little detachment of men in the farmyard, Robert Colindale stood to attention with his gun across his shoulder. The gun was cleaned and oiled, its bearer freshly shaved, his uniform was brushed and spruce and his buttons were bright.

Nothing, though, could brighten his tired eyes. He was remembering the events of 31 October in the littered environs of the village called Gheluvelt. It had been a day that came closer to his concept of what hell must be like than anything he had previously experienced. He was remembering, too, the subsequent roll call when the names of his fellow-soldiers were read out one by one.

'. . . Barter, Private William.'

No answer.

'Anyone know anything about him?'

No answer.

'Bayliss, Corporal John.'

'Wounded in the neck, sir, when they got the machine guns on us. I saw the RAMC blokes took him off but it looked pretty bad.'

'Bridges, Private Clive.'

'Dead, sir, when they stormed the orchard.'

'Bright, Private Arthur.'

'He's bought it too, sir. Bayonet.'

Against his will Robert saw again the moments when the dawn mists began to clear and wave after wave of dark figures in spiked helmets poured into the orchard held by the Queen's. Every night since they'd pulled the shattered battalion out of the front line he'd been reliving that scene in his dreams. He'd killed the Jerry bastard who did for Arthur, jabbing his own bayonet upwards into the man's throat, feeling the blade jar against the spinal column, deriving a vicious satisfaction from the sensation. And then, oblivious of the mayhem around him, he'd stuck his heel on the fallen man's chest, dragged out his blade and plunged it in again and again, sobbing for his mate.

'*Vel Exuviaie Triumphant.*' 'Even the remnants triumphant', said the regimental motto emblazoned on the banners. But Robert didn't feel particularly triumphant. The only emotion he could summon up with any strength now was a longing to go home.

Daisy hurried up the sloping street near Guildford station. She had just a few minutes to spare between finishing her list of shopping for Mrs Driver and being picked up by Nichols and Blackie outside the station, and she wanted to seize the chance to pay a visit to Mrs Bright.

The trouble was, now that she was here she wasn't sure which house was the right one. She hadn't really noticed details that day she came with Arthur . . . but at last she recognized the pattern of the front-room curtains and the plant pot for the aspidistra on the table behind the window.

Daisy hoisted her wicker shopping basket further up her forearm and summoning all her courage, reached for the knocker. Before she could raise it, the door opened a foot or so and Mrs Bright peered through the gap.

'I saw you come along the road,' she said. 'What do you want?'

'Arthur . . . have you heard anything about Arthur . . . ?' But already Daisy could guess the answer to the question that had been tearing her apart for days, ever since she'd heard the news about the battalion. All of Mrs Bright that was visible was garbed in deepest black, not the dusty black of the skirt she'd worn on the day Daisy met her but the horribly immaculate 'best' black of a mourner. Her seamed face was haggard with grief and unmistakably hostile as she stared at Daisy.

'We just got the telegram this morning,' she said. 'What's it to do with you?'

'Wounded . . . ?' It was hopeless, but still Daisy clung to hope.

'Dead.' Hope crashed. Mrs Bright began to close the door.

'Please don't. I have to talk to you.' Desperately Daisy wedged her toe in what was left of the gap so that Mrs Bright couldn't shut her out. 'Please. Arthur and me, you know we were going to get married.'

'Well you can't do that now, can you?'

'You don't understand,' Daisy whispered. She drew a long, shaky breath. 'I'm going to have a baby.'

There. She'd said it. Dumbly, she waited for Mrs Bright's

hostility to fade. The woman who should have become her mother-in-law put out a hand, but as Daisy groped for it, she was given a calculated shove that sent her staggering backwards.

'You little slut,' Mrs Bright hissed. 'Be off with you, you're not wanted here. This is a place of proper grief.'

'But it's your grandchild,' Daisy protested, hardly audible.

Mrs Bright sneered. 'That's what you say. My Arthur was a cleanly brought-up boy. He was going to marry Adelaide Stringer. That little bit of silliness with you was just on account of him being muddled up for a while and I dare say you took advantage of him. I never took it seriously! He loved Adelaide. He wrote to her just a few days before he died to say he hoped to see her when he came home on leave. Why should a boy like that be bothered with a trollop like you?'

The door closed.

Shivering with reaction, Daisy crept away, her arms tightly folded around the basket held against her stomach as if Mrs Bright's verbal blows had been physical. It couldn't be true, it *couldn't*, that Arthur had written to Adelaide Stringer. . . . As if that matters now, she reminded herself wearily.

'Hey! Hang on!'

A man ran down the road after her. He was middle-aged, with thinning hair, dressed all in black like Mrs Bright.

'Arthur's dad,' he said, catching up with her, panting for breath. 'I heard the missus just now. She was a bit hard on you. I'm sorry. She's upset about Arthur. We're all upset.'

Daisy couldn't find anything to say. Her brain was frozen. She watched him fishing for words. His face was Arthur's face grown older and harder.

'Was it true what you said about a baby?'

She nodded.

'That's bad. Very bad. It'll be illegitimate, like.' He chewed at his lip, his face furrowed. He groped in his pocket.

'You'll be hard up. Here.' He looked down at what he had extracted, hesitating, then with sudden decision transferred a few coins from his closed fist into her cold hand.

'Best I can manage. Sorry. Good luck,' he said, and walked rapidly back up the street. Daisy looked down stupidly at the coins in the palm of her hand. He'd given her five shillings.

At the beginning of December Rupert spent a week in London learning the details of manufacturing procedure at a shell factory whose output he hoped to emulate. Miss Jessie, haunted by Daisy Colindale's wan face and pinched expression, took advantage of his absence to grant Daisy an extra few days' holiday.

At least the girl's brother had turned out to be safe and well in the aftermath of First Ypres. Sadly, though, her fiancé had been on the battalion's horrifyingly long casualty list printed by the *Advertiser*. Jessie had cried when she read it, coming across familiar names and connecting them with faces she'd known around the district. The harsher realities of war had come very quickly to Guildford.

Rupert, on hearing the news, had expressed the view that Daisy's bereavement would be best coped with by encouraging the girl to throw herself into her work. Hard work, he said, was the best cure for heartache, as he had discovered himself after his dear wife died. When Jessie demurred, he had suggested that showing 'favouritism' to Daisy would cause resentment among the rest of the staff in view of the maid's other unscheduled absences this autumn. Now Jessie crossed her fingers and hoped he would be proved wrong. She couldn't believe that Mrs Driver or Joan or Susan would begrudge their fellow servant a break in her duties, not when she had been wandering around like a sad little ghost for the past few weeks, dodging into dark corners and cupboards to wipe the tracks of tears away from her face.

It was because of Miss Jessie's small mutiny against Mr Rupert's decision that Daisy was at last able to get home, to break the double bad news about Arthur and the baby to Mrs Colindale.

Louella, who had realized Daisy's condition for weeks, ever

since she'd witnessed her early-morning dose of nausea, stood silently at the kitchen table slicing carrots for the midday meal, while Daisy laid the bald facts before her mother.

After all the strain of waiting to hear that Robert was safe, Mrs Colindale felt additionally aggrieved about being called upon to absorb the information that Daisy was in the family way and that the prospective husband was no longer a prospect. Sitting propped in her wheelback armchair by the kitchen range, she had worked her way through *How could you be so silly?* And, *What will the neighbours say?* Then, *What will become of us all?* And now she was on to pragmatic suggestions.

'You could get rid of it.'

Louella and Daisy stared at her, united in shock. Granted, Daisy's situation was a catastrophe, but the solution proposed was drastic indeed. Louella abandoned the chopping board and moved to lay a supporting hand on Daisy's arm.

'Mother Colindale, she can't do that. It's all she's got left of Arthur.'

'Sentiment,' said Mrs Colindale bleakly, 'lasts a short while. Babies go on being a trouble to you for ever. Even when they grow up,' she added, rubbing it in.

'Were we that much trouble, Mum? Robert and me?' said Daisy. She cast her mind back over scenes of childhood. She'd had a straitened upbringing: there had never been quite enough to eat, always a need to patch clothes and make-do-and-mend. She could remember acutely the humiliation of being teased at school when she hobbled in wearing her brother's hand-me-down boots, too wide and too long for her slender feet, held on only by tight lacing and thick socks. Treats were few and far between, the Christmas stockings had contained nothing more than an orange and a few sweets. Her mother had often scolded or slapped and been too weary to sympathize or congratulate over their small triumphs and disasters . . . but through it all Daisy had had a sensation of being loved, even when her behaviour was at its most exasperating. Had that been an illusion?

'Did you wish you didn't have us?' she asked with difficulty.

'Yes,' said Mrs Colindale. 'Often.' Then she saw Daisy's face. 'No. I mean, you were there, you were mine, I made the best of it. And you were lovely children . . . only there's no denying it would have been a lot easier without you once Harry died. And you, Daisy, you're not even starting out with a husband and hope for the future, like I did. It'll be people pointing and staring and calling you names, on top of all the scrimping and starving . . . and it'll be the same for all of us,' she added with a hint of pleading.

'But to get rid of it, Mum? To kill a living thing?'

'And it's dangerous,' Louella put in grimly.

'It can be,' Mrs Colindale admitted. 'But I know of a woman, lives out Wood Street way. Ma Turner. She's good, so I've heard. Very clean. None of her girls have ever died of it.'

'So far,' said Louella. 'Oh, this is ridiculous. She can't possibly. We'll just have to cope, somehow.'

'I'm a bit old for coping,' said Mrs Colindale. She leaned back against the worn patchworked cushion behind her head and her face had that look that Daisy remembered from bad times gone by, a look of deathly tiredness. And she hadn't been well for a long time . . . that day she'd fainted, back in the autumn, it hadn't just been the starvation diet of the previous weeks, or the worry about the money. She'd admitted to long-standing pains in her stomach, and what she called 'women's troubles'. It was true, she was too old for coping.

There was a long silence.

'This woman in Wood Street . . . what's her address?' said Daisy, avoiding Louella's accusing eyes.

Once she had agreed in principle to her mother's solution to her problem, Daisy would have liked to go straight out to Wood Green and get it over with. But Mrs Colindale urged that an appointment must be made first, which involved the sending of a discreet note via the most reliable child in the neighbourhood. While she waited for the messenger's return, Daisy agonized about alternatives . . . but it seemed that there weren't any. The birth of a baby with no father, complicated by the absence of a marriage certificate and lack of money, would pose insoluble problems.

The appointment had been made for the evening when there was less chance of anyone witnessing the visit and guessing the errand. Daisy had asked Louella along to provide moral support, but she wasn't giving any. It had been apparent from her pursed mouth and her unaccustomed taciturnity as she and Daisy trudged with a lantern through the outskirts of Guildford, that she disapproved of the whole proceedings. Daisy, who badly wanted her hand held and her conscience quietened, wished dismally that Louella would understand the desperation of her choice and stop blaming her for her weakness.

'Come in, dear. I'm all ready.'

Ma Turner was stout and short of breath, smelling of cabbage underlaid by a fainter smell of unwashed old lady. Her smile, which was probably meant to be reassuring, was rendered sinister by the dark gap where a canine tooth was missing from her upper jaw. Daisy and Louella followed her silently down the tiled passageway into a small, square back parlour. The room was poorly lit by an overhead gas lamp. The only furniture consisted of a low iron bedstead, with a threadbare blanket spread over the striped ticking of the mattress, and a table in the corner furthest from the window. That the householder could afford to dedicate a room to her sideline was an indication of the popularity of the service she offered, but there was no fire in the black iron grate and the room was bitterly cold.

'Take your things off, just your lower half, and lie down on the bed. How many months are you, dear?'

Daisy took a moment to understand the question.

'Four months. Since the beginning of August.'

Ma Turner whistled through the gap in her teeth. 'Leaving

it late,' she said. 'More trouble to shift when you leave them. Still, I dare say we'll manage.'

Fumbling with the waist buttons of her skirt, Daisy looked over her shoulder at the equipment assembled on the table. A chipped enamel basin half-full of cold water, a cake of soap and a none-too-clean towel was the basis of Mrs Turner's reputation for hygiene. A large brown-tinted glass bottle contained some unspecified liquid and beside it lay a coil of rubber tubing, a funnel, a long steel knitting needle and a small bottle of brandy. Daisy's hand moved instinctively to her stomach. The shifting sensation might have been the baby, or it might have been a spasm of fear.

'What's in the brown bottle?' she asked huskily. Mrs Turner followed the direction of her gaze.

'Carbolic.'

'What for?' The question, sharply put, had come from Louella.

'Well, we pump it in, see,' said Mrs Turner comfortably, 'and then we poke about a bit. It's a stubborn baby that hangs on in those conditions. Don't worry,' she added. 'You won't feel much, dear. The drink'll see to that. Take as much as you need.' She was unscrewing the smaller bottle as she spoke, and now she thrust it towards her client.

Dimly, Daisy was aware of Louella's hand gripping her arm above the elbow and shaking her.

'Come away,' said Louella fiercely. 'You can't do this. You *can't*.'

Daisy looked again at the bottle, the tubing and the knitting needle. She thought of the baby, whose faint stirrings she had become aware of in the last day or two, whose small shape had been forming inside her for almost four months now. She imagined it drowning in carbolic, writhing on the spike of the needle. Briskly, Mrs Turner pushed the brandy bottle into Daisy's hand and rolled back her sleeves over her forearms.

'Hurry up, dear, it's parky in here. And I haven't got all night.'

'I'm sorry,' Daisy whispered. She put the brandy down on

170

the table and blundered towards the door. 'I've changed my mind.'

'Suit yourself.' Mrs Turner shrugged her shoulders. 'More fool you.' Then she stepped across the doorway, barring retreat, and held out her hand. 'You'll have to pay me something anyway, seeing as I got in the booze and the carbolic specially for you.'

'How much?'

'Let's say five bob, shall we?'

'For a bottle of carbolic and a dribble of brandy that you'll use anyway?' Louella objected furiously. But Daisy was too tired and shaken to argue. She dug into her coat pocket and handed over the five shillings which had been the baby's endowment from Arthur's father.

9

Griffin stretched lazily, spreading his hands out behind his head. Even the officers in their linen-sheeted beds in the nearby farmhouse, he told himself, couldn't have had a better night's sleep than he and his fellow rankers had had in the barn, half-buried for warmth in a litter of straw. Pity they couldn't have arranged to bring the horses along with them and given them a dose of the same luxury.

Outside in the farmyard a cock was crowing. How long before somebody scragged that cock? Without it, he could have slept on for another hour.

It was the last of the battery's six rest days, ten miles behind the front lines. Rest days came periodically, just when you felt that you couldn't stand the tension any longer, strung up as you were by the constant assault on your senses of the day-and-night booming of the guns. Then they'd march you back along the muddy roads and you could get a shower and a change of clothes and, at last, a decent night's sleep – away from the furtive journeys with a jumpy team, a cartload of high explosive and the ever-present expectation that a Minen-werfer or Whizzbang would arch down out of the sky without warning and blow you to kingdom come.

Not that you couldn't hear the guns in the rest camp. Griffin thought they could probably hear them across the Channel in England. But at least here you knew that unless the enemy did something very fast and unexpected, for the time being it was some other poor devil who was on the receiving end of all that artillery.

Griffin scratched at his side, revelling in the knowledge that the itch he was experiencing was due to the prickliness of the straw which had made up his bed, and not the usual crawling sensation that marked the progress of small armies of lice across his body. Lice were endemic by now among the soldiers, a fact of life to be borne stoically while in action, but since he'd arrived at the rest camp he'd painstakingly burned them out of the seams of his clothes with a match flame, the clothes had been washed, and until the next lot hatched he was blessedly free of parasites.

From somewhere outside he could smell bacon frying, the aroma working on the saliva glands in his mouth even though he knew from experience that the bacon allocation would be too little and too fatty to live up to the promise of that glorious smell. Still, better than the everlasting plum-and-apple jam of front-line rations, about which the troops were likely to stage a mutiny one of these days. He stretched again. Soon he'd have to get up. There'd be work to do.

Even in the rest camps there was work to do. 'Smarten yourself up, soldier. Polish this. Burnish that. At the double!' Hours of bull, shining your boots and brushing out the dried mud from the long woollen puttees that wrapped your legs from ankle to calf. Fiddling about with a little tin of 'Soldier's Friend' and the U-shaped metal guard that slipped behind your buttons to keep the brass polish off your tunic. Someone, somewhere, probably a Red Tab on the Staff sipping brandy in his château, had decided that keeping the soldiers spruce and busy was good for their morale. That someone should be staked out under the flight path of the next Minnie Werfer and see what that did for *his* morale.

'Shut that flipping door!'

Burnes, the brigade's postman, had edged in through the doorway of the barn, closing the heavy door carefully behind him in response to a chorus of complaints about the icy draught that had swirled in from the farmyard. Outside it was snowing. Again. Rivulets of melted snow trickled down the back of his waterproof cape as he sent an envelope spinning in Griffin's direction. ''Ere you are, mate. Letter from your lady love.'

The letter, damp from Burnes' clammy grasp, landed on

173

Griffin's chest. He struggled up on to one elbow and snatched it, just in time, as his nearest neighbour made a grab.

'Who's been writing to you, then, Griff? Your mum, is it?'

'Well, it ain't your mum who's been writing to you, Lockett.' The postman stood over the driver thus addressed, legs braced, and drew another envelope appreciatively under his nostrils before dangling it tantalizingly just out of reach. 'Leastways, if she has, can you please give us a letter of introduction to 'er next time I get any Blighty leave? She don't 'alf use seductive perfume.'

'Go on. Give it here.'

'Who's going to make me, son?'

While they wrangled happily over Lockett's mail, Griffin opened his envelope. He knew who it was from. Nobody wrote to him except Mrs Driver, for whose rambling stream of gossip about the Grange and its inhabitants he was grateful. He drew out the thick, ivory-coloured sheet, filched, he suspected, from Miss Jessie's private stock of hot-pressed writing paper. It was covered on both sides with the cook's large, untidy handwriting. She wasn't the world's greatest speller . . . he carried the page over to the door and frowned over it in the grey light coming through cracks in the warped planking, deciphering the information that Mrs Driver was sorry not to have written sooner, only they had been very busy getting ready for Christmas. And that on account of Miss Laura's having learned to drive with some School of Motoring during her stay in London, Mr Rupert had now sent Aldridge off to volunteer for the New Army; that Mr Oliver was away somewhere or other practising to be a gunner; that Ferry had had some more trouble with his arthritis; and that poor Daisy was very low about her Arthur, killed in the big battle at Ypres.

Afterwards, Griffin was ashamed of the way his heart leapt at the news. *She's free . . .* was his first thought. Followed by, *She's free, and she's unhappy.* And I'm stuck here in bloody Belgium for the forseeable future. Assuming I don't get killed.

*

At the breakfast table at Maple Grange, Laura opened the first of a clutch of letters and having scanned the contents, waved a sheet delightedly at Rupert. 'Good news, Pa, Oliver's finished his course at The Shop.'

In September Oliver, nervous and proud in his brand-new uniform, had been instructed to report to Deepcut, where he was taken aback to be shown a bunch of raw recruits and told to initiate them in the finer arts of gunnery. On protesting that he didn't know very much about the subject himself, he had been told to watch the other officers and pick it up as he went along. By dint of persistent reminders he had eventually persuaded his commanding officer to send him on a training course at the gunnery school at Woolwich, known throughout the Royal Artillery as 'The Shop', from where he had posted home detailed reports of his activities which Aunt Jessie couldn't follow and Rupert was too busy to read. Only Laura had understood what was required and written back the appropriate notes of appreciation and encouragement.

'The course is down to eight weeks now instead of six months, because of the war. Apparently he's been really burning the midnight oil to get through all the manuals. Anyway he's rejoining his battery who've just moved to the Godalming area for training. I expect it was them we saw travelling along the Hog's Back the other day, Aunt Jessie, with the guns. I wonder where he'll be billeted? Claire Lawrence's family live in Godalming, perhaps he can get in touch with Claire. She used to have an enormous crush on him when we were at school together . . . though Oliver just thought she was bossy. Mainly because she kept shouting "Mine!" when they partnered at tennis. Anyway he thinks he might be able to get leave at Christmas. Won't it be fun to have him home again?'

'Magnus will certainly think so,' Jessie commented drily. The dog had been noticeably pining since his master had disappeared and his mournful expression and his habit of lying obstructively across the first-floor landing outside Oliver's bedroom door had so irritated Rupert that Magnus had been sent over to the Home Farm, where Inglis was instructed to 'train him for something useful'. So far the only aptitude that Magnus had shown was for escaping and finding his way home.

From behind the pages of *The Times*, Rupert's response was a grunt. He was in a bad mood on several counts. Already it was early December, but production of shells was not yet under way at his newly converted factory. Recruiting suitable staff for what was necessarily meticulous and dangerous work was proving harder than he'd anticipated. So many local men, including members of his mower-manufacturing work force, had volunteered in response to the big posters pasted up everywhere with their eye-catching message that was backed by Lord Kitchener's face and pointing finger. 'Britons! He wants YOU. Join your country's army. God save the King.'

That the recruits were still coming forward with such alacrity was very praiseworthy; but the result, as Rupert had learned with deep reservations during his recent trip to London, was that all sorts of vital labour like munitions work would have to be entrusted to mere women. Meanwhile, the provision of Oliver's kit and Laura's London junketings, to say nothing of her driving lessons, had proved more costly than he'd anticipated – and Lloyd George's first wartime budget had just doubled income tax to two shillings and sixpence in the pound. Rupert didn't need reminding about the forthcoming expense of Christmas.

'Is anything the matter, Pa? Shall I ring for some more coffee for you?' Laura smiled solicitously at her father as she pushed her chair back and headed for the bell pull by the door. She was really becoming very pretty, more and more like her mother every day, Rupert reflected with a faint lightening of his gloom.

He had genuinely loved Sylvia. Perhaps she was the only person in his life towards whom he had felt such undiluted emotion, unless it was the nanny who had cared for him until he was five years old. Nanny had been sent away after some uncomprehended adult squabble and Rupert had suspended trust and affection for the next quarter of a century until Sylvia had unlocked long-forgotten feelings. He had been undemonstrative with his wife, even pompous sometimes, but he had secretly wanted to give her the earth and everything on it. It wasn't so much the sex – that had never been particularly earth-shattering and after the twins were born, even less so because of Sylvia's terror of repeating the experience. But she'd been someone to share with. And then, suddenly, it was over. Sylvia brought home from Italy in a coffin and laid under a stone in the churchyard, Rupert alone. He'd thought he could do without love. His male urges he took care of, prosaically and at infrequent intervals, with a young woman living in Greenwich to whom he paid a retaining fee to ensure that she was always clean and always available when he made his business trips to London. He felt no trace of involvement with her whatsoever.

But lately he had thought he would like to be closer to Laura. It would be nice to know that she *liked* him, not just in a dutiful, daughterly way, but as a person.

'Actually, Pa,' Laura said as she returned to the table, 'I was going to ask you about Christmas.'

'What is it?' he asked, jarred, suspicious, detecting the traces of a wheedle in her voice. 'A new dress?'

'No. At least that wasn't what I meant, though a new dress *would* be very welcome . . . but what I meant to say was, don't you think it would be a good idea for us to have a party?'

'*A party?*' Rupert echoed, his tone unpromising. He hated any upheaval that had not been created by himself.

'Just a little one, to celebrate having Oliver home. We haven't done any proper entertaining for ages, not since my "coming out" dance last year. It won't be any trouble, Aunt Jessie and I can see to it all.'

'Hmm,' said Rupert.

'Oh, *thank* you, Pa. What a darling parent you are sometimes.'

Laura whisked out of her seat and wrapped her arms around

her father's neck from behind, laying her smooth cheek against his for just long enough to remind him again of the similarity to Sylvia, who had been prone to such fleeting but sweet gestures of affection.

'I didn't say yes,' he pointed out with feigned dourness.

'But you meant it, didn't you?'

'I suppose so.'

Laura's growing ability to winkle concessions out of him seemed to be another trait she had inherited from her mother.

Rupert might have been right in his assertion that hard work was a good way of handling grief. Miss Laura's party was a godsend for Daisy. Coming on top of all the normal preparations for Christmas, it created so much labour for the staff that she was on the run from dawn till midnight and staggered up the steep back stairs to her attic bedroom each night, too exhausted to dwell on the fact that Arthur had gone for ever, or even to worry about how much longer she could conceal her pregnancy from the sharp eyes of Mrs Driver. Every morning she would wake to heartache and desolation, but there was food to prepare, decorations to fix, floors to polish to an ultra-perfect gloss and all the best china and silver and glass to be washed and dried and burnished. Then there were the spare bedrooms to be made ready for those guests who had been invited to stay overnight after the party.

'. . . Alice Delamere as was,' Joan said, ticking off on her fingers, 'and Miss Duffus and Miss Johnson from Guildford and Miss Lawrence from Godalming, and two or three of Mr Oliver's friends from the artillery. We'll be bulging at the seams and no mistake, *and* I doubt if Miss Laura's spared a thought about whether we've got enough of the good sheets to go round.'

Laura had not. She was too preoccupied with other problems – the guest list, for instance. There were so many considerations to be borne in mind. Who among her local acquaintances had a right to expect an invitation, having entertained Laura or Oliver in the past few months at a similar event? Who would not get on with whom? Most importantly, how on earth was she to balance the numbers of male and female guests?

'It's hopeless, Aunt Jessie. If I leave any of my school-friends out they'll never forgive me, but almost every young man I think of inviting turns out to be unavailable because of his "military commitments". Even Edward Allingham's gone to France.'

The two Brownlowe ladies were seated by Jessie's desk in the morning room, Laura with a notepad in front of her on which she was doodling rather than adding names. At the mention of Edward Allingham, Jessie looked up sharply. She thought she had detected a forlorn note in her niece's voice. But Laura's expression was irritable rather than anguished.

'I would have asked his brother James, he'll be on vacation from Oxford. But when I wrote to mention it to Oliver, he said absolutely not to. I think they've fallen out,' said Laura, 'because of Oliver volunteering and James not. It's all rather awkward. I mean we all know James, not just Oliver. And at this rate,' she went on, 'we'll have the most awful party with all the girls standing about like wallflowers and everyone will despise me for arranging it. Perhaps,' she added hopefully, 'we could ask some of your Canadians? You've got some coming to tea today, haven't you?'

'Yes, I suppose I have,' said Jessie with visible apprehension.

The Canadians were not so much Jessie's as Rupert's. On hearing that a contingent of Princess Patricia's Rifles had newly arrived at Aldershot as part of a volunteer force from the Colonies, he had contacted their commanding officer and issued an invitation to 'tea and entertainment' at the Grange. He had then delegated the responsibility for hospitality to his sister. He had assumed that his invitation would be understood to apply only to officers; he had forgotten to be specific. Jessie was taken aback, when the Canadians arrived, to find that she was hosting a sizeable gathering of Other Ranks.

Putting aside her misgivings about what Rupert would say

when he heard about the misunderstanding, Jessie did her best to welcome the visitors. It was too cold to use the gardens, but she had instructed Ferry to shift every moveable chair and occasional table in the house into the drawing room and had provided packs of cards, a variety of newspapers and magazines and an excellent tea wheeled in on two creaking trolleys by Joan and Daisy.

Jessie moved among the tables, making sure that the plates of refreshments circulated and that the teacups were full. She was rewarded by smiles and comments of appreciation.

'This is real nice cake, ma'am. You make it yourself?'

'Oh, no!' Jessie had a brief vision of Mrs Driver's reaction if she ever proposed invading the kitchen to the extent of making a cake. The private who had spoken looked embarrassed, suspecting that he had made a gaffe. Jessie hurried to smooth over the mistake. 'But I think the recipe came from my mother, originally.'

'Well, she certainly knew her stuff, ma'am.'

'Thank you,' said Jessie. The Hon. Mrs Brownlowe, unlike her self-effacing daughter, had been the terror of her kitchen staff and had seldom allowed a dish to her table without personally dictating its precise contents. It might indeed be said that she had known her stuff.

'Excuse me, Miz Brownlowe.'

Jessie became aware that a young corporal was trying to catch her attention.

'Excuse me, ma'am,' he repeated. 'I understand that you've been so kind as to consent to give us a little concert?'

The words sent a chill of dismay through Jessie. In fact, Rupert had volunteered a piano recital on Laura's behalf, but this morning Laura had treacherously claimed a prior commitment.

'I'm awfully sorry, Aunt Jessie, but I won't be here this afternoon. I'm driving Pa to the factory and then going on to tea with Claire Lawrence before I collect him again at five o'clock. I want to get Claire organized to make sure Oliver's well looked-after in Godalming.'

'But you were supposed to be doing the music for the Canadians.'

'Never mind. You're much better at it than me.'

There was no help for it. Jessie would have to play the piano.

The Lawrences lived in a tall grey stone house with steeply pointed gables, built on a hill overlooking the town and the valley below. Claire and Laura had been through six or seven years of schooling together at the Academy for Young Ladies, where they had begun by detesting one another and had gradually gravitated together because they were the brightest girls in their age group and correspondingly the least popular with everyone else. But they had gone abroad to separate finishing schools and, what with the upheaval of the war, had scarcely met during the last year.

In the interim Claire, like Laura, had changed. She was now at least four inches taller than Laura, had discovered a flattering way to manage her thick auburn hair by coiling it in a plump crescent of a roll behind her neck, and had adopted a particularly enviable French scent. Her blunt manner which Oliver had labelled 'bossy' remained the same, as Laura discovered when they had completed the formalities of admiring each other's appearance and taking a polite cup of tea in the company of Mrs Lawrence, and had then climbed the broad stairs to Claire's pretty bedroom on the first floor to settle themselves for a proper private chat.

'So tell me everything. What have you been doing with yourself since you came back from Paris, Laura?'

'Various things. Learning to drive, for one,' said Laura.

'Oh, so have I. What else?' With six unthinking words, Claire reduced Laura's proud achievement to a commonplace. Worse, she went on to ask about Edward Allingham. Years ago, when her agonized adolescent longing for Edward had reached a particularly intense phase, Laura had confided her passion to her schoolfriend in one of those late-night-and-hushed-whispers sessions while Claire was staying at the

Grange for a weekend. She had been ruing her indiscretion ever since.

'Any progress?' said Claire. 'This was going to be the year he noticed you.'

'He's engaged,' said Laura between her teeth. 'To some nurse he knew at Oxford.'

'Oh, bad luck.' Claire, belatedly recognizing her tactlessness, hurried on to other subjects. 'And how's your beautiful brother?'

'He's volunteered for the Royal Artillery. That was mainly what I came to tell you. He's going to be in Godalming for the next few weeks, training. I thought you'd be interested.'

Claire had responded to the confiding of her friend's adoration for Edward with an admission that she personally weakened at the knees in the vicinity of Oliver. Laura had been stunned. How could *anyone* feel like that about her tedious brother? But Claire, unabashed, had said baldly that Oliver was an idiot like all boys of his age, but had the glimmerings of a human being in there somewhere, and besides he was so awfully handsome that it made up for a lot. Her opinion on this matter had not wavered in the ensuing years despite Oliver's failure to recognize her frank pursuit of him. Claire, thought Laura, was uncrushable.

'I thought perhaps you could arrange for him to be billeted with your family,' she suggested.

'Wonderful idea! Unfortunately, we have a rather horrible little captain with us already, *and* his groom, *and* his batman, and I have a nasty feeling that he would object most strongly and vociferously if we tried to bump him out of the way for the benefit of a junior officer! But I'll certainly get Mother to invite Oliver to tea and supper at very frequent intervals. Thanks for telling me, Laura.'

'And we're planning a party,' said Laura, 'for the day after Boxing Day, and you're invited to stay the night afterwards so you won't have to worry about bringing your chauffeur out late to collect you.'

'Lovely. Though getting home wouldn't have been any

problem,' Claire said carelessly. 'We don't have a chauffeur any more, he's gone to drive ambulances in France. But I can drive myself over. Father has a new car, a little runabout, hideously cold in this weather, but it takes less petrol and it's much more fun to drive than the old one! You probably saw it outside.'

'Yes,' said Laura with a spasm of jealousy. Rupert certainly wouldn't have let her take *his* car out for her own activities – it was only when he wanted to go somewhere that she was permitted to climb behind the wheel. So far, all her cajoling had not shaken him on this particular point and indeed he would probably be very annoyed with her if he knew that instead of going straight home from the factory today, she had taken a detour into Godalming to see her friend. Moreover, the car in which Claire was free to roam about was a glorious scarlet Austin with a fold-down hood. Beside it, the Landaulette looked like a hearse. 'However do you manage to get the petrol to use it for yourself?' she asked icily.

The shortage of this commodity and the dubious ethics of using it for non-essential travel were Rupert's main excuse for restricting his car to his own use. But as usual Claire was impervious to any hint of ill-feeling and only replied equably that her father's occupation as a doctor meant that he received preferential treatment at the garage but that luckily most of his patients lived within the town and he liked to visit them on foot for the sake of the exercise, so petrol had not, so far, been a problem. She was impossible to offend, Laura remembered from school. It was fortunate in a way, because Laura herself had a knack of coming out with comments to which most other girls took umbrage, but it could be very frustrating when what you wanted was a quarrel. And having to own up to failure over the situation with Edward Allingham had made Laura feel distinctly waspish.

'You haven't told me yet what you've been doing,' she said.

'For the war effort, do you mean?'

Laura didn't. She heard far too much about that already at

the breakfast table at Maple Grange. But it seemed that nobody could talk about anything else for long, not even Claire.

'First, I tried to volunteer to drive ambulances in France, like our chauffeur. They will take girls, apparently, but you have to be over twenty-three. I was told I could drive the military around at home instead. Somehow, running staff officers to and fro didn't appeal. I'm not sure what else to do, the minimum age limit seems to apply to anything really useful. Perhaps they'll drop it if the need increases. Meanwhile I'm still considering the alternatives. I could be a canteen worker at the YMCA.'

'Aunt Jessie does that at Aldershot once a week. I can't really see you dolloping custard on to jam roly-poly for the troops all day, Claire.'

'Neither can I. Though someone has to do it I suppose. Anyway, in the meantime one decisive thing I *have* done is to join the Women's Suffrage Movement. It's rather in abeyance at the moment because of the war, but there are still plenty of ways in which they can influence people with the way they behave. In fact the war gives increased opportunities to impress those in power with the abilities of women. And I know you're going to remind me,' Claire added, as Laura opened her mouth to interrupt, 'that I used to say I didn't believe in all that rot. I still rather disapprove of the wilder fringes of their activities like setting fire to churches and that silly girl who killed herself trying to bring down the King's horse at the Derby. That kind of thing only makes the opposition more determined and repels the moderates who might otherwise recognize the justice of women's claims. But fundamentally I do agree that we are not given our proper place in society, excluded from decisions that shape our lives and then expected to shoulder the consequences when the men who do order everything get it wrong.

'This war is a prime example. Nobody asked *us* what we wanted before they started it! And it's true that the men are doing the fighting, but the women are very much affected. It's them that lose the breadwinners, lose the sons they've raised, it's them that fill the gaps when the men go. Last week we had a delivery of coal and I looked at the labourer who was tipping it down the chute and underneath that black dust and those shapeless overalls, there was a woman! She said her husband had joined up and somebody had to replace him or the business would fail.'

Laura fidgeted. She had been vaguely aware of the suffrage movement, you couldn't entirely ignore it when its supporters chained themselves to railings in Downing Street, were force-fed in prison and, as Claire had said, even set fire to churches to draw attention to their cause. There had been a panic last summer in the Guildford area, when some warden had spotted a light in his church and turned out half the parish on a suffragette hunt which proved to have been founded on nothing more sinister than the vicar forgetting to extinguish an oil lamp. But she regarded such events as nothing to do with her. It was a shock to find that her old schoolfriend was now spouting such radical views.

'Don't look so worried,' Claire said. 'I'm not inviting you to march up and down Godalming High Street with me, waving placards and shouting "Votes for Women!". Not yet, anyway. But when you have a spare moment you might think about what the movement stands for.'

'Yes, of course. When I have a moment,' Laura muttered, embarrassed. From somewhere in the house, a clock chimed and automatically she counted. Five strokes. *Five?* She consulted the enamelled watch pinned to the lapel of her woollen jacket. It was the one that James Allingham had rescued from the river at Oxford and it had been distressingly unreliable ever since. Today it was evidently running slow. Pa would be waiting at the factory. And Pa hated being kept waiting *anywhere*.

Jessie loved music and had been well trained as a child. Alone, she could tackle virtually any sheet of music manuscript, but given an audience she was reduced to a quivering bag of nerves and her fingers were distressingly apt to fumble the notes. Knowing this, she leafed hastily through the assortment of music in the Canterbury beside the piano and selected a Brahms lullaby which could be played so quietly that, with luck, anybody who wasn't familiar with the music wouldn't spot the mistakes. She hated the hush that fell over the room as she seated herself at the keyboard. If only her visitors had gone on talking, clattering their cups and saucers or slapping down their cards, she could have coped so much better.

'Shall I turn the pages for you, ma'am?' the corporal offered. He had a nice, open boy's face and hazel eyes. She had an idea that he had spotted her apprehension and sympathized with it.

'Oh. Yes, thank you, that would be very helpful.'

Jessie opened the music book and placed it on the rack, her fingers already beginning to tremble with that wretched, familiar nervousness. She got through the Brahms creditably enough. The corporal knew about music; enough, anyway, to be efficient at turning the pages. There was a spattering of applause from the men when she finished. The fluttering sensation in Jessie's stomach settled a little. She rather hurried through an eighteenth-century piece which was over-ambitious for the occasion, full of intricate cadenzas which ought to have been played on a spinet. As she reached the last bars, she felt able to glance over her shoulder at the expressions on the faces of her audience and wished she hadn't. Boredom was overlaid with polite attention on every face, but it was unmistakably boredom.

'Do you think I should go on?' she whispered to the corporal. 'I have a feeling this isn't really the sort of thing they enjoy.'

The soldier stooped a little to catch what she was saying, and replied while bent towards her conspiratorially. 'What you played was good. But what they *really* like, ma'am, is a sing-song.'

'You mean, like "Tipperary"?'

'That's the idea. Music-hall songs. But I guess that's

probably not the kind of music you English ladies include in your repertoire?'

The words might have been sarcastic, but his smile and gentle intonation robbed them of any possible sting.

'I don't think you should write us English ladies off too readily,' Jessie said. She spread her fingers across the ivory keys, summoning resolution to dare something very new and unconsidered. ' "Tipperary"? Now, let's see . . . how does that go?'

Everyone knew 'Tipperary', roared out by the soldiers in Aldershot and Guildford or hummed by the servants like Joan as she swept the stairs and daydreamed about her soldier friend. Long ago in the schoolroom, Jessie had enjoyed improvising or strumming nursery rhymes by ear in the days before her piano tutors became more exalted and less permissive than the old lady who had been her first governess. She launched into the first bars of the song, at first tentatively, then with growing confidence, and around the drawing room the visitors straightened up with a murmur of satisfaction as they recognized the tune. Soon they were all singing.

An hour later Rupert arrived back from the factory, only to wince as he handed his outdoor clothes to Ferry in the hall and heard two dozen hearty male voices bellowing 'Sister Susie's Sewing Shirts For Soldiers' from the direction of the drawing room. He raised his eyebrows at the butler.

'It's them Canadians, sir,' said Ferry, as if that explained everything.

'Some soldiers send epistles,
Say they'd rather sleep in thistles
Than the saucy, soft, short shirts for soldiers sister
    Susie sews. . . .'

Someone, Rupert recognized disapprovingly, was thumping the tune out on his Broadwood semi-grand with a gusto that showed scant respect for the quality of the instrument. Still, that was the sort of thing one had to put up with these days

– sacrifices for the War Effort, making allowances for our Empire cousins and all that.

He paused to congratulate himself that he hadn't bought a Bechstein – some people were chopping them up these days rather than house a Teutonic artefact. The Broadwood had cost him a hundred and thirty-five guineas from the Army and Navy, so it was fortunate that it posed no such moral obligations. He wondered whether he ought to go in and play the genial host but decided against it. He was rather tired and irritable, having been kept hanging about for twenty minutes by his disgracefully unpunctual daughter. He wanted his tea and a cigar, and anyway they were Jessie's guests he told himself, conveniently forgetting that the invitation had been issued at his insistence. She might as well get on with it.

Lockett's girl had sent him a body shield for Christmas.

'Silly cow,' Lockett said as he showed it to Griffin. It consisted of a sectional metal lining between two layers of course canvas, with straps to attach it to his chest. In return for restricted flexibility of the figure, it would offer protection from a very small, half-hearted piece of shrapnel – assuming, that was, that the projectile in question was targeted at the limited area thus shielded. Most pieces of shrapnel were not so well behaved. 'Someone should have told her we get blown to bits out here, not slightly dented,' grumbled Lockett. 'I'd have been better off if she'd spent the money on fags.' But when Griffin saw him again, he was penning the young lady an effusive letter of thanks and detailing an entirely imaginary incident in which the gift had already saved his life.

'She meant well,' he excused himself, blushing.

Griffin had received a small brass gift box from Queen Mary, duplicates of which had been dispensed to all serving soldiers. It contained cigarettes, tobacco or chocolate for the non-smokers. Griffin had asked for chocolate and been told the supplies had run out. He supposed he could swap the cigarettes for something useful. He had also been sent a card from the staff at Maple Grange.

188

They had each signed their names and added a brief message: 'Hope they are feeding you properly', from Mrs Driver. 'Teach those Jerries a lesson!' from Mr Ferry. Joan had scribbled that they all thought of him, Susan the little scullery maid said she hoped the war would soon be over. . . . He searched but the signature he most hoped for wasn't there. And then he saw it, a small pencil drawing of a daisy with eight petals. The message was: 'Keep safe'.

Oliver, far from appreciating his sister's efforts to render his Christmas leave memorable by the giving of a party on the day after Boxing Day, had failed even to produce the required number of fellow officers to save Laura from social disgrace.

'I had to really scrape around,' he complained. 'Most of the chaps had their own plans for leave. Morrison's people are in India, but even he had to disappoint an aunt in Cheltenham by leaving her early. And he and Felthorpe have made it embarrassingly clear they were only doing it as a favour to me.'

'Oh, really?' said Laura, mortified. She resolved, if at all possible, to flirt very hard indeed with Morrison and Felthorpe, to enslave them utterly and then to make them rue their reluctance to attend her party. After all if Charles McKay thought she was wonderful, why not these rather ordinary young men? Making a start, she flashed a dazzling smile towards the two youthful officers loitering in the background before turning back to her brother. 'Well, I'm sorry if it was a nuisance for you. But we couldn't have a party with more girls than men! And you told me not to invite James Allingham. . . .'

'James? I should think not. I couldn't have trusted myself to talk to him. He's a shirker,' said Oliver, thinking sourly of James loafing in the comfort of a book-lined study while he drilled gun teams in the December fog on Frensham Common, or crouched in a rowing boat for hour after cramped hour teaching recalcitrant horses to swim attached to the lines rigged across the murky waters of the Little Pond.

189

'Well, anyway, come and talk to Claire. You remember Claire Lawrence, you've been her partner at tennis,' said Laura, taking her brother's arm and steering him across the room. Oliver looked splendid in uniform and she was proud of him, but he was no more obliging about being polite to her schoolfriends than he had been in the past.

'Do I have to?'

'Yes,' said Laura firmly. 'You do. And do be nice to her, Oliver. You know she likes you.'

'Oh, lord,' said Oliver, dismayed. This wretched Lawrence girl had apparently turned up at the battery on several occasions asking for him, leaving messages that he should contact her. He had been teased about it unmercifully in the mess, and the pity of it was that he couldn't even recall which one of Laura's female acquaintances was Claire. The little pasty-faced one with the stammer? The blonde one with the overpowering scent and the giggle? The lanky, auburn-haired one with the bossy manner?

The latter. But he'd forgotten how pretty she was . . . or maybe it was the way she did her hair nowadays instead of those awful plaits.

'Hullo, Oliver. I hear you're with the Royal Artillery. How do you like it?'

'Er . . . it's not too bad,' said Oliver. Laura had meanly led him to Claire and abandoned him while she dealt with the enslavement of his fellow officers. 'Though of course I'd rather be with the cavalry.'

'Why?' said Claire. 'The *arme blanche* is outdated as a weapon of war, isn't it?'

'I don't agree.' Oliver was shocked that a mere female should consider herself entitled to give an opinion on a military matter, particularly when it was in opposition to his own views. It was worse than being told which way to serve to exploit your opponents' weaknesses in a doubles match – though in that respect Claire had always proved irritatingly right. 'The cavalry is essential,' he explained coldly, 'to press home the advantage of a gap created by the infantry and artillery. There's nothing so demoralizing to an infantry force as a determined attack by cavalry.'

'Oh, that's absolute rot,' said Claire candidly. 'You can't send the horses in against machine guns, whatever those old ex-cavalry generals may think. It may have worked in the Crimea, but this is the twentieth century. And I bet there's nothing so demoralizing to a cavalry squadron as being mown down by a hail of bullets!'

Oliver turned scarlet. Girls weren't supposed to tell you that you were talking rot. They were supposed to listen and learn and hail the conquering hero. He decided, as he had done in the past, that he didn't like Claire Lawrence, pretty or not. While he fished about in his mind for an excuse to cut short the conversation, someone on the far side of the drawing room put a record on the gramophone and the assembled guests moved to find themselves partners.

'Do you know how to quickstep?' said Claire, brightening.

'No,' said Oliver, with a brevity just this side of rudeness. 'I don't dance.'

'Oh, don't be so stuffy. I'll teach you.' With that, she tugged him into position, planted his left hand determinedly on her waist, then snatched it up again and studied it. 'Goodness, your hands are rough! All that soldiering, I suppose. Never mind, can't be helped.' The hand was once more manoeuvred into position against the warm silky surface of her russet-coloured dress, just above the hip. Oliver glared at her. Claire smiled sunnily back and a groove appeared in one cheek.

'You do look cross,' she said. 'Am I so very awful?'

Quite suddenly, to his dismay and confusion, Oliver's heart was hammering away at an unaccustomed rate and his guts were performing back springs.

Jessie was trying to keep out of the way of the young people. This was Laura's party. But she had wandered into the drawing room a few moments before to make sure that her niece was managing and didn't need her help. She saw Laura near the fireplace, chatting away animatedly to a couple of mesmerized young officers while the other guests danced.

She was wearing her mother's pearls, Jessie noticed, and the new dress in dove-grey silk which Rupert had sanctioned at that breakfast in almost the same breath as he had agreed to the party. He had made up for it, of course, by insisting on a particularly mean Christmas box for the staff – a fact of which Laura remained in blissful ignorance.

The rhythm of the dance made Jessie want to tap her feet, even to join in, though she reminded herself that it was ridiculous to suppose that anyone, ever again, would think of quickstepping with her.

A couple swayed by, and she moved quickly back to avoid the swing of their clasped hands. It was another second before she recognized her nephew as one of the dancers. His expression, as he gazed at his laughing, breathless partner, was even more absorbed than that which Laura was currently achieving from his friends.

'I do believe,' Jessie told herself, amused, 'that Oliver has discovered girls! And not before time. . . .'

But as she closed the drawing-room door quietly on the music and the buzz of voices, the smile left her face. The truth was that for Oliver and all the young men of his generation, there was so little time left to snatch at happiness before they faced the horrors of war.

10

The war, which was to have been over by Christmas, showed no signs of being resolved, and on the third of January intercession services were held in churches throughout the country to remind the Almighty whose side he was meant to be on. There had been an unsubstantiated report, dismissed as an hallucination by sceptics, that He had sent a platoon of angels to help the Allies out at Mons, but since then He seemed to have left the warring nations to get on with it.

Rupert felt that the service was important enough for the entire staff to attend as well as the family, even if it meant a cold Sunday lunch afterwards. Other households in the area had reached the same decision, so the little church was well packed and the special collection produced a satisfying amount for the Red Cross fund.

'Have you heard about the truce?' said Ferry to Mrs Driver when they were back in the warm kitchen at Maple Grange, divesting themselves of the many layers of clothing which had been needed to keep the chill of the church from their bones.

'No,' said Mrs Driver, her attention on the coordinated production of game pie for the dining room and cold sliced pork for the kitchen. She moved purposefully towards the larder, then stopped dead as Ferry's words sunk in. 'What truce?' she demanded.

'Mrs Inglis' nephew Fred, the middle one of her sister's boys, he got a Blighty wound on the twenty-seventh, bullet in the thigh she said it was. Well, she and her sister met him off the Hospital train at Charing Cross last night and she told me he says the soldiers in the front-line trenches stopped firing over Christmas. They sang carols and played football and gave each other food and cigarettes instead. Those Germans, they were singing "Silent Night", so he reckoned. Different language, of course, but it's the same song. Same God really, I suppose. Makes you think, doesn't it?'

'But if they've stopped fighting, how is it we haven't heard? I put a whole shilling in the Red Cross collection because the vicar told us it was sorely needed. And if the war's over, how did Fred get his Blighty wound?' asked Mrs Driver shrewdly.

'Oh, well, truce didn't last, did it? Wasn't official, and the commanders, they ordered the guns to start firing again on Boxing Day.'

'Seems a shame, doesn't it?' said Mrs Driver. 'Oh well, I suppose those generals know what they're doing.'

Between his knees, Oliver's horse was shivering. He hooked the reins over his left arm, transferred his drawn sword from his gloved right hand and slapped the freed hand against the animal's shoulders, trying vainly to warm it up. His own teeth were tightly clenched but even so his jaw juddered helplessly. The wind was blowing from behind and the snowflakes that had settled on the back of his head and neck, beneath the peaked cap, were thawing from his body heat and snaking down into the gap between his collar and his skin. The temperature was hovering around zero and Lord Kitchener wanted to inspect the Division.

Unfortunately, Lord Kitchener, and the French general he was bringing to impress with the sight of his New Army in training, were one and three quarter hours late. On the common behind Oliver, four brigades of artillery and thousands of infantry had been drawn up at the ready, the splendour of their uniforms undiminished by greatcoats – the theory being that they looked smarter that way. Now, after hours of standing frozen rigid in the snow, the men were no longer at their visual best.

Parked along the side of the road were a number of cars belonging to local people who'd come along to see the review and cheer the Secretary of State for War. There had been more spectators earlier, but one by one the arctic conditions had defeated them, though Oliver could still make out the distinctive scarlet Austin Tourer of the Lawrences at the end of the line. He hoped Claire and her mother had brought some good thick carriage rugs and hot-water bottles – the Austin's folding hood couldn't be much protection against the cold. He transferred his reins and sword back to his right hand and buffeted his mount's other shoulder, though his action by now was prompted more by a need to bring life back into his numbed fingers than because he thought he was benefiting the horse. He tried to think warm thoughts. Flickering log fires. Steaming hot baths. Toast and crumpets and Earl Grey tea in translucent china cups wreathed with roses, like the ones they had at The Laurels where he was due to have tea when the parade was over.

Intermittently, in the massed lines of the infantry, a man would keel over and be hauled out of sight, the ranks closing again at once because gaps were unsightly and surely Kitchener would be here any moment now.

There was a stir of anticipation to Oliver's left. Hastily he returned his drooping sword blade to the perpendicular. Two large closed cars could be seen speeding along the road.

'Eyes front!'

Several thousand soldiers straightened their aching backs and threw out their chests. The cars shot past without slowing down. The waiting troops, eyelashes clogged with snow, caught a brief glimpse of a stern profile in the back seat of the first car. Under the red-banded cap, its peak decked with bronze oak leaves, was a hawklike nose and an unsmiling mouth topped by a luxuriant moustache. Kitchener was engrossed in conversation with his guest. He didn't turn his head to look at the men, but his gloved hand gestured towards them as the car swept by, as if they were the illustration to some point he was making.

The cars disappeared in the distance. Behind Oliver, another of the infantrymen sagged silently to his knees in the snow.

*

195

'I thought it was awful,' said Claire, quivering with indignation, 'the way they made all those poor men stand out there in the cold all that time, and then he didn't even look!'

It was tea time at The Laurels. On being released at last from the parade on the common, the battery had trotted hard all the way back to Godalming, trusting to miracles that the horses wouldn't come down on the ice. The animals had been rubbed down, fed and stalled, the men had been congratulated on their steadiness in adverse conditions and dismissed to their billets, and at last Oliver was free to attend to his own bodily comforts. He had had the anticipated hot bath, restoring circulation to his cramped limbs, and now, seated on the deep-buttoned Chesterfield in Doctor and Mrs Lawrence's comfortably shabby drawing room, he was enjoying the log fire, the toast and the tea. The close proximity of Claire Lawrence, firelight flickering on her auburn hair and the soft folds of her olive green woollen dress, was another contributory factor to the contented warmth he was feeling.

'Oh, well,' he said philosophically. 'Couldn't be helped. Something must have delayed Lord Kitchener.'

'But I've heard he's always late,' Claire said. 'My cousin Dilys lives near Windsor Park and she told me that he was *four hours* late for an inspection there. And it was pouring with rain at the time. And Dilys said she heard some of the soldiers died of pneumonia. Mother and I brought one of those men who'd collapsed back to Father's surgery today, in our car, and he was absolutely blue. He couldn't speak. I wouldn't be surprised if he hasn't caught his death of cold. But I suppose if you're a Brass Hat you don't worry about little things like that,' she added scathingly. 'I suppose you've got more important matters on your mind!'

Oliver reached for another slice of hot buttered toast. 'Well, yes, I suppose you have,' he said, trying not to notice the sarcasm. He still found Claire's forthright manner hard to deal with, though a part of him rather admired it. 'You do have to be tough in the army,' he added. 'I dare say today was good practice for the men.'

'Not if they die of pneumonia! What's the point of calling up thousands and thousands of volunteers to fight if you just waste them needlessly before they even get there, by being unpunctual?' demanded Claire.

Oliver, though he would not admit openly to such a mutinous attitude, privately felt inclined to agree with her. Parades and practising for the hardships of the Western Front were all very well, but when were they going to graduate to the real thing and prove their resilience in ways more directly related to the winning of the war?

'Anyway,' said Mrs Lawrence soothingly from behind the tea trolley, 'you all looked very smart indeed, Oliver. Lovely, shiny guns. Claire, dear, can you look after Oliver and make sure he has enough tea? I must just have a word with Cook about dinner tonight.'

As she left the room, Oliver felt a momentary panic. Being alone with any girl other than his sister was a new experience for him, and the fact that the girl in question was as pretty and soft and generally desirable as Claire Lawrence made it particularly nerve-racking. Ever since the Christmas party he had been conscious of a powerful wish to advance his acquaintance with Claire – he had an idea that it would be rather delightful now, for instance, to be able to slip his arm around her slender waist. He had a vivid memory of the way it had felt during that quickstep. But there was no music to excuse the move, and he was at a loss for the appropriate steps to take in order to bridge the gulf between the polite taking of tea and such an intrepid act.

'*Do* you want any more tea?' inquired Claire when her mother had closed the door behind her.

'No thank you.'

'Toast? Cake? Another muffin?' She lifted the lid from the silver dish stacked above its reservoir of hot water, in which the muffins were being kept warm.

'No thanks, I've had loads already.'

'In that case . . .' said Claire. She removed the cup from his hand and replaced it on the tea trolley, then swivelled

197

deliberately sideways on the sofa to face him. She smiled and the groove in her cheek which he found so appealing made its appearance.

'I think it would be a good idea if you were to kiss me, don't you?' she announced in a businesslike way.

Oliver goggled at her with the paralysed air of a rabbit looking into both barrels of a shotgun.

'Ordinarily,' Claire continued, 'I'd wait for it to occur to you. But times are rather exceptional.' She rested both hands on his shoulders and leaned forward, face tilted and eyes already closed. Oliver swallowed. Her mouth was a couple of inches from his, lips invitingly puckered. He took the line of least resistance and did as she had suggested.

It was a very tentative kiss. She tasted faintly of honey. He maintained the slight pressure of his mouth against hers for a few seconds then withdrew it. Claire opened her eyes.

'Well, that wasn't so difficult was it?' she said in an encouraging tone. Oliver studied her face suspiciously.

'Are you laughing at me?' he demanded.

'No, Oliver.' Claire linked her hands in her lap. 'I wouldn't dare,' she said, eyes downcast. Oliver hesitated, torn between a wish to bolt from the room and a desire to kiss her again.

'Oh, Oliver.' Claire let out a long breath and touched a finger gently to his jaw. 'You are so *deliciously* serious.' That decided it. He pulled her into his arms and this time he did not break off the kiss until footsteps could be heard in the corridor outside. Then instinctively they sprang apart and when Mrs Lawrence came back into the room her daughter was sitting demurely at the far end of the sofa while the young officer intently examined the watercolour painting above the fireplace.

His first attempt at kissing a girl hadn't been too impressive, Oliver admitted to himself afterwards as he strode jubilantly back to his lodgings. But his second had been better . . . and hell's bells, he intended to go on improving!

'Jessica, will you come in here for a moment? I want a word.'

Rupert's study doubled as a gun room. Tall glass-fronted cases against one wall held his collection of shotguns, with which each year he took part in the grouse and pheasant shooting seasons of the Hampton estate nearby. He was rather proud of his marksmanship and one of the few occasions when he had shown any warmth towards Oliver, Jessie remembered, had been when the boy brought down his first bird. Oliver had been so pleased. . . .

There was no warmth about Rupert's manner now. He had crossed to the fireplace and was standing with his back to it, his features harshly shadowed by the lamplight. Jessie wondered tiredly what new contribution he had decided she owed to the war effort.

'Jessica, you know how reluctant I am to interfere in household matters which are your domain. . . .'

Then why do you do it, Rupert, all the time? But Jessie's face registered only polite attentiveness.

'What steps, exactly, are you proposing to take with regard to the condition of Daisy Colindale?'

Oh, damn! He's finally noticed.

'Condition, Rupert?' Jessie echoed, playing for time.

'Unless you are becoming remarkably short-sighted, Jessica, you cannot have failed to observe that she is, not to put too fine a point on it, expecting a child.'

'Ah.'

'Well? I repeat, what are you going to do about it?'

'I'm not sure.'

'She can't stay here. I won't tolerate those kinds of goings-on among my staff.'

'But Rupert. . . .' Jessie nerved herself to contradict her brother. 'Her fiancé was killed, you know, at Ypres. It's a war baby, Rupert, so many of those poor young girls have made the same mistake, and when you think about the circumstances it's hardly surprising. . . .'

'That is no business of ours. If she has behaved like a slut, she'll have to take the consequences.'

'I do feel some responsibility,' persisted Jessie. After all it was she who had given the courting couple time to say their goodbyes, time that they'd clearly used unwisely. If she had been strict like Mother, it would probably never have happened.

'Don't be silly, woman! On what grounds? Send her packing, the sooner the better.'

Something in his brisk, impatient voice reminded Jessie of the day when, as a child of five or six, she had fallen out of an apple tree in the orchard at home. She'd hurt her arm and cut her forehead open, and the fright of seeing the blood on her hands had made her roar with unaccustomed volume. But Rupert, who was reading his paper close by, had only glanced up with irritation and ordered her to shut up and stop being such a baby. Later, when it turned out that her arm was broken, he had remained singularly unsympathetic. The years had not mellowed him.

'As for wages, I suppose you'll have to give her the usual month's notice – and that's generous considering her behaviour.'

'But how will she live?'

'That is her problem.' Rupert stalked to his desk and placed his hands squarely on the embossed leather surface. He leaned forward, his scowl obdurate. 'You may dismiss her tomorrow.'

'But Rupert. . . .'

'I have said what I have to say on the matter, Jessica. I am not willing to be troubled further by the distasteful predicament of a domestic servant who has let her base instincts get the better of her – and at a time, too, when the nation has most need of a high moral standard from all its citizens, to counter the depravity of the Hun. Ring the bell on your way out, will you? The fire needs stoking.'

'I'm sorry to lose you, Daisy, I really am. You've been a good worker since you've been here.'

'Thank you, ma'am,' Daisy said woodenly, standing to attention in the morning room. She fixed her eyes on a row of decorative Meissen plates arranged in a rack on the wall opposite, to avoid meeting Jessie's troubled gaze. Poor Miss Jessie, she was obviously deeply embarrassed by the scene, but it was ridiculous for Daisy to be feeling sorry for the mistress at this moment. What would *she* do now? Not that her dismissal was unexpected; she had known ever since she and Louella came away from old Ma Turner's house that the day of reckoning would come at Maple Grange. Letting out the side seams on her dress and tying her apron loosely wasn't going to disguise her rapidly-expanding waistline for ever. The staff probably had been aware of it for weeks, carefully making no comments for fear of precipitating a disaster. Miss Jessie had known too, Daisy was sure, and Miss Laura had hesitantly initiated inquiries about her health from time to time, only to abandon them because she was fearful of having her dawning suspicions confirmed. Only Mister Rupert seemed to remain in ignorance, being too wrapped in his shell-factory conversion and his war-work committees to notice what was under his nose. Well, now he had noticed.

That the crisis was expected didn't make the situation any easier.

'If . . . when . . . you are looking for work again, Daisy, I should be glad to give you a reference,' said Jessie.

'But I can't come back here when the baby's born? Not if I find someone to look after it?'

'No. I'm sorry. If it was up to me . . . but I am afraid that my brother feels very strongly about such things.'

'I see,' said Daisy. At her sides her fingers pinched tightly at the crisp cotton of her apron. Jessie extracted a buff envelope from one of the pigeonholes of the desk beside her and laid it down on the surface.

'I hope this will help for the time being. And I have left a parcel of baby clothes and linen in your room, which may come in useful. If there is anything else I can do, please let me know.'

Daisy leaned forward and picked up the envelope, dropping it automatically into the deep pocket of her apron.

'Thank you, ma'am.'

An hour later she sat on the narrow iron-framed bed in her room at the top of the house. Inside her stomach the baby kicked and she glanced down, laying her hand on the place.

'Keep still, will you? Haven't you caused enough trouble for one day?'

Down in the kitchen regions, Mrs Driver and Joan and Susan were probably still discussing the latest turn of events in shocked whispers. Daisy had left them to it while she packed her suitcase, and now it was closed and strapped, topped by the generous bundle of baby linen which Miss Jessie had shamelessly plundered from the stock for Soldiers' and Sailors' Wives.

Daisy looked around the room: at the faded flower-patterned wallpaper on the sloping eaves, the familiar curtains, the chest of drawers and the rag rug on the dark-stained floorboards. She and Joan had worked together on that rug over a succession of winter evenings. There'd be no more cocoa and cake in the servants' hall, no more good-natured banter and moans with the people who had been her friends. Nichols, instructed by Miss Jessie, was tacking up Blackie and when he was ready, the governess cart would transport her away from Maple Grange for ever.

You don't know what you've got until you lose it.

She'd had a good job in congenial surroundings, three square meals a day, two kind mistresses in Miss Jessie and Miss Laura. She'd even managed to put a little each week in her post-office savings book. And now, because of an hour's madness in the hay barn – with a man who hadn't even been honest with her if his mother's jibe about Adelaide Stringer had been true – she was having to say goodbye to all that, to crawl back home, bringing trouble and disgrace to her family and somehow she must bring up a bastard baby on no earnings and a squandered reputation.

Pressing her lips tightly together, holding back the tears, she untied the strings of her apron and hung it on the hook behind the door where she had hung it every night before going to bed.

It was then that Daisy remembered the envelope. She slid her hand into the apron pocket, lifted it out and ran her thumb along under the flap, tearing the thick paper.

Inside were banknotes. She counted, clumsy-fingered.

A whole year's wages.

Daisy stumbled back to the bed and sank down, her legs shaking. Miss Jessie, for the time being at any rate, had saved her.

'You did *what*?' said Rupert.

'From my own money, of course.' Jessie found to her shame that she was shivering. She tried to remind herself that she was a grown woman and that her bellicose brother had no real power over her, but it was no use. Faced with his anger and contempt, she was like a small child threatened with a whipping.

'Your money? You've precious little of it! You're a fool, Jessica, and you'll die a pauper!'

Rupert's father, Frederick Brownlowe, had been the old-fashioned kind, a believer in the system of patrimony. For the sister who married, Alice's mother, there had been a dowry. For Jessie, who was expected to look after her parents in their old age, nothing had been arranged when Elizabeth Brownlowe had died suddenly of a heart attack. Nor, in the year before his own death, had a shocked and grieving Frederick found the energy to consider Jessie's future. Her release had meant her simultaneous ruin. Rupert inherited the family money.

He had made provision for her – board and lodging at the Grange in return for her supposed assistance as acting mistress of his house. That was all. Her half-share of her mother's jewels she had converted into cash, an act for which Rupert – with a lofty disregard for the realities – had found it hard to forgive her, and it was on the small income produced by this amount that Jessie provided her clothes and the other expenses that her brother chose not to defray.

She had been hoping he would never need to know of her

gesture to Daisy Colindale; she would have found it far easier to accept the scrimping it was going to necessitate in the coming months without his scornful scrutiny. But Daisy, too grateful to be circumspect, had been effusive in her thanks; regrettably, she had expressed her breathless sense of eternal obligation outside the door of Rupert's study . . . into which, five minutes after the maid's departure, Jessie had been summoned to account for the gross disregard of his instructions.

'I couldn't just turn her away,' Jessie defended herself. 'She has been a loyal servant for as long as I've been here.'

'She's done the job she was paid for.'

'I was fond of her. Laura was fond of her,' Jessie added, hoping vainly that mention of his daughter would deflect some of Rupert's wrath. At least it might remind him that Daisy, among other things, had been Laura's personal maid. But he only snorted with disgust.

'I'm fond of my horse. But if he misbehaves, by God, I teach him a lesson!'

It was true; hence Plumbago's sour and stubborn nature. Jessie waited silently. There was no point in arguing any more. Rupert would rail on for a little longer, would remind her of her folly at every opportune moment for a few weeks . . . but at least she wouldn't have the utter destitution of Daisy Colindale on her conscience.

'Well, I shan't be replacing her,' Rupert said meanly. She was sure he had made the decision on the spur of the moment, to spite his sister. 'The other servants can take over her work. There is less for them to do anyway, with Oliver away.'

It wasn't true. Oliver had needed very little attention. Without him the house hadn't shrunk. The silver tarnished and the fires shed ash as rapidly as they had always done. And now that Aldridge had gone, a tight-lipped Ferry, aided by a verging-on-the-mutinous gardener, had already been obliged to take on the extra responsibility for keeping the motor clean and maintained. Jessie did not relish the prospect of conveying the latest news to the staff. Daisy had been an extremely hard worker and, sentiment aside, would be sorely missed.

'And another thing!' Rupert remembered. 'I discover that you have been entertaining Canadian soldiers here. In my drawing room.'

'You invited them, Rupert.'

'Officers. I invited officers. Not *troops*!'

'I hadn't realized,' Jessie murmured. 'I welcomed those that I had assumed you'd invited.'

'Well, sort it out.'

'It will be difficult, without causing offence,' said Jessie.

'Hang it, who cares about the offence? I don't want my house invaded by a mob of uncouth Colonials with heaven knows what diseases! Give them tea, by all means, but in the stables or the barn at the farm!'

'If you insist, of course I shall try to make this suggestion to their commanding officer on your behalf,' said Jessie delicately, 'but he may find it hard to understand your attitude when so many of the local gentry have offered their hospitality.' She watched her brother's face darken with frustration as he realized, slowly, that he was indeed in a difficult position. He could not now refuse to receive the soldiers without being criticized throughout the district as a snob. He searched for a way out, and found it.

'You say other people of my position . . . ?'

'So I have heard,' Jessie said.

'Hmm. Well in that case it may as well continue, I suppose. So long as there is no damage.'

Outside the study door, Jessie drew a sigh of relief. Fortunately Rupert had not demanded details. It was true that other prominent families in the area were now offering to entertain the troops . . . but only after the Brownlowes had set an example. Jessie permitted herself a small, private smile of satisfaction. *Her* teas were by far the most popular!

Indeed Jessie had been bewildered but gratified by her unexpected success as an entertainer of the Canadian troops. Every week the numbers who came to the Grange from the camp at Aldershot seemed to get larger. She'd even bought some sheet music to keep up with the songs they roared for.

> Private Perks is a funny little codger
> With a smile, a funny smile.
> Five foot none, he's an artful little dodger
> With a smile, a sunny smile. . . .

As each batch of soldiers was sent away for intensive training on Salisbury Plain, another would arrive, having heard of the good food and the first-rate sing-song that was on offer from Miz Brownlowe.

Jessie liked the Canadians. She liked their humour, their self-confidence and the way they managed to treat her simultaneously like a lady and like one of themselves, with none of the awkward subservience that had sometimes made her cringe when she'd encountered it from the English Tommies at the YMCA. She was aware that the Other Ranks at the recreation hut found her presence inhibiting and would rather have been sold their tea and cigarettes by someone with whom they could have a bit of banter, someone like Joan or little Susan, the scullery maid. She had wondered sometimes why on earth middle-class ladies felt compelled to volunteer for these menial duties and then carry them out badly, when they could actually have helped the war effort more effectively by making do with less help in their homes and sending their staff along instead. Her attempts to propose this sensible arrangement to various war-work coordinators had not been well received, so she went on doing the best she could. But with the unselfconscious Canadians she felt she could relax and even venture to laugh at their jokes without shocking anybody.

But the bitter cold weather of the new year, following on the heels of the long, wet autumn, provided a fertile breeding ground for flu germs and spinal meningitis in the vast encampment on the plain where the volunteers of Kitchener's

New Army were gathered under canvas. Some died, and among them was the Canadian corporal who had first turned Jessie's pages at the piano in the drawing room of Maple Grange.

Jessie, remembering with gratitude the comment that had prompted her first timid rendering of 'Tipperary' had counted the cheerful young man as a friend. It struck her as particularly ironic that he should have crossed an ocean to fight a war and then died before he could play any part in it. He had volunteered on impulse, he'd told her, having gone down to the station to see off a friend who had joined up. The recruiting sergeant had called out, 'Come on, lads, room for a couple more,' and in one of those fateful moments that can change a life, or end it, he had stepped forward. Now he would never sail home again, to the sweetheart to whom he had forgotten to say goodbye. The thought of that unknown girl's pain was like a needle in Jessie's own heart; it seemed to her that the words 'if only' and 'never again' were among the saddest in the language.

'Pack up your troubles in your old kit bag and smile, smile, smile,' sang the troops who had not yet gone to war.

'There's not much for the cavalry to do here,' wrote Charles McKay from Belgium. 'So we take our turn in the trenches with the infantry. A spell in the front line generally lasts for six days if we're lucky and there's someone to relieve us, and the conditions are less than comfortable! The trenches are perpetually flooded – there's no way of draining them because of the high water-table round here. Gradually we are getting supplies of wooden duck-boards to lay along the bottoms to keep us from losing our footing, but they rot soon enough, as do the sandbags that hold up the sides. Keeping them repaired is a constant task in the daytime. Any of the men who aren't engaged in rebuilding, cleaning up the after-effects of a shelling or on a burial party, tend to fall asleep on the "fire step" on the side of the trench and have to be climbed over to get from "A" to "B".

'At night, we bring up our supplies, mend the wire in front of the trenches and keep watch for raids from the enemy or go on raids of our own, crawling across No Man's Land and praying that no one will send up a star shell to light the place up and pick us off. With luck we'll collar a few Jerries to haul back for interrogation and with a lot more luck we'll lose nobody in the process. The Jerries are a funny lot. Some of them are the real Teutonic stereotypes, full of bombast and *Deutschland Uber Alles*, some of them seem like quite decent chaps.

'They shell us with shrapnel day and night but our guns give as good as they get, and the trenches are constructed in a zig-zag so the effect of an explosion is contained in its own little area. You know when there's been a hit somewhere along the line, though, as you hear them calling "Stretcher-bearers at the double!" and then the bearers run by – if they can run, given the state of the ground! After a while, they come back more slowly with a load of casualties. I used to find it too harrowing and look away if the body on the stretcher was moaning, but I'm getting quite hardened to it now.

'I'm writing this by lamplight in a snug little dugout. As the name suggests, it's really just a big hole scraped in the wall of the trench and shored up by boards. There are a couple of bunk beds and not enough blankets. I wish you could taste the tea – no, on second thoughts, I'm glad you can't! It's made from filtered water, they tell us, which is brought up in carts, but I suspect it's actually ditch water dosed with something to kill the germs. Anyway it tastes foul! The men mutter that there is something else in the water, to make them stop thinking about women. I don't think it's working with me, though. . . .

'I hope you won't think that's an awful cheek. I do think of you a lot, Laura, when we have a peaceful spell like we're having now. I keep remembering you at McKinley's, you looked like an angel with the lights shining on your hair. Please will you send me a photo, so I can show off to the others about the beautiful young lady I know in Blighty? Or

I won't show anyone, if you'd rather I didn't, but please send the photo anyway.

'Hugh sends his regards. He's writing to Alice from the other side of our little hovel – which means his boots are two inches from my shoulder! He says Alice is nursing, now. I hope this doesn't give her problems in getting leave at the same time as Hugh. Won't it be wonderful if he and I have leave together, and we can all meet up in London again and go dancing . . . ?'

Laura sent back a photograph as he had asked. She had sat for a portrait at Mendoza's in Bond Street during her London visit, on one of the dreary days when Alice was busy and she'd nothing else to do, and she had been pleasantly surprised by the result. Careful lighting had made the most of her classic features and cast a halo around her crown of hair. She looked like one of those sculptured goddesses that eighteenth-century gentlemen used to bring back so enthusiastically from the Grand Tour and set up on plinths in their grottoes.

She hesitated over what to sign on the photograph, and finally wrote simply, 'Laura' which could be noncommittal or intimate depending on how you wanted to interpret it. She was still unsure how she felt about Charles. He wasn't Edward . . . but his open admiration was a very satisfactory consolation for Edward's indifference. She thought it would do no harm to go on corresponding with him and it would be pleasant, as he suggested, for the four of them to meet again. She had been too preoccupied with her duties as a hostess to spend much time with Alice at the party, but she had noticed that her cousin had lost weight and looked haggard – pining for Hugh, presumably. As she deposited her letter to Charles on the silver salver on the hall table, for the gardener's boy to take to the post later, she made a mental note to write to Alice and arrange a visit or outing to cheer up the deserted bride.

But other distractions intervened, and before she could carry out her intention, Hugh Molloy stood up too quickly and too carelessly behind a damaged parados in a front-line trench near Messines. A sniper's bullet spun him from the fire step and when Laura saw Alice again, her cousin was dressed from head to foot in the black waterproof crape that Courtaulds were promoting profitably nowadays as 'fashionable mourning'.

'It was instantaneous, his commanding officer was absolutely sure of that. He didn't suffer.'

Jessie and Laura were paying a condolence visit to Alice, now at home with her family near Dorking to recover from the shock of her early widowhood. They sat uncomfortably in the drawing room whose tall sash windows overlooked a valley of bare-branched wintry trees, while she told them what she had heard of Hugh's death.

'And Charles is going to send me a photograph of the grave,' said Alice, the white knuckles of her tightly clenched hands betraying the pain she was feeling. She looked simply awful, thought Laura: her hair was dull, her face was tinged a goblin yellow and there were great purple smudges under her eyes, which peered out between lids puffy with weeping.

'What will you do now, Alice?'

'I'm going abroad with a VAD unit. Margaret Churchill is leaving next month and she said I could join her. I'll be just old enough by then. I won't give way to grief,' said Alice steadily, 'I shall go where I can help to keep other wounded soldiers alive and perhaps save their wives and sweethearts from suffering what I have had to endure.'

Laura looked at her cousin with new respect. Under her soft, little-girl manner, it seemed Alice had a backbone of steel. 'I wonder,' Laura asked herself, 'if I could cope as well if I lost someone I cared for?' She had been more shaken than she would wish to admit by the news of Hugh's death. It didn't just happen to other people, it happened to someone you knew. It could happen to Charles, or Oliver, or even, she recognized with a tremor of fear, to Edward, now serving with the Queen's somewhere in the region of Ypres. It could have happened already . . . how would she know? Who would tell her? She would learn of it from a line in a newspaper casualty list or a few words in a casual conversation. *Heard about young Allingham? Pity.*

Beside her, Aunt Jessie cleared her throat.

'You are very brave, my dear,' she said gently to Alice, and quite suddenly the stiff figure in black crumpled.

'I don't feel brave,' she wailed. 'I feel – oh, torn and battered and terrified. And *angry*! Why did it have to happen? We were so happy! *Why?*'

Jessie rose from her seat and crossed quickly to Alice's side. She put her arms round the shaking girl and they rocked together while Alice sobbed, all her restraint abandoned. Laura, to whom such extremes of emotion were alien, looked on helplessly and for the first time in her life wished she could be more like her aunt.

'Do you think I'm very selfish?' she asked Jessie as they drove home.

'Why do you ask?' said Jessie, after a telling pause.

'I don't know . . . this war is so terrible and so many people are having a dreadful time because of it, and I've just been carrying on as usual, not wanting to let it disturb me. I *am* selfish, aren't I?'

'Not exactly, dear. Unthinking sometimes, perhaps.'

'But I can't go on ignoring it, can I?'

'No,' said Jessie quietly. 'I don't think you can.'

11

It was one thing for a chastened Laura to resolve to abandon selfishness and 'do her bit'. It was another matter, she discovered, to find anyone willing to accept her services. Like Claire, she was too young to be allowed to drive ambulances overseas, she was considered too much of a lady to turn postwoman or bus conductress, and when she offered herself to the various genteel organizations at home that had appealed for volunteers at the outbreak of war, she was met with coolness rather than gratitude. The committees and teams that had been set up to provide comfort parcels, convalescent facilities for wounded soldiers or advice and practical assistance for the dependents of the departed troops, had already shaken down into effective working units and did not much want the trouble of incorporating a new and possibly disruptive member into their midst.

She made a half-hearted approach to the Countess of Onslow, who had offered Clandon Park as a hospital within days of the declaration of war. The stately mansion had met with more favour from the Red Cross Committee than Maple Grange. 'Though heaven knows why,' Rupert said, on hearing the news. 'Everybody knows that it's the coldest house in England and the Onslows gave up trying to live in it themselves years ago! The wounded would have been far more comfortable at Maple Grange, even if the ceilings *are* ten feet lower!'

Whatever had motivated the Red Cross Committee, Clandon had been declared a Private Military Hospital and, having been given a comprehensive coat of whitewash, had been receiving the wounded since the preceding October – with Lady Onslow as Commandant.

Faced with Laura's inquiry, the countess eyed her dubiously. She had many well-born girls from old county families working as VADs at Clandon, and in general they did a wonderful job. But this one didn't look the type. In fact, in that precisely angled velvet hat with the feather, she looked more like a fashion plate out of *Vogue*. Lady Onslow was reminded of a story she'd heard about a society butterfly who'd arrived for hospital duties with her personal maidservant in tow, on the grounds that one couldn't possibly do without one's maid. However, the countess told herself, appearances can be deceptive. She reached for a sheet of paper and a pen and uncapped her inkwell.

'Of course you have taken your examinations in hygiene, home nursing and first aid?' she said as a preliminary.

'No,' Laura admitted, dashed. 'I did start . . . but something intervened.' Those were the studies, she recalled, which she had abandoned with such alacrity to go to London and had managed to postpone on her return.

'Oh. I'm sorry, my dear, but you can't possibly become a VAD without them.' Lady Onslow's closure of the inkwell had an air of finality. 'I suggest you enrol in some classes,' she said with kindly dismissal, 'if you are sure that VAD nursing is the right course for you.'

Laura left Clandon feeling a mixture of profound relief and wounded pride. She knew she was basically squeamish and Margaret Churchill's talk in London last autumn had confirmed her suspicions that she would make a thoroughly inept nurse, but all the same it was galling to realize that someone else thought so too. In fact it was beginning to seem as though *everyone* else regarded Laura as useless.

On her way home from Clandon she made a detour to call on Claire Lawrence in the hope of collecting some sympathy.

'Nobody wants me,' she said plaintively as the two girls climbed the stairs to Claire's room. 'I even asked Pa if he'd take me on as a munitions worker at the factory but he said don't be silly, and it's best if I just go on driving him around. But that doesn't seem to be a particularly enormous

213

contribution, does it? Though I suppose he would be in difficulties if I went off to do something else,' Laura admitted, 'now that Aldridge has gone for a soldier.'

'He could always learn to drive himself,' said Claire, rather tartly. Laura regarded her with astonishment. The idea that her father might perform in person a task that the Brownlowes would normally have expected a servant to carry out had never occurred to her . . . though Claire's father did it, she realized, and nobody thought that was odd.

'Anyway, I don't see the problem. If you need the examinations to become a VAD, why don't you just *take* the examinations?' Claire continued. 'You're perfectly capable of passing them.'

'Because I can't stand that ghastly Mrs Snelling.'

'She isn't the only instructress in Surrey. There are plenty of others,' Claire said, opening her bedroom door. 'My aunt, for instance. I don't think you'd find her classes too awful. I don't, anyway.'

'Are you taking nursing classes?' Laura said with astonishment.

'Started this week. What's so surprising about that?'

'I knew you'd considered nursing, Claire, but I thought you gave up that idea when they said you couldn't go overseas until you were older.'

'That was when I thought it would be a bit tame, doing it at home,' Claire said. 'But some of the hospitals here are getting the wounded straight from the Front, which is much more the real thing, and Aunt Phyllis is a decent old stick, so I decided I might as well get the exams just in case I do decide to volunteer. Well, how about it? Shall we do the classes together?'

'All right,' said Laura cautiously. Her reservations about her nursing potential remained, but . . . life *was* very slow at the moment, and she'd told Aunt Jessie she was going to get involved in doing something practical for the war and, as Claire had said, she didn't actually have to commit herself at this stage to becoming a nurse.

214

Claire and Oliver sat together in Doctor Lawrence's scarlet Austin beside the road that crossed Witley Common towards Haslemere. It was far too cold for a drive to be a pleasant experience, but the wish for privacy had made them opt for the common rather than drawing room at The Laurels, where Mrs Lawrence might interrupt at any moment. Even here, five miles out of Godalming, there was the danger that someone who knew Claire might see the car and report that the doctor's daughter had been spotted spooning with an officer out Witley way . . . but she was prepared to take the risk. Anyway, attitudes over what it was or wasn't permissible for a young lady to do had relaxed considerably since last autumn. Most of the nation was too busy with higher concerns to spend much time worrying about propriety.

In practice, the windows of the car were too misted over for any prurient passer-by to identify its occupants, much less what they were up to. So far, to Claire's disappointment, this was not much, though Oliver had taken hold of her hand as a prelude to breaking the news that he had received his expected posting overseas.

'I'll miss you awfully,' he said, absent-mindedly stroking his thumb across the back of her fingers.

'I'll miss you, too. When do you have to go?'

'Tomorrow.'

'Not much notice.'

'No. They need a replacement quickly for a wounded officer and my CO said I was the most suitable.' Oliver was still wondering uneasily whether this had been a gratifying accolade or whether the CO had wanted to palm him off on someone else.

'So it's just you that's going tomorrow, not the whole battery? Oh, bad luck,' said Claire gently.

'Well it's what I've been trained for, isn't it?'

'But it must feel a bit strange and lonely, going on your own, when you've got used to being with a team.' Coming from Claire, the comment was an unusually perceptive one;

she didn't often seem very aware of other people's more sensitive feelings. Moved, Oliver raised the captive hand momentarily to his cheek.

'You will write to me, won't you?' he said.

'Of course.'

A minute passed. Oliver rubbed with his sleeve at the misted windscreen. Claire watched his profile and thought that if he didn't kiss her soon she'd have to suggest it yet again. It was rather humiliating that every time they met, Oliver was so backward at coming forward, as it were, where kisses were concerned . . . though once started, like the Austin, he tended to run on quite happily until she applied the brakes.

'Claire . . . actually I asked you to meet me because there is something special I wanted to ask you before I go.'

'Ask away,' said Claire steadily. She didn't feel steady inside. Was she about to be proposed to? If so, it was not before time – after all those snatched entwinings on the sofa at The Laurels. Oliver was going away into danger, and she shrank from the prospect of empty days and the waiting for news which might be bad news. It would be some consolation to have their relationship placed on an official footing before he left her.

'It's a very big favour, I know. I mean we haven't known each other all that long. Not *well*, anyway.'

Claire waited, her hand passive in his, her nerve-ends tingling, while Oliver sought for the right words.

'What I was wondering was. . . .'

'Yes?' Claire prompted, controlling an urge to scream.

'Would you look after my dog?'

Engrossed by his problem, Oliver didn't notice his companion's sigh of punctured expectation. 'You see, Pa doesn't really want a dog about the place and Inglis at the farm hasn't got time for him, and Laura keeps muttering about going away to do something for the war effort. And Aunt Jessie would keep him for me but Magnus won't obey her. But he'll obey you,' said Oliver. Dogs, like young men, tended to do what Claire told them. 'So I wondered if you could possibly give him house room while I'm away? I'm afraid that Pa might get rid of him, and I'd be sorry to lose the little brute.'

He watched her anxiously. Claire's expression was difficult to read as she stared down at their linked fingers on his lap. At last she raised her head.

'Yes of course, Oliver. I'll be glad to look after him for you until you come back.'

She had her reward, though it was not precisely the one she had hoped for. Oliver, his anxieties about Magnus' future shelved, was free to concentrate on other matters. Unbidden for once, he slid his arm around her shoulders and bent his head towards hers.

But when it came to saying goodbye to his family, he found the occasion unexpectedly emotional. Laura gave her brother a hug and told him, in a voice which shook, to be a hero but not a reckless hero, and to come home safe. Aunt Jessie speechlessly handed him a small parcel which, unwrapped, proved to be a leather pocket case containing gelatine lamells of sedative drugs and a bottle of chloroform. It was an impressive present: it had cost her twenty-seven shillings, at least a week's pay for a working man, nearly a month's pay for a private in the infantry, and after the hole that Daisy's final wages had made in her bank balance, it was a considerable outlay for Jessie. Oliver knew nothing of the Daisy incident; he had barely registered the maid's absence, much less felt any curiosity about it, but he did appreciate that Jessie's gift was both generous and practical. When he tried to thank her, she shook her head.

'It's nothing, just a token. I hope you won't need to use it. You will look after yourself, Oliver? Keep as dry and warm as you can and don't take any silly risks? Oh dear, that was wrong. You know what I mean, don't you?'

Rupert pumped his son's hand and quoted the soldier poet Rupert Brooke, whose stirring verse in response to the outbreak of the war had inspired a legion of volunteers. 'Now, God be thanked Who has matched us with His hour, And

217

caught our youth, and wakened us from sleeping . . .' he said hoarsely, his eyes bright with rare affection. 'I'm proud of you, my boy. I envy you this chance.'

Well that was something, Oliver thought, as he climbed aboard the London train at Guildford and stowed his kitbag in the luggage rack. It wasn't often that Pa was proud of him. He alternated between intense excitement and equally intense apprehension – at last, at last, he was going to the war . . . ! But it was all very well to concoct visions of a shining military career, just suppose he made a mess of it? Suppose he turned out a coward? For a minute or two he tortured himself with imagining a shameful, rather than a triumphant homecoming, the rumours about some less-than-glorious exploit preceding him. Nobody at the station to meet him, the door opened to his knock by a sternly silent Ferry, Laura and Aunt Jessie tearfully reproachful, Pa turning away with his lip curled in disgust . . . and finally, Claire Lawrence looking through him with stony eyes.

He'd die first, Oliver vowed. And as the train swayed and clattered along the line, he reverted with relief to a daydream in which he led a fearless charge, or galloped out to retrieve a gun from the teeth of disaster as its fear-crazed team stampeded towards the enemy. . . . By the time the train pulled into Waterloo he had awarded himself a medal and the King himself had pinned it gratefully on to his heroic chest.

'Dear Daisy,' wrote Griffin, 'I was sorry to hear from Mrs Driver about your friend Arthur. . . .' He frowned at the notepaper resting on one drawn-up knee. He scratched out 'friend' and substituted 'fiancé', chewed on the end of his pencil, scored a line through the whole page, ripped it off the pad and crumpled it into a ball. It was no good: he never got any further than that one statement, which wasn't much better than a lie anyway.

More than three months had passed since the big battle for possession of Ypres. If he was going to send a letter of condolence it should have been written long ago. He supposed that the conveying of his sympathy would have to wait until he got a Blighty leave – not that this seemed imminent. With the war a little over six months old, officers had begun to get home leave as and when their units could spare them, but none of the rankers that Griffin knew had so far been blessed. It was said that they were being granted leave at the rate of one per cent of the army at a time, and knowing his luck, he'd probably be at the end of the queue. The only realistic way to get home was on your back on a hospital ship, with bits of you missing. There were times when it seemed like an attractive option.

'Griffin? Have you got a few spare minutes?'

'Yes, sir.' The driver removed his feet from the flour sack stuffed with straw in which he had been keeping them warm and stood up stiffly, shoving the scrap of paper into the pocket of his greatcoat as he did so. In fact these were the first spare minutes he'd had in a hard morning, having had to play veterinary to a wounded horse on top of all his normal duties. But the sentence had been a polite preamble to a request, not a serious question and besides, it was Forsythe who had spoken, poking his head in under the low lintel of the doorway into the dugout. Forsythe was a decent bloke; some of the officers would have bellowed 'Driver Griffin, out here at the double!' and to hell with the niceties.

Forsythe was an acting captain now. Promotion these days came by stepping into dead men's shoes, and there had been plenty of those since the war began. In six traumatic months the young subaltern who had first spoken to Rupert Brownlowe's groom in the market place at Guildford had become a hardened campaigner. In most situations you'd have taken him for a man of thirty, Griffin reckoned. His youthfulness showed through when he laughed; but at present, following the demolition of his guns by a particularly well-placed couple of *minenwerfers* and pending their replacement, he was in charge of an ammunition column engaged in the nightly process of bringing supplies forward from the depot, and there wasn't much to laugh about as they ran the gamut of the

German guns. All along the Menin road out of Ypres lay shattered wagons and the carcases of horses; in the fields nearby, rows of rough wooden crosses sprouted in the snow like young trees, etched with the names, ranks and units of dead men.

'How's Diamond?' said Forsythe, who took the trouble to learn the names of all the horses. He came a little further into the dugout. His army greatcoat covered two layers of woollen cardigan jackets and a flannel shirt; the collar, turned up as a protection from the biting wind, rubbed against the stubble on his chin and the tip of his nose was raw-red with cold.

'Not too bad, sir.'

Last night, as Griffin's team galloped hell-for-leather along the potholed road with a wagonload of ammunition bouncing behind, amidst descending shells from the German batteries, one explosion had been too close for comfort and a sliver of ricocheting stone from the road surface had buried itself in the cheek of Griffin's mount a couple of inches below the eye.

'I've cleaned the wound out and bandaged her up,' the driver said, his matter-of-fact tone giving no clues about what a struggle this operation had entailed. The mare had been in a state of shock and correspondingly uncooperative. Soothing words having failed to do the trick, he'd had to strap up one hind leg under her belly to put her off-balance and stop her striking out with her forelegs while he swabbed at the deep gash with stinging disinfectant; even so she'd hopped around on the remaining three limbs with remarkable agility.

'Will she be fit for work tonight?'

Griffin hesitated, thinking of the dark road and the careering teams. They were short of horses. Would a panicky Diamond make much of a difference to the normal state of affairs? 'I reckon she'll do, sir,' he decided, 'if I pad her up enough under her bridle. Mind you, she'll be nervous.'

Forsythe nodded. 'So shall we all,' he said wryly. 'I'm sure you'll cope. Now, can you do something for me? Our new subaltern's just arrived. He managed to get separated from his allocated valet in Poperinghe. I'm on my way to HQ for a briefing and I haven't time to deal with him. Can you show him where to put his kit and generally tell him what's what around here? He's replacing Second Lieutenant Matthews.'

'Yes, sir.' Griffin followed the officer out into the frosty air, flexing his mittened fingers which were cramped with the cold. Outside the dugout stood a youth in a remarkably clean khaki greatcoat and what, until an hour ago, had been the glossiest boots in Ypres. With his back to them, he was staring gloomily across the sea of trodden snow, churned mud and ice-rimmed puddles, and towards the front-line trenches from which the occasional staccato burst of rifle fire could be distantly heard.

'Sounds as though the Jerries have put a new sniper into that coppice north of the salient,' commented Forsythe, shielding his eyes against the pale sunlight as he too peered eastwards, assessing the source of the firing. 'I expect the battery will flush him out this afternoon.'

The newcomer turned. Like Forsythe, he had been screwing up his eyes against the sun, but they widened momentarily at the sight of Griffin. The reaction was mirrored by the spasm which crossed the driver's face.

'Do you two know each other?' Forsythe was still alive, unlike many of his fellow officers of the BEF, because he had a watchful eye for small details.

'Yes, sir,' said Griffin guardedly.

'This man was my father's under-groom before the war,' said Oliver.

Forsythe's gaze flicked between the two wooden expressions and he recognized that relations between employee and employer's son had not been of the most cordial. He suppressed a sigh. Life was complicated enough out here without adding old tensions to the situation. He hoped there wasn't going to be any trouble. For a moment he considered withdrawing the order he'd just made to Griffin to settle the new man in. But he was too pressed for time to find a substitute and Second Lieutenant Brownlowe could not be left standing around in the mud for ever.

'Well, if you'll excuse me . . .' He glanced at his wristwatch, an invaluable innovation for gunnery officers. 'Driver Griffin will take you to your quarters. Glad to have you here, Brownlowe; we'll talk later.'

As Forsythe walked quickly away, Oliver and Griffin faced one another warily, Oliver's kit bag on the ground between them. Eventually Griffin stooped and swung it up to his shoulder, since Oliver clearly wasn't going to.

'This way, sir.'

The officers' billet was a small and decrepit stone building, sited in what had once been a sizeable clump of trees and which was now largely reduced to a collection of polled and fractured stumps. The roof tiles being mostly gone, it was covered with corrugated tin and disguised with earth and tangled branches; more earth than branches because too healthy a covering of foliage would have been a giveaway to German reconnaissance planes. For the benefit of the enemy's spotters, who periodically swooped overhead to photograph the area, the battery had painstakingly rigged itself up some fake dugouts and bogus guns some distance away from the genuine articles. They were constructed from spare wagon-wheels and felled timber, with just the wrong amount of camouflage. The intention was to make a German artillery officer smile with satisfaction at his own perceptiveness and aim for the false target; so far the ruse had worked, as the encircling shell holes testified.

Crammed into the confined interior of the genuine accommodation thus protected were several narrow iron-framed beds and a makeshift table covered with maps. A collection of haversacks hung by their straps from nails fixed to the battens that supported the roof. Griffin ducked under a dangling haversack to dump Oliver's kitbag on one of the beds.

'Here you are, sir. Home, sweet home. This is your bed.'

'What exactly happened to the previous occupant?'

'Stopped a load of shrapnel, sir.'

The Germans peppered the Allied side of the salient with a variety of explosive devices, one of which was designed to detonate in the air and to shower an umbrella of lead balls over a wide area. Matthews had been some distance from the centre of the blast, but even so his back would probably look like an old dartboard by the time the surgeons had finished digging little bits of metal out of it. But it was definitely a Blighty, they'd assured him as they dosed him with morphine, and despite the pain he'd been grinning as the stretcher-bearers carried him away, face down and thumbs pointing triumphantly skywards.

As he stepped forward, Oliver's shoulder bumped against a haversack, tipping it on to the floor. Griffin scooped up the canvas bag and restored it to the nail.

'Silly place to hang it,' Oliver complained irritably.

'It's to keep things off the floor, sir. You'd best do the same.'

'Why?'

'Rats, sir. They'll eat anything you put down. Food, letters, books, just about everything except your gun.'

Oliver flopped on to the bed, wincing at its lack of springing, and surveyed his new quarters with distaste. His eyes lit upon something that moved among the rumpled blankets under his thighs and he stood up again so rapidly that his head collided with the tin ceiling.

'Christ!' he said, straightening his cap. 'What are those?'

Griffin peered, and identified the minute insects as lice.

'*Lice?*' Oliver's voice climbed. 'Good God. I'd heard the *men* had lice . . . but not the officers!'

'I'm afraid so, sir. We've been trying to requisition a better class of parasite for the officers, sir,' said Griffin, poker-faced. 'But you know how it is. There's a war on.'

Oliver reached for the offending blanket, lifted it from the bed between an extended forefinger and thumb and dropped it on to the beaten earth of the floor. Having completed the manoeuvre, he wished he hadn't. The mattress thus revealed was crawling with the beastly creatures. Grimly, he postponed that problem and turned to the soldier at his side.

'Griffin, let's get one thing straight from the start. Just because you worked for my father, that doesn't entitle you to any familiarity.'

'Perish the thought, sir,' said Griffin gently.

'I will not take any lip from you. I am an officer, you are a ranker, and if you forget that fact for one moment, I will make you wish that you hadn't. Is that understood?'

'Yes, sir,' said Griffin after a pause. It had not been a long pause but, combined with his steady stare, it reminded Oliver of past unsatisfactory exchanges with the former groom, and left him wondering how you defined 'dumb insolence' for the purposes of a court martial.

'Do you require anything further, sir?'

'No,' said Oliver curtly, and turned his back.

Normally Griffin would have hunted out a straw-bag footwarmer for the new arrival and told him that an effective treatment for a louse-infected blanket was to seep it in a bucket of petrol – obtainable through the usual processes of theft and barter from the Service Corps boys or a friendly ambulance driver – to hang it up while the petrol evaporated and then to scrape all the unhatched eggs off the surface of the material with your thumbnail. Of course the downside of this procedure was that the bed's occupant stank of petrol and had to be extremely careful when lighting a match, but at least the little blighters would be temporarily discouraged.

On this occasion he decided not to bother with the handy hints. Somehow, he didn't think they would be appreciated and anyway he didn't feel particularly generous. Someone else could give the full welcome to Mr Oliver.

Left alone, Oliver hesitated between the lice-ridden mattress and the floor. Eventually he perched himself gingerly on the extreme edge of the bed and waited for somebody to tell him what to do next.

It was bad enough, he reflected miserably, to be hived off arbitrarily from the battery you'd been involved with for months and dumped among strangers for your initiation into front-line operations. It was worse when you had to maintain the discipline and the fearless mask of an officer in front of someone who had known you as a spotty schoolboy and showed every sign of having despised you from the outset.

Oliver groaned. He had handled the encounter with Griffin all wrong, and he knew it.

Forsythe had not been impressed by his brief acquaintance with the new subaltern. Oliver had occupied the walk down to Griffin's dugout by telling his superior officer how thrilled he was to be out here at last, and how much he was looking forward to fighting for his country and dying for it if he had to. To be fair, the captain reminded himself, he'd been that green once and Oliver Brownlowe couldn't help having swallowed whole the hogwash they were fed on at home, to the effect that *Dulce et Decorum Est Pro Patria Mori*. He'd know better when he'd witnessed a few deaths devoid of sweetness and decorum.

Meanwhile he ought to be broken in gently. It was therefore with some misgivings that Forsythe found himself compelled to send a message, later that evening, to his First Lieutenant: 'Dear Davidson, I'd hoped to be back tonight but I'm held up at HQ. They are waiting for some aerial reconnaissance information and then there's to be a conference about relocating some of the batteries. I am afraid you'll have to see to the run and take the new boy with you. Tell him not to do anything spectacular, just go along with the men, they know the job. Keep your heads down, see you tomorrow. Good luck. Donald Forsythe.'

He would have been even more concerned if he had realized that Davidson would receive his message while curled up on his bed in the unmistakable throes of a dose of dysentry; and that consequently, the task of commanding the night's operations would fall, *faut de mieux*, on the inexperienced shoulders of Second Lieutenant Brownlowe.

The casualty rate for the ammunition run had dwindled

lately, not because the amount of high explosive devoted to impeding it had lessened, but because one evening Forsythe had realized that his opposite number behind the enemy lines was only human. The Oberleutnant in charge of laying the German guns that covered the road issued the appropriate instructions to his teams at the beginning of the nightly barrage . . . and retired to his bed. So that once you had taken note of the range and order of the deliveries, provided that the same man was in charge, you could expect the shelling to continue in the set pattern for the rest of the night. Like the participants of a schoolgirl skipping game, who choose the right moment to duck into the circling rope, the wagon drivers waited, poised, before slotting themselves in among the shells exploding in series down the road.

Of this refinement, Oliver was unaware.

When he arrived at the dump the requisitioned French farm carts known as Jacob wagons, their sides fitted with large ramps to take a full load, were already piled high and waiting. Oliver was as unsure of his new horse as he was terrified of his new responsibility, but he determined not to give any sign of it. He had been given a list of the ammunition to be delivered and where, and had roughed out a schedule for the movement of the shells. Being new to the area, this had been difficult because he didn't know how long the journeys ought to take. But it had made him feel calmer.

'Right, men,' he announced busily. 'Captain Forsythe and First Lieutenant Davidson are unavailable for various reasons, so I'm in charge. Let's get on with it.'

Since the death of Dawson during the retreat from Mons, Griffin had been lead driver of his team. Hunched in the saddle on the lead horse of the nearest wagon team, keeping a sharp eye on the hand horse of the pair because she was a sweating and agitated Diamond, Griffin emitted a soft groan. Oliver heard it and recognized it for what it was, a comment on his qualifications as controller of the operation.

'Driver Griffin, your team can go first.'

'We usually do, sir. That's why we're at the front, sir,'

Griffin informed him helpfully. It was pushing his luck with Oliver, he knew. The fledgeling officer was strung taut with nerves and about as ready to explode as Diamond. But he couldn't resist it.

Oliver gave him a long look, sure that the driver was mocking him, unsure how to deal with it. *Better stop sniping at the poor little devil from now on*, Griffin chided himself, *and get on with the job in hand*. Raising his whip as a signal to the other drivers, he closed his legs on his horse's sides and the team moved forward, the rest of the convoy fitting into place behind. Oliver's horse danced edgily alongside the leading wagon.

Ahead of them in the moonlight stretched the road to the front line. The snow lay unmelted in the fields but on the road it had dissolved and been churned into a toffee-coloured mud by constant traffic. At intervals, shell craters showed like patches of spilled ink between the vaguely defined mounds of wrecked carts and slaughtered animals that no one had the time to clear away. Along the verges, a rough canvas barrier had been erected to shield the road from the eyes of the German gunners who covered the salient, but this was the main supply route to the line and even the most random shelling would yield results.

Tonight the usual heavy barrage was in operation. Oliver licked his dry lips. Already, in the few hours since he'd stepped from the train at Poperinghe, he had learned how not to shudder visibly in automatic response to the whine-and-crash of explosions. But this was the first time he had seriously had to offer himself up to their effects. He tried to blank out the realization that his life could end in the next few minutes. The wagons, having formed a line astern, had halted. He turned to the team waiting beside him and forced his voice down a scale as he addressed the lead rider.

'Carry on, Griffin.'

The wagon didn't move.

'I said, carry *on*!'

'Not yet, boys,' said Griffin quietly to the two drivers

behind him. He was watching the explosions as they travelled the length of the road, concentrating too hard to remember to give the reasoning behind his refusal to the officer who had issued the instruction.

'Griffin! I gave you an order!' Already Oliver's schedule was running late. To encounter such disobedience was completely unforeseen and he didn't know what to do. He was beginning to panic.

'Sir,' said Griffin, without turning his head, 'we don't go yet. Didn't Captain Forsythe tell you about the guns?'

'Never mind that! Do as I say! What are you, man, a fool or a coward?'

'Neither,' said Griffin. His temper snapped. 'And I'm not sacrificing my team because some little pipsqueak of a baby officer is too green to know the difference between courage and suicide.'

'Right! That's it,' spluttered Oliver. 'I warned you, Griffin. I'm charging you with gross insubordination and refusing to obey orders.'

Griffin shrugged, his attention still infuriatingly elsewhere. Oliver wheeled his skittering horse and kicked her closer, his grip on the whip in his right hand tightening. He didn't know whether to bring it down on the flank of the horse or the shoulders of the intransigent driver. Suddenly, Griffin twisted in the saddle.

'All right, one more blast and we'll go,' he shouted over his shoulder.

'It won't do you any good now,' said Oliver. 'I'm pressing that charge.'

'To hell with the charge,' said Griffin. 'Let's get this damned ammunition to the gun pits and *then* you can do what you bloody well like. GO!' he bellowed, kicking hard, and the horses bounded forward, hauling the swaying, jolting wagon at full tilt along the Menin road.

'You've done what?'

Forsythe was less than thrilled by the news that the battery's

228

newest subaltern had seen fit to put a man on a charge within twenty-four hours of his arrival. Forsythe himself operated on the basis that discipline problems usually arose from poor communications or stupid orders, and he took care not to have any.

'I'm sorry, sir, I had no choice. He was very clearly insubordinate.'

'Griffin? He's one of our best drivers. You must have misunderstood him,' said Forsythe, exasperated. 'You knew him before the war began, didn't you?'

'In that he was one of my father's grooms, yes I did, sir.'

'Well, I dare say it was the old familiarity, then.'

'With respect, sir, familiarity was no more permissible when Griffin was an employee than it is now,' said Oliver stiffly.

'For heaven's sake . . .' muttered Forsythe. 'Then you won't drop this charge business?'

'I can't, sir,' said Oliver. 'It was dealt with by the major, first thing this morning.'

Forsythe uttered a word that his mother would have blanched at. 'What was the outcome?' he enquired grimly.

'FP1, sir. Twenty-eight days.' In Oliver's opinion this was far too light a sentence for the offence.

'Hell!' said Forsythe.

Field Punishment Number One involved taking the miscreant thus sentenced and attaching him by the wrists and ankles to the wheels of a gun or limber, one hour per day, for whatever number of days was prescribed by the officer presiding over the disciplinary proceedings. In the cold weather it was particularly uncomfortable for the soldier concerned to be held immobile for any length of time. It was also supposed to be a shaming experience and to make sure that the offender got the point, it was coupled with extra fatigues and loss of the cigarette ration.

Griffin, when approached by Forsythe and Oliver, didn't look remotely ashamed. His face bore an expression of detachment verging on boredom. He didn't care about the cigarettes apart from the loss of bartering power. He could stand the fatigues. He conceded that he'd been silly to needle the new subaltern and he probably deserved what he'd got. But the being tied up seemed to him to be a complete waste of everybody's time and energy. He calculated that he had been standing spreadeagled for approximately three quarters of an hour and was resignedly anticipating a further quarter of an hour today, with a repeat of the whole palaver tomorrow and the next day and the next. . . . He raised his dark eyebrows slightly as Forsythe unfastened the straps that pinioned his arms to the wheel.

'Sir?'

'Your FP1's cancelled.' Forsythe, crouching down to release the prisoner's ankles, was still in a flaming temper about the whole affair. In a few terse sentences he had explained to Oliver the reasoning behind the driver's behaviour of last night and had insisted that the crestfallen subaltern should accompany him to search out and release the victim of his error. However, the senior officer who had issued the sentence need not be distracted by the news of its curtailment, Forsythe had decided. It was unfortunately possible that the major would hold the crime of insubordination to be valid even in a situation where the order issued was plainly ill-conceived. Forsythe was prepared to argue the point with the major – but only if he had to.

'Brownlowe's got something to say to you,' pronounced the captain as he straightened up. 'Haven't you, Brownlowe?'

Griffin was still leaning against the wheel, his fingers now curled around the spokes because he was rather afraid that if he let go, his paralysed limbs would buckle under him. He didn't much want to fall down in front of Oliver Brownlowe, who was now confronting him, his smooth cheeks pink with all the humiliation that Griffin was declining to feel.

'I gather I misunderstood your actions last night, Driver Griffin,' he muttered reluctantly. 'Sorry about that.'

Griffin carefully relinquished a spoke and lowered

one stiff arm. Pain flared in his shoulder as he did so. He gripped his other wrist and rubbed at the marks left by the tight strap.

'That's all right, sir.' But his eyes conveyed a different message.

'And Griffin, it may be that you weren't entirely effective or respectful in your communications with Second Lieutenant Brownlowe?' prompted Forsythe with deceptive gentleness.

'No, sir,' Griffin admitted. 'Sorry, sir.'

'But it won't happen again,' said Forsythe, giving an order that masqueraded as a mere polite suggestion.

'No, sir.'

'Don't let me down on that, Griffin.'

'No, sir.' And for the first time Griffin looked abashed.

'I hope,' said Forsythe as the two officers walked back to their billet, 'that you've learned a little sense, Brownlowe – the sense to listen to a more experienced soldier, even if he is a ranker and even if he doesn't couch his comments in drawing-room language. Otherwise, frankly, you won't last long. And I'm sick of writing notes of regret to the next-of-kin of boys like you!'

Oliver did not realize that his superior's scathing words came from a man who was barely two years older than the 'boy' now squirming under the lash of his tongue. But it occurred to Forsythe, belatedly. He stopped dead and turned to the unhappy subaltern.

'What am I doing? It's me that should be on a charge, for stupidity. I've been tearing you off a strip and hang it, you'd only just arrived and you got thrown in at the deep end. You weren't to know who is or isn't a troublemaker. You did pretty well, considering. Cheer up, in a couple of months you'll have leap-frogged over me, rank-wise, and then you can give *me* a hard time.'

The impulsive gesture had been characteristic of Forsythe. Along with his common sense, his efficiency and his willingness to take a share in whatever dangerous tasks he required of the men, it was a trait that had won him the loyalty of his subordinates in the battery; though his senior officers, when they encountered it, regarded it as slightly suspect. On cue, it netted him something like adoration from Oliver Brownlowe.

12

'What about a perambulator? Have you thought about that?'

Mrs Colindale seemed to take a dour satisfaction in confronting her errant daughter with the harsh economic realities of having a baby which would have been better 'seen to' by Ma Turner. When Daisy first 'brought her shame home', as her mother had put it, Jessie Brownlowe's generous parting gesture had blunted the edges of this tendency. But even a year's worth of the wages paid to a servant over and above her keep 'all found', were not likely to last long when she had to do all the finding herself, and as the money dwindled, so the sharpness of Mrs Colindale's remarks grew.

'Usually, people would rally round. Someone who'd stopped using their gear would lend it. But we can hardly expect that in *your* case.'

As if illegitimacy were catching, Mrs Colindale's neighbours were determinedly ignoring Daisy and her bulge in public, though in private they doubtless had plenty to say about it.

Daisy sighed. When Robert was born, she knew, her mother had had a new perambulator . . . but then, unlike Daisy, she'd had a husband earning good money. Coach-built, mounted on Cee-springs, upholstered in best American leather cloth, the baby carriage had been Mrs Colindale's pride and joy, and she'd extracted the maximum pleasure from showing it off. But such a perambulator, even from the cheaper end of the range, would cost four pounds or more. Realistically, it was more likely that Daisy's baby would have to take the air in a drawer from an old cabinet, mounted on a set of salvaged wheels if any could be found.

'There's my old perambulator still, out in the coal shed,'

Mrs Colindale recalled reluctantly when she had sufficiently dwelt on the problem. 'I suppose you could use that, though lord knows how we'll cart the coal come the winter.'

Daisy wrapped a shawl round her and followed her mother out to the lean-to shed behind the house. It was almost empty, with only a small heap, mostly slack and dust, piled in a corner. In more prosperous times, with Robert's money from the Dennis works coming in, the family had been able to order fuel by the cartload. This winter the rising prices and their reduced income had meant that Louella had been forced to collect fuel from the coal merchant by the sack, or even the half-sack, as necessity dictated.

The perambulator was so uniformly filthy that it was hard to tell its colour, but Daisy remembered navy blue, with a picked-out garland of tiny white flowers on the sides as a trim, and a white lining. Now it sagged on its springs, the insides of the wheels and the handle were speckled with rust spots, the interior cloth was torn and the hood had rotted along its folds so that the metal of the frame showed through.

'Well, better get cracking on it,' said Mrs Colindale briskly in the face of Daisy's dispirited silence. 'I'll fetch you a bucket of water and a cloth, shall I? No, better get Louella to do that. My insides are giving me trouble again.' She turned from the derelict pram towards her daughter. 'No use looking so gloomy,' she said. 'Needs must when the devil drives. And you made your bed, Daisy.'

She trudged back into the house and a few minutes later, Louella brought out a steaming bucketful of soapy water.

'No, I'll do it. Move over,' she said, as Daisy knotted her shawl to keep the fringed ends out of the way and rolled up her sleeves. 'You should be taking things easy in your condition.'

'I don't see why you should have extra work because of my baby.'

'Don't be silly. I like to help. Anyway,' said Louella, 'you'd do the same for me, wouldn't you? Not that you'll ever get the chance, the way things are going,' she added gloomily.

'He'll be back one day, Lou.'

'Will he? It's been more than seven months. It feels like seven years, or seventy and any day there could be a knock at the door and a telegram to say he's dead. I keep thinking I'm used to it, and then something happens to remind me that he isn't here, or bring to mind the way we were, and then it hurts just as much as it did the day he went.' Louella wrung out the cloth with bitter vigour. 'Anyway even if he does come back safe, I don't know if we'll have children.'

'Course you will.'

'Reckon so? I'll tell you something,' said Louella, her arm working in methodical circles as she attacked the begrimed side of the perambulator. 'Right from the day we were married, we were trying. Four months, no luck. Then after he went away, I missed my courses. I didn't tell anyone in case I was wrong, I didn't even write to him about it, but I was so excited that I had to bite my tongue not to shout it down the High Street. Especially when you came home, that time when Mother Colindale was sick, and I saw you were in the same situation. I thought your Arthur'd come back with my Robert, and you'd get married and our babies would be born together and grow up together. . . .'

She rinsed the rag out in the bucket and lifted it, sloshing water over the dirt through which the flower garland was beginning to show. 'Then in November, I lost the baby.' The streams of blackened liquid flowed down and ebbed out around her shoes. 'So maybe it isn't so easy to have one when you want one, after all.'

'Oh, Lou, I'm sorry,' said Daisy inadequately.

'Seemed so silly. Me wanting mine and losing it, you going down to Ma Turner to get rid of yours. I nearly told you then.'

'Why didn't you?'

'Oh, well, you'd got enough on your plate.' Louella looked at Daisy's tragic expression and smiled raggedly.

'I shouldn't have said anything now, should I? Never mind. That's life. Anyway it's all for the best, isn't it? This way if

I have a baby, Robert'll be there to watch it growing. If he ever comes home.'

'Cuppa tea and a packet of Players, please miss.'

Behind the soldier, the khaki queue stretched almost to the door of the recreation hut, though every one of the scarred wooden tables and chairs was already occupied. Properly speaking, this was Aunt Jessie's shift at the YMCA hut, with Laura functioning as a spare pair of hands. But Jessie had been called away 'for a moment or two' almost two hours ago.

Where on earth was she?

Laura reached down the requested pack of cigarettes from the wooden rack behind her and pushed it across the counter, dumped a thick earthenware cup on to its saucer and shunted them towards the gigantic teapot. She'd just topped the pot up with boiling water and from bitter experience she knew it was going to take all the strength left in her aching wrists to pour out a cupful of the tongue-furring brown liquid the troops were prepared to accept as 'tea'.

'I'd rather have milk in first, if you don't mind, miss.'

'Oh. Yes, of course.' Wearily, Laura splashed milk into the cup.

'That's a bit too milky, miss.'

Gritting her teeth into the nearest thing to a smile she could manage, Laura tipped half the dispensed milk into a neighbouring cup.

'How's that?'

'Fine, miss. Just right.'

Laura poured. The soldier sorted out coppers with nerve-jangling slowness.

'Cuppa tea and a packet of Woodbines, please miss.'

'Milk in first, please miss.'

At last Jessie reappeared in the doorway. Beleaguered, Laura waved. 'Can you help? We're awfully busy.' But Jessie was accompanied by the two co-workers who'd arrived earlier and carried her off after a whispered consultation.

Instead of Jessie it was Mrs Jarvis who joined Laura at the counter.

'All right, I'll take over here. You go and talk to your aunt.'

Jessie and Mrs Simpson had gone back outside. Stepping out into the cold February sunlight, away from the clatter of cups and the clamour of conversation, the cigarette smoke and the smell of crowded humanity, Laura drew a long, appreciative breath. A cab was drawn up at the roadside, the elderly driver waiting resignedly in his seat. She caught sight of a pale, averted face behind the glass of the passenger compartment before she turned to her aunt.

'You wanted me, Aunt Jessie?'

'There's a job for you, Miss Brownlowe, if you are willing to take it,' said Mrs Simpson briskly. 'But it involves going to France – not for long, just a few days. Your aunt tells me that your French is good. Though we were hoping to find someone a little more *mature*,' she added, eyeing Laura dubiously.

'But in the circumstances, as speed is so very vital . . .' Jessie murmured.

'What is it I'm supposed to do?' said Laura, looking from one woman to the other. She resented the suggestion that she, a young lady of almost twenty – well, nineteen-and-three-quarters, anyway – was not sufficiently mature for whatever was proposed, though it was a refrain she had heard to exasperation point over the past few weeks.

'There is a lady waiting in that cab over there,' Mrs Simpson explained. 'She has received a telegram to say that her husband has been very seriously wounded. He is in hospital in Calais and she wants to go to him at once. But she can't go on her own, she's in such a state, poor soul, and quite unused to foreign travel. It's clear from the way the telegram is worded that the husband is likely to die. We can arrange for her children to be cared for while she's away, that's being done now. But she needs someone to go with her to help her through her ordeal, sort out her passport in London and any

237

other travel problems, interpret with the authorities and so on. Will you go, Miss Brownlowe?'

Laura hesitated. She turned to Jessie. 'What about my nursing classes? And Pa? And I'd need to pack. . . .'

'The classes will wait. I'm sure Mrs Lawrence will understand,' Jessie said. 'And your father can find another driver for a few days. As for the packing, I've done that for you in the hope that you'd agree.' Jessie gestured towards a leather valise lying beside the hut door. 'I think I've remembered everything. Will you go?'

'I suppose so,' Laura said doubtfully. She disliked making rushed decisions under pressure from other people, and she was mentally distracted by considerations like the probable deficiencies of her aunt's valise-packing technique. It was a very *small* valise. But she allowed herself to be shepherded over to the cab and when she met Mrs Emery, the woman's strained courage reminded her so painfully of Alice, holding out gamely against heartbreak, that she could have kicked herself for her first, ungenerous reaction to the appeal for help.

'Here is Miss Brownlowe who will go with you to France,' said Jessie. Mrs Emery's mouth managed an automatic smile, though her frightened eyes did not.

'Thank you,' she whispered. 'You are very kind. Everyone is being so kind.'

But as Laura was about to climb into the cab, Jessie put out a detaining hand.

'Perhaps I should be going myself,' she said in an undertone, reverting to her normal hesitant manner. 'Your French is far better, Laura, and I have to admit I'm so horribly seasick that I would probably be more of a handicap than a help . . . but it's rather a delicate situation.' She glanced at Mrs Emery, who was twisting her fingers together inside the cab.

'I'll manage,' said Laura with more confidence than she was feeling. She had an idea that this task would constitute some kind of benchmark of her capabilities, not just for Aunt Jessie, but for herself. 'Anyway, as you said, speed is the important thing here and it's my clothes that you've packed.'

'I suppose so.' Jessie handed in the brown valise, Laura's coat and an envelope containing money and instructions. Laura remembered that she was still wearing her tea-serving apron and passed it out to her aunt as the cabbie shook his reins and began to turn the vehicle round. A moment later they were trotting down the road and it was too late to back out of the assignment. She looked at Mrs Emery's pallid face and racked her brains for something to say that might take her companion's mind off the reason for their journey.

'My aunt says you have children . . . ?' she began tentatively.

It was an inspired opening. The Emery children, their ages, personalities, illnesses and a selection of their infant misadventures successfully occupied the cab journey to Guildford, and the subsequent train journey to London.

The next step detailed on the sheet of instructions supplied by Jessie and Mrs Simpson was to take Mrs Emery to the Foreign Office to obtain passports. This required a very strict examination as to their motives for the journey, and also, as Laura discovered to her dismay after more than three hours of waiting and questioning, the presentation of a form signed by a person of authority such as a magistrate or a lawyer, testifying to the bona fides of the would-be travellers.

'But we don't have one. I didn't realize,' said Laura.

'But you must,' said the man behind the desk, with the blank obduracy of officialdom.

'Can't you overlook it this once?' Laura pleaded, exerting all her charm.

He remained unmoved. 'Certainly not. Rules are rules.'

At the point of despair, Laura remembered seeing another sheet of paper in the envelope which had contained her instructions and the money for the journey. To her relief, it fulfilled the specification. On the payment of four shillings, two passports bearing the signature of the Foreign Secretary, Sir Edward Grey, were issued at last, and they were free to proceed to France. Except that by the time the train from

Victoria pulled into the station at Folkestone, it was too late. They'd missed the boat.

A night in a hotel in Folkestone did nothing to ease Mrs Emery's state of mind, nor did the scramble for tickets the next morning. The ship on which they had obtained their passage was crowded with officers going back to their units after home leave and the sight of the seething mass of khaki uniforms, so sharply reminiscent of her husband's, distressed Mrs Emery as much as the overheard snatches of conversation about particularly hellish experiences at the Front. To make matters worse, like Jessie she was a poor traveller. Eventually she was persuaded to lie down in a cabin and rest, and with a sense of escape Laura went on deck, but the sea wind whipped at her face and spattered her clothes with salt spray. Added to which, she was being stared at by young men in uniform in a way that only the iciest air of un-approachability could discourage. And she kept remembering snippets of war news as relayed by Pa over the breakfast table.

It was true, or ought to be, that Britannia Ruled The Waves. The German battle cruisers, after their dastardly bombardment of Hartlepool, Whitby and Scarborough just before Christmas, had been chased back into the North Sea by the navy and were currently penned inshore, not daring by virtue of their inferiority to venture out again, so Pa said. Nevertheless, in recent weeks a number of ships had been torpedoed and sunk by submarines in the Channel, and it was only a week or two ago that the hospital ship *Asturias* had been attacked off Havre – though fortunately that attack had failed. Laura found herself obsessively scanning the waves for the straight, foaming track of a torpedo. The grey sea slapping against the sides of the ship looked so cold and deadly.

Depressed, she decided to go below deck instead. She found a chair in the saloon and re-read her instructions. On reaching Boulogne, they would need to apply for a *laisser passer* from the commissioner of police and to make contact with a representative of the YMCA, who would provide transport and conduct them to the right hospital. It sounded relatively simple.

But the issuing of a *laisser passer* by a French official, it transpired when they had docked, was at least as arduous a procedure as the obtaining of a passport from an English one. The French policeman who examined their request seemed to start from the assumption that they were a pair of spies and Mrs Emery, still green from the crossing and exhausted by the effort of not thinking about what might be waiting for her at the hospital, was not a good witness under cross-examination. She fumbled her answers, contradicted herself, and Laura could see that the man's suspicions were increasing by the minute.

'*Eh bien, Madame, Mademoiselle. Restez ici, s'il vous plaît. Je dois vérifier.*'

He left them alone in his office while he went into the neighbouring room.

'What's happening?' Mrs Emery asked, in a scared whisper.

'I don't know. Shhh.' Through the closed door, Laura heard the low, rapid mutter of the man's voice on the telephone.

'*Oui, bien sûr. Ils ont des passeports véritables. Un mari blessé, à l'hôpital. Mais il y a quelque chose de faux . . . je ne peux pas mettre le doigt sur la cause de mon soupçon, mais. . . .*'

Laura stiffened. Didn't the silly man realize that he was dealing with two English ladies and that the English were their allies?

'*Je regrette*,' the policeman said as he came back into the room, '*que vous devrez attendre encore un peu.*'

More waiting? 'Oh, this is absolutely ridiculous!' Laura exploded. Summoning up her rusty French, she managed a flood of protest about the delay even if it was peppered with grammatical errors. The man's expression became, if possible, even more stubborn. He spread his hands in a classically Gallic shrug. Once more they were left alone.

'Not even a cup of tea,' said Mrs Emery with sad resignation. Laura scowled at the door which had closed in the policeman's wake. A sense of failure washed over her. Mrs Emery's husband was mortally ill, perhaps every moment counted and here they were, stuck in a French police station, and all because she, Laura, couldn't deal firmly with a policeman whom Pa would have had for breakfast. She couldn't even think of anything reassuring to say to Mrs Emery.

An hour crawled by. Laura fumed. At last the door opened again.

'Ladies.'

In the doorway stood an Englishman. Laura recognized him as such because of his calmness and because of his clothes, which were recognizably Jermyn Street in their origins. He looked rather like Pa, she thought, but more benign. He bowed slightly, from the waist.

'Miss Brownlowe? Your aunt sent a cable. I am Geoffrey Quiller of the YMCA.'

'We are delighted to see you,' Laura said with relief. 'The people here seem to be absolutely convinced that we're up to no good.'

'Perhaps they are a little over-cautious at present, but it is understandable in the circumstances. I must apologize for not being here to greet you, but I was a little delayed. There was a Zeppelin raid on Calais last night.'

'Oh!' said Laura, catching her breath. She had thought herself safe once they stepped on to dry land, away from the submarine menace. She hadn't thought about bombing. Zeppelin raids had been anticipated in England ever since the start of the war and one enemy raider had actually dropped a bomb on Dover just before Christmas, but in Guildford the threat had receded to the point where for some people, including Rupert Brownlowe, fear of death from the skies had given way to impatience with the lighting regulations and the shortage of holland cloth for making window blinds in order to comply with them. Here in France it seemed, the risk was very real.

'It wasn't too severe,' Mr Quiller reassured her. 'One

Zeppelin, a clutch of incendiary bombs. One house wrecked, five people killed.'

'Ah, Monsieur Quillair.' The obstructive policeman had joined them again, his formerly stony features rearranged in a smile. He discussed the situation briefly with the YMCA representative whom he obviously knew well and, with newfound courtesy, he issued two pink slips of paper which authorized Madame Emery and Mademoiselle Brownlowe, British subjects, to journey without hindrance to the YMCA hostel and the military hospital at Calais.

Mr Quiller led them to a waiting car. 'Hospital first, I think. Then we'll go on to the hostel.'

On the way, driving through the centre of Calais, they passed the bombed house – now reduced to nothing more than three crumbling walls and a heap of steaming debris. Groups of bystanders had gathered in the street to stare and discuss the event. Laura caught herself imagining her return to the nursing classes in Godalming, giving a nonchalant account of her journey. *Oh, yes, they bombed the place the night before we arrived. If we'd caught the right boat, I suppose we'd have been in it. No, I wasn't the least bit frightened. Rather excited, really. . . .* Then she scolded herself for being so heartless.

Later, at the hospital, nonchalance fled entirely. The beds in the wards they passed through were full of wounded men. Not just the sick, unconscious bodies she'd expected, but men who were visibly suffering and horribly maimed. Laura shuddered and walked on with averted eyes, fighting an inclination to run, to push past her companions and find fresh air, away from the human smells hanging in the atmosphere despite the disinfectant. She remembered Margaret Churchill talking about the foul stench of gas gangrene, and her stomach heaved.

For a man with severe internal injuries, Sergeant Herbert Emery was surprisingly animated when they found him in a small back room. His face was grey and sunken, his voice was little more than a whisper, but his conversational powers were unabated.

'Well, Annie, I didn't believe it when they said they'd send for you. They're angels, these nurses, proper little Florence Nightingales. They said to me, if you had three wishes, what would they be? And I said, well, first wish would be for a nice bit of chicken for my dinner and second wish would be a glass of champagne, and third wish would be for a sight of my Annie. Never thought I'd get any of them, did I? Thought it was a joke. But I've had the chicken and the champagne, and blow me, here you are. Should have asked for a thousand pounds while I was at it, shouldn't I?'

'Oh, Herbie. . . .' In the face of this greeting, Mrs Emery sat down on the end of his bed and burst into tears.

Mr Quiller touched Laura's arm. 'Let's see if we can wheedle ourselves a nice cup of tea out of one of the nurses before we go to the hostel. We'll come back later and collect her. I expect she'll want to stay with him for the rest of the day.'

The hostel was a private house which had been leased to provide visiting relations of the wounded with somewhere to stay that would be comfortable, quiet and more sympathetic than a hotel. At sixpence per day, it was also far cheaper, added Mr Quiller. 'Without the YMCA hostels, many of the soldiers' families would have to let them die without a last sight of their nearest and dearest. They simply couldn't afford to come.'

It was difficult for Laura to imagine a level of poverty in which a trip to France in such extreme circumstances was beyond a family's means. 'Do you think Sergeant Emery will die?' she asked in a subdued voice. 'He seemed so lively.'

'Hard to tell. Cheerful chap, isn't he? Sometimes if it's touch-and-go, a visit from a loved one helps to turn the balance. Let's hope he pulls through.'

Late in the evening, Mrs Emery came back from the hospital to a cold supper at the hostel. Her pale face was as drawn as it had been during the journey, but her eyes shone with contentment.

'He's ever so much better than I thought,' she said happily.

'I was so afraid I'd be too late and there he was, talking the hind leg off a donkey, same as ever.'

Laura and Mrs Emery shared a bedroom. Laura was so tired out by the unusual stresses of the past two days that she fell asleep as soon as she lay down in the rather spartanly furnished room, but in the night she was wakened by a soft tapping at the door. Mrs Emery slept on, while Laura dragged herself out of bed, fumbled for her wrap and opened the door.

Mr Quiller, a shade less impeccably dressed than before, his thinning hair unbrushed, stood on the landing with a candle in a holder. He was shielding the flame from the draught with his hand. 'Sergeant Emery has had a relapse,' he said quietly. 'The hospital has sent for his wife.'

Laura woke Annie Emery and got her dressed. After her revived hopes, the change in her husband's condition was too much of a shock for her to absorb and it was like manipulating a large rag doll, Laura thought, as she tugged at sleeves and buttoned and twitched garments straight.

'Sorry,' the woman kept saying in automatic apology. 'I'm all fingers and thumbs.'

At the hospital a nurse led her away towards the ward she had left earlier. Laura and Mr Quiller waited. It was another hour before Mrs Emery returned, moving as if controlled by strings.

'I'm glad he had his champagne,' was all she said.

'There was a funeral,' Laura told Aunt Jessie later, 'at a cemetery outside the town. There were twenty burials that morning in the one long grave, but Mrs Emery was the only relation there to mourn. The matron of the hospital came, and Mr Quiller. There were proper oak coffins with flags to drape over them, and a little detachment of men with rifles to fire a salute and buglers to sound the last post.'

Jessie watched her niece's face. Had she done the right thing in sending Laura to Calais? At the time, making a hasty decision and chivvied by Mrs Simpson, she had thought it a good thing that Laura's new awareness and sympathy should receive some focus, lest it should wither. Afterwards she realized what a gamble she had been taking: not just with the inexperienced and sheltered Laura, who had gone to a bombed town across a submarine-infested Channel, but also with the anxious wife, now a widow, who had needed support and might not have received it.

'How is Mrs Emery?' she asked.

'Bearing up. Rather dazed. She kept saying "Everyone is so kind",' said Laura sadly. 'But I didn't do anything, Aunt Jessie. I felt so helpless. I couldn't think of a single thing to do or say that would make it any better. All I did was listen and cry with her.'

'That is just what she needed,' said Jessie.

Laura's time in France had one practical effect on her daily routine at Maple Grange. In her absence Rupert had decided to dispense with her services as a driver.

'I thought I could rely on you, Laura, but if you are going to keep dashing away on your own concerns. . . .'

'Didn't Aunt Jessie explain?'

'She did. Some nonsense about the YMCA. I gather that I do not come high on your list of priorities, so I have made other arrangements.'

Rupert's alternative arrangement was a chauffeur called Walker whose employer had recently sent him, as Aldridge had been sent, to volunteer for the armed forces. On the brink of being too old anyway, he had been medically examined and pronounced unfit for active service, but on returning to his old workplace he had found that the family car had been donated for military use. He was deeply grateful to find employment with the Brownlowes, he was very respectful and Aldridge's uniform fitted him without alteration. Rupert liked him.

It stung Laura that her father was angry with her in such circumstances. Oliver was used to it, but she had always been Rupert's favourite. She knew that his occasional coldnesses towards her tended to be short-lived, easily melted by some small show of contrition on her part, but on this occasion she had no intention of being contrite. She resented his attitude. Pa claimed to honour and support Britain's fighting men and was active in promoting the work of the Parliamentary Recruiting Committee, to the extent of making personal calls on the young men of the district who had not yet volunteered and demanding that they justify their failure to do so. It seemed hypocritical of him to put his own convenience before the needs of a soldier's widow.

In the meantime she told herself with a shrug, the hiring of Walker was an advantage, giving her time and transport for the nursing classes she had agreed to undertake with Claire. Her brief exposure to the wounded in the Calais hospital had made her even more sure than before of her unsuitability as a VAD, but she felt a restless need to do *something*. And while she waited for that something to present itself, the acquisition of the rudiments of first aid would fill the gap.

'Pa, can I ask you a favour?'

Laura posed the question with caution. Several weeks had passed since her Calais adventure and, as expected, Rupert had long forgiven her for her temporary desertion; but Laura had not forgiven Rupert for his reaction to it. Years of assuming that he was the model for right-thinking behaviour had accentuated her disappointment at the discovery that he could be selfish, a trait which she had just learned to blame in herself. Instinct told her to avoid any action that might further highlight the differences between them.

So she had looked for a moment when he was in a good mood. It wasn't easy to pinpoint one. These days Pa was available for conversation only at the breakfast and supper table. Apart from his munitions production, he was forever being coopted on to new committees for the more efficient running of the war on a local level. This morning he had been in a distinctly bad mood, snorting furiously over the latest edition of the *War Illustrated* and crashing his fist on to the table so hard in reaction to one photograph that he spilled his third cup of coffee.

'Look at that! German Red Cross members marching to the battlefield with rifles and *pickelhaube* helmets! Succouring the wounded? Hah!'

But by suppertime, things had looked more propitious; it seemed that the day at the factory had gone smoothly, he had a staff of fifty now working on the production of 13-inch shells and the Ministry of Munitions was satisfied with his output. Payment for the first completed consignment had been received and Rupert was anticipating a profitably busy time ahead. Particularly satisfying was the thought that one day soon, as he told Laura and Jessie, *his* shells would be crashing down on the heads of the Huns, possibly even on those rifle-carrying impostors from the enemy Red Cross.

'And what would this favour be?' he inquired, helping himself to more wine from the silver-topped decanter on the sideboard.

'I'd like to invite somebody to stay.' Laura watched her father's good humour fade. 'His name's Charles McKay,' she said hurriedly. 'He's a lieutenant in the Royal Horse Guards – you remember, he was Hugh and Alice's best man.'

'Mmm,' said Rupert, considering. 'Good-looking fellow. Thought he went off to Belgium with Hugh?'

'He did. But he was wounded last month, helping to get some casualties in from No Man's Land, so he's back in England now, at Clandon.' She waved a folded letter. 'He's supposed to be ready for moving to a convalescent home and I thought we might have him here for a while instead.'

Rupert considered the request. *I think you should investigate the situation as soon as possible*, Caroline Delamere had written to her brother back in the autumn of the previous year, once she had grasped what lay behind Alice's prattlings about Laura and a young cavalryman. *For that poor girl has no mother, and I am sorry to say that as a guardian of reputation and an arbiter of decorum, Jessie is far too feeble to be of any use at all.*

At the time Rupert had merely tossed the letter over to Jessie to read and be mortified by, before disappearing into his study to look up the McKay family in one of his maroon-bound volumes of *Burke's Landed Gentry* and check that the chap was a suitable prospective son-in-law. This point settled to his satisfaction, Rupert had rather forgotten about young McKay. He wondered now whether his sister Caroline's reporting of Alice's artless comments was right and that the boy was really smitten. Laura was very young of course, but it didn't hurt to get your future sorted out good and early, provided you made a sensible choice.

'Very well,' he said. 'As you wish. I look forward to meeting that young man again.'

In fact Lieutenant McKay's letter informing Laura of his arrival at Clandon was three weeks old and she had already coaxed the new chauffeur into driving her to the hospital on a number of occasions. Luckily, Walker, when asked not to mention the journeys to Mister Rupert unless his employer specifically questioned him about them, had been flattered by his involvement in what he presumed was a romantic intrigue, and had agreed to cooperate. Rupert's views on what was or wasn't proper conduct for a young unmarried girl had softened considerably since the war began, but his indulgence was not to be relied on. He might insist that she should be chaperoned by Aunt Jessie, and Laura was too unsure of her feelings about Charles to want a witness to their encounters.

Laura's first reaction to Charles' brief note that barely mentioned his wound had been to assume the worst. He might be lying blinded, limbless, incoherent, like the maimed men she had seen at Calais. Then she realized that if so, he would not have been capable of writing a letter. All the same, it had been a nerve-wracking experience, making that first hospital visit, and she had been fervently wishing herself elsewhere as she drove along the avenue of trees towards the tall, square bulk of the red brick house over which the Red Cross flag fluttered.

Charles, she learned, was in one of the upstairs wards, which might have reassured her if she had known that the most serious surgical cases were kept nearest the operating theatre on the ground floor. A dark-haired VAD with a sallow, unhealthy complexion led her past the rows of beds that filled even the marble-flagged entrance hall, towards the main stairs. On the newel post at the bottom was a carving of a hawk attacking a thrush.

'Oh, that's nice,' said Laura, because the stark, uniform whiteness of the place was chilling and the carved birds were at least a decoration, reminiscent of the house's former glory.

'It's a devil to polish,' the VAD said flatly. 'The sharp bits catch at your hands.'

Laura stared at her in surprise. The girl, for all her pasty face and lank hair, had sounded quite well-born, yet here she was talking about the difficulties of polishing as if she'd been a servant.

Charles was in one of the smaller rooms, the anteroom to a great bedchamber. His iron-framed bed was by a long window with shutters folded back to give a view of a sweep of neglected lawn ending in a stone grotto. The gardens of nearly all the great houses were suffering now from a dearth of the manpower needed to maintain them, but Clandon had been on the slide even before the war and there were numerous weeds sprouting in the already overlong grass.

'Lieutenant McKay, you have a visitor.'

As she followed the nurse between the beds, Laura's heart was thumping and she fixed her gaze on the scrubbed oak boards of the floor to avoid looking at the wounded men. Downstairs in the hall, she had neglected to take this precaution, and had regretted it when she saw a blanket which rose over a cradle frame then dipped far short of the end of the bed to show that its unconscious occupant had lost both legs.

How awful if Charles had been similarly afflicted. Laura forced her eyes upwards and relief flooded through her. Under the blankets, his long legs were still in place. He had been shot through the shoulder which, while no doubt painful, was a very *picturesque* wound. It enabled him to sit propped up against his pillows, with swathes of white bandage showing at the open neck of his pyjama top and his left arm arranged in a sling. Under the tousled fair hair his handsome face, undamaged, creased into a wide smile.

'Laura! How marvellous to see you!'

His unchecked delight was infectious.

'And you. Charles, you can't imagine how good it is to see that you aren't badly hurt. I was so worried when I read your letter.'

The nurse had set a chair beside the bed before she hurried away to her other duties. Moving towards the chair, Laura bent and touched Charles' uninjured arm. It had been intended as a momentary friendly gesture, nothing more, but he reached his hand up to the nape of her neck and tugged her towards him. Caught off balance, mentally and literally, and afraid to pull away in case she hurt him, Laura found herself being soundly kissed, before the appreciative eyes of the other wounded soldiers sharing the anteroom. From those who could operate both hands, there was a spattering of applause.

'I'm sorry,' Charles apologized unconvincingly as he released her. 'You just looked so beautiful, I couldn't resist it.'

'Well!' said Laura and sat down, her heart pounding. Her first ever kiss from a man. In all her daydreams, she'd never imagined it happening like this! But then she'd never imagined it happening with anyone but Edward.

'You're not angry with me, are you?' Charles said, worried that he'd gone too far.

'No, I suppose not.'

After all, Laura told herself afterwards, there wasn't anything to be angry about was there? Charles was a wounded hero, and the nurse who showed her to the room had obviously thought he was wonderful. It had been satisfying to be aware of her envy as Laura passed her again in the hall at the end of her visit, and to know, too, that Charles was equally envied by the other patients because he had someone so pretty to visit him. She had arrived for her next visit in a flutter of expectation, but Charles didn't repeat the kiss. She didn't know whether to be relieved or disappointed. On the whole, she finally admitted, she was disappointed. She consoled herself with the thought that if he came to stay at Maple Grange, there'd be plenty of opportunities to test his enthusiasm, and her own reactions.

13

'I met young Allingham yesterday in Guildford,' said Rupert from behind *The Times*.

'James?' Laura paused on the verge of slicing the top from her boiled egg with an ivory-handled knife.

'No, the other one. Edward. Home on leave,' said Rupert.

Laura dropped her knife on to her plate with a clatter. Charles McKay, on the far side of the table, observed that as she picked it up again, her hand was shaking. Warning bells rang in his head. Did Edward Allingham mean anything to her? Wasn't he supposed to be engaged to a nurse?

'How *is* Edward?' Laura asked, after a short pause. From her disinterested tone she might have been inquiring after the health of any distant acquaintance, but Charles thought he could detect a pulse thumping away under her jaw, above the embroidered collar of her blouse.

'Oh, very fit,' Rupert said, spreading Gentleman's Relish on his toast. 'Bit down in the mouth, though. I gather his fiancée, Miss What's-her-name, was supposed to have arranged leave from her nursing outfit in France at the same time, but it turned out she couldn't make it. So he's rather at a loose end, poor chap. I invited him over here for lunch.'

Laura was staring steadily down at her plate as if she expected her boiled egg to hatch. Charles laid his linen napkin beside his own plate. Only a minute ago he had been about to embark on a healthy helping of sausages, bacon and tomatoes from the range of covered dishes on the sideboard. Now his appetite had gone.

He had been at the Grange for three weeks and still he didn't know where he stood with Laura. He'd thought, when she invited him to convalesce at her home, that it was a clear signal. But when he'd arrived, confident and eager, she'd slapped him down. She'd called him by his rank and surname, though at the hospital it had been 'Charles', and said that 'we' hoped he'd enjoy his stay. Since then her behaviour had varied. Sometimes she was warm and approachable, though after the setback of the formal welcome, never quite warm enough for him to dare to repeat the kiss he'd given her in the ward at Clandon. Sometimes she was so cool and distant that he felt like a worm. He knew he was in love. But was she? His shoulder was almost healed, he had a medical-board assessment coming up in a few days, after which he expected to be sent back to his regiment. It was time to get the matter sorted out.

'Can I talk to you?' he said in an undertone, as he followed her from the room at the end of breakfast.

'Yes, of course. Now?'

'I meant privately.' Charles glanced over his shoulder. They were alone in the hall, but the door through to the kitchen regions was only a few yards away and behind them in the dining room, Rupert was gathering his morning post together prior to setting out for the factory. They could be interrupted at any moment.

Laura looked up at him and smiled with her normal self-possession that he would have given anything to be able to disturb in the way that one reference to Edward Allingham had apparently disturbed it.

'All right,' she said. 'Let's take a walk in the garden and make the most of the sunshine.'

She led him to the peony garden which Sylvia Brownlowe had established soon after she came to the newly built house, the extravagant gesture of someone with so much land at their disposal that they could afford to devote a quarter of an acre to one expensive species of plant with a short flowering season. Despite the war, it was immaculately maintained. The Maple Grange gardens had not suffered from the drain of manpower like some others because the gardeners were too old and the gardeners' boys too young to volunteer, though last August, in the first wave of patriotic fervour, Billy Marshall had walked to Stoughton Barracks and lied about his age. Being short even for his fifteen years, he had failed to convince the recruiting officer that he was old enough to fight and had been sent back with a kindly injunction to grow a bit first.

Between the head-high privet hedges, the garden would be crowded from May to July with exotic, heavy blooms but in mid-April the new buds on the bushes between the grass pathways were still tightly closed, showing only a crack of colour.

Laura had chosen the peony garden for its privacy. 'To think that last week this was all skinny red stalks like rhubarb and now it's in full leaf already. It'll be glorious in a few more weeks, when the flowers are out,' she said. 'A bit boring now. But I think the sundial's beautiful all the year round.'

Inside the protective hedging, away from the wind, it was warm in the sunlight. On a stone plinth in the centre of the garden where the grass paths met, three fat and joyous lead cupids danced with abandon, facing in different directions. Balanced improbably on their heads was a stone circle with the sundial set into it.

'My mother bought it from the breaking-up sale of a country-house far grander than Maple Grange. I remember it being brought home on a cart, wrapped in layers of sacking, and Pa and Oliver and I were summoned to the drive to witness the great unveiling. Mother cut the string with such a triumphant flourish.' Momentarily, Laura's expression was wistful as she touched her finger to the tip of the style which sent its shadow across the blackened bronze surface of the dial. It occurred to Charles that he had never seen her vulnerable and sad like this and he felt a surge of tenderness towards her which was almost unbearable. As a distraction he leaned forward to read the words engraved in flowing copper-plate around the rim of the sundial.

Gather ye rosebuds while ye may, Old Time is still a-flying:

And this same flower that smiles today, To-morrow will be dying.

Probably three hundred years had passed since Herrick had written the poem, but Charles, with Laura standing at his shoulder, felt the immediacy of the message. *Get her while you can, you fool. . . .*

He turned to face her. He was as apprehensive now as he had been on the day that his regiment first went 'up the line' to take their turn in the trenches. He drew in a deep breath and tried to keep his voice steady. 'Laura. I think you know what I want to say.'

'Do I?' said Laura. She wasn't making it easy for him. He tried to find the right words but it mattered too much. His brain fogged.

'I love you,' he muttered with difficulty.

'You sound as if you're ashamed of it.'

'Do I? Good God, no, I'm not! But I'm horribly nervous, I'll admit that. This is the first time . . . I've never felt about anyone the way I feel about you.'

'*How do* you feel about me, exactly?' Laura said without mercy.

'I . . . I think you're the most wonderful, beautiful . . .' stammered Charles despairingly. 'Every time I'm alone with you it takes all my strength not to . . .' He bit his lip, staring at the sharp line of shadow across the sundial. He couldn't possibly tell her how he felt about her – he didn't know himself. A moment ago he had felt tender. Not any more. Remote, untroubled Laura. He had the sensation that she was watching him make a fool of himself as calmly and consideringly, damn her, as if he'd been a butterfly struggling on a pin and she had put him there. He wanted to haul her into his arms and bruise her mouth with his, to demolish her self-possession and somehow force her into returning his passion. Because he knew she didn't return it, not yet, and the realization was agonizing.

Laura sensed his confused and suppressed desire and found it exciting – and also exasperating, because like a true

Englishman he set so much store by controlling it. She had fully expected, as they walked through the wrought-iron gateway into the garden, that Charles was going to declare his feelings. Come to that, she had been expecting it for weeks. She knew perfectly well that he was in love with her, but until he actually said it in so many words, she had had to pretend not to be aware and it had been a sore test of her patience. She would have liked to provoke him into overstepping that invisible mark that gentlemen observed in their dealings with young ladies. He had done it just once, at the hospital, and it had been exhilarating, but since then he had been a model of propriety and it made her feel diminished in her power over him.

'Will you marry me?' blurted Charles.

Her first proposal. It should have been a wonderful event. She had imagined it a number of times in the weeks he had been at the Grange, had mentally scripted their exchanges up till the moment when he asked her to be his, just as she had done with Edward Allingham for all those years. The difference was that in rehearsing the scenes with Edward, she had always known what her answer would be. With Charles she didn't. He was handsome, he was sweet . . . but. . . .

. . . But today Edward Allingham was coming to lunch. She was over Edward. It had been a silly schoolgirl obsession which she had now grown out of and in any case he had demonstrated that he had absolutely no taste by becoming engaged to that very ordinary nurse. But all the same her heart had hammered at the news of his visit; her mouth had gone dry and something had moved in the pit of her stomach in the same shameful way that it had always done.

Decidedly today was not the best of days for Charles to make his proposal. He stood there, waiting for her answer, hopeful and afraid.

'I don't know,' said Laura. 'I'll have to think about it.'

Edward rode over from Hindhead on a rangy bay gelding.

257

'Nice-looking animal,' said Rupert, 'if a bit long in the tooth?'

'Yes, that's why the army exempted him from service when they were requisitioning last year,' said Edward.

'Bit like me, eh?' said Rupert with heavy good humour. 'Spirit is willing but the old frame's not up to it.' He slapped the gelding on the neck before passing the reins to Nichols, who led the bay into one of the empty stalls in the stable yard. In the next stall Plumbago turned his head and nipped viciously, and there was a brief flurry of rearing and snorting.

'Is it all right to leave him?' Edward said. 'He's not my horse, he's on loan from my uncle.'

'They'll settle down. Plumbago means no harm,' said Rupert. In this he was not strictly accurate. Plum was persistently anti-social. He had even had to suffer the indignity of a red ribbon tied at the top of his tail when out hunting, to warn the other riders of his tendency to kick, though Rupert had always contended that his mount only succumbed to this temptation when crowded by idiots.

'Well, if you're sure . . .' Edward said, unconvinced. 'Only I'd hate to take him home with any damage. Uncle Henry has volunteered as a special constable and he relies on Mackintosh to do his rounds.'

Laura, who had come out behind her father and had hung back with unusual reticence while he greeted the guest, went sensibly into the long building, emerging a few moments later to announce that she had moved the visiting horse further down the row and that he was now exchanging friendly whickerings with Blackie instead.

'There was no need—' said Rupert irritably, but Edward gave her a grateful smile.

'Why is he called Mackintosh?' Laura asked, to cover up the fact that the sight of Edward was making her feel breathless and light-headed.

'Oh, I expect it's because he's such a useful old thing and a steady goer in all weathers.'

The Brownlowes laughed at the joke, Rupert politely and

Laura because anything Edward said was wonderful. The fiction that she was over him had been sustainable – just – until she saw his face again. Already she was making frantic calculations inside her head about how long his visit could be made to last.

'Come inside and have some sherry,' said Rupert. 'And meet our house guest. Charles McKay of the Blues. You've met him, haven't you? At Alice and Hugh's wedding.'

'Yes,' said Edward, surprised. 'But I heard he and Hugh went out to Belgium together, and Hugh, of course—'

'Killed,' Rupert agreed. 'Yes. Too bad, too bad. And Charles was wounded, though not in the same incident. Bringing in some of his men from No Man's Land after a trench raid, under heavy fire. Might be a medal in it, I believe. Anyway, that's why he's here now, convalescing. Or at least, that's the ostensible reason,' he added, directing a roguish smile in the direction of his daughter. 'But I suspect there's rather more to it than that, hey, Laura?'

'Oh, *Pa*!' protested Laura, squirming with genuine anguish, which her father mistook for coyness.

'Well, time will tell,' said Rupert comfortably as he ushered his guest in through the back door. 'Don't mind coming in the back way, do you, my boy? Don't need to stand on ceremony with you, eh? You know us too well for that. Ah, Ferry,' he greeted the butler in the hall. 'Lunch in twenty minutes? And sherry now in the drawing room, please. The *good* sherry.'

It wasn't often that Rupert gave his guests the old amontillado, but Edward was a particular favourite of his. Nice-mannered, respectful young chap, thought Rupert. And if his political ambitions ever came to anything, potentially useful.

'The battalion's coming back to strength gradually, but it's been a slow process.' Over lunch, at his host's request, Edward was giving an account of his war experiences so far. 'They keep sending us drafts of men, but some of them are the wounded of last October at Gheluvelt, coming back, and to be honest they aren't up to it yet. We had to set up a special medical board to examine one lot and sent seventy per cent of them straight home to England.'

'Still,' said Rupert, 'it's cheering to know that they are so keen to get back to the action. That's the bulldog spirit for you.'

Edward was about to say that in some cases it might be the doctors who had judged the men fit who were the keen ones, rather than the soldiers themselves. Then he thought better of it. He sensed, correctly, that Rupert would prefer any account he might give to be amusing or stirring rather than accurate, and he was too habitually polite not to oblige. He noticed, too, that Charles McKay was being reticent about his own exploits. So he said nothing about the hardships of the weakened battalion manning waterlogged trenches near Givenchy in the icy rain, the steady draining of their numbers by snipers and shelling, the exhausting marchings to and fro in accordance with some dimly comprehended and soon-countermanded order. Instead, searching his memory for humorous anecdotes, he told his fellow-diners about finding a family of frogs in his boots in one particularly damp billet and about the idiot subaltern, fresh out from England, who'd made up some pills with ammonia and iodine crystals – which exploded with a loud bang when dried out.

'He dropped a couple on top of the stove when no one was looking. Everyone dived for cover thinking it was a whizz-bang – and when we crawled out from under the table, brushing the dust from our uniforms, there he was, looking smug. The captain was *not* amused.' He didn't add that the subaltern had died the following week in a mishap with an unstable hand grenade, having failed to learn in his short time in France that things that go bang are not to be played with.

Throughout lunch Edward was watching Charles McKay and Laura. He was curious to know whether Rupert's heavy hint about the pair had been justified, an interest partly prompted by self-protection.

He'd made light of it when Margaret drew his attention to

signs of infatuation on the part of Miss Brownlowe, that day at Oxford, but in retrospect it had explained a lot of Laura's behaviour over the years. Edward was not the type of young man who enjoyed collecting admiration from the fair sex. He'd had plenty of it, but it embarrassed him. He was engaged to Margaret and his loyalty, once given, was unshakeable, even though the relationship was currently so unsatisfactory. He was also kind-hearted and he hated the idea of Laura being unhappy because he couldn't return her feelings. It would be a relief, he thought, to learn that she had transferred her affections to the cavalryman.

If she had, she gave not the slightest sign of it during lunch.

'Pity I didn't know you were arriving on horseback,' Rupert mentioned, as the remains of the syllabub were cleared away by Joan and the cheeseboard set down in the centre of the table. 'Plumbago's desperately short of exercise. I have no time, and poor old Nichols finds him a bit of a handful these days. Laura doesn't, but Laura hates riding alone and she won't ride with Nichols on Blackie, she says that's too tedious for words . . . and of course, lately she's had other things on her mind.' Again he twinkled at his daughter. Charles McKay looked self-conscious but Laura kept her eyes on the pattern of roses on her plate and ignored the comment.

'I dare say I could give him a quick ride out for you, sir, though I have to be home before dark,' said Edward.

'Oh, I wouldn't put you to that trouble. I only meant we could have had a canter together. But now I've agreed to see a man from the Poor Law Committee at three. They want me to join the committee. No peace for the wicked,' said Rupert.

'So why don't I take Plumbago out with Edward and Mackintosh?' suggested Laura. 'Just for an hour or so.'

Edward felt a twinge of alarm and told himself not to be silly.

'What about your guest, my dear?' said Rupert.

'Charles won't mind, will you, Charles? You can write some letters.'

Edward glanced across the table. In fact, Charles was looking as though he minded quite a lot.

'Well,' said Rupert, puzzled by the vibrations in the air around him. Whatever was Laura up to now? Making young McKay jealous? Maybe he was being a bit slow in coming up to the mark? In which case, good for her! He raised his eyebrows at Edward. 'Say if you'd rather not,' he said.

'It sounds like a very pleasant idea,' Edward said, there being very little else that he could say in the circumstances. Laura pushed back her chair and tossed her napkin down on to the table beside her plate.

'I'll go and get changed,' she said.

'Laura!' protested Aunt Jessie faintly. Even her impulsive niece didn't normally leave the table while a meal with guests was in progress. But Laura only said that she didn't want any cheese or coffee, thank you, and continued on her way out of the room, leaving an uncomfortable silence behind her.

It took her half an hour of frantic preparation before she emerged from her room in a severely cut riding habit of black superfine wool with a high collar and Russian-style frogging on the jacket. It had been made for her before her departure for finishing school, and for a few worried moments she'd been afraid it wouldn't fit as she struggled with the looped cord fastenings. *Damn* Pa for dismissing Daisy. . . .

It occurred to her in passing that Daisy's baby must be almost due now. She made a mental note to ask Mrs Driver or Ferry whether they'd heard anything. Not that it was excusable, of course, to have a baby in the way that Daisy had done it, but all the same it would be nice to know if she was all right and if the baby was a boy or a girl. She might buy it a silver rattle or something. No, perhaps not a silver rattle. Something more practical.

The jacket, once fastened, fitted her perfectly. She tugged at the lace ruffle at the neck of her blouse so that it rose a snowy half-inch above the collar of the jacket. A little round cap with a feather completed the ensemble. Laura had a weakness for feathers in her cap.

'There!' she said, and bit her lips to make them redder, telling herself that this ride with Edward meant nothing, nothing at all, but she might as well look her best for it.

'Plum's pulling like a train. Shall we gallop?'

'If you like,' said Edward. Laura didn't appear to move in the saddle, but somehow she conveyed a signal to Plumbago that sent him streaking away across the valley with his long neck stretched out. Mackintosh followed at a more sensible pace for his age and the wind condition, and when Edward finally caught up with his companion on the fringe of the wood on the other side of the valley, she was riding her horse in calm figures of eight to cool him down gently.

'By jove, Miss Brownlowe, you can certainly ride!' said Edward with spontaneous admiration. Laura's lashes swept down over her sparkling eyes and she coloured at the compliment. Edward thought fleetingly how pretty she was, and realized that on some level he was attracted by her. It was purely physical, he had no intention of giving way to it, but he immediately felt guilty because by his own strict standards of loyalty to Margaret he shouldn't even have noticed Laura's prettiness.

'There are bluebells further into the wood. But the branches are a bit low for the horses. Shall we walk for a bit?' She had dismounted as she spoke and was already looping Plumbago's reins over the branch of a tree.

'All right,' said Edward. He experienced again a faint *frisson* of danger, though venturing on foot into a wood with Laura should be no more hazardous than riding with her outside one.

They strolled along a sandy footpath under the trees. The kick-pleated skirt of Laura's riding habit brushed over the long grass at the side of the path as she walked. Flicking a sideways glance towards her, Edward thought her expression mirrored his own tension.

'Here are the bluebells. Every year I get thrilled all over again by the sight of them. I always have, ever since Nanny used to bring Oliver and me out to pick them when we were small,' said Laura. 'They'd always wilted by the time we got them home, which seemed terribly sad.'

Edward admired the bluebells for a suitable length of time and wondered in passing whether Margaret liked flowers and if so, why he had never given her any. She was always so down-to-earth, that was why. It seemed to rule out extravagant gestures.

'I suppose we'd better get back to the horses,' he said eventually.

'I suppose so. Does Miss Churchill ride?' Laura asked as they picked their way back along the path.

'A bit. Not much.' He knew Margaret had owned a pony as a child, as children of her class were expected to, but it had been of the Blackie variety – an elderly plodder and not what Edward thought of as a 'proper' mount. If she rode now it was as a way of getting from one place to another, rather than for pleasure.

'Does she hunt?'

'No.'

'I expect she'll do a lot once you're married,' said Laura.

'I don't suppose so. She doesn't really like it.' The Reverend Henry Churchill was far too poor to keep hunters, Edward knew, and his daughter was basically opposed to blood sports anyway.

'It must be difficult when someone doesn't share your interests.'

'Margaret shares many of my interests,' Edward said curtly.

'But she isn't exactly from the same background, is she?'

Edward frowned. Margaret's dislike of activities that involved the killing of animals was one of the areas of potential friction between them, because Edward enjoyed his hunting and shooting and had no intention of giving them up. He was aware of the problem, but like most men his technique for dealing with relationship problems was to ignore them in the hope that they would go away. Laura's words probed in sensitive places.

'Not like you?' he said with a flash of anger. 'Is that what you mean? Look here, Miss Brownlowe. Laura. I'd like to make this clear. Margaret is my fiancée and I won't hear any criticism of her. And I don't have any interest at all in anyone else.'

Laura stood quite still for a moment, with her chin up. Then with a quick movement she scooped up a handful of skirt and stalked towards the horses.

'It's getting late,' she said, over her shoulder. 'You'll be wanting to get home.'

Edward's indignation collapsed. He'd distinctly felt that Laura was crowding him towards some sort of admission. Making a play for him, not to put too fine a point on it. But suppose he'd been wrong in his assumption? He'd been an arrogant ass. No wonder she was angry.

'Laura, I'm sorry if I've upset you. . . .'

'Why ever should I be upset?' said Laura, her flushed cheeks giving the lie to her words. 'I'm a bit puzzled by what you've just said, or rather why you felt you had to say it, but it doesn't matter to me at all.' She stood by her horse's head, unlooping the reins from the branch. 'Please would you help me to mount?'

Edward stooped, making a stirrup of his hands, and she sprang lightly up, arranging herself in the side saddle with practised efficiency.

'I'm so sorry Miss Churchill doesn't ride much. She probably doesn't realize what she's missing,' said Laura. 'Race you back.'

Plumbago streaked away like a Derby favourite and Edward mounted hastily, but Mackintosh wasn't up to the pace and Edward didn't attempt to match it. He watched Laura disappear into the distance, riding as if her neck meant nothing. She'd be lucky if her mount didn't put a foot in a rabbit hole, going at that speed, and come a cropper.

When he reached the stable yard at the Grange, there was no sign of Laura.

'She came back a few minutes ago, in a muck sweat,' said

Nichols. 'Leastways, Plumbago was in a muck sweat,' he amended. 'Will you be wanting to leave your horse here overnight, sir?'

'No, I must take him home. I'll hack him back very quietly,' Edward said in the face of Nichols' disapproval.

'In that case I'd better give him a rub down, sir, and throw a rug over him while you're saying your goodbyes to Mister Rupert.'

On reaching home, Laura had tossed her reins to a startled Nichols and gone straight to the drawing room, where she found Charles alone and reading a book.

'Charles, this morning you asked me to marry you and I said I'd think about it.'

'Yes?' said Charles, his mouth dry.

'I've thought about it. If your offer still stands, I would like to accept it.'

So when Edward came into the house to thank Rupert for the lunch and Laura for her company on the ride, he was confronted with the news of her engagement.

'And that,' Laura told herself, 'should scotch his conceited supposition that I care two pins for him!'

That she was being dishonest, and using Charles, and cheating herself, was something that she refused to acknowledge at the time.

Rupert was delighted by the news of his daughter's engagement; Charles McKay's family included at least two elderly bachelor uncles from whom Charles could justifiably be said to have expectations, not to mention his parents' very adequate financial status. But Jessie had some qualms, which she voiced privately to her niece in the drawing room on the day after the announcement.

'Laura, are you absolutely sure about this engagement? Forgive me, I don't want to intrude, but you are so very young to be committing yourself like this.'

'Ah well, you know how the saying goes – *Gather ye rosebuds while ye may*,' Laura said airily. 'At the rate the young men are getting themselves killed, I'd better take what I can, while I can, don't you think?'

'But do you love him?' Jessie said gently.

'*Love?*' Laura's laugh was artificial. 'Oh, love! Well, of course I'm mad about Charles. He's perfectly sweet, but even if he wasn't, surely anything's better than ending up as an old maid?'

. . . *Like you.* The words were unspoken but as clear to Jessie as if Laura had shrieked them at her. She said, with dignity, 'I do hope, then, that you will be very happy.'

Looking at her aunt's anxious face, with the patches of colour high on her cheekbones, Laura felt a belated pang of regret. It was tinged with irritation. No matter how awful you were to her, Aunt Jessie never bit back, and then you invariably felt bad about it afterwards. She sighed and said contritely, 'Thank you, Aunt Jessie. And thank you for all the good things you've done for me. You're a dear, really you are, and I'm sorry I'm unkind to you sometimes.' She kissed her aunt's cheek and went to join Charles in the garden, where she proceeded to salve her conscience and quieten her doubts about the wisdom of what she'd done by being very, very nice to him.

It was Jessie's turn to sigh. She wasn't quite sure what she'd hoped to achieve in broaching the subject with Laura, but one thing was sure: she had made a mess of it as usual. When would she ever find the right words? Yet she knew with certainty that Laura was making a mistake. Prompted by heaven knew what disappointment and wounded pride, she was rushing into a hasty engagement with someone to whom in the long term she was unlikely to find herself suited. Jessie had watched Laura now for nearly eight years and had observed that although her niece was too impatient and careless over her lessons to have shone at school, she had a brain at least as sharp as that of Oliver. And under her superficial vanity and self-centredness, there was a good heart waiting to be touched. One day, she was going to want to use that brain and that heart.

As for Charles McKay, Jessie suspected that though a pleasant enough young man and unarguably good-looking, he was not particularly bright. He had joined the army because his family expected it of him, he had pursued his military career conscientiously but without much ambition, he had gone to war and would 'do his bit' without complaint, and as soon as peace and the anticipated inheritance permitted, he would settle into being a quiet, unadventurous country gentleman with a pipe, a brace of gundogs and a copy of *The Times*. She was afraid he was going to find Laura a real handful.

In his first year at public school Oliver had hero-worshipped the Captain of the first eleven, Edward Allingham, opening batsman and fast bowler *par excellence*. His longing to impress his idol had prompted him to volunteer for the most perilous fielding positions like Silly Mid On or First Slip whenever Edward was lending a hand with the coaching. It had brought him some hard knocks, but the occasional 'Well done, young Brownlowe' had made it all worthwhile. Now, despite being a foot taller and sprouting the wherewithal for a beard, he felt the same desperate anxiety to please the object of his admiration. So when Acting Captain Forsythe needed a man to carry out some difficult or dangerous duty, Oliver was invariably first in line. He would have been disconcerted to find out how much of a headache this gave Forsythe, who was more interested in getting necessary tasks carried out efficiently and preserving the life of his new junior officer than in promoting Oliver's dreams of heroism.

It was the wish to be thought a good chap that made Oliver raise a hand when a driver galloped down to the billet late one afternoon with the news that the horses hitched to a water cart had done a bolt, dragged the cart off the road and ended up in a flooded shell hole nearby.

'We cut the traces and managed to get the horses out, but the cart needs someone to get a line round it.'

'I'll go and sort it out, shall I, sir?'

'All right,' said Forsythe. 'Better take a team of our men with you.'

To Oliver's disappointment, among the men who fell in behind him as he set out to the rescue of the water wagon were Griffin and his two fellow drivers Lockett and Chepstow. Since the incident on the night of his arrival, he had done his best to avoid Griffin and anyone else who'd witnessed their exchange.

The hole was the product of a howitzer shell and wide enough to hold a house. It was filled to within a foot of the brim with yellow-brown liquid, out of which only the tips of the cart shafts projected unpromisingly.

Oliver stripped off most of his uniform and tied one end of a rope round his waist, wishing the bolting horses had chosen a warmer day for it. Several of his men ranged themselves along the rope and lowered him cautiously over the rim of the hole with another coil of rope looped round his shoulder. The water was colder than he expected, making him gasp.

'All right, give me some free line,' he called, treading water. He took a deep breath, gauged where the wheels of the wagon ought to be, and dived.

It was like swimming in cold soup, impossible to see anything. After an eternity of groping and fumbling he managed to get a drag rope knotted around one front wheel. He shot to the surface, his lungs bursting, handed over the remains of the attached line and collected another rope. The second time, his legs tangled in his own tow line and for a few frantic seconds he thought he was drowning, but he kicked free, took another gulp of air at the surface and eventually got the second rope into place. As he towelled down and shrugged back into his tunic, he realized that from the vantage point of Hill 60, to the South, the German guns were beginning to pitch a stiff barrage.

'Better get this over with as quickly as possible.'

In the mud of the salient, manual hauling of heavy objects had become a daily occurrence. Rapidly, without discussion, the men formed into two teams and began to pull, leaning backwards into the drag, each new effort marked by a concerted gasp of 'Heave!'. The wagon, with a lurch, reared up out of the water and the men's boots tracked steadily back from the shell hole's edge.

'That's done the trick,' Oliver announced, satisfied, pushing filthy wet hair out of his eyes. Then he heard a screaming sound, like an express train hurtling closer, followed by the swish of something heavy falling and turning through the air. He stood frozen.

'Whizz-bang!' somebody shouted. Before Oliver's uncomprehending eyes, the two teams of hauliers abandoned their ropes and flung themselves flat on the ground. The cart slid back into the water, spreading ripples. Oliver stared. Something cannoned into him, sending him flying to the ground. He lay on his stomach, arms spread, winded. A khaki-clad arm across his shoulders kept him from rising.

Somewhere ahead there was an almighty explosion. A column of earth rose heavenwards and a wave of hot air struck his face, along with a considerable quantity of mud and bits of gravel. Instinctively he closed his eyes in the fraction of a second before the onslaught. Seconds after the blast, he dared to open them again.

He raised his head. Earth was still raining down. The man who was lying half on top of him rolled over and stood up stiffly: Griffin, whose face, spattered with mud and pin-points of blood where the flying grit had pierced the skin, must be a mirror of Oliver's own. Looking at the debris of earth and rock and metal fragments littering the ground around him, Oliver recognized reluctantly that the driver had probably saved his life.

Someone was screaming.

There was a new hole by the road, and close to its lip lay a khaki-clad figure thrashing uncontrollably from side to side. Oliver climbed to his feet and ran towards him.

The wounded man was Driver Chepstow. His legs were footless and the bloody scraps of his puttees and the shreds of his trousers flapped as he kicked and clawed at the air. As

Oliver reached the body he was already tugging Aunt Jessie's case of sedatives free from his breast pocket, but the most cursory glance at Chepstow told him that a lamell of morphine would never overcome this kind of pain. Chepstow's stomach was spurting blood like a punctured water pipe and what remained of his legs had been stripped of skin from the knees down. Fragments of unexploded gunpowder buried in the flesh were burning his flayed limbs like acid.

Lockett and Griffin pounded up, gasping. Chepstow screamed steadily, dragging air into his lung between each bellow. Lockett turned his back, his hands over his ears, his face contorted. Oliver uncapped the bottle of chloroform and began to spill liquid on to the lint wad of his field dressing with jerky, frantic movements.

'He's had it, sir,' said Griffin. 'You've got a gun. Put him out of his misery.'

'I can't,' said Oliver, his face pale. 'Bad for morale.'

'Sir,' said Griffin urgently, 'is it good for morale to let the men know that if they're hit, they'd be left in this kind of agony?'

'I don't know.' Oliver pressed the lint down over the wounded man's nose and mouth, holding it in place with difficulty because Chepstow's movements were so violent. 'It isn't my job to know. I'm doing what I can.'

The screaming, though muffled by the lint, continued with an animal intensity.

'For pity's sake, sir,' said Griffin. 'If he was a horse—'

'Shut up, Griffin.'

Chepstow thrust up one flailing hand and tore the chloroformed pad aside. With all his force, he shrieked.

'If you won't, let me,' said Griffin, white-lipped. Suddenly Oliver couldn't stand it. He thrust his revolver at the driver.

Griffin straightened up. He'd done this before, given the *coup de grâce*, at Néry, or on the Menin road. Only then it had been horses. The handle of the service revolver pressed into the fleshy pad below his thumb. The wounded man screamed on but the buffeting sound of it seemed to have

271

receded beyond a vibrating wall. Griffin stood with the barrel of the gun pointed directly at Chepstow's forehead. Sweat gathered on his brow.

He couldn't do it. He couldn't pull the trigger.

Oliver looked up into Griffin's face and silently tipped the chloroform bottle on to the wad of lint again. This time when he laid it across Chepstow's nose and mouth, there was less resistance. Gradually the screams turned to groans and then to silence. The subaltern removed the lint as a party of stretcher-bearers ran along the road towards them, bent double.

'Over here,' said Lockett, raising his arm.

'I think he's dead anyway,' said Oliver. Perhaps the chloroform had done it and not the shell. It was too much for his tired brain to contemplate. He stumbled away towards the verge and was sick. When he returned, Chepstow had been loaded on to a stretcher and was being carried away across the rough ground. Griffin was standing staring down at the soaked patch of earth where the man's mangled legs had been.

'I'm sorry,' said the driver, raising his head. 'I was out of line there, sir.' He passed the revolver back to Oliver, who restored it to its holster.

'It's all right,' said Oliver. 'Bloody war,' he added wearily. They exchanged a look which recognized that each had learnt something about the other. Griffin knew that Oliver, under stress, had been prepared to let him shoot Lockett to stop him screaming. Oliver knew that Griffin, having claimed the right of merciful execution, couldn't carry it out.

Griffin peeled off his tunic and held it out to the subaltern. 'You're cold, sir,' he said, standing in his shirtsleeves.

Belatedly, Oliver realized how violently he'd been trembling. He was grateful for the warmth of the extra tunic round his shoulders.

It was his most unnerving encounter yet with death. Once, seemingly a lifetime ago, he'd thought the old man by the railway path at Ash Green was a preparation for the Front. Wrong.

The pounding in his ears wasn't his own blood. It was the

guns. A big barrage of some kind, somewhere. In fact, though he did not yet know it, the Germans were launching an all-out assault on the stretch of the line running from Hill 60 to Langemarck and the French contingents near Langemarck and Pilckem were at that moment discovering the effects of chlorine gas. 22 August 1915. Second Battle of Ypres.

14

Daisy was cleaning the last of the knives with cut potato, finishing off with a piece of cork. She worked fast and furiously. She'd been feeling absolutely charged with energy all day, which made a welcome change from the swollen lethargy of the past couple of months and the recent acrobatic gyrations of the baby. Thankfully, these had quietened down of late and she proposed to make the most of her restored vigour while she could.

Already she'd cleaned the windows, smeary in the spring sunshine, and given the kitchen floor a good scrub. Now she'd finished the knives, she decided she'd go out into the garden. Those leggy old lilac bushes would be a sight in another month when they flowered, but you couldn't eat lilac and food was so dear. The Separation Allowance paid by the army during Robert's absence was coming through regularly now, and it had even been increased in March in recognition of the soaring cost of living, but it was still much lower than the pay packet he'd brought home from the Dennis works and Daisy felt very conscious of having added a mouth to be fed to the family budget, with yet another due shortly. The more of the little garden that could be turned over to food production, the better. She'd root the bushes out and dig the ground up ready for potatoes.

The garden was narrow, with a wavering paling fence all down one side. The other side was partly bounded by the scullery-with-boxroom-over that jutted out at right angles from the main house and, leaning against it, accessible only from the yard, stood the coal shed, the garden store and the 'convenience' which had been installed around the turn of the century when the sewage works opened up in Guildford. This

274

was still much less 'convenient' than the flower-patterned china thrones of Maple Grange in their pretty rooms with stained glass windows and embossed tiles from the William de Morgan company, but it was considerably more hygienic than the hole in the ground covered over with a brick plinth and a wooden bench seat, which it had replaced.

As a small girl, Daisy had hated to venture out at night to the blackness of the sheds in the yard, afraid of encountering one of the long-legged racing spiders that lurked in their recesses. Nowadays she was used to spiders. She'd seen plenty of them in the murky basement regions of the house where she'd been a servant before she moved to Maple Grange. Even so, she unconsciously braced herself as she unlatched the door into the narrow shed next to the WC, which held the garden tools and the tin bath in which the Colindale family had their Friday night all-over wash in front of the kitchen fire.

To get at the tool she most wanted, a wooden-handled sickle, Daisy had to shift the bath to one side. For once, nothing scuttled out from under it and she expelled a sigh of relief. At the Grange, she recalled nostalgically, there had been proper indoor bathrooms – even one for the servants' use, though the sheer number of those using it had meant a rota which had to be strictly observed. Not just having a bath when you felt like it.

That, Daisy thought, was her definition of luxury. Being able to take a bath in privacy any old time you liked, as Mr Rupert could do, and having someone else to mop up the scum and the soapsuds afterwards, and deal with the soggy towels . . . not much chance of that if you weren't born into the gentry.

She selected a fork along with the sickle and advanced on the lilacs, hardening her heart to the memory of fragrant blue-purple panicles of blossom. She couldn't afford to give them one more flowering or it would be too late to set in the potatoes. Determinedly, she grasped a handful of bush, but as she raised the sickle a wave of cramp spread across her stomach, making her gasp. She dropped the tool and bent forward, her hands pressing at her sides.

'You've started!' Louella had been watching from the window. She hurried down the path, with Mrs Colindale following more slowly behind her.

'No, it's not due for nearly another week,' Daisy said, taking shallow breaths.

'Babies come when they're ready,' said her mother prosaically. 'I thought this one was on its way when you came over so busy. That's always a sign.'

Gradually the cramp ebbed away, but Mrs Colindale adhered firmly to her diagnosis that Daisy had gone into labour and that consequently the lilacs must be reprieved for the time being. In this she was partly influenced by sentimental considerations that she would not have dreamed of voicing: her Harry had planted those lilacs the year they were married, and had placed a vaseful of them by the bed when young Robert was born. She had seen the sense of potatoes instead, but her heart had cried out against the destruction of the bushes, and now it seemed that fate was on her side in the matter.

Between them, Louella and Mrs Colindale marched a protesting Daisy into the house and deposited her in the Windsor chair by the kitchen stove, just as a second spasm tightened its iron fingers inside her pelvic cradle.

'Louella, go and tell Mrs Randall,' Mrs Colindale instructed, already poking vigorously at the glowing coals behind the bars of the range in readiness for the heating of water. 'I dare say it'll be hours yet, but we may as well make sure she's available when the time comes.'

Mrs Randall was Ma Turner's opposite number in the field of pregnancy. Where Ma Turner unofficially helped babies out of the world, Mrs Randall helped them in, though for the past five years she had done so at the risk of prosecution. Nowadays all practising midwives were supposed to be inspected and certified by the county council, but Mrs Randall had never bothered to apply for the seal of approval, on principle. She knew practically all there was to know about childbirth and her knowledge was derived, not from books but from a lifetime's experience. How could some meddling busybody of a male official presume to judge her competence?

'I still think we ought to get the doctor,' said Louella. 'Or at least a proper, registered midwife.' But she was outvoted. Mrs Colindale didn't approve of anything so highfaluting and newfangled as a certified medical practitioner, and at fifteen shillings per confinement Daisy couldn't afford one.

'Half a pound of twopenny rice, half a pound of treacle. . . .' Daisy recited nursery rhymes and snatches of poetry inside her head. Anything to distract herself from the pain in her abdomen. The trouble was that as each new spasm surged over her, it forced the words from her mind, leaving her floundering. Evening had come, night had fallen as the contractions got stronger. 'Pop Goes the Weasel . . . *Pop Goes the Weasel*. . . .'

Another contraction. She felt as if she were struggling on the point of a lance. As Louella laid a cool flannel across her sister-in-law's sweat-drenched forehead, Daisy dredged up another fragment of verse from her memory:

'And some they mounted the black steed
And some they mounted the brown
But Janet mounted the milk-white steed
To ride foremost through the town.

O who will guide your horse, Janet?
O who will guide him best?
O who but Willie, my true-love?
He kens I love him best. . . .'

Out of the blue the words conjured up the image of Will Griffin, bending at Starbright's side in the stable yard at Maple Grange. Her breathing quietened. Griffin. Where was he now? she wondered. Was his body rotting in the ground in one of

277

those far-off places that she couldn't pronounce, his blood all spilled and wasted like Arthur's had been?

She was having Arthur's baby at this very moment and yet another man had crept into her mind. Ashamed, Daisy turned her head aside on the pillow as yet another irresistible muscle cramp took hold. She heard Mrs Randall's words of encouragement.

'I can see its head coming. Here we go, dear. Deep breath and *push*.'

It was a girl, they told Daisy a few minutes later.

'One of the easiest birthings I've ever seen,' added Mrs Randall. Daisy smiled weakly. Now it was over, she was prepared to accept that it hadn't been too bad, in spite of all the dire things she'd heard beforehand from her mother about the agony involved. She cradled the small bundle against her, its damp, puce and wrinkled face muffled by the shawl that had come courtesy of Jessie Brownlowe and the Soldiers' and Sailors' Wives Association.

'Well, you were lucky,' said Mrs Colindale. 'With my first I was thirty hours in labour.'

Daisy hardly heard her. Awed, she touched the tip of one forefinger to the baby's face to move aside the shawl. Instinctively the small thing turned its unfocused gaze at the contact and pushed and nuzzled.

'Let her feed,' said Mrs Randall. 'It'll bring down your milk, dear.'

Daisy slipped aside the fabric at the open neck of her nightgown and the tiny mouth closed upon a nipple. A feeling of utter contentment flooded through Daisy.

'What are you going to call her?' Louella said from the chair beside the bed.

'I don't know. I hadn't made up my mind.'

'I thought "Harriet",' said Mrs Colindale. 'After your father.'

Her expression was softer than Daisy could remember it. If a name could help reconcile the baby's grandmother to her bastard status, it seemed a small price to pay.

'All right. *Harriet*,' said Daisy.

By the time Harriet Colindale was one month old, fifty-nine thousand men had been killed or wounded in the struggle for Ypres. The town itself was a ruin, its ancient stone houses demolished by a ceaseless rain of artillery fire, its medieval Cloth Hall no more than a gaunt skeleton rearing out of a heap of rubble. The Germans held all the high ground of the Passchendaele Ridge to the North and the Messines Ridge to the South, and the line of the salient had been forced back to a flat curve within a few kilometres of the town walls and the Menin gate. There it held, and the overstretched enemy accepted that for the time being there would be no break-through to the Channel ports.

'Things have been a bit hot here,' wrote Oliver Brownlowe to Claire Lawrence. 'But they've calmed down now.' He was rather pleased with the understatement. There was no need to labour the point about the dangers of the last few weeks. The casualty figures spoke for themselves.

Oliver had settled in. You could tell by the merest glance that the young officer was a different man from the starchy subaltern who'd arrived at the Front at the end of the winter, bleating about death or glory. These days his attire had been adjusted from the smart to the practical. Drooping below the edge of his tunic, Oliver wore a knitted cardigan, wonderfully striped, which would probably have given Lord Kitchener apoplexy if he saw it on a representative of his smart New Army. It had been acquired in an off-duty moment in 'Pop', which was how the soldiers familiarly referred to the town of Poperinghe, and had become known in the region as Brown-lowe's Coat Of Many Colours. Wound about his neck was a muffler with ragged fringes and several sinister stains which owed their origins to the German howitzer gunners' habit of sending 5.9 shells over while Oliver was drinking his tea. His face was dirty and he hadn't shaved for a week. He had acquired a pipe, though he had not yet learned how to keep it lit. The other day, to his pride and joy, a new arrival with the battery had assumed he must be an Old Contemptible of the original BEF.

One further source of satisfaction was that he seemed to have come to a tacit understanding with Driver Griffin. In the crowded days that followed the abortive attempt to rescue the water cart, Griffin had come to acknowledge that for a cosseted sprig of the gentry, Oliver had some hitherto unsuspected pluck. And Oliver, secure in the knowledge that his father's groom no longer viewed him with scorn, was able in return to accord the driver recognition for his abilities.

One practical manifestation of this new entente cordiale was that Griffin and his partner in crime, Lockett, had obtained a horse for Oliver. Gunner subalterns were supposed to have two horses and a groom to look after them, but ever since his arrival Oliver had been without a regular horse. One of his predecessor's mounts had been wounded by the same shrapnel bomb as its rider and had been taken away for treatment by the army vets, and the other one had been quietly stolen by another battery before the replacement subaltern could arrive to lay claim to it. Pending a new draft of remounts, Oliver had had to borrow any nag that was going and he had rather resented the indignity.

One May morning he emerged from his billet to find a grinning Lockett on the doorstep, holding the reins of a pretty bay mare.

'We've won you a horse, sir. We 'eard you were short, so when we came by this one we thought of you.'

'Hmmm,' said Oliver. By now he was familiar with the concept of 'winning', which was an euphemism for stealing. 'Who's "we"?'

'Griffin and me, sir.'

'Where did you find her?'

'Well, sir, there was a pack of remounts going by last night, and I suppose a couple of them must've broken loose. We caught this one round the back of the horse lines this morning. D'you reckon she'll do, sir?'

'She looks very nice. But won't somebody come looking

for her?' Oliver stroked the mare's nose, summing up her conformation. Nice clean hocks, intelligent eyes. A little on the light side for him, but he thought she'd make a cracking good ride. His hand felt sticky, and on inspection he discovered that a dark brown substance had transferred itself to his fingers. 'Boot polish?' he hazarded.

'That's right, sir. Just for the time being. She's got a little white wheat ear on her forehead, you see, quite distinctive. And Griffin's changed the number on her hooves, so that's all right.'

'Hmmm,' repeated Oliver, visualizing the scene: the horses trotting by, with too few drovers to supervise them; the shadowy figures of a battery driver or two slipping in amongst them; the wielding of a knife on a lead rein and the spiriting away of a likely looking mare. All done with the silent efficiency that marked Griffin's other activities.

The mare nibbled softly at the palm of his hand, her breath warm. He thought she was a peace offering from the former groom, and a very adequate one at that. Trust a gypsy type like Griffin to know how to rustle a horse.

'Poor old Magnus,' said Claire. 'Just when he's got over pining for Oliver, I'm leaving him too. I'll have to give him one of my old shoes to chew to cheer him up, along with that cricket boot of Oliver's.'

Laura was reminded that she hadn't yet written to tell her brother about the boot, which she had dug out of a school trunk stored in one of the attics at Maple Grange. Claire had been persistent in her pleas for some discarded item of clothing with Oliver's scent attached to it, to console Magnus for the disappearance of his owner, and Laura had thought the boot, long outgrown but still undeniably smelling of Oliver, would never be missed. But after she had handed it over, it had occurred to her that it might be a precious childhood talisman, possibly a memento of his first century for the school eleven or some equally earth-shaking occasion.

'Will you miss me, Magnus? Never mind, it can't be

helped,' said Claire, fondling the mongrel's ears as he gnawed ecstatically at the boot. 'Mother will take care of you, won't she?' She turned to Laura. 'Did you hear,' she said, 'that some beastly person was going round the London parks, just before the war began, pouring petrol over German shepherd dogs and dachshunds and setting them alight? As if they could help their origins! Honestly, people go on about the atrocities of the enemy, but some of our own people are just as bad!'

Laura said vaguely that there were beastly people everywhere. She wished that her visitor would go home. Charles had gone back to his regiment yesterday and she was feeling dismal and headachey with anticlimax. The excitement of the engagement had pumped her up for the last few days, but now that he had gone, doubts about the wisdom and decency of her conduct were beginning to surface. She wanted to be alone to think the situation over, and she was finding Claire's energetic presence distinctly wearing.

'What am I thinking of? I haven't congratulated you on your engagement, Laura. But then you haven't mentioned it either. Is there a reason for this maidenly reticence?'

'How did you know about it?' said Laura, surprised.

'Saw it in *The Times*.'

Pa must have sent in the announcement, Laura supposed. Or Charles' family. There had been a hurried trip to Inverness-shire before he left, to introduce Laura to her prospective in-laws. They had been kind and welcoming and had told her that having met her, they perfectly understood why Charles had chosen to spend his convalescent weeks in Surrey rather than come home. Laura had liked them very well . . . but she couldn't imagine a future spent in the Highlands, which it had dawned on her was a distinct possibility if she married Charles. And it made her feel uneasy, the speed with which everything was going ahead. She'd said *Yes* to Charles in an impulsive moment and now all the world and his wife knew, and Charles had begun to treat her like his affianced bride. She was still on a pedestal as far as he was concerned, but somehow the pedestal had been lowered. He'd kissed her goodbye with an air of possession and called her 'Darling'.

'I must say I'm surprised,' said Claire. 'I didn't think he was your type.'

'Why not?'

'The only time I met him, he seemed rather too slavishly devoted to you to appeal. He's not at all like Edward Allingham.'

'That's the attraction,' snapped Laura.

'Well, congratulations anyway. Now you're an engaged woman, does that mean you can chaperone me?'

'No one can chaperone you, Claire, you're far too wilful.'

Claire smiled, immune to insult. 'That's what Mother says. Anyway, Laura, the other thing I came to say, apart from the congratulations of course, is that we've both passed our nursing examinations wtih flying colours and now we're eligible to apply as VADs.'

'Oh.'

'You don't sound very thrilled.'

'To be honest,' said Laura, 'I don't think I'd make a very good VAD.'

'Oh, nonsense, you'll be excellent.' Claire brushed the comment aside. 'I'm hoping to go to Clandon, then I can still get home to keep an eye on Magnus occasionally and I'll be on the spot when Oliver comes back on leave. I'm applying tomorrow. Will you come too?'

'I don't think so,' said Laura.

'Why not?'

'I told you. I don't want to be a VAD,' said Laura. Claire stared at her disbelievingly.

'But you must! It won't be nearly so much fun without you. You can't let me down now Laura, I'll never forgive you if you do.'

It was bewildering to Laura that she could have been so much in charge with Charles – up until the moment when she'd accepted him, anyway – yet with Claire Lawrence she was always the follower. They seemed to have set the pattern in their schooldays and however hard Laura tried to assert herself, she had a sensation that Claire had her on the slide, like the loser in a tug of war, and that nothing she said would save her now.

She was right. She could no more withstand Claire's determination than Oliver had been able to. By June they were at Clandon.

'Nurse Brownlowe, isn't it?'

'Yes, Sister.'

'Fetch a bucket and cloth and clean up this floor.'

Laura scowled after the departing back of Sister, who at that moment seemed to her to bear a sinister resemblance to the hated Mrs Snelling of her earlier training days. She was standing in the middle of the ward kitchen which had been partitioned off from one of the staircase halls next to the great entrance hall. The floor here, as in the main hall, was in pale-grey veined marble. It was covered in footmarks. The kitchen was the way through to all the other rooms on that side of the ground floor: it was raining outside, the grey marble showed the tracks of everyone who walked across it and Laura had already wiped it over with a wet cloth four times this morning, on her hands and knees. Her hands were red-knuckled and her back ached. Nowadays she understood only too well the comment from the VAD whom she'd met when she first visited Charles, about the staircase carving being difficult to polish.

She was sick and tired of being treated like a scullery maid. Not for the first time since her arrival, Laura considered making a bolt for it, home to Maple Grange. It would mean facing Pa and Aunt Jessie, of course. Pa had been pleased with her for volunteering, so pleased that he had given her a diamond-and-ruby brooch as a reward, pinning it to the front of her jacket like a decoration for valour and calling her a good girl . . . but oddly enough it was the prospect of explaining her retreat to Aunt Jessie that kept Laura at Clandon. Aunt Jessie didn't give any jewellery, she had none to give. 'Well done, Laura,' was all she had said, in her quiet voice, but in a way that Laura didn't fully understand, lately it was as if her aunt had come to represent the standards to which she felt she must hold. Disappoint Aunt Jessie, she felt, and she would be letting herself down.

'Hurry up, Nurse. You haven't got all day. It's almost time to do the patients' morning tea.' It was Sister Soames back again, the buff labels from last night's convoy of new arrivals in her hands. Her lips were pursed with concentration as she sorted through the labels that briefly categorized their injuries and the treatment received so far. Occasionally her eyes narrowed as she came across a particularly bad case.

Laura fetched the bucket and cloth as instructed. At least she wasn't going to be the one who stood by, later this morning, holding the stump of a leg as the surgeon applied the first dressing after an amputation. Sister might well be.

From the old nursery on the top floor at Clandon Park where Claire and Laura shared a room with three other VADs, there were eighty back stairs to the ground floor, a hundred and five to the basement. The girls who 'lived in' were privileged because it gave them a precious extra half hour or so in bed, compared with the others who came in from their billets in the surrounding villages by ambulance. And yet Laura was always rushing to be punctual. Every morning she flew down the stairs and along the landings, round and round the stairwell, fastening her apron and cuffs as she ran. To be late for breakfast was regarded as disgraceful and Laura, who felt herself to be the least valued of the VAD nurses, needed no extra sources of shame.

Breakfast was at seven in the basement kitchen with its vaulted ceiling and its old-fashioned stove which would have given Mrs Driver forty fits; it entailed a hurried taking-in of necessary sustenance, not the leisured meal with servants in attendance that had been the normal experience of many of the girls. Then came the task, allocated to the newest recruits, of preparing the breakfasts of the patients.

'If I survive my time here,' said Claire, dropping the last of nearly a gross of pungent kippers into the boiling water of a vast cauldron, 'I swear that I'll never look at another kipper.'

Laura didn't answer. It was her turn to empty the wire traps that were dotted around the scrubbed brick floors of the many-roomed basement area to keep the resident rat population under control, and she was trying to blank out all conscious thought because that was the only way she could carry out the procedure. If she once let herself imagine what would be waiting for her, she knew she couldn't do it. Stiff corpses with bared teeth and dull, clouded eyes, or worse, not quite dead – eyes still bright, paws still twitching. . . .

'Claire, it's my turn to do the traps. I suppose you wouldn't be an absolute angel . . . ?'

'Certainly not.' Claire didn't mind the rats, or said she didn't, but she felt it was character-forming for Laura to learn to live with the tasks that were her lot as a VAD. 'If you don't do it, you'll never get used to it, will you? Anyway, I haven't very much time before I have to help with the fomentations.'

Claire was good at nursing, perhaps because she had less imagination than Laura about what it felt like to be on the receiving end of her ministrations. Brisk and unqueasy, she was already being allowed to help the 'proper' nurses with treatment more skilled than the rubbing of embrocation into backs – which was the limit, so far, of Laura's progress beyond bed-making and general skivvying. It was thanks to her partnering with useful and dependable Claire, Laura suspected, that she was lodged in the enviable nursery quarters. But there remained the rat traps.

'Shall we go into Guildford this afternoon?' Claire asked as she scooped cooked kippers out of the boiling water and slid them on to the stacked plates. 'It's our afternoon off, don't forget.'

As if Laura could. She'd been counting the days. 'All right. I'll meet you out in the park shall I?'

'I'd rather you met me upstairs,' said Claire. 'That Australian Lewis gunner who came in last week, the one who

286

keeps sending me poetry . . . he's on his feet again now, and if I come down through his ward on my own, he's apt to make a grab.'

Laura hooted with delight. 'Wonderful! I wouldn't *dream* of interfering with your little romance, Claire. I wonder what Oliver will make of it?'

'You wouldn't tell him?' said Claire, turning pale.

'I might not,' said Laura, considering. 'It all depends how I'm feeling after I've done the rat traps.'

She waited.

'Oh, all right,' said Claire reluctantly. 'I'll do them while you finish the breakfasts. Just this once. So long as you swear you won't mention the Australian to Oliver.'

On their afternoons off, the VAD girls tended to ride in by ambulance to Guildford where they could stock up on delicacies like Bovril, biscuits and potted meat to supplement the rather lean diet on offer at the hospital.

'. . . And a Tommies' Cooker.' Claire had made a shopping list which, besides food, included a practical present for Oliver.

'What on earth is that?' Laura said.

'Solidified methylated spirits in a tin, with a collapsible stand. Some of the men on the wards say they're a godsend in the trenches,' she explained to Laura. 'It means they can heat up water for hot drinks.'

'Oliver isn't in the trenches.'

'He is sometimes, when he's on Observation Post duty.'

Oliver's letters to Claire were clearly more informative than those to his sister – which was perfectly understandable. Laura, after all, had letters from Charles at least as detailed. But she wished she'd thought of the Tommies' Cooker.

A shop stocking the desired article proved hard to find. They trekked in vain up and down both sides of the granite-paved High Street, and Laura was ready to abandon the quest as they paused by the Tunsgate arch. She heaved an exhausted sigh, then sniffed again.

'Claire, you stink of ether.'

287

'I know,' said Claire smugly. 'I sprinkled some on before I came out.'

'What on earth for?' Laura, in contrast, had tried in vain to erase all traces of the odour of hospital with soap and scent.

'I'm a nurse. I'm dealing with the wounded. I'm proud of it.'

For the first time, Laura noticed that Claire had somehow bleached her apron to fade the Red Cross emblem on the front. She looked like a long-serving, hardened VAD and beside her, Laura looked – and smelled – like a novice. There were times when Laura detested her friend.

'Oh, look,' said Claire. 'Isn't that Victoria?'

On the far side of the street under the clock, Victoria Duffus, last seen at Laura's party, was engaged in hot discussion with a young man in a Norfolk jacket. As they watched, she pushed something into his hand, turned her back on him and walked quickly across the road towards them.

'Whatever is Victoria up to? Surely not an assignation?' said Claire intrigued. She waved. Victoria, recognizing them belatedly, came up with her cheeks burning with indignation.

'The language of some people! He ought to be ashamed of himself!'

'Who is he?' said Laura.

'I don't know! The only thing I do know is that he isn't in the army, and when I asked him why not, he said it was none of my business in the rudest possible way.'

'But why on earth were you asking?' Claire said. Then she saw what Victoria held in her hands. 'Feathers! Oh, Victoria, you aren't in the White Feather League, are you?'

'As a matter of fact I am,' said Victoria. 'My brother has joined up. And my cousin Wilfred. Wilfred didn't even wait for a commission, he joined the Artists' Rifles as a private rather than hang back. It was rather a nuisance, actually,' she added, frowning, 'because some hotels and restaurants wouldn't take bookings from Other Ranks, only officers, which limited the places where we could all meet up. But he's in France now and he's certainly doing his bit. And it makes my blood boil that because shirkers like that chap I just spoke to won't do *their* bit, boys like Wilfred and Reggie have to take twice the hardship and twice the danger to make up for them.'

'Still,' said Claire, 'I'm not sure about this feather business. Some people can't volunteer, because of their health, or their family responsibilities, or because their occupation is too vital and their employers won't let them go. And some people genuinely in all conscience believe that war is evil, whoever you fight against. It must be awfully embarrassing for them if they're confronted by someone waving feathers.'

'Then they can explain,' said Victoria. 'I gave that fellow every chance to explain and all he did was swear at me. No, he was definitely a shirker, and men like him should be shown how disgraceful their behaviour is by being forced to accept the badge of shame. Don't you think so, Laura?'

'I suppose so,' said Laura. She wasn't sure where she stood on the matter, and nor, probably, was Claire. But Claire and Victoria had clashed at school and could not be expected to agree on anything now.

'Good! Then you can help me to hand these out,' said Victoria. 'It's better if there are more of us, it means they can't intimidate or ignore us so easily. Phyllis Morris was with me, but she's gone over to North Street to cover more territory, so it'll be super to have you instead.'

'Count me out. I've an errand to run. I'll see you here a bit later, Laura.' Claire prepared to leave them to it. Laura threw her friend a look of agonized supplication, but it was too late. Claire was already walking briskly down the street in her blue cotton uniform with the VAD cloak around her shoulders.

'Claire was always a bit unsound about patriotic considerations,' said Victoria. 'But you'll help won't you, Laura?'

'What do I have to do?' said Laura reluctantly.

'Just keep an eye out for young, fit chaps who ought to be in the army and aren't. Take that fellow, for instance. He should be in uniform.'

Laura followed the direction of Victoria's pointing finger

and saw a familiar figure, brown-haired and angular, striding down the street, hands in pockets and sunk in thought.

'Oh, it's James,' she said.

'Do you know him?'

'Yes,' said Laura. 'He's a friend. That is, he used to be a friend of my brother Oliver.'

'Well, you give him a feather then,' said Victoria.

'Oh, no. I'd rather you did.' Laura had not bargained for confronting anyone she knew. But Victoria thrust a feather towards her impatiently.

'No, it'll be much more effective if it comes from you. More shaming. Go on.'

Laura accepted the feather reluctantly. James had altered since she'd last seen him a year ago at Alice's wedding. His figure had filled out a little from stick-insect-thin to lean. There was a faint blurring of golden-brown stubble on his jaw. She supposed even schoolboy acquaintances had to grow up eventually. She stepped forward with Victoria's badge of shame held unobtrusively at her side, wishing herself any-where else. But Victoria *was* right she reminded herself. A young man like James ought to be in uniform, not strolling round Guildford in a grey striped flannel suit and leaving it to others, like Charles and Oliver and his own brother Edward, to shoulder the burden.

'James!' she said.

'Oh.' Her voice jolted him from his introspection. He hastily removed his hands from his pockets and held one out to her. On the slope of the street he seemed to tower above her.

'Hullo Laura,' he said. His face under the nondescript fringe of brown hair lit up with pleasure. 'It's been ages since—'

'Never mind that.' Ignoring the outstretched hand, Laura cut him short, conscious of Victoria Duffus' expectant eyes on them both. 'Have you enlisted in the army yet?'

'No,' said James, puzzled, beginning to take in the aggress-iveness of her manner. 'How are you? How's Oliver? I haven't heard anything for ages. Are you busy at the moment? We could go and have some tea and catch up on news.'

'Do you have any intention of joining the army?' Laura demanded. The colour began to mount in James' face as he recognized the purpose of her questions. He gave her a long, truculent stare and stuck his hands back into his pockets.

'No,' he said. 'Though there is a reason for that actually.'

'Are you unfit? Have you been turned down by the Medical Board?'

'No.'

'Then take this! You deserve it.' Laura had intended to hand him the feather, but found she was at a loss now that his hands were out of sight. She thought she had better push the quill into the top buttonhole of his open jacket and stepped up to him with that intention, but found her wrist caught and held.

'Thank you for this token of your opinion of me,' said James. Still holding her wrist with one hand, he took the white feather between his forefinger and thumb and studied it. Then he released her and transferred the feather into the palm of his other hand, closing his fingers over it to stop the breeze from snatching it away. The expression in his eyes was difficult to read, but it wasn't shame.

'James Allingham,' said Laura, embarrassed and angry at the fiasco of the presentation, aware that Victoria must be thinking her a fool for the mess she had made of it. 'If you think that I or any decent girl would take tea with a – a *shirker*, then you are very much mistaken.'

'None but the brave deserves the fair. Eh?' said James softly.

'I beg your pardon?'

'Dryden,' said James. 'I was quoting a line from Dryden. You're an idiot, Laura,' he added. 'Stop striking dramatic poses and take some note of what's really happening around you.'

Unclosing his fingers, he released the feather. It drifted downhill on the breeze as James stepped round Laura's stiff, furious figure and walked away down the High Street. She was left with a keyed-up, unsatisfied feeling. She didn't know what she'd anticipated – maybe some attempt at a defence on his part, some dialogue in which she could have convinced him where his duty lay. Somehow she had not expected him to take the insulting token so calmly and contemptuously, or to leave her so abruptly. Her cheeks burned.

'That's right,' said Victoria. 'You told him. Good for you!'

'I don't know,' said Laura uncertainly. 'There was something. . . .'

'Success!' said Claire's voice behind them. Laura turned. Claire was flourishing a parcel wrapped in brown paper. 'One Kampite Tommies' Cooker complete with refill blocks. I asked an old lady who knew exactly the place, she'd just bought one herself for her nephew. Are you going to carry on sorting out the tardy heroes with Victoria, or shall we go for some tea? Wasn't that James Allingham?' she added as an afterthought.

'Yes,' said Laura. In the distance James had crossed the road and was about to disappear down Swan Lane. His hand had been warm, she was remembering illogically, the fingers strong. No longer a schoolboy . . . so he really had no excuse for not having joined up by now! she told herself, trying to overcome the feeling that she had done something wrong.

'I suppose he's back to collect his medal. They get a fortnight's leave don't they, along with the investiture?'

'*Medal?*' Laura echoed. The sinking feeling deepened.

'DFC. I saw it in the *Advertiser* last week, didn't you?'

'But he said he wasn't in the army,' quavered Laura.

'That's right. The Distinguished Flying Cross is for airmen, dear. He's in the Royal Flying Corps. Quite an ace, I believe – five victories in his first few weeks at the Front. Didn't you know?' Claire studied Laura's dismayed expression. 'Oh dear,' she said with heartless amusement. 'You didn't. Oh, Laura, *don't* say you've given him a white feather!'

Forsythe's acting captaincy had been confirmed and the

battery had been supplied with replacement guns. At the same time they were moved south to a quieter sector of the line for a spell away from the hazards of Hellfire corner. Here the shelling was comparatively desultory. Nobody complained of boredom.

Driver Lockett's girl, endlessly concerned for his welfare, had sent him a packet of two hundred and fifty Black Cat cigarettes to supplement the fifty a day which were the army ration for men in front-line service. Along with the cigarettes, the makers included a free gift to the troops, a phrase book to facilitate their dealings with the local peasantry.

'Excoosay mwa mis-sure, je shersh dew pan,' Lockett rehearsed phonetically, his forehead creased with effort. The buying of bread from a farmer was theoretically possible. The French and Belgian farmers were still phlegmatically working their acres on the edge of the battlefields, there being a tacit agreement between the opposing armies that they would confine their shelling to a band of about three miles either side of the lines. Here in this relatively inactive section where the soldiers were separated by hundreds of yards of No Man's Land, the range had been further decreased and the gun teams passed horses working the ploughed furrows and women feeding chickens as if the war were only a nasty rumour and the thunder of the guns a distant storm.

Lockett tried his phrase book on the farmer down the road from the horse lines and returned with an air of exultation.

'Did you get some?' asked Griffin. Fresh French bread would make a welcome change from the iron-hard biscuits which had to be smashed with the butt of a rifle and soaked in water to render them edible.

'No,' said Lockett, momentarily deflated. The book, he had discovered, told you how to ask for bread but it didn't tell you how to interpret the farmer's idiomatic response. Comprehending that was down to sign language. This farmer's signs being particularly expressive, Lockett had gathered that the man hadn't any bread, that Lockett's misbegotten friends had stolen it all yesterday, and that if any more Tommies came around leering at his daughter their lives would be in danger. This latter information he had conveyed with a dramatic scoop of his finger from ear to ear.

Lockett was considerably younger and fitter than the farmer, so he wasn't impressed by the threat. He was more preoccupied by the fact that the farmer's daughter, hovering in the background, seemed less averse than her father had suggested to an admiring glance from a soldier.

'Cor, she was a smasher,' he reported, sketching a shape in the air with his hands. With Madeleine, too, he had overcome the language barrier when he'd encountered her again by the gate as he was leaving her father's property. For two hundred and fifty Black Cats she'd be happy to make a rendezvous. She'd even bring a friend, if wanted.

'How about it, Griff? Fancy a bit of *parlez-vous*?'

'No. Thanks all the same,' said Griffin, feeling a passing sympathy for Lockett's girl at home who had unwittingly supplied him with the wherewithal for his proposed entertainment.

'Oh, come on. Tomorrow we may die. What are you saving yourself for?'

It was a good question. For months now, Mrs Driver's letters hadn't mentioned Daisy Colindale. Griffin put oblique little questions into his replies, but without result, and to ask outright would be to admit his interest. He was instinctively reluctant to do that . . . and he was afraid, too, that it might produce something he didn't want to hear. She might have found a replacement 'best boy' for Arthur. No news was good news. He watched Lockett and his second choice of companion preparing for their amorous encounter with the French girls and thought of Daisy's picture, which he had torn out from the Grange staff photograph last August before the battery embarked for France. It was tucked inside his paybook in his breast pocket. He didn't often bring it out now, partly because of the general lack of privacy and partly because it was getting so cracked and frayed at the edges that he was afraid it would disintegrate altogether. Anyway he knew her features by heart. And all the Madeleines in Europe couldn't make him forget them.

15

Another heat-wave summer. In Gallipoli, as the Dardanelles offensive against the Turks floundered, flies settled thick on the eyes and mouths of troops sweltering in the trenches, carrying disease from the rotting corpses to the living. Along the Western Front the wells of the farmers were drunk dry by thousands of redundant cavalry horses as they waited to exploit a gap that never came. The artillery pounded on, sweating gunners stripped to the waist to manhandle the heavy shells from wagons to pits to gun breeches. At home in England, crops ripening in the fields had no farm labourers to harvest them. Belgian refugees, soldiers in training, school-boys and even that perennial last resort, women, were taken on to fill the gap.

By August, the Colindale family were scraping pennies. Daisy's money was almost gone and the Separation Allowance, designed to supply rather meanly the wants of two women, was spread too thin when it came to feeding three-and-a-bit.

Mrs Driver, putting old friendships above moral considerations, had agreed to be godmother to Daisy's baby and, popping in on her day off for a quick discussion about the christening arrangements and a coo at Harriet, mentioned that Inglis at the Home Farm was desperate for harvest workers. Louella borrowed a bicycle from one of the neighbours, rode out to Seale early one August morning and was hired for haymaking.

It was backbreaking work for those who weren't used to it. Thirty men and women walked side by side through the long grass, scything, till each field was cut, then raked the hay into heaps, turning the piles over to dry in the days that followed before forking it up into the big farm wagons to be transported to the stack. Louella cycled home each night tanned brown by the sun but hardly able to speak from exhaustion.

On a blazing day towards the end of August, Daisy pushed her perambulator along the lane past the double iron gates of Maple Grange. Despite the heat she was walking fast, almost running. Under an improvised canopy of bent wire and pinned tea towels, the baby smiled and gurgled up at her, enjoying the unusual jolting motion as her mother steered without regard to the bumps in the road. Normally Daisy would have been smiling back, talking to Harriet or singing softly as she walked, but today her face was flushed and grimly concentrating. It had been a long, long trek from the outskirts of Guildford and she had no idea if she would manage to get home again. But what other way could she carry the news to Louella?

She heard the sound of a motor and looking up wearily, she saw the Brownlowes' Landaulette coming towards her along the lane. She paused to mop at her damp brow with the back of her hand. The motor bowled past her, an unfamiliar man in a chauffeur's uniform at the wheel. In the passenger compartment were Miss Laura and Mr Rupert.

The Landaulette came to a halt a few yards further along the road. Without waiting for the driver to open her door, Miss Laura emerged and ran back towards the perambulator. She was wearing one of the new, shorter skirts, Daisy noticed, ending several inches above the ankle. In the old days of hobble skirts, she had never seen Miss Laura run.

'Hullo! Daisy. How are you? Is this your baby? Oh, isn't she sweet!' said Laura, arriving rather breathless beside her. Mr Rupert was also descending from the motor. His expression did not echo that of his daughter.

'What's her name?' asked Laura, bending over the perambulator.

'Harriet.'

'What a pretty name. Hullo, you darling,' said Laura, tucking her forefinger into Harriet's grasp in the way that all baby-admirers do. In her enthusiasm she had forgotten that Daisy's daughter was a product of sin. Rupert had not.

'What are you doing here?' he demanded of Daisy as he arrived.

'Taking a message to my sister-in-law, sir. She's working on the farm.'

It did not occur to Rupert that it was none of his business what his former employee was doing on a public road. Anyway she was about to venture on to his land with her errand. When he dismissed a servant he dismissed them for good, and having closed the door of employment on Daisy, he was annoyed to find that one of her relations had apparently crept through it on to some part of his property.

'Any message can wait,' he said curtly, 'until she is finished for the day. I won't have my workers interrupted in the time that I'm paying them for.'

'But sir, it's important,' said Daisy.

'I said it can wait. I don't want you wandering about on my land. And if I find you've disobeyed me, I'll have you arrested for trespass.'

Laura stared in consternation at her father. She had known he had sent Daisy away because of her pregnancy, it was a normal reaction by an employer to such news. But she hadn't realized with what acrimony he had done it. Daisy stood staring into the pram and Laura could see she was on the verge of tears.

'Come on Laura. We're wasting time,' said Rupert and strode back towards the Landaulette.

'I'm sorry, Daisy,' said Laura irresolutely. She, too, was about to go. This was her precious whole day off from Clandon, a freedom that came only once a month, and she had planned in detail how she would use it. But Daisy's agonized expression couldn't be ignored.

'What was the message? I'll see it's passed on.'

'Oh, thank you, Miss Laura,' gasped Daisy. 'It's for Louella Colindale, with the haymakers. Could you please tell her, Robert's come home.'

Robert had a week's leave, part of which was already used up by the journey back to England and the queuing in a long line of soldiers for train tickets at a series of stations. He had pictured coming through the door and finding Louella standing at the kitchen table like she always did, concocting some delicious meal, with her dark hair tidily coiled at the back of her head and her white apron tied over her sweetly curving figure. Instead, he had found an empty kitchen. He walked through. The back door stood open and his mother, her Windsor chair set down on the brick paving outside, was dozing in the sunlight. A battered pram was parked on the small area of yard which had once ended in a patch of grass and a few flowerbeds. Apart from the old lilac bushes, it now abutted row upon row of vegetables. Among the vegetables stood his sister Daisy, picking runner beans into a woven cane basket. No Louella.

For a moment the disappointment was acute. Then Daisy saw him and dropped her basket, and his mother woke up and said his name on a long note of wonderment. He was hurried inside, and the kettle put on, and his kitbag eased from his shoulders, until it began to seem true that he was home – even though the most important part of his homecoming had yet to materialize.

'She's out at Seale, working on the Maple Grange Home Farm. I'll fetch her,' said Daisy as if the trip she spoke of were a hundred yards and not a long seven miles. She thought of leaving Harriet – it would make the journey quicker and easier – but then she realized that Robert was tired out and Mrs Colindale was too distracted by his sudden appearance to be capable of sensible behaviour. And anyway she would never be back by the time Harriet's next feed was due. There was nothing for it but to take the baby with her. She unbraked the perambulator.

'Whose is the baby?' asked Robert. 'Louella hasn't—?'

'No. She's mine,' said Daisy. She hadn't included the difficult subject of illegitimate Harriet to Robert in her cheerful

299

letters, having a vague feeling that the mentioning of problems at home was unfair to a soldier in action and was best saved for when it could be properly explained. Before Arthur's death it had been a potential source of trouble between him and Robert. Afterwards it would only have added anguish. Without discussing the situation, Louella and even Mrs Colindale had apparently come to the same conclusion.

'It's a long story,' was all Daisy said. 'I'll tell you later.'

Louella, on receiving the message that Miss Laura sent down to the field with Billy Marshall, had dropped her scythe on the ground where she stood and simply run. Finding Daisy waiting in the lane outside the farm gates, she had been torn between helping to push the pram home again and doing what her every instinct cried out to do, which was to abandon all handicaps and hurry on.

'What about your bicycle?' said Daisy.

'I'd forgotten.' Louella shook her head to clear it. 'This news has knocked all the sense out of me.'

'Go back and fetch it and then get on home. I'll manage,' said Daisy. Harriet was beginning to grizzle, her feed overdue. Daisy lifted her out of the pram and sat down on the verge beside the road, unfastening her blouse. The relief to her aching legs and back was immense. She watched Louella cycling away and thought with a small pang of regret that but for fate and a German bayonet it might have been her now, hurrying back to Arthur. Then she reminded herself that by all accounts if he had come home, he'd have had a hard job deciding which girl to visit first, her or Adelaide Stringer.

When Louella reached the terraced house, Robert was asleep in the back bedroom upstairs, so deeply that it was impossible to wake him. His boots stood beside the bed and his tunic was tossed over a chair, but he had been too tired to undress further. She carefully unwound the puttees from his legs, folded them and laid them on top of the tunic, then sat by the bed and watched his face.

He looked older, thinner, the lines deeply carved across his features even when relaxed. A man of less than thirty, she thought sadly, shouldn't have such lines. Sleeping, his limbs sprawled out, he might have been a dead man except for the steady heaving of his chest. The sight of him hurt her, the longing to hold him to her was so intense.

Moving quietly, even though shaking her husband's shoulder and saying his name had failed to penetrate his unconsciousness, she unpinned and brushed her hair. She poured cold water from the jug on the washstand into the china basin patterned with tiny flowers and washed herself all over, then with the threadbare towel clutched to her, she searched in the chest of drawers for a nightdress, the one she'd worn on her wedding night last year. The lawn fabric, with its bodice of fine tucking, was so thin as to be almost transparent. She pulled it over her head, settled the clinging material over her hips and thighs, and lay down beside Robert to wait for his waking.

It was almost dark when Daisy came in.

'Where's Robert and Lou?' she asked her mother as she carried Harriet into the house.

'Upstairs. Don't disturb them.'

'I wasn't going to.' But it occurred to Daisy that with Robert lying alongside Louella in the double bed in the back room, and Mrs Colindale in the single bed in the front, there was nowhere for her and Harriet to sleep tonight. Harriet could be accommodated by bringing the pram indoors. Pragmatically, Daisy resigned herself to the prospect of the small, hard sofa in the front room. At least it was a warm night.

'What's it like out there?' said Louella on the last night before Robert's leave ran out. Her husband hadn't said much about the subject of life in the trenches; though to be fair he hadn't said much about anything really, being too busy reminding himself what he'd been missing for the past year in the way of conjugal comforts.

There was a long silence while Robert considered the

question, lying on his back with one arm folded under his head. 'I can't begin to tell you,' he said. He was just starting to talk in his normal voice, having at first spoken only in a hoarse whisper which he said was on account of being so used to keeping your voice down in the trenches. Talk out loud and you'd call down a shower of shrapnel around your ears.

'But you've been all right? Properly fed and all that?'

Robert didn't answer.

'I want to know,' said Louella. 'I want to be able to picture you, sometimes, doing what you're doing.'

'All right,' said Robert with sudden violence. 'Picture this. Living like a rabbit in a slit in the ground. Flooded all winter and half the summer with muddy water, sometimes up to your waist or higher. Nowhere to sleep but a hole in the wall. Stick your head above the parapet and someone shoots it off. Rations that some bastard steals half of before they get to you. Shells falling anywhere, any time, that can blow you to shreds. Cannon fodder, they call us. Sitting ducks. The din of the guns day and night. Burying the bodies of the ones they got and waiting for someone to have one of those bright ideas like a trench raid, which involves you climbing up out of this comparatively cushy existence and nipping across No Man's Land in the dead of night. All you've got to worry about then is drowning in the mud or getting hung up on the wire as target practice for a few thousand machine-gun bullets. If you're *really* lucky you get to the enemy trenches where they throw grenades at you and if all else fails they skewer you on a bayonet with a jagged edge. This is what it's like, turn and turn about, six days at a time. More if they haven't got anybody lined up to replace your platoon. And that's when it's quiet.

'And all your mates dying, one by one,' Robert went on flatly, staring at the ceiling. 'New ones come and then they die, too. So you can't have mates, because to actually *like* somebody is to bring them bad luck.' He turned and punched his pillow viciously. 'You shouldn't have asked,' he said.

'Is it really that bad?' Louella's voice shook, remembering

the way her husband had writhed and muttered in his sleep beside her during the past few nights. His first, angry tirade had made her flinch as if physically battered, but his closing words were somehow more frightening. Robert sighed, his anger ebbing. Now he'd have to try and make her feel better about something over which there wasn't any way to feel better. Bloody women, how could they understand?

'Sometimes it's all right,' he said. 'Anyway, got to be done hasn't it, until we beat the Boche?'

But how much longer would it take? And how much longer could he stand it?

Daisy had viewed with apprehension the prospect of telling Robert about the fathering of Harriet. Arthur'd been his mate and she didn't want anything to sour her brother's feelings about the dead man. She needn't have worried. Robert seemed to hold her solely to blame for the baby. He said, when asked, that Arthur hadn't really discussed Daisy but had seemed a bit undecided about the women in his life. Men often were. Anyway, Daisy had rushed into engagement and any girl who was fool enough to trade her good reputation for a seed pearl ring deserved what she got.

'All right,' said Daisy with a flash of spirit. 'What I got was Harriet. And I'm glad. I wouldn't part with her for anything.'

Louella understood better than her sister-in-law that it was envy that made Robert so unkind. Arthur Bright's one hurried coupling with Daisy had produced what he and Louella had tried for in vain for months.

On the day that Robert's leave ended, there was a small sensation in the row of terraces. Neighbouring curtains twitched as a delivery van pulled up outside the Colindales' house and unloaded a cream-coloured baby carriage of glossy splendour, complete with alternate summer and winter hoods, an apron to keep the rain off and an embroidered quilt.

Miss Laura had sent a new perambulator for Harriet.

'Come and look Mother Colindale, it's the most beautiful

present,' said Louella, thankful for a distraction in the hollow aftermath of Robert's departure. But Mrs Colindale, sitting in her Windsor chair, only gripped the armrests and shook her head. Her face was twisted with pain.

This time Louella had her way. A doctor's visit might cost as much as three pounds, but no home-brewed infusion of tansy or camomile could ease the pain and Mrs Colindale's condition, even though partially masked by her habitual endurance, frightened her daughter-in-law. The doctor, when he came, said he should have been called long ago. He arranged tests at the hospital, which revealed that the cancer was too advanced for treatment. Mrs Colindale, given permission at last to be ill, came home and went to bed and stayed there.

Food for a sick person costing more than food for a healthy one, and Louella's harvesting wage having been forfeited because of her unauthorized departure from the Home Farm, Daisy pushed the new perambulator into Guildford and sold it to a second-hand shop for less than half its value.

'The Tommies' Cooker was a wonderful idea,' Oliver told Claire on his first home leave, which came at the beginning of September. 'I sit in my little nest up at the Observation Post and brew up cups of Bovril on it. Luxury!'

He was seated on the familier Chesterfield at The Laurels. On one side of him, head resting on his knee, Magnus panted happily. On the other side, equally happy if not panting, Claire rested her head on his shoulder. Having had seven months at the Front to identify his wishes and rehearse his speech, Oliver had proposed to Claire within ten minutes of seeing her again and as a consequence their moments on the Chesterfield were no longer subject to supervision.

'You make it sound like fun,' said Claire. 'But I know it must be hell, really.'

'It is and it isn't,' said Oliver. 'In some ways it's more awful than I could have imagined and in other ways, well, it *is* fun. I mean, if you take away the death and the danger, it's

304

like a glorious OTC camp at school, everybody mucking in together and ragging each other to lighten things up. The captain's a terrific chap and the men are a good lot, too, once you get to know them. When we're out of the line for a bit, we have games – football, boxing, or tug of war on horseback, which is a big laugh. The men hang on like grim death, they won't give way even if the horse gives up the struggle. It's the funniest sight, a pony standing still with his hooves dug in and the rider going on without him, still hanging on to the rope.'

'Death and danger?' said Claire, homing in on the one fragment of his speech that concerned her.

'Well, yes. It was pretty hot round Ypres, though we're in a quieter bit of the war for the time being.'

Claire looked at her fiancé. In language and attitudes he was still an overgrown schoolboy she thought affectionately.

'Oliver, it's so hard to see you as a ruthless killer.'

'I'm not,' he said. 'It's a funny thing being a gunner. I mean, I do the sightings and send the positions through by telephone; or if I'm at the guns I'm passing those instructions on to the bombardiers, and I know that if the job's been done properly, someone is going to get killed or wounded once the shell's been fired. But it's all at a distance, not like shooting a man at point-blank range or running a bayonet through him. I know the enemy is out there and the whole point is to kill him, before he kills you or somebody else on your side. But knowing it isn't believing it, somehow. Or it wasn't at first. . . . As a matter of fact, for the first few months the only Germans I came across were dead ones, apart from seeing a few prisoners go by now and again under guard. Then I did meet one of our enemies and wished I hadn't, because it sort of put a face to them if you see what I mean, and then it's harder to fire off shells at them.'

'What happened?' said Claire.

'Well, there I was with one of our signallers, sitting in the mud up at the OP. Then the line went dead and he sneaked out to do a repair. He came back and said there was a Jerry

305

sitting in a shell hole a few yards away from us, wounded. Must've been there for a day or two, he reckoned, ever since their last trench raid. I thought that seemed a bit rough, so when my relief came along I crawled over to take a look.

'He was sitting there, very scruffy but quite resigned, smoking a cigarette my signaller had chucked him. He was an *unter-offizier*, like me. He'd got shot in the knee and he'd bandaged himself up, but he knew he couldn't make it back to his lines and he hadn't got quite to the stage of desperation where he was prepared to head for ours, though by the time I arrived he'd used up his water and his rations. I got the old cooker out and made him a cup of Bovril and we had a talk.'

'I didn't know you spoke German.'

'I don't. No need. He spoke absolutely fluent English. It turned out he had an English uncle living in Weston-super-Mare, his mother's sister had married an Englishman. And he'd studied at Oxford, at Balliol, would you believe? I was quite shaken up. I mean, they tell us the Boche are all savages, and then you meet one who's just like you, more or less. And from some things he said, I gather they hear the same stuff about us. That we're arrogant and merciless and all that. He said some friends of his had been taken prisoner in a trench raid and that news had come through that they'd been tortured for information and then shot. I told him it was rubbish, we wouldn't do that sort of thing, and he said did he look like a man who'd cut the hands off little children?'

'I suppose some of them do,' said Claire.

'I don't know,' said Oliver. 'I don't know what to believe. Anyway, he showed me a photograph of his family and his girl and I showed him mine, and then I persuaded him to hand me his pistol and I hauled him back to the OP and down the communication trench. He's probably over here in Blighty now, behind the wire. We said we'd get in touch when the war ended. Of course we were both sure that our side was going to win it. But like I said, these days when I know I've scored a direct hit on something – and sometimes you do see the men, flung up in the air along with the earth and the

306

sandbags – I think about Jurgen Reinhardt and his girl Kirsten, his family and uncle in Weston-super-Mare, and I feel rather bad about it. But what can you do?'

The price to be paid for the pleasures of home leave was the wrench of returning to the Front. Oliver returned as an engaged man, which was a mixed blessing because it meant he had more to lose now. He reminded himself that some of the men hadn't had any leave at all yet, despite thirteen months in action; Griffin, for instance, whom he encountered in the horse lines on his first day back.

'Did you have a good leave, sir?'

'Yes thanks, Griffin.' Oliver realized that Griffin was eyeing him hungrily. He dragged a crumpled envelope out of his pocket and the driver's expression brightened momentarily until he recognized his own handwriting. Oliver cleared his throat, uncomfortably conscious that he was conveying disappointing news.

'Sorry, but I couldn't deliver your message after all. Daisy Colindale isn't employed at the Grange any more, I don't know why.'

Griffin took the letter without comment and walked away. Oliver saw him collide with a tethering post and right himself, before he continued on his way like a man sleepwalking.

The letter had been the product of hours of agonizing on the part of Griffin. He'd weighed up the possibility that Daisy would snub his approach against the frustration of knowing he'd let slip an opportunity to get in touch with her. But what could be more natural than to send a friendly word via the subaltern, coming home on leave?

'Dear Daisy, just a few lines to say, how are you? I was sorry to hear from Mrs Driver about your bad luck. If you have time to write, I would appreciate a word or two about how you are getting on. If you can remember who I am after all this time. Best wishes from Will Griffin.'

Alone in a distant part of the horse lines, with a friendly black mare nudging at his shoulder, he read his own letter through again, his eyes bleak, before tearing it into shreds. Too late, too late. Like every other bit of bad luck that came his way, he absorbed this blow in silence.

The British commanders had decided that the time was ripe for a 'push' to counterbalance the German advances of Second Ypres, and Robert Colindale rejoined his battalion in time for the Battle of Loos which began on 25 September 1915.

The weapons of war were growing steadily more ingenious. Now they included flame-throwers, introduced by the Germans at Hooge in July, and chlorine gas, lethal if inhaled for more than two minutes, which had broken the French lines north of Ypres in April. The French had used tear-gas grenades in 1914 and the Germans, recognizing a clever idea when they saw it, had developed the weapon to such an extent that they'd made it their own.

'Here you are, Colindale. Stick that with your kit.'

Robert examined the latest in gas masks which the lance corporal was doling out. It was at least an improvement on what it had replaced: a handkerchief soaked in bicarbonate of soda or a nose-and-mouth cover tied on like a surgeon's mask, containing a pad of cotton wool which had a filtering effect so long as it was kept moist. It being impossible to maintain the moisture level ready for use at all times, its effectiveness had been virtually nil. The new mask was a hood made of thick blue-grey cloth, with a clear rectangle of mica over the eyes.

'That'll steam up,' said Robert. The lance corporal flipped him a small tin.

'Stuff to clean it with. Anti-condensation.'

Robert tried the cleaner. It didn't work particularly well. He supposed it was better than nothing.

Five minutes past six in the morning. The Givenchy sector. 'A' Company, first battalion, the Queen's, stood in line – trench ladders propped against the sandbags in front of them – waiting for the signal to go over. Bayonets fixed. The taste of the extra rum ration still burning in their mouths. *When you hear the artillery barrage stop and the whistle blow, lads, up the ladder, through the cut wire, run like hell. Theory is, the bombardment and the gas canisters we're using this time should have knocked out the enemy front-line before you get there. Giving the Hun a taste of his own chlorine.* That was the theory.

Gas masks on.

Seven minutes past six. The guns stopped. In the sudden, uneasy silence, the whistle blew.

On an intake of breath, Robert blundered at the ladder, scrambled up, heavy boots slipping on the rungs, the face of the man behind him crowding close, dodging his heels. His head reared above the sandbags. Through the plastic oblong of the gas mask he saw a waste of mud and water and blasted tree stumps, viewed till now only through the similarly limited aperture of a trench periscope. Puffs of smoke from the enemy trenches. Noise. Shouting. The staccato crack of rifles, machine guns stuttering like morse code. Robert cleared the parapet and ran, leaping the wire tangles. A voice, bellowing insanely, muffled through cloth, was his own.

At first the lack of response from the enemy lines was eerie. Then halfway across No Man's Land all hell broke loose. Something hammered into his chest and flung him backwards. Hooded figures stumbled over him and ran on, eyes behind the clear shields veering momentarily sideways and down. Pain in his chest. He couldn't breathe. Clawed at his mask, tore it upwards. Air, fresh air. Gulped it in. Choked and coughed. Someone fell to their knees beside him and dragged at the thick cloth, hauling it down again over his nose and mouth. Robert fought. Words, incomprehensible, rained down on him.

'Put it back on, you stupid bastard! For Christ's sake, put it back on!'

The British gas, lifted on a treacherous wind, drifted back over the Allied lines. In the act of replacing the mask on Robert, Private George Deacon was shot in the back.

Robert, suspending his creed of non-involvement, had started lately to like young Deacon, who played the mouth organ and told deeply profane jokes with an air of innocence that only increased their humour. He lay with the body across his thighs until a gang of stretcher-bearers came to take him in. There was no point in taking Deacon, whose eyes had stared into Robert's, unblinking and for some hours now, through the mica of his gas mask. Robert, his own eyes under the hood scoured by the chlorine, was unaware of that fact, but he knew the feel of a dead body.

At the casualty clearing station they handed him a buckled piece of metal, his Princess Mary's gift box of the previous Christmas which he had used to keep his cigarettes dry and uncrushed. It had deflected a bullet from his heart and flung it past his shoulder.

'Do you want this, mate? It's not much use now.'

Robert, unseeing, his chest bruised by the impact of the bullet, still gasping for air like a stranded fish because the gas had got to him in the seconds before Deacon, nodded while froth oozed and bubbled from his mouth. He fumbled and wrenched until he had the twisted box open. He felt among the mangled cigarettes and his fingers closed weakly over a dented scrap of silver. Louella's Vesta case. His good luck.

The buff Field Service postcard distributed in the trenches had printed lines informing the recipient that the sender was quite well/had been admitted to hospital. If the latter applied, he was sick/wounded and was going on well/hoped to be discharged soon. He had received the recipient's letter/telegram/parcel or, alternatively, had received no letter lately/for a long time. Letter followed as soon as possible.

A further line warned that if any information not covered by the printed options was added, there would be no delivery. Scanning the card, forgetting to breathe while she did so, Louella managed to decipher from the uncancelled lines that Robert was wounded in hospital somewhere. There was nothing to cover the eventuality that he was not 'going on well'. His signature looked as shaky as her legs felt when she read it.

Some days later, the promised letter arrived. 'I hope you didn't worry too much. I couldn't write more, I was gassed. The nurses helped me with the card as I couldn't see, but my sight's coming back now. At least it was a Blighty. I'm in hospital in Portsmouth. Can you manage to come?'

She was on the next train. Daisy stayed at home with Harriet, partly because they couldn't afford more than one train fare, but mainly because however much she longed to see her brother, someone had to look after Mrs Colindale who was sinking fast.

Ferry was late. Mrs Driver kept glancing anxiously at the mitre clock on the mantelpiece in the servants' hall. She was dying for a cup of cocoa, but traditionally the staff had their last beverage of the day together and somehow it felt like bad luck to go ahead without the butler.

'Oh dear, where can he have got to?'

'I expect he'll be back soon,' said Joan from the comfort of the opposite side of the fireplace. She spoke in an undertone because in the chair furthest from the fire (as befitted her lowly status), Susan had already nodded off, her head lolling sideways and her mouth agape. They were all tired these days, trying to keep Maple Grange going at the level Mr Rupert expected despite the reduced staff. It didn't help that Ferry was also much occupied by his duties as a voluntary special constable – out at night in all weathers patrolling the district on Blackie.

Ferry had been a 'Special' since April. News of the gas attacks that had nearly let the Germans through to the Channel ports had driven home the conviction that a man had to do *something* to help beat those Jerries, even if he was too old for the fighting. When Mr Rupert came up with the scheme of Maple Grange supplying a special constable and agreed to loan Blackie for the purpose, Ferry had been glad to step

311

forward. He was a singularly unconfident horseman, having ridden nothing more lively than a seaside donkey in his youth. But if the boys in the trenches could handle their side of things he told himself, he could at least brave the hazards of a dark night in the Surrey countryside.

His duties so far had consisted mainly of searching out offenders against the blackout rule and instructing them to muffle forthwith any gleams of light that might be shining from the windows of their homes. At first there had been heated exchanges with the offending householders, who condemned him as over-officious, but lately any complaints had been muted. With the spate of Zeppelin raids over London, the prospect of the war coming to Guildford in some form seemed very much more real.

He was also supposed to keep an eye out for the activities of spies, but there was not much sign of those after the first flurry of arrested pigeon-fanciers who might be sending cryptic messages to the Kaiser; though there had been one unfortunate incident soon after the war broke out, when a party of ladies conversing in French for the sake of practice had been dragged out of a railway carriage on the Reading line on the grounds that they were 'talking foreign', and another when an indignant Swiss gentleman had come home to find that the police had been through his mansion with a fine toothcomb in search of evidence that he wasn't Swiss after all but something more sinister.

Ferry was thinking about spies as he rode down the lane between Compton and Puttenham. He was also, at the back of his mind, thinking wistfully about cocoa. He was already late back because he'd had a slight altercation with an old lady in Puttenham who wouldn't believe that light was shining from her shuttered upstairs windows until marched out into the street to see for herself. The point proven, he'd had to help her cover a warp in one of the old wooden shutters with a tablecloth – in the course of which she had mentioned that while on her way home from her sister-in-law's house at Compton earlier in the day, she had spotted some strangers lurking on the edge of the woods and she thought that maybe it was 'them German spies'.

The spot she had described was well off his normal track and he suspected her concern had been aroused by nothing more than a few local lads setting illicit traps for rabbits. But duty insisted that he should check her story. To his relief the area of the reported activity seemed perfectly normal when he inspected it in the faint and wavering light of a torch. Not that his investigation was particularly thorough. Ferry wasn't sure what espionage would look like if he did come across it and anyway he doubted his ability to deal effectively with it.

It was a clear, starlit night, but cold, and his arthritic hip was aching dully. It was one of those evenings when his physical endurance was tested and he allowed the disloyal thought to surface that men like Mr Rupert looked after their own comforts very well for all that they were so free with suggestions that interfered with the comfort of others. It was hard to imagine Mister Rupert out on Blackie on a night like this, though he had the advantage of a lifetime's horsemanship to make such an activity easier for him. Ferry had to nerve himself every time he put his foot in the stirrup.

Fortunately Blackie was mostly too old and bored to misbehave. But she was pulling hard at the reins now, which was odd because she was too far from home to be anticipating the delights of a warm stable and a well-stuffed haybag. Her pricked ears flicked forward and back and she snorted softly, jogging about in a way that sent her rider lurching in the saddle.

Then he registered what had made her nervous. A low thrumming sound was coming from somewhere behind him. It sounded, he thought, like a bluebottle trapped in a confined space. Soft and eerie at first, it gradually increased in volume. Ferry's skin crawled. 'All right, old girl, all right,' he said, but his voice wobbled and the words did nothing to reassure the frightened mare.

The noise came from the East, somewhere in the region of St Catherine's on the edge of Guildford. As he strained his eyes towards it, he saw the brilliant blue light of a parachute flare slowly descending, then the pale finger of a searchlight stroking the sky and finally, hovering against the stars, the long cigar-shape that he had heard described and never quite expected to see.

'Blimey, it's a Zeppelin!'

In time with the realization, there came a flash that lit up the sky, followed by a violent explosion far away in the direction of Pewley Downs – but so intense that it shook the ground under Blackie's hooves. It was too much for the mare. With a snort she wheeled round, shedding her rider halfway through the turn, and headed for home. Some minutes later, Ferry followed rather more slowly and with a limp. Behind him, the explosions continued at intervals.

The sound of the bombs falling on Guildford had been heard at Maple Grange, and Blackie caused something of a sensation by appearing riderless in the stable yard with broken reins, a wild expression and a badly gashed foreleg. Ferry, staggering home nearly two hours later, met with a hero's reception from the staff, particularly when it was learned that he'd actually seen the Zeppelin. But as the shock of the incident receded, glory being transitory, the butler found to his chagrin that Rupert was blaming him for the damage to Blackie.

'Another time, keep hold of your horse's reins if you come off. First rule of horsemanship.'

'Sir,' said Ferry, hurt, 'I did my best, but it was all a bit sudden.'

'Well, never mind,' said Rupert irritably, and went off to confer with Nichols and the veterinary surgeon who'd been summoned to stitch up the mare's leg at some expense. Ferry took his own injuries off to be salved with Mrs Driver's embrocation and thought bitterly that life could be very unjust sometimes.

The raid on Guildford, which took place on the thirteenth of October, was one of several across the home counties that night. Afterwards it was deflatingly suggested that the

Zeppelin had not been targeting the town at all, but had managed to get lost while looking for somewhere more significant. One good outcome of the bombing for Daisy Colindale was that it got the neighbours talking to her. A sense of being partners in adversity brought them into one another's homes to exchange information about the damage caused by the seven bombs.

'I've heard they tore up a whole load of trees and broke ever so many windows. But there's nobody dead,' said Mrs Dean from next door, 'though a lot of chickens were blown up. A miracle I call it. I spent the whole time sitting under the table praying to the Lord, I can tell you.'

Harriet, too, had passed the raid under the kitchen table, further protected by the upturned tin bath; but since Mrs Colindale was too sick to be moved, Daisy had sat by her bed and held her hand throughout. Louella, in Portsmouth with Robert, had missed the whole thing.

A few days later the incident was replaced as a topic for indignant discussion by the news that a nurse called Edith Cavell had been executed in Brussels by the Germans for helping Belgian soldiers to escape to Allied lines. The execution of Nurse Cavell, coming hard on the heels of the menace from the air, sent many men who had so far held back into the recruiting offices. From Maple Grange, Billy Marshall, gardener's boy, unrolled his shirtsleeves and walked again to Stoughton Barracks. At sixteen, he was barely taller than he had been on the day of his previous rejection, but this time a less selective recruiting sergeant let him through.

16

In a year of wartime nursing at Number 4 General Hospital, Camiers, Margaret Churchill thought she had seen it all. The bodies of the men carried in on stretchers were so many lumps of meat: composed of stripped skin to be regrafted; torn muscle and pulverized flesh to be trimmed away; raw-lipped open wounds to be sutured, pumping veins to be clamped. A shattered limb, dangling by a shred of skin, would be whipped off by the surgeon and fed to the furnace by a steady and unflinching Margaret. At first the casualties of liquid fire had made her gag, with their stink of charred flesh when she peeled back the lint dressings, but she'd controlled the reaction. She could carry out the four-hourly irrigation of a gas gangrene wound without visible emotion, despite inwardly cringing at the agony in the patient's eyes as the cold Hypochlorous Acid solution pumped into the wound. It had to be done.

The gas victims had been another shock to absorb. Blue faces, rasping breath, drowning slowly in the liquid of their own lungs . . . and often dying blind and terrified, the chlorine burning their eyes. Now, in November of 1915, she had learned to live with that horror as well. The wounded men thought her heartless – though they might grudgingly concede that her ministrations hurt less than those of other, more approachable nurses. It was the VADs, tiptoeing around the ward behind her who dispensed the sympathy.

They'd nicknamed her 'Maggie Marble'. Margaret found the tag unfunny, even hurtful, but she made no attempt to alter the manner that had inspired it. She appeared hard because she knew she couldn't afford emotion. If she once started to pity the wrecked men who passed through the wards, she'd be finished.

'Sister Churchill, you're wanted in Matron's office.'

'I'll go when I've finished this.' Margaret was absorbed in the delicate process of extracting the packing from a stomach wound, inch by painful inch, prior to repacking with fresh solution-soaked lint. After days of this treatment, she and the boy who was her patient both knew exactly how long the process would take and she knew he counted the seconds that he had to stand it without screaming. She didn't even look up at the nurse's words.

'Matron said straightaway. Should I take over here?'

'I said I'll go when I've finished.'

Matron wasn't used to being kept waiting. But Sister Churchill was one of her best nurses and the occasion was exceptional. She smiled good-humouredly as Margaret came into her office. When she spoke, it was not to Margaret but to the young officer in khaki seated by her desk.

'Here she is.' She might have been presenting him with a particularly valuable present. Indeed, Matron saw it that way.

Edward Allingham stood up. He and Margaret faced each other awkwardly, like strangers.

They were strangers. They'd had no sight of one another since last November, when Margaret had gone to Camiers and Edward to his battalion at Hazebrouck. Their postal communications since then had been studies of how much can be left out rather than how much can be told. Edward had gone on bleeding inwardly over Margaret's refusal to marry him before he left for active service; Margaret had not known how to deal with his stilted sentences so she had echoed them.

Her failure to be available at the time of his last leave, when another nurse's illness had made it difficult for her to leave the hospital short-staffed, had added a further drop of poison. She felt she had made the only choice she could, but at the time the stress of that choice had been almost unbearable until the relentless flood of casualties from the second battle of Ypres forced it to the back of her mind.

'Hullo, Meggie.'

Margaret went on looking into Edward's eyes without

317

speaking, trying to gauge his mood. The nickname had been spoken lovingly, but after such a long time she couldn't quite trust it.

The silence stretched. Matron stirred in her chair.

'Sister Churchill, Lieutenant Allingham is on leave and has asked that you be granted leave at the same time. I have agreed to his request.'

Margaret darted her superior a shocked glance before her eyes returned to Edward's face. 'We are so busy,' she said, to him and not to Matron. 'How can I go now?'

'No one is indispensable, Sister Churchill,' said Matron. 'Enjoy your leave. We shall still be here when you get back.'

Her voice brooked no argument. When Margaret had gone to sign off, she turned to Edward. 'She is as nearly indispensable here as any human being can be, but she is desperately in need of rest and restoration. Look after her.'

'I'll do that,' said Edward.

On the path outside Matron's office, he took Margaret's hand.

'I'm sorry to spring things on you like this. I thought if I came on the off-chance there'd be less time to get my hopes up and it would be less disappointing if you wouldn't come.'

'I'm sorry about last time.'

'I'm sorry about the way I took it.' His hand tightened on hers before he lifted and studied it. 'You aren't wearing your ring?'

'It would tear rubber gloves,' said Margaret, smiling at the impracticality of his question. 'And sapphires can't stand carbolic.' But she lifted a thin gold chain around her neck to reveal the ring that had been tucked inside her dress behind the tight, almost clerical collar.

'Doesn't it scratch?'

'Sometimes. I don't care.'

'Will you marry me now, this leave, Meggie? Or do I have to go on waiting?'

'Yes. I mean, no. I don't want to wait any more either.'

*

318

'Quietly, in Paris, on 15 November. . . .'

Laura read the wedding notice in the *Advertiser* in the drawing room at Maple Grange. The six months of her initial VAD contract were almost up and she had been having an inner struggle over whether to regard honour as satisfied and think of some other way to help win the war, or to go on punishing herself and probably the patients by asking to renew the contract.

She had another choice to make as well. She carried in her pocket a love-letter from Charles McKay to which she had been postponing an answer. The newspaper announcement of Edward's wedding seemed to provide that answer. She borrowed Aunt Jessie's desk in the morning room and wrote hastily.

'Yes, I think it would be a good idea for us to get married on your next leave. I'll set things in motion at this end.' She added a few incidentals about life as a VAD before she signed her name, underscoring it heavily. It was a habit she'd developed lately, this slash of the pen across the page under 'Laura'. Lending her words a sureness that she didn't feel.

What would it be like being married to Charles? What did it matter? There wasn't anything else in prospect for her now.

She dropped the envelope on to the salver on the hall table as usual, for Billy Marshall to take to the post. Then she remembered that it was no longer Billy who carried the Grange's mail to the pillar box. He was training on Salisbury Plain. She couldn't imagine the gardener's boy, with his small, skinny figure and gap-toothed grin, taking part in a bayonet charge. Easier to picture him in a hospital bed, trying to be brave when the dressings trolley came round. So many of the casualties in the wards at Clandon were young lads who must have left their homes as full of patriotic fervour as Billy. Some had even managed to retain it. Others had lost their ideals along with an arm or a leg or the ability to breathe without torturing scarred lungs.

It was becoming increasingly hard to balance the daily sight of the wounded at Clandon with the 'triumph' and the 'glory' that her father kept talking about.

In mid-December Charles McKay was granted leave and held Laura to her word. In a flurry of preparation, Maple Grange laid on a wedding.

'Do you, Laura Sylvia Brownlowe, take this man . . . ?'

What would happen, Laura wondered, *if I just said, 'No, sorry, I don't, this is all a silly mistake,' and walked back down the aisle?*

But it wasn't a serious consideration. She was cemented in: by a promise given unthinkingly; by the expectations of a church full of well-wishers; by all the fuss about the gown and the flowers – almost impossible in December – and the exhuming from a trunk, and layers of tissue and lavender, of her mother's wedding veil.

'Reminds us what we're fighting for, doesn't it?' Pa had said, as he presented her with the yards and yards of filigree-dainty Bruges lace which had swathed Sylvia Cathcart on her wedding day. 'Gallant little Belgium and its craft and culture, overrun by those barbarians.'

At the time Laura had felt a mixture of pleasure that he should have felt able to let her wear the precious veil with its train of memories, and of irritation that he had to drag the war into it. Pa was at her elbow now, sweating lightly in his black tailcoat because he'd supplied great sacks of hard-to-come-by coal for the church boilers so that Laura could look her best in silk and lace without shivering – with the result that everyone else within range of the blast was overheated. She stole a glance at him and saw that the glow of pride and sentimentality that he'd been emanating all day was overlaid by a shadow of anxiety. An uncomfortably long time had elapsed, she realized, since the vicar's last question.

'I do,' she said hastily, and on either side of her Pa and Charles expelled twin sighs of relief. When they knelt for the blessing Charles' eyes met Laura's and she felt another inward twitch of the alarm that had assailed her when he'd arrived at the Grange yesterday, fresh from the Front. He'd seemed worn and haunted, and she'd had a sensation then that this wedding was like a lifeline to a drowning man for him. Now the sensation was repeated and she knew she was entangled with emotions too deep for her experience.

Oh well, thought Laura, as she'd thought when faced with a marble floor at Clandon and a cloth and bucket, *better get on with it, I suppose.*

In the drawing room at Maple Grange the guests sipped champagne and ate slices of fruitcake. It was a far cry from the lavish spread that Rupert would have wished to provide for his daughter's wedding, but after all there was a war on and the event had, of necessity, to be a scratch affair since no one had been sure when the bridegroom would be available until he'd actually turned up. For those closest to the family there would be a dinner party to redress the balance.

Rupert didn't feel he was losing a daughter, but gaining a son as he told Charles McKay. Charles smiled wanly and mumbled something inaudible, scarcely dragging his eyes off Laura as she chatted with his parents on the other side of the room. The McKays had travelled down from Inverness overnight and were too tired to contribute much to the conversation, so Laura was supplying all the animation.

'Beautiful, isn't she?' Rupert said. 'Reminds me so much of her mother, you know. In that veil.'

'Yes, sir.'

'She's got plenty of spirit, has Laura.'

'Yes, sir.'

Rupert thought that at this moment spirit was something in which young McKay appeared to be sadly deficient. He should be at his new bride's side, dealing with his family, or getting to know her friends, not wilting at the edge of the crowd. *Like a ghost at a wedding . . .* was the phrase that flitted across Rupert's mind. Still, one shouldn't judge too harshly. The poor chap was fresh from the war. His hand was shaking as he downed his champagne. Terrible times for soldiers.

Rupert moved to refill Charles' glass. The bottle he picked up from the tray on the sofa table was empty. Nor were there any further glasses. Where was Ferry who ought to be doing this? And Joan? He realized with irritation that the room was quite devoid of servants. Even Jessie had disappeared. He muttered an excuse to Charles, whose eyes were still following Laura around the room with dog-like devotion, and hurried towards the kitchen regions.

The large kitchen was full of staff, which was quite proper because shortly they'd be called upon to give the young couple their good wishes. Except that at least two of them should be in the drawing room now, circulating the champagne. And except that there was an extra figure present: Will Griffin, the former groom who'd joined up in the first week of the war.

'Ferry! Joan! What's going on here? You should be with my guests.'

'Sorry, sir,' said Ferry, spinning round, guiltily apologetic. 'I came through for some more champagne and got a bit distracted, sir, on account of Griffin turning up unexpectedly.'

'That's all very well, Ferry, but there's a somewhat important occasion going on next door.' Normally Rupert would have been pleased to see Griffin, would have offered him a glass of beer and quizzed him genially about his exploits. But today was not a normal day and he was merely exasperated by the distraction. 'What does he want?'

'Well, sir . . . he's on leave and he came inquiring after Daisy, sir. Daisy Colindale.'

'Oh. Her,' said Rupert. His exasperation mounted. Across several yards of kitchen, his eyes met Griffin's. 'The girl isn't here any more.'

'He already knew that, sir. He was wanting to know where she'd gone.'

'Has anybody told him why she's gone? I sacked her for immoral conduct. And I hope,' said Rupert, as the possibility dawned, 'that you weren't responsible, Griffin, for that young slut's deplorable condition?'

Griffin took a step forward, his sallow face suddenly suffused with colour. 'What did you say?'

'The girl has had a bastard child. And if you fathered it, then you can think yourself lucky that you are no longer in my employ.'

Without warning, Griffin's right fist shot up towards Rupert's jaw. But Jessie Brownlowe had slipped in between them. Griffin aborted the gesture abruptly.

'Don't!' Jessie said breathlessly. 'Griffin, don't. It would cause you such trouble.'

'Good God.' Rupert dimly comprehended that he had been menaced in his own kitchen, by a member of the serving classes. He had difficulty in believing it. 'Get out of here!' he said, over the smooth crown of Jessie's head. 'Before I call the police!'

As Griffin stood with his hands clenched, breathing rapidly, Jessie tugged at his sleeve. 'Come away. It's no good.'

'No,' said Griffin at last, and followed her meekly out of the kitchen.

Even on Laura's wedding day, Jessie wore her mother's old-fashioned châtelaine belt around her waist, from which dangled the keys of Maple Grange on a silver chain, together with scissors, a propelling pencil, a small notepad in an engraved silver case and a purse of change. In the stableyard, trembling with the cold and with reaction from the unpleasant little scene in which she had just been involved, she wrote rapidly on a page of the notepad before handing it to the soldier.

'That's her address in Guildford. Griffin, it's a lovely little baby, I've heard Mrs Driver say so. A little girl.'

'The baby's not mine,' said Griffin rather dazedly. 'Mr Rupert was wrong there. But I wish it was.'

He spent the seven miles of the walk from Maple Grange to Guildford, under a grey sky that threatened snow, trying to decide how he felt about Daisy Colindale's baby. He had told Miss Jessie that he wished the little girl was his. But the fact remained that she wasn't, that there existed a living, breathing testimony to Daisy's feelings for someone else. She had loved Arthur Bright. Enough it seemed, to risk everything for him. Job, reputation, everything. Inside Griffin, demons of jealousy warred with sympathy for Daisy's plight.

By the time he reached the downward slopes into the town, the sympathy had won. It must have been hell for her over the last few months with not only her lover gone, but her livelihood too and the shame of an illegitimate child to contend with on top. He'd loved her before, knowing of Arthur's existence. How could he love her less, now that she was alone and down on her luck?

He found the road from Miss Jessie's directions, still unsure of what he would say when he saw Daisy, but sure of that one thing – that he did desperately want to see her.

At first sight, as he turned the corner in the gathering twilight, the terraced rows of houses facing each other across the road seemed deserted, though when he looked closer there were drawn blinds at every window with only slivers of light showing at the edges. Mrs Driver's letters had mentioned the blackout and the excitement of the Zeppelin raid, though Griffin had only been wryly amused by the death toll of seventeen chickens and a swan.

The impression of desertion was being dispelled, now, by curls of smoke rising from the chimneys and cooking smells and the clatter of crockery emanating from the houses. It had been a long time since Griffin had sat down at a table for a civilized meal. He imagined hopefully that Daisy might invite him in and make him welcome. The sick feeling he'd carried away with him from Maple Grange began to fade. But at number seventeen although the blinds were undrawn, no lights showed. Griffin knocked, the sick feeling returning. There was no sign of life inside the house. He knocked again, more loudly because despair was setting in, and from the neighbouring front door a few feet to the left, a woman emerged.

'No good knocking, there's nobody there. Martha's died, the funeral was yesterday. And the young one's gone to Portsmouth with the baby.'

'Portsmouth?' Griffin echoed in dismay.

'Did you come for the funeral? You didn't miss much. But then they hadn't two pennies to rub together, that family, not since the young one's bit of trouble. Not many people went. But I did. Martha Colindale was an old friend. Must be twenty-five years we've been neighbours, ever since she and Harry first—'

'Do you know where in Portsmouth?' Griffin broke in.

The woman considered. 'Can't say as I do. She didn't say. Kept herself to herself since her bit of trouble, did Daisy.'

'Do you know when she'll be back?'

'Can't say as I do,' the woman repeated. She studied Griffin's stricken expression with curiosity. 'Are you the father?' she asked. But the dark-haired young man in khaki was already walking away, with a face that would have been well-suited to a funeral.

Griffin didn't normally drink anything more than the daily rum ration issued to the troops, and that only because it kept the cold out. Tonight he went from Daisy's empty, blank-windowed home to a public house in the town and drank steadily, transferring most of the contents of a bottle of whisky down his throat in return for the pay he'd saved up for sixteen months for this precious leave. At first he was left alone because his black expression was forbidding, but the pub was crowded and eventually a man blundered up to the bench he'd chosen.

'All right to sit here? Not lousy, are you?'

Griffin didn't answer, but the question rankled. He'd been very careful about that, getting himself clean and decent and smartened up for his return to Guildford. The man was in his fifties, too old to be a soldier, and belligerent. The tankard of beer he clutched was evidently a long way from being his first.

'A lot of the troops we get in here are lousy, if they're newly back. Sit around scratching. Probably all they do when they're out there, too, the way things are going.' He peered at Griffin's shoulder badge. 'Artillery? Bombardier, are you?'

'Driver.'

'Oh. Well, you want to pull your socks up, lad, you and your mates. War's been going on far too long. All these food shortages, all this bumping about in the dark, it isn't good enough. Country's going to the dogs. Should have smashed the Hun to pieces long ago if you people knew your job. And what's more,' he jabbed an offensive, black-nailed finger into Griffin's chest, 'my son's out there with the infantry and he says they get more shells in the trenches from the lousy shooting of their own gunners than they do from the Hun. He reckons the artillery's bloody well useless.'

It was the last straw. Since the man was clearly trying to pick a fight, Griffin obliged, giving him the right hook he'd earlier been tempted to deposit on the smoothly shaven jowl of Rupert Brownlowe. He was subsequently transported to the police station on a charge of being drunk and disorderly. He compounded the damage by punching a couple of constables and spent the remainder of his leave locked in a cell. At least it solved the problem of where to go and what to do. They let him out in time to catch the boat train back to France.

Was that it? Laura asked herself, on the night of her wedding. Was that the giddy sensation that was supposed to have inspired poets and tempted desperate lovers throughout history? It hardly seemed worth it, this clumsy mauling.

She lay on her back in the best guest bedroom at Maple Grange in an eighteenth-century four-poster bed with a canopy and hangings of flowered linen. Beside her, Charles was asleep. Or was he? At any rate, his eyes were closed. She thought something had happened, for him, that ought to have happened, though the whole process had been so uncomfortable and embarrassing that she couldn't be sure.

If only he hadn't kept saying 'Sorry'.

After three months in hospital at Portsmouth and an all-too-

326

brief spell of recovery at home in Guildford, Robert was sent to Ripon to be retrained. It seemed a gassing was not sufficiently disabling to release him from the obligation to fight for King and Country.

'Bad chests over here!' bellowed the Ripon physical training instructors, who had very little medical knowledge and less human compassion. 'Bad arms over here! Bad legs over there!'

Robert shuffled over to join the bad chests. The man who was bawling out instructions was an archetypal sergeant major, without any experience, Robert guessed sourly, of what it was like to be recovering from war wounds. He had ordered his victims into a field, tunics off, braces down, shirts unbuttoned to the waist and now, he promised them as they shivered in the wind, he was going to separate the men from the boys. To put it another way he was going to undo what the nurses at Portsmouth had spent three months achieving. Soft soldiers.

'Get in line. Round the perimeter. Quick march,' commanded the instructor. And all too soon, 'Trot.' The little troupe of gassed men broke into a shambling run. 'Faster. Come on, you pathetic bunch of miserable specimens. Get those knees up! Forgotten how to double, have we?'

On and on they ran. Pain tore like a knife at Robert's chest. He struggled for breath. When he couldn't stand it any longer he stopped dead, bent forward from the waist, hands propped on his knees, dizzy with the pain.

'Oy, you. What's your game?' At his side, the sergeant stood with his hands clamped to his hips.

'I . . . I can't . . . run . . . any . . . more . . .' gasped Robert.

'Ho. Is that so?'

'Gassed . . .' wheezed Robert.

'Well that's why you're here, my son. To get you ungassed. Put a troop of Uhlans behind you and you'd soon remember how to run. Now get on with it. Trot.'

'No,' said Robert. The rest of the reluctant runners had also halted and stood watching his rebellion.

327

'Insubordinate, eh? Is that your game?'

'It's no game,' said Robert. He could breathe more easily now, but the ache in his chest remained. 'I can't run any more. If you want to kill me, you'll have to do it officially.'

'We'll see about that.'

Robert was extremely lucky, he realized later, that when he was marched down to see the medical officer, the man on duty happened to be one with a shred of pity for the convalescents. Many of the army MOs were not so sympathetic. Injuries, in their opinion, were being exaggerated, even self-inflicted. By now they were coming up against a certain reluctance on the part of the Poor Bloody Infantry to fight. They took a dim view. This one gave Robert the benefit of the doubt when he said he'd been worked too hard, too soon.

'All right, I'll have you transferred to a different instructor. How's that?'

The new instructor was more of a pragmatist, ready to let the gas cases work their way up gradually from walk to run, and to rest when they had to. After six weeks of the regime Robert was passed as fit again for active service.

'Fit enough for cannon fodder, anyway,' said his bête noire the sergeant major, with a leer. Robert thought that if there was any heavenly justice the NCO would spend eternity running along an unending network of communication trenches in the Flanders mud with a full pack on his back, pursued by all the hounds of hell and with a constant barrage of mortar shells raining about his ears. But Robert didn't believe in justice any more.

His mother was dead, shrivelled with the pain of the cancer that had eaten her insides, and he hadn't even been there to say goodbye. His family was dragged down into poverty because the war that should have been over by Christmas of 1914 had lasted a further year already and showed no sign of ever coming to an end. Worst of all, Louella reckoned she might be pregnant. She'd told him of the possibility, though it was too early to be sure, because she thought it would cheer him up in the wake of his mother's death. But it didn't. Coming now, it just made it that much harder to be apart from her.

He'd come back from Portsmouth just before the New Year with Louella and Daisy, and in mid-January he'd been transferred to Ripon. But on their return, they had been confronted by a landlord demanding unpaid rent and threatening eviction. All through her twenty-five year tenancy Mrs Colindale had been scrupulous about paying the rent on time, and the money owed was only the two weeks' worth during Daisy's absence, but the man was a stern Methodist and Daisy had an uncomfortable feeling that the existence of Harriet coloured his attitude.

To help pay for Mrs Colindale's funeral, Daisy had sold her seed pearl and tourmaline ring and her mother's wedding ring. To finance her trip to Portsmouth and contribute towards a rather cheerless Christmas in lodgings there, she had sold the kitchen sideboard. To stave off the landlord, every last item of furniture in the house that was not absolutely essential had had to go, including the Windsor chair in the kitchen and the patchwork quilt under which Mrs Colindale had slept every night of her life since the day she was married. She'd sewn it in her maiden days and it had been a work of art. In a way the losing of the quilt and the chair brought the fact of her mother's death home to Daisy in a way that nothing else had. She'd sat on the denuded bed and cried for an hour, until the distant bellowing of Harriet reminded her that life went on. Then she picked herself up and went downstairs to see what could be assembled for supper out of the unpromising contents of the larder.

Mrs Driver's arrival one January afternoon on a friendly call was doubly welcome because she brought with her a fruitcake smuggled out of the Grange under a folded teacloth in the bottom of her shopping basket. It was a brave gesture in view of Mr Rupert's known antipathy towards Daisy since her dismissal and his notoriously stern views on pilfering. The cook also brought the news of Will Griffin's untimely arrival at the Grange in the middle of Miss Laura's wedding reception.

'He seemed quite upset,' she reported. 'We thought there was going to be a proper dust-up with Mr Rupert.'

Louella filled the kettle for tea and sliced up the cake. Daisy tried to concentrate on the conversation with the visitor while Harriet clung to her shoulder, tugged at her hair and bounced on sturdy legs on her lap, uttering a constant, distracting 'Ahhhh' for the mere joy of hearing her own voice.

'The little love,' said Mrs Driver fondly. 'Full of herself isn't she?'

Mrs Driver had never married. The 'Mrs' was a courtesy title accorded to cooks as part of the perks of their rank. She'd worked her way up from scullery maid and was happy enough in her work, but contact with babies like Harriet made her broody, though it was long past the time when she might have had a family. Marriage, that was another thing. She had hopes of netting Ferry eventually, when they reached retirement age, and she had a nest egg put by for a dowry which would secure them a comfortable home somewhere.

Daisy agreed that Harriet was a little love. She was also a little tyrant, strong-willed and exhausting. Her red hair and pale skin came from her mother, but so far she showed every sign of having inherited Arthur Bright's forceful personality along with his physique.

'Let's hold her for a bit,' said Mrs Driver. With difficulty, Daisy detached Harriet from her neck and passed her over to the cook. Harriet, mercifully, didn't object to the transfer but closed in on Mrs Driver's bright coat buttons with fascination and attempted to discover whether they were edible.

'But are you sure he was asking for me?' Daisy said, reviving the topic of conversation that had been interrupted by her small daughter's insistent performance.

'Sure as I sit here. "Daisy," he said. "I want to find Daisy. Mr Oliver said she's gone from here, but you must be able to tell me where." Joan reckons she always knew he had a soft spot for you.'

Daisy blushed and looked at her hands rather than at her visitor.

'Anyway just as we were about to tell him, in came Mr Rupert and started demanding why Ferry and Joan weren't doing the honours with the guests, and then he said something rude about you and the next thing we knew, Griffin was shaping up to him. Might have knocked him down, too, only Miss Jessie stepped in and calmed things down. I think she gave Griffin your address. Didn't he come along here afterwards?'

'No. When was this?' said Daisy.

'Just before Christmas.'

'Oh,' Daisy said on a forlorn note. 'I'd have been in Portsmouth.'

At that moment Harriet succeeded in actually detaching one of Mrs Driver's buttons and putting it into her mouth. The process of getting it out again, and of placating Harriet for the deprivation, occupied the rest of the cook's necessarily short visit – she was supposed to be shopping in Guildford – and meant that Daisy was unable to ask any more questions about Griffin.

But when Mrs Driver had gone, Louella piped up, 'So who's this Griffin?'

'Groom at the Grange,' said Daisy, going pink to the tips of her ears. 'At least he was till the war. Then he joined the artillery.'

'Is it true what she said, about him having a soft spot for you?'

'I don't know,' said Daisy. 'I did sometimes wonder.'

'Well how did you feel about him?'

'I don't know,' Daisy said again. 'He used to make me nervous.'

'Do you mean he frightened you?'

'Not exactly. Only sometimes he'd stand there watching and I'd go funny inside.'

'Oh, that. Better write to him then,' said Louella.

'Do you think I should?'

'Can't do any harm.'

'But with Harriet and everything?' Daisy said doubtfully. 'I don't even know if he knows about her. What do you think I should say?'

In the end, she and Louella composed a careful letter.

Dear Mr Griffin, (or Driver Griffin, I don't know what to call you.) Mrs Driver said you came to the Grange and asked about me. I think you came here as well. I am sorry I was not at home to see you. My brother was in hospital in Portsmouth as he was gassed at Loos, and his wife and I were staying down there to be with him.

Did you know that I have a baby now, born in April? Her name is Harriet. She is lovely but very determined and has quite a temper. You may have heard that my fiancé Arthur was killed in the first fighting at Ypres.

Well, I won't go on now, but I hope you are well and will think of coming to see us when next you are back in Guildford. With all best wishes, Daisy Colindale.

PS I would like it if you would write to me.

Daisy wondered, as she posted it, how long it would take him to reply.

''Ere you are, Lockett, letter from your lady love.'

Burnes, the brigade postman, didn't bother to vary his badinage since so many of his customers became casualty figures before they reached the point of finding the repetition tedious. Lockett took his letter eagerly, ready to feel sentimental about his girl. The battery was back in a 'hot' part of the line and he'd almost forgotten the delights of Madeleine of the farm.

'Seen Griffin?'

'He's in the horse lines, helping the blacksmith with the shoeing.'

'Can I leave his letter with you, then?'

'Stick it in my haversack,' said Lockett without looking up.

He was already immersed in the affectionate outpouring of his Emily.

Burnes pushed the letter into the haversack dangling from the ceiling of the dugout. A few minutes later Lockett emerged to water his horses, and while he was away a German gunner dropped a lucky hit on the dugout. Lockett, surveying the ruins, remembered to lament the loss of his bedding, his spare shirt and his photograph of Emily. He forgot all about Griffin's letter.

Back in Guildford, Daisy waited for an answer, and when none came, concluded sadly that the news of Harriet had damped down whatever interest in her had ever been felt by Will Griffin. It was a painful thought. But less painful than the alternative explanation for his silence – that he might have joined the long list of those 'Killed in Action' on the Western Front.

Laura found it hard to return to Clandon as a married woman. The other girls seemed to treat her differently, leaving her out of their late-night gossiping sessions about 'best boys' and the over-bold or attractive patients in the wards. It was as if the few days with Charles and those uncertain night-time fumblings had altered her in some way, turning her into a sober matron. She remembered her own reactions to her cousin Alice after her marriage to Hugh. Laura, too, had looked for signs of change in Alice . . . and had found them. The girl had been so obviously happy, transfigured by the experiences of her marriage. Laura was not.

Perhaps it would be better when Charles came home again, when she'd had a chance to get used to the idea? And perhaps next time he would be less haggard, less silent and twitchy. It had been hard to inject any joy into their days together when her new husband said so little and only watched her all the time with that awful, anxious expression, reaching for her hand as if he expected her to snatch it away.

She envied Claire who had no doubts at all about loving Oliver, though she was far from blind to his faults. A letter from Laura's brother could lift Claire in to a sunny mood for an entire day, so that she'd accept with perfect equanimity the teasing of the soldier-patients.

''Ullo, she's 'ad another letter. Oh, Nurse Lawrence, if only it was I that could bring that sparkle to your eyes!'

The Australian with the roving hands even put it into one of his odes, though nowadays he had accepted the hopelessness of his attachment.

> She walks in beauty down the ward,
> Her smile is kind but cruel.
> She little cares how she's adored
> By this unlucky fool.
> Alas, she has no time for me,
> There's one that she loves better.
> Her sweetheart's in the artillery,
> Today she's had a letter.

This offering sent Claire into gales of laughter. 'Isn't it *sweet*? Oh dear. Shakespeare he isn't!'

It was surprising how cheerful Claire could be amid the daily routine of the hospital. Christmas at Clandon, Laura gathered, had been great fun. The wards had been decorated with holly and paper garlands and the VADs had crept round in the night, tucking presents into the socks that the patients had hung from the ends of their beds – oranges and peppermints, chocolate and tobacco, penknives and handkerchiefs with the Union Jack on them, all bought in Guildford on afternoons off and carefully gift-wrapped by the night nurses in the long, quiet hours. There'd been carol-singing, and the commandant and Matron had performed a duet that was received with rapturous applause. There'd even been mistletoe, under which the Australian had cornered Claire and obtained his first and only kiss.

At Maple Grange, Laura and Charles had exchanged solemn gifts under the eyes of a benignly smiling Rupert. A luxurious dressing gown for Charles, a pair of diamond-and-pearl drop earrings for Laura: neither present remotely appropriate to their current lives. It had been rather depressing.

At Clandon, as winter dragged on, Laura lay awake in the night nursery listening to the steady breathing of the other girls who shared the large room, and wondering how she had got herself into such a mess. Outside on the ruined lawns, the peacocks that were leftovers from the house's gracious past sometimes screamed in the darkness. She felt like joining them.

17

On 22 March, 1916, the First Battalion, the Queen's, was in the front line near Beuvry. For the time being the war was static, a state brought about by the total exhaustion of both sides.

The enemy might be exhausted in terms of manpower, but they had not run out of artillery ammunition. In mid-morning, Robert Colindale lay in his shallow dugout among a group of fellow-soldiers, all trying to snatch some sleep because there'd been a trench raid on the German lines last night and there was likely to be another tonight. Eyes closed, head buried in his overcoat to keep the rats off his face, he heard the shriek of a land mine coming over and the woosh-woosh of it turning in the air. He emerged from the coat and sat up, along with every other occupant of the dugout, staring at the shored-up roof. The hair on his scalp lifted.

'It's going to be close,' someone said.

The blast picked up everything in the dugout and hurled it down again in a tangle of legs and arms. Robert came down bottom of the heap, with another man, unconscious or dead, lying across his head and shoulders. Above them, the sides of the dugout had caved in.

Robert lay pinned down in total darkness. He could scarcely breathe for the pressure on his chest, but there was a small clear space around his nose and mouth, created by the arm of the man above him. The air he dragged in stank of mud and sweat and blood.

Previously, in the hospital at Portsmouth, struggling for each breath in the aftermath of the gassing, he'd dreamed of being buried alive. It was the worst of his nightmares.

Time passed and he knew he would die. He thought of Louella and her baby that he'd never see: and of his mother who should be waiting in heaven, except that he'd never really believed all that stuff about heaven. The tears ran down his face and trickled into his ears. 'Oh, God,' he said, 'Oh, God,' knowing that nobody could hear him.

And then, unbelievably, the weight on his body was shifted. Daylight blinded him. Cold air in his lungs. He was lifted and propped into a sitting position on the fire step of the trench, back against the sandbags of the parados. Concerned faces peered at him.

'This one's OK. You're OK, mate. Talk about lucky.'

He was shaking uncontrollably. Someone pushed a tin mug into his hand but he couldn't keep his hand steady enough to get it to his mouth. It jerked in front of his dazed eyes as he sat there crying.

'Here you are, mate.' A hand guided the mug to his lips. It jolted against his teeth. He swallowed the contents down, then choked at the unfamiliar stuff burning the back of his throat. Brandy was for officers. But it got his brain working again. He began to take in the important things: that he was alive, and whole, though his hands still trembled and there didn't seem to be any strength in his aching body. Out of the corner of his eye, he saw a hand sticking out of the heap of earth and split sandbags beside the place where the dugout entrance had been. He recognized the scar on the thumb where Anderson had jammed it last week when helping the artillery boys to shift a gun stuck in the mud back in Bethune. Shouldn't someone dig the poor blighter out? He dragged himself to his feet and took a step towards the heap of earth and found that someone *had* dug Anderson out. And laid him in tidy sections on the far side of the heap.

They put Robert on a stretcher and carried him down the communication trenches to a field dressing-station, where a harassed MO gave him a cursory going-over and announced that he was undamaged. He walked back on his own legs, wading through the muddy water in the flooded parts of the trench network, in time to be briefed for the night's forthcoming raid.

'You've got some legal experience, haven't you, Allingham?'

'Yes, sir. I was training as a solicitor before the war.'

'Fine. Then you can be Prisoner's Friend.'

Edward grimaced. He'd heard about that job. Any soldier who underwent a Field General Court Martial on a charge of Desertion or Cowardice, for which the sentence might be death if found guilty, was entitled to the help of an officer in presenting his case. But out here at the Front, a court martial was such a far cry from a civilian trial that to have any knowledge of civil processes of law, he suspected, was actually a disadvantage.

'What's it about, sir?' he asked the captain who'd appointed him.

'Some soldier who went on strike the other night. Detailed to take part in a trench raid, but when the party got back they found him still sitting in our own trench. Wouldn't say a word when questioned, blank refusal to obey orders. Open-and-shut case, really.'

It was a last-minute duty. When Edward arrived at the *estaminet* where the court martial was to be held, the other members of the court were already assembled in an upstairs bedroom. The bed, a ponderous construction with tall wooden posts at the four corners and a grubby lace bedspread, had been pushed back against a wall to make room for an ill-matched assortment of chairs. Downstairs, the normal business of the establishment continued noisily. In another room the prisoner waited under guard.

'Come on, Lieutenant Allingham, let's get this business done with.'

'Sir,' Edward said, to the major in charge, 'can I have a consultation with the prisoner before we begin?'

'I hope we aren't going to have too much of this legal smart stuff,' the Major said, looking at him with disfavour.

338

'If I'm to function as "Prisoner's Friend", sir, I do have to have at least a few minutes with him.'

'Oh, all right, if you must. Coffee, gentlemen?' said the major, looking at his watch.

The prisoner was a gaunt young man with reddish brown hair and a pallid complexion. He gave the impression of having lost interest in everything that happened to him. Questioned, he confirmed that he'd failed to go on the trench raid as ordered.

'Why did you do that?'

'I'd had enough.'

'But you've been on raids before?'

'Yes.'

'So what was different about this one?'

'I'd had enough.'

'You're an experienced soldier, aren't you?' said Edward. 'You've been out here a long time?'

'Too long,' said the man.

'I think we all feel that,' Edward said. He rubbed at his forehead. The prisoner's attitude wouldn't get him anywhere with the court. He didn't display any contrition; he simply repeated with the obduracy of a stone wall that he'd had enough. Edward wished he knew more about the soldier. The man's face wasn't familiar to him. There should have been a report from his NCO, but the whole event had been too hurriedly staged. There was only his paybook, which in itself didn't convey much beyond the fact that the accused hadn't been in any serious trouble before. He had come out with the BEF at the beginning of the war, which ought to count for something.

'Can you think of anyone in the regiment who could speak up in your favour? Say what a good record you have?' Perhaps, Edward was thinking, he could plead for an adjournment in order to get some kind of defence together. But the prisoner looked at him blankly.

'Any friends who know you well?' Edward persisted. The man laughed.

'Friends? They're all dead. Every last one of them.'

'Well,' Edward said helplessly, 'we have to consider whether you wish to plead guilty or not guilty.'

'Might as well be guilty. I did what they're saying I did. I stayed behind when I should have gone. If they gave me the same order again I'd do it again. I've had enough.'

Did the man realize, Edward wondered, what was going to happen to him if he were found guilty?

'You know the sentence for Cowardice?' he asked. Just for a moment, there was a spark of life in the man's dead, closed expression.

'Is that what they call it? Cowardice?' he said. Then he spread his hands in a gesture of indifference. 'They'll shoot me. What does it matter who kills me, them or the Boche?'

Edward was about to say, 'It'll matter to your family.' But the major appeared in the doorway and cut the interview short.

'Ready, Allingham? For God's sake, get a move on or we'll be here all night.'

The Field General Court Martial found the soldier guilty of cowardly behaviour and sentenced him to death by firing squad.

'This is only the first stage,' the major told Edward, who was unhappy with the proceedings. 'After this, the findings of the court get passed up through the chain of command, all the way to the top. There's every opportunity for the man's record to be properly taken into account, as you say it should be, and for his officers to put in a recommendation for mercy.'

In the days that followed, Edward learned by questioning members of the battalion that the prisoner had recently returned from hospital in England, where he had been getting over the effect of a gassing at Loos, that he was thought to have family worries and that he had been buried alive by a shell explosion for a short while on the day of the incident. The few fellow-soldiers and officers who had been around long enough to remember him from his pre-gassing days considered that he was a good soldier, if a bit morose. Edward nagged his captain about the case and the captain nagged the major. The major grudgingly conceded that a recommendation for mercy might be appropriate, and duly appended one.

The papers were sent to the commander-in-chief for what was termed 'consideration', though Edward gathered that the c-in-c never interfered with the decision of the court.

'Then what's the point of a recommendation for mercy?' he asked the captain, who shrugged. He had more pressing matters on his mind. Despite the non-cooperation of one miserable soldier, the trench raids conducted by the rest of the battalion had been so successful that they had earned a commendation from HQ. A general was to come on a visit of inspection and congratulate them personally, which would involve immense efforts of 'bull' on the part of the troops to render themselves sufficiently smart for the occasion.

The general came. He reviewed the artillery emplacements and the ammunition depots and picked his way carefully along the reserve trenches, though not the front-line area, in his jodhpurs and well-polished boots, pointing with his cane at anything that interested or displeased him. Before leaving, as an afterthought, he passed on confirmation of the sentence of death on the convicted coward.

'Could I have a word with you, sir?'

The general looked ostentatiously at his watch. There would be a meal waiting for him back at the château: there were reports to read tonight and he'd had a difficult day in the mud. And he could tell by the young officer's nervous, apologetic manner that he was about to be subjected to some impracticable request. He hoped it wasn't going to be a desperate plea for a transfer to a staff post – they were over-supplied with staff officers already, many of them there because some powerful relation had been pulling strings. And at the rate the division had been losing officers, they needed to keep every last one of them at the Front. He sighed.

'Very well. What is it? Briefly.'

'Sir, do we have to do this execution? It's not as if the poor devil's shirked his share of the fighting. He's been in the front line regularly since the beginning of the war – he was a reservist who came out with the first batch in 1914. He's stood everything the Boche hurled at him so far, and he's been gassed and sent back after it. Can't we let it go?'

'No, Lieutenant, we can't let it go. In the first place, the case papers have been seen and the death warrant has been signed by the commander-in-chief. And secondly, the purpose of such a court martial is to make it clear that shirkers and cowards will receive short shrift. In the field, every soldier must pull his weight or be a danger and a liability to his comrades. If we overlook a serious case of disobedience like this, every soldier who felt he'd done enough would be dropping out of the line at crucial moments. And then where would we be?'

I know where you'd be, Edward thought with a sudden wave of revulsion. *Back in your nice, comfortable office at GHQ, standing in front of a marble fireplace, playing with your cane and looking at a relief map on which the men are smaller than pinheads, the way you always are whenever there's any actual fighting to be done. Pontificating about how one determined push will do it and how it's all worth the sacrifice. . . .*

He looked at the general's implacable face and reflected bitterly that it was these old commanders who were the soldier's enemy, not the poor devils of Fritzes who just heard the same old lies and the same bungled orders in a different language.

It was Edward's job to supervise the execution, which took place in a nearby farmyard at dawn, in keeping with tradition. The firing party turned out grumbling into the grey light. Nobody liked the duty and the habitual wrongdoers of the battalion had been nominated, without the option to refuse, by a hard-hearted sergeant.

At least it wasn't going to be one of those public shootings, with the man's comrades lined up to watch and be warned.

The soldier who was to die seemed in a daze, as indeed he had been ever since his arrest. Last night the brief ceremony of 'Promulgation of the sentence' had confirmed his fate. He sat on the ground with his back against the scarred stone wall of the barn, head lolling, stupid with misery. The padre was squatting beside him, going through his routine, but it was plain that the condemned man wasn't even listening.

The protocol required the officer in charge of the execution to bandage the man's eyes. At Edward's approach, the soldier scrambled awkwardly to his feet.

'Not much of a way to go, is it?' he said, his speech slurred, his eyes bloodshot and unfocused. 'Still, got to make an example. Poor Bloody Infantry won't fight if you don't give them an example.'

Judging by the smell of his breath, someone had slipped him a stiff measure of brandy and Edward did not feel disposed to hunt out the culprit.

There was a ring in the wall of the farmyard which might once have tethered a bull, and to this the prisoner's hands were tied behind his back. Adjusting a folded handkerchief clumsily across the man's eyes and knotting it behind his head, grazing his own knuckles against the rough stonework in the process, Edward was aware of laboured breathing and the warmth of a human body beside his.

This is murder, he thought. *And I'm carrying it out because I can't think of anything else to do.*

The sergeant handed him a small square of white cloth to be pinned over the man's heart, as a target for the firing squad. For a moment Edward was unable even to remember which side of the chest the heart lay. Tactfully, the sergeant plucked at the tunic of the unresisting victim in the appropriate place and handed the officer a pin.

'All set, sir?'

Edward had loaded the men's rifles for them in advance. One rifle contained a blank round. If they felt squeamish about what they were doing, the executioners could delude themselves until they had pulled the trigger that their particular

343

gun was the one with the blanks. Afterwards they would know. Any experienced soldier could tell a live round.

The sergeant, standing by the ten men of the firing party, waited for the prearranged series of signals that would tell them when to fire. In an ironic mimicking of compassion, someone in high office had decreed that though a deserter or coward must die, he need not be subjected to the words, 'Ready' and 'Present'. No doubt whoever was responsible had congratulated themselves on their humanitarian gesture.

Edward's heart was hammering the way it did before they went over the top last year at Loos, or before one of the trench raids which had finished the nerve of this particular soldier. He hesitated. But it was no kindness to prolong the moment. He raised his right arm and made the three signals, the last with his fist clenched.

The braced figures of the firing squad jerked in unison at the recoil of the guns. The blindfolded man shuddered, then jackknifed, legs splayed below the knees, wrists still dragged upwards behind his back by the tethering ring. Edward walked forward with his revolver in his hand. If the man had not died instantly, it would be his duty to administer the *coup de grâce*.

The MO had a pocketknife out and had cut the body loose by the time Edward reached him. He squatted on his heels, hand over the man's heart inside his tunic. It came out bloody. He looked up and motioned Edward away.

'No need for that. Instantaneous.'

'Burial party,' Edward said and turned away, heartsick, from the huddled corpse. He thought this was probably the worst action of his life, and the one of which he would always be most ashamed. . . .

When Louella saw a buff envelope that was not a telegram in the delivery boy's hand, she breathed more easily and gave him a penny for his trouble. It would be some communication from the Powers That Be about the Separation Allowance, now much reduced since the death of Robert's mother. She filled the kettle at the sink and placed it on top of the stove before she investigated the envelope's contents. The words hit her harder because of the moment of false security that had preceded them.

'I am directed to inform you that a report has been received from the War Office to the effect that No. —, Private Robert Joseph Colindale, First Battalion, Queen's Royal West Surrey Regiment, was sentenced after being tried by court martial to suffer death by being shot, and his sentence was duly executed on 7 April 1916.'

After the shock's first impact came the enduring reality. Robert was dead. Louella and Daisy wore black and exhibited obvious signs of grief, but the local paper carried no notice of the soldier's death in battle. The whispers started. Later, when men of the battalion came home on leave and told what they knew, the whispers intensified.

Some were sympathetic. 'Robert Colindale. Who'd have thought it? Must've seen some terrible things to make him behave that way.'

Others were quick to condemn. 'Good thing too. Teach the shirkers that they can't go foisting the danger on to other mens' shoulders.'

Louella dragged herself wanly about the house, hunched over her sorrow. It was Daisy who braved the stares and pushed the perambulator down to the shops to buy the family's food, only to find that Louella refused all sustenance – not that there was much to refuse. The Separation Allowance had stopped and there was no pension to replace it. The War Office had taken no decision on the question of pensions for the families of men executed for desertion or cowardice.

Robert's effects were sent home in a packet, together with a well-meant letter from a junior officer who clearly didn't know about the Record Office communication and who wrote, with no details, that Private Colindale had died in action, had been much liked in the regiment and would be missed by his comrades. Inside the packet was a soldier's will, written out on the back of an envelope, which left what Robert had to his wife, Louella. What he had, it seemed, was a few shillings from his last week's pay, a crumpled pack of Woodbines, a prayer book, a couple of dirty, finger-printed sepia photographs, a bundle of letters from Louella and Daisy – the latest of which were returned unopened, stamped 'Deceased' – and a badly dented silver Vesta case.

In the end Louella's longing for oblivion came up against her hard core of common sense. She and Daisy examined their prospects and their assets. It was a brief discussion.

'No money. Nothing left to pawn. What shall we do?' Daisy said.

'I don't know,' Louella said hopelessly. 'I'd say, I'll work. But I'm pregnant. If I do anything strenuous I could lose the baby. And he wanted it so much,' she added. The tears she'd thought were exhausted welled again in her eyes.

Daisy absent-mindedly scooped up a determined Harriet, who was swarming on all fours towards the stairs. 'What about your family?' She had never met Louella's people.

Louella had come down one summer with a party of hop-pickers from London and standing among the tall poles near the lane at Seale, stripping the bines, had caught Robert's eye as he strolled along to meet Daisy on one of her days off from the Grange. The hop-pickers were an annual event in the district, a cheerful, raucous and disreputable invasion from the East End of London, but Louella had been different from her companions, quieter, more refined. Daisy had never known whether her sister-in-law's reticence about her family was because she was ashamed of them and wanted them kept away from Robert, or the reverse. Now Louella said, 'I'd rather not go to them.' No explanation.

Daisy shifted Harriet to the other hip and said, 'Well . . . there's the Poor Law Relief.'

Frequently administered with the utmost meanness and incorporating the utmost humiliation for those obliged to seek it, the Relief was a last resort.

'Who are the Guardians?' said Louella.

'The only one I know of is Mr Brownlowe at the Grange.'

They stared at each other. It was not a propitious thought.

346

Strictly speaking, Rupert should have passed on the Colindales' application to a properly convened committee of the
Guardians for a decision. But he didn't see the necessity. He
eyed the two women who stood before him with cold distaste.
Daisy Colindale had brought her bastard child along with her,
perhaps in the hope of rousing more sympathy. Well, it hadn't
worked. The Colindales were clearly a bad lot – first a slut
of a servant and now a cowardly soldier. And the widow was
visibly pregnant, too. Doubtless expecting the good people of
Guildford to keep her and her progeny. He wholeheartedly
approved of the verdict of the Field General Court Martial
and of the sentence carried out. He didn't see why the parish
should have to pay for the consequences.

'If you are given Poor Law Relief,' he pointed out, 'it would
be to place you on a par with the families of decent men, men
who have fought and died for their country, not abandoned it
like cowards. I hardly think that this is what the fund is
intended for.'

Louella had been slumped in apathy. It was Daisy who had
made the request, standing apprehensively in the morning
room at Maple Grange with Harriet in her arms. But now the
widow spoke, with a shaking vehemence that took Rupert by
surprise.

'Decent men? Decent like you, do you mean? My husband
fought. My God, he fought. He went out with the first of them
in 1914. He was at Ypres when the battalion was torn to
pieces. He was at Loos. He was gassed, it took months in
hospital to get well again. They made him go back. You call
him a coward, and you . . . you've sat here on your well-padded
backside the whole of the bloody war, making money out of
your shells, pointing your fat finger in con- demnation at those
who were better men than you'll ever be. I wouldn't take your
charity,' said Louella. 'I'd rather starve.'

'As it happens my charity is not on offer,' said Rupert.
'Starve away.' Louella stepped forward and for one in-
credulous moment, he thought she was going to strike him

across the face. Another one? First that groom and now this coward's relict had threatened him, and both in his own home! The decent world was going crazy.

Instead she spat. The glob of spittle landed on his clean-shaven cheek and he recoiled in disgust, groping in his trouser pocket for his linen handkerchief.

'One day I'll pay you back for what you've said and done today, Mr Brownlowe,' said Louella. Harriet, frightened by the angry voices, began to cry.

'Come on, Lou.' Daisy hadn't had high hopes of the interview anyway. She was half-horrified, half-impressed by Louella's behaviour. But she recognized that if she didn't get her sister-in-law away now, anything could happen. She clutched Louella's wrist and tugged her towards the door, balancing a screaming Harriet on her shoulder with one hand as she did so.

When the women had gone, Rupert owned himself shaken by the incident. The widow had spoken with such suppressed violence that he could almost believe her capable of murder. He pulled himself together. A hysterical female, turned wild by the news of her husband's very proper execution. What power had she to harm a man like Rupert Brownlowe?

'What now?' said Daisy at home.

'One of us will have to work,' said Louella. 'And one will have to look after Harriet.'

Since Louella was nearly five months pregnant, the appropriate division of labour was obvious.

'But not here,' Louella added. 'I can't stand to stay here and know everyone's talking about Robert behind my back. We'd better go to London.'

Daisy was willing. She too was tired of putting a brave face on things in Guildford, being pointed out as the sister of a man who'd been shot by his own side. The problem was how to afford the move. So the next day she took Harriet into the town in search of work, wheeling the battered old perambulator round the shops.

'No work here,' was the general response. 'But Mr Brown-lowe's taking on women for his shell-making,' one shopkeeper suggested, meaning to be helpful because the girl's gaunt face troubled his conscience. 'Why don't you try there?'

With a sense of hopelessness, Daisy turned for home. As she manoeuvred her perambulator round the corner of Market Street, she almost collided with a couple of young women in VAD uniform.

'Why, it's Daisy!' said one. 'Daisy Colindale!'

Daisy raised her tired eyes. Miss Laura, now Mrs Charles McKay, was staring at her in consternation.

'How are you? You don't look very well.'

'Don't I, miss? I mean, ma'am.'

'Your perambulator,' said Laura. 'What happened to the one I sent you? Wasn't it any good? I chose it out of a catalogue, but it sounded very nice.'

'Oh it was, ma'am. It was beautiful.' Daisy was red with shame. 'Only we had to sell it,' she whispered.

'Hard times?' said Miss Laura's companion sympatheti-cally. She was a tall, auburn-haired girl whom Daisy re-membered as a guest at the Grange. Miss Lawrence, wasn't that her name? 'Yes, miss,' Daisy agreed humbly.

'But doesn't your family get the Separation Allowance for your brother?' asked Laura. 'I know it's not much, but—'

'Not any more, ma'am. Robert was shot, you see.'

'Shot?' Laura echoed blankly. 'Oh Daisy, I'm so sorry. But surely there's a pension?'

'No, miss. *Ma'am*. Not if he's shot.'

'I don't understand,' Laura said.

Claire Lawrence nudged her. 'Court martial,' she hissed.

'Oh, *Daisy*.' Laura was appalled. She didn't know what to say. She racked her brains.

'Have you spoken to my father? I'm sure he'd do some-thing.'

'No, ma'am, he wouldn't. Louella and I went to ask about the Poor Law Relief, with him being one of the Guardians, but he said we couldn't have any as Robert didn't die for his country but for what he did. He said it wasn't right to put us on a par with decent people,' Daisy recalled bitterly.

'I'll talk to him,' Laura said.

'I don't think it'd do any good, ma'am.'

'Well, then, let me help.' Laura reviewed the contents of her purse. 'I haven't much money with me now,' she added apologetically, 'but I'll send you what I can tomorrow.'

'Would you, ma'am? I'd be ever so grateful. I'd pay you back soon as I can, ma'am,' said Daisy, the heat scorching her cheeks.

'You'll receive something tomorrow. I promise.' Laura tried to smile at Harriet, who was regarding her with curiosity.

After Daisy had gone on her way, pushing the decrepit old perambulator, her shoulders slumped with weariness, Claire turned to Laura.

'Sometimes . . .' she said, 'I know he's your father, Laura, but I have to say that there are occasions when Rupert Brownlowe behaves rather nastily.'

Laura didn't argue the point. She wanted to believe that Pa had some justification for his harshness to Daisy, but it was hard to find an excuse. After all, whatever Daisy's brother had done, it wasn't her fault, or his wife's, and it certainly wasn't the poor baby's.

Next day she despatched a five-pound note to Daisy from Clandon, with a message that more would follow when she could manage it. Daisy sent back a letter saying that there was no need for more and thanking her very much for her kindness, which would be repaid at the earliest possible date. With the money, the Colindales went to London.

In May of 1916, Margaret had started to drop things. First a cup or a plate as she took her hurried tea on duty at Camiers. Then the more important things: a bottle of ether, a disk full of surgeon's instruments, a thermometer as she shook it.

'My fingers are numb,' she said apologetically to Matron. 'And I seem to have lost my judgement about where things are in relation to one another.' She was perpetually tired, too, dragging herself around the wards on leaded legs and with odd blank places where her memory should have been.

'You are working too hard. It's a habit of yours, I've noticed,' said Matron. 'You'd better take some sick leave.'

Margaret complied. The constant fatigue had sapped her confidence as much as it had interfered with her ability to carry out her duties. She was increasingly afraid that she would make mistakes, lethal ones.

In June, Edward arrived at her parents' home in Iffley and carried her off for what he called a 'proper' honeymoon, though for Margaret the few days in Paris last November had been as proper as any bride could wish. She still found it difficult to believe that Paris and Edward had happened to her, they were so much in contrast with the horrors of her daily life at the hospital.

'Where are we going?' she remembered to ask in the train.

'Someone has lent us a cottage in Surrey. I happened to meet him as I was changing trains at Guildford. He has a little place on his estate that's empty at the moment but in good order and he said we were welcome to use it. The staff at the main house will pop across and "do" for us, so we don't even need to worry about hiring a help, and it'll be far more private than a hotel or our parents' homes. I thought it sounded just the job.'

'Who's the benefactor?'

'Rupert Brownlowe. He was at Alice Delamere's wedding in August 1914. And you met his son and daughter, that day at Oxford. The day the war began,' Edward said.

'Oh, yes. Laura.'

Margaret supposed it was unreasonable and childish of her to mind, just a little, that her time with Edward was to be spent on the premises of, if not under the actual nose of, Laura Brownlowe.

'Will she be around?'

'I don't know,' said Edward. 'She was about to start VAD nursing the last time I saw her.'

'Really? I had the impression it wasn't her kind of activity.'

'Maybe it wasn't. She's married now,' said Edward. To change the subject, he started to tell Margaret about the court martial he'd been involved with, about the execution afterwards and the way it had affected him.

'I felt horribly guilty about it. I still do. I feel I should have argued more, insisted on having more time to prepare a proper case. The man wasn't interested in saving himself, that's the way it seemed at the time, but he'd been blown up the day it happened. Direct hit on his dugout. Most of the men with him were killed. That sort of experience is bound to knock you sideways for a while, isn't it? There should have been some recognition of that . . . but nobody cared.'

'You did your best,' Margaret said. 'By the sound of it you did more than most people would for someone they didn't know.'

'But it wasn't enough. And I took charge of the execution.'

'Obeying orders.'

'Should one always obey orders? Even when one knows they are wrong? I keep thinking of the hymn that begins "Once to every man and nation comes the moment to decide. . . ." I should have stood out against that order.'

'That's asking too much of yourself,' said Margaret gently. 'You're only human. I'm only human. There have been patients who've died, whom I sometimes suspect might have lived if I'd acted a little more quickly, or spotted a complication sooner, but we do the best we can at the time. It's no good blaming yourself afterwards.'

'But that poor devil of a soldier. . . .'

Jasmine Cottage was at least a hundred years old, with stone walls, a chimney at each end of the wavy-tiled roof and four small-paned windows set around the front door like a child's drawing. It had been part of the Maple Grange land long before the new house was built, and from time to time it had housed workers from the Home Farm. Its last occupants had been a family with nine children, now moved to a larger house on Rupert's estate, after which Jasmine Cottage had been cleaned up and repaired, and a new dog-leg staircase installed instead of the ladder up which the nine children had climbed to their sleeping quarters on the first floor.

Rupert had been apologetic about the smallness of the cottage he was lending to the young couple, but when the cab deposited them at the wicket gate, Margaret and Edward found it delightful with its old rose hedging and the sweet-scented jasmine that swarmed over the porch.

Edward produced a key and opened the white-painted front door. Then, in accordance with tradition, he carried his wife over the threshold.

'Why did you marry me?' Margaret asked him after their first night at the cottage.

'Because I didn't think you'd let me do this otherwise,' said Edward, lifting her nightdress over her arms and head as he spoke.

'I mean seriously. Why choose me?'

'Because of your honesty. And your intelligence. Because you see what's good and what's evil, for all their complexities, more clearly than anyone else I know. But you don't judge harshly. What's the matter?' said Edward, noticing her rueful expression.

'You could have a grandmother with those qualities,' said Margaret.

'But I don't.'

'Sometimes,' said Margaret wistfully, 'I know it's silly but . . . I wish I was the kind of girl that men wrote poems for. I wish I could be loved for something less *worthy* than my sterling character. Something like my eyes, or my hair,' she added, with a recollection of the blue-and-golden beauty of Laura Brownlowe in a punt at Oxford.

Edward looked puzzled. Then understanding dawned.

'Oh. That. That goes without saying.'

'No, it doesn't.'

'All right. I'll say it.' Edward knelt above her in the bed and kissed the top of her head. 'I love you for your hair.' He lifted a handful of it and momentarily buried his face in the thick masses. 'And for your understanding eyes.' He kissed her closed, quivering eyelids. 'And your lovely, generous mouth.' He spent a long time on that before his lips travelled to her throat and downwards. 'And this . . . and this. . . .'

With her old habit of insecurity, Margaret wondered if he meant any of what he was saying. Then she decided that she didn't care, she would take it anyway.

18

Margaret opened her eyes and it was mid-afternoon. The scent of jasmine drifted in through the open sash window. Edward had just set down a tea tray on the bedside table.

'Earl Grey,' he said, 'and Mrs Driver's jam sponge. And I was going to write you a poem, but Skelton has already done it better than I could. Here.' He laid an open book in front of her. Margaret sat up with the sheet pulled up against her body, held in place by her bare arm, and leaned forward. Her unpinned hair, falling on either side of her face, softened her features. She looked happy, and rested, and Edward thought that at this moment his supposedly plain, prosaic wife was more beautiful than she would ever realize. He wished he could convince her that he loved her in the way she wanted. He read her the opening lines of the poem that John Skelton had written to Mistress Margaret Hussey, towards the end of the fifteenth century.

> Merry Margaret
> As midsummer flower
> Gentle as falcon
> Or hawk of the tower.'

'I've always wondered about that,' said Margaret. ' "*Gentle*" isn't the word that usually springs to mind when you think of hawks and falcons. Did Mistress Margaret have a nose like mine, do you suppose?'

'It's a very nice nose,' said Edward, kissing it and returning to the poem. 'With solace and gladness, Much mirth and no madness, All good and no badness. . . .'

'*Merry Margaret?* Not much mirth nowadays,' said Margaret wryly.

'We'll find it again,' said Edward. 'When the war's over.'

'Are you sure you don't want me to come to the station?'

The discussion of all parting lovers.

'No. Better not to.' Edward shrugged into his tunic and Margaret ducked under his arm to fasten the buttons. Her fingers were still numb and clumsy and she managed to make the task last a long time, but finally it was done and he picked up his cap and his valise.

'Edward. . . .' By the front door of Jasmine Cottage, Margaret took hold of his lapels. In a way they had already said their goodbyes but she couldn't quite let him go yet. 'Come back to me, won't you?'

'Through hell or high water,' he promised. He put the valise down again and wrapped his arms round her. 'I love you, Mrs Allingham.' He laid his cheek against her hair for a moment and his arms tightened.

'I love you,' he repeated, with a catch in his voice.

Then he was walking briskly down the garden path. At the bottom he closed the gate carefully and crossed the road towards the Grange, where Rupert's chauffeur was waiting to drive him to the station in Guildford. He looked back once before he disappeared.

It was with obvious reluctance that Louella took Daisy and Harriet to her old home in Bethnal Green: a row of terraced houses in a mean street. Mrs Colindale's Guildford house had been small and cheaply built but was always kept clean and respectable even in times of financial hardship. This area was noticeably down-at-heel. Ragged children squabbled on doorsteps that hadn't seen a whitening stone in years. Skinny dogs nosed at scraps in the gutters. A small boy, his bare legs streaked with dirt below the oversized trousers tied around his waist with string, was trundling a rusty iron bicycle wheel instead of a hoop among the grass tufts that disfigured the road surface.

'Hullo Jem,' said Louella. The boy had been intent on his

game, but he stopped in his tracks to stare at her, wordlessly, before resuming his solitary occupation. He nudged the pram as he passed, but Harriet slept on amid the bags that held Louella's and Daisy's clothes, tired out by the long railway journeyings and the walk from the station in the June evening sunlight.

Louella knocked at a scarred front door beside a grimy window. After a pause it was opened by a thin, dark-haired woman in whose face a faint echo of Louella's prettiness could still be discerned.

'Hullo Mother.'

The woman looked at the visitors with eyes that were too tired and demoralized to register surprise.

'Are you going to ask me in? Or do I stand on the doorstep?' said Louella sharply.

Her mother moved aside and Louella pushed past her. Daisy followed, leaving the door open so that she could keep an eye on the perambulator in the street. The front door of this house opened directly into a living room, shadowy and shabby. An unshaded light bulb dangled from the ceiling, a flyblown sepia picture of Queen Victoria in a chipped wooden frame hung askew above the ugly cast-iron fireplace, which was clearly lacking the attentions that had kept the fireplaces at Maple Grange shining. Patches of damp stained the walls.

Facing them on a chaise longue with crudely carved legs, its rubbed and torn velvet upholstery shedding horsehair stuffing, lay a man. Beside his dangling hand, cold tea stagnated in a saucerless cup. He hauled himself upright as the two girls came in, swinging his bare feet to the ground, and surveyed them with suspicion.

'My mother, Agnes,' Louella told Daisy briefly. 'My stepfather, Bert Wilkins.'

The man was heavily built, with small eyes buried in swollen red cheeks and downward lines of cruelty on either side of his full-lipped mouth. The broken veins on his nose advertised the fact that he drank too much for his own good, and the yellowing bruises on Agnes' cheek and jaw showed that she shared the consequences.

'So you're back,' he said without enthusiasm. 'To what do we owe the honour? Left your husband?'

'No,' said Louella. 'He's dead.'

The man grunted. 'So what do you want? You can't come back here. No room. There's been another little 'un since you left, not that you've ever bothered to ask.'

'No need to ask,' Louella said. 'Nothing changes, does it?'

'None of your lip, my girl.'

'I'm not your girl,' said Louella. 'Mother, I came to see how you were, and to ask if you know of anywhere that we can get cheap lodgings?'

'You could try Mrs Jenkins round the corner,' said Agnes Wilkins, ignoring the first part of the question. 'I've heard she's got a room empty.' She had showed no emotion, no joy in seeing her daughter after what must be well over two years' absence. Nor was she interested in Daisy or the perambulator parked outside the door. Nobody offered the visitors any refreshment.

'Thank you. That's all. Come on, Daisy.'

It was the briefest call that Daisy had made in her life. Taken by surprise, she was left standing as Louella moved towards the door.

'Call again, Lady Muck, feel free,' sneered Bert from the chaise longue as his stepdaughter made her exit.

Louella stalked down the street, her mouth set with disgust. Daisy hurried after her with the perambulator.

'I should have known better than to go there,' Louella said. 'Any port in a storm, but that man will never even be that.' She turned her head as Daisy caught up. 'He still hits her,' she said. 'Did you see the brusies?'

'Yes,' Daisy said uncomfortably.

'She should never have taken up with him.'

'No.'

'My father was killed. A hay wagon overturned and crushed him. We lived in a tied cottage on a farm out in Essex and she didn't know what to do. Married the first man that'd take us on – and it had to be Bert Wilkins, passing through. Can't blame her, really, widow and a child, no money. But she could have done better than *him*! And she goes on having children, she goes on letting him at them . . . no woman should just stand by and tolerate that, not to her own kids, even if the man is a brute and a bully. She couldn't do any worse if she left him, but she won't.'

Daisy had stopped dead, her expression horrified.

'Oh, Lou . . . you don't mean . . . ?'

'He likes interfering with little children,' said Louella baldly. 'He was always after me on a Friday night when he'd got a few drinks in him, but I was smart enough to give him the slip. And later, when I got old enough, I'd keep him off with a broom handle. But the kids that came later, they weren't so good at defending themselves.'

Now Daisy understood Louella's reticence about her family.

In a neighbouring street, slightly cleaner, Mrs Jenkins at Number Seven agreed that she had a room to let. But the rent she demanded for the small downstairs front room with a bed crammed into it was exorbitant.

'Take it or leave it,' she said. 'Someone else'll want it if you don't. And not everyone'd take in a baby,' she added, eyeing the perambulator. 'Not sure I want to, come to that. Noisy, is she?'

'We'll take it,' said Daisy hastily. They could afford a week's rent but after that, if she didn't find work quickly, they'd be running out of cash again. She wished for a moment that she'd taken Miss Laura at her word and waited for more money, but then more borrowed would be more to repay.

'Want feeding, will you?' said Mrs Jenkins. There was nowhere in the room to cook a meal.

'Yes, I suppose so.'

'That'll be extra.'

After Edward went back to France, Margaret stayed on for a

while at Jasmine Cottage to complete her recovery. She offered rent but Rupert refused it. He was pleased that Edward's wife extended her stay, though Jessie worried that Mrs Allingham might be lonely and kept inviting her over to the house for tea whenever she could spare the time from her own activities, which now included the sewing of sacks for sandbags for the trenches.

'I'm not lonely,' Margaret assured her on one of these visits. 'I miss Edward, of course, but this is good for me after the hospital where one is never alone and there's always something rather unpleasant waiting to be done. You probably think it's a bit odd that I haven't gone back to my parents, but they did keep fussing on while I was there, trying to turn me into an invalid, and that's the last thing I need. I have to get strong again.' She sipped at her tea. 'I shall have to go back as soon as the numbness in my hands and legs has gone. I hope it won't be long – I feel so much better for this rest. Edward thinks there's going to be a big "push" soon on the Western Front. That'll send the casualty figures soaring,' she added grimly.

'Oh dear,' said Jessie. She put down her own teacup and saucer. 'It goes on and on. It seems to have been with us forever, doesn't it? I find it hard to remember what life was like before the war began. And these days I can't remember, if I ever knew, what it is we're all supposed to be fighting for. My brother would be horrified if he heard me say that,' she added ruefully.

'I'm the same,' said Margaret. 'Do you think any one of the nations involved really wanted this war, or had the faintest idea of what they were letting themselves in for when it started? I sometimes wonder if there couldn't have been something said or done by somebody, somewhere, to avert it. And then all those lives would have been saved.'

'Yes,' said Jessie, after a moment. 'I wonder just when and how it *will* end? Whether the enemy will swarm over England, as they are supposed to have swarmed over Belgium and France, committing acts of brutality, and then we'll understand properly what it was all about . . . or whether we'll win and everything will be all right again.'

'I don't think,' said Margaret, 'that things could ever be "all right" again in the way they were before the war, whoever wins the battles.'

On 1 July, 1916, the Allied 'push' that had been the subject of rumour and speculation became a reality on the Somme. After two days of waiting under drenching rain for the signal, the day dawned bright and clear and potentially sweltering. The British troops climbed out of their trenches and walked forward steadily, in parade-ground formation as ordered, towards the enemy trenches whose occupants were supposed to have been destroyed by six days of intensive artillery bombardment. Instead the Germans had been waiting in their deeply fortified dugouts for the bombardment to stop, at which point they emerged, set up their machine guns and slaughtered the oncoming troops.

The sunlight glinted on newly issued tin helmets. Once the German machine-gunners had their sights lined up, they could pick off most of the emerging Tommies before they'd even succeeded in climbing completely out of the trenches. In due course the German commanders ordered a counter-attack, with the same results for their own men. And so it continued.

In 1914 Lord Kitchener had said of the conflict in the trenches, 'This isn't war. I don't know what to do.' But Lord Kitchener had been drowned at the beginning of June, when the *Hampshire* was sunk by German mines off the Orkneys, and in any case he had already given way to commanders who believed that they *did* know what to do: throw men at the enemy, and when they died, throw more.

The first day bought a gain for the British troops: an advance of a mile and the villages of Montauban and Mametz, what was left of them. For this advance they paid a price of fifty-eight thousand casualties. Nineteen thousand were killed outright, the rest crawled or were carried to the first-aid posts, where the stunned staff ran out of wound labels. Commanding officers who had hitherto sent individual letters of condolence over deaths-in-action were forced to abandon the attempt. Instead they wrote to their regiments' local newspapers, expressing their general sorrow.

At Clandon, as at every other hospital in England and in France, the casualties came flooding in.

Nowadays Laura and Claire wore a white stripe on their sleeves to show that they had a year's experience. It distinguished them from the new VADs who had been drafted in to help cope with the seemingly endless flow of wounded. The two girls worked as a team to blanket-bath the new arrivals who came in day and night, straight from the front-line first-aid stations, still streaked with the mud of the battlefield.

'Another red tag.' Claire studied the label on a head-wound case, unconscious on a stretcher before her. 'Prone to convulsions. Better leave this one alone for now.' The head case had been carried from the ambulance into the great hall, but as yet nobody with sufficient medical qualifications was available to supervise his careful transfer from the stretcher to the bed. So many of the wounded were arriving with the broad red stripe on the tag that signalled the need for extra care. In some cases the warning was superfluous. The nurses had just skirted a stretcher whose occupant had lost both legs and one arm.

'They never should have shipped them home in this condition,' said Laura. 'They should have been treated in France.'

On the next stretcher another 'head wound' lay with his eyes open. The bandage wrapped around his forehead was stained rusty where the blood had soaked through the dressing, and dried, during the jolting of the journey.

'There's no room to nurse them over there,' he said matter-of-factly. 'Too many casualties. All the French hospitals can do is slap on a dressing and a tag and shunt us through.'

Claire and Laura carried on, tight-lipped. Like all the other nurses at Clandon, they had someone at the Front, anxiety for

362

whom could not be allowed to distract them from the job in hand.

In the gap between the opening of the Somme offensive and the reporting of it, Margaret Churchill began to have nightmares. Night after night, sleeping in the small, flower-papered bedroom at the front of the cottage, with the sash window open to let in the cool night air, she dreamed of men who climbed out of the trenches and ran, only to have others run across their backs, treading them into the mud.

One night the dream was the worst she had ever known. Under a pale sliver of moon, a figure crawled across a wasteland punctured by deep holes half-full of slimy water that reflected the moonlight. Behind him the night sky was lit with the flashes of explosions, against which the stumps of trees and tangles of barbed wire were briefly silhouetted. In places the wire was festooned with huddled forms that were vaguely human. Other hummocks on the ground might be a raised knee, an outflung arm. The crawling man's hands clawed at the earth. His head and shoulders inched closer. Hatless, under his disordered hair dark rivers trickled down his face. His laboured breathing rasped in her ears.

Margaret's eyes flew open. The breathing had been her own.

There was someone sitting on the edge of the bed. She was aware of the tilt of the mattress and a man's shape outlined against the faint light from the window. A hand touched her cheek in a comforting gesture.

'Edward?'

Gradually, full consciousness returned. Her cotton nightdress was drenched with perspiration. The figure had been there. Now it was gone.

Margaret sat up, alone in the house, rigid with terror.

After a while she made herself reach for the box of matches and light the candle on the bedside table. She felt swamped by the emotions of the dream. In an effort to restore calm, she picked up the book she had been reading before she slept. Chaucer's *Knight's Tale*. The well-handled volume fell open, as she might have predicted, at the page and the passage that had always moved her with its aching sadness.

'What is this world? What asketh men to have?
Now with his love, now in his colde grave
Allone, withouten any compaignye.'

'Oh, Edward . . .' said Margaret. And prayed that it had been only a dream.

Daisy sat on a bench amid a line of women, waiting. In her hand she held a green admission ticket from the labour exchange opposite Plumstead Station, which had gained her admission to the Woolwich Arsenal. She had already spent more than two hours outside the office of the lady superintendent, in a shed containing the overflow of a crowd of would-be employees. Now, having moved gradually up the queue, she had reached the right-hand end of the front bench of sixteen girls.

Back at their lodgings, Louella would be wondering what had happened to her. She'd left at seven o'clock that morning to look for work and already it was mid-afternoon. Her daughter would be missing her. This was the longest they'd been separated in the whole of Harriet's short life. Daisy shifted her position on the hard bench and sighed.

'Cheer up,' said the girl next to her. 'It may never 'appen.'

'By the time they get to us, there'll be no jobs left,' said Daisy.

'No fear of that. They're taking on all they can get at the Arsenal, churning out supplies for the big offensive.'

Daisy's neighbour was in her early twenties, with a thatch of blonde hair. Her thin cheeks were artificially reddened and her natural lip-line had been redrawn, a trifle clumsily, into a pouting cupid's bow, but her round blue eyes were friendly. Having broken the ice with Daisy, she seemed disposed to go on chatting.

'You ain't from round here, are you?'

'No,' admitted Daisy. 'I come from Guildford, in Surrey.'

'Thought you wasn't local, from the way you talk. You ain't a nob, though. You'd be surprised, the nobs they get turning up here, all lah-di-dah, asking for a job with the munitions. Wanting to "do their bit".' Her voice mimicked the cut-glass precision of an upper-class accent. 'That's what my sister Dora says anyway. She works here sewing bags for cordite cartridges and gas masks. That's where I'm hoping to get in. How about you?'

'I don't know,' said Daisy. 'I don't know anything about it except that they're taking on workers.'

'Well, don't you let her talk you into going in the Danger Buildings. Tries it on with all of them and if they don't argue, next thing they know, they're on the mercury or the trotyl. And it ain't good for your health, for all Lady Barker'll try to say it don't do you no harm.'

'Who's Lady Barker?' said Daisy.

'Oh, that's Lil. The lady superintendent. She'll be the one that does the interview. She's a good sort, Dora reckons, but she's got to find someone to go in the Danger Buildings I suppose. Only it ain't going to be me. Not on your life.'

'Next row, you can go in now,' called a woman from the doorway. As the girls filed past her she collected their green passes. Daisy and her companion found themselves shepherded towards yet another bench in another large room. In front of them, seated at a table, were three women. Other smaller tables set out in rows behind them were occupied by more women, filling out forms.

'Next.'

''Ere we go,' muttered Daisy's friend. She advanced to the table, clutching her handbag. The middle one of the three women studied her calmly.

'Name?'

'Elsie Parrish.'

'Where do you live, Elsie?'

'Silvertown.'

The interviewer was in her forties, heavily built, wearing a double-breasted khaki jacket and tie reminiscent of army uniform. Under a mannish round hat with a small brim, her broad, bespectacled face was creased with laugh lines but her manner was brisk and businesslike.

'What's your working experience, Elsie?'

'I was in service, ma'am, till yesterday.'

'Reason for leaving?'

'Well, partly I want to help our lads to win the war, ma'am. I've got me two brothers out there. And partly,' Elsie added frankly, 'I've heard the pay's much better here.'

The woman smiled. 'It can be, if you're prepared to work hard.'

'I always do, ma'am. Even for five bob a week, which was what I got in service. Along with me keep and uniform, but they wasn't all that open-'anded about the keep.'

'You can certainly better that at the Arsenal. Would you be prepared to work with yellow powder?'

'You mean the trotyl, ma'am? I'd rather not, ma'am, I've got young brothers and sisters who depend on me now our mam's not well and I don't think it'd be right to take the risk. My sister's in the sewing, I'd like to work with her.'

'I'm afraid the only vacancies today are in the Danger Buildings.'

'Oh,' said Elsie. She considered. 'Well, I don't know.'

The superintendent sighed. 'The term "Danger Buildings" is to warn people to take proper care, not to say that everyone who goes to work there is in danger. It's not dangerous if you follow the precautions you are shown. You look like a sensible girl, I am sure you would make an excellent trotyl worker.'

She waited.

'All right,' said Elsie. She was not the first interviewee that day who had found Lilian Barker hard to resist. Out of the corner of her eye she saw Daisy watching her, and pulled a rueful face.

'Good girl. Take this blue paper outside and you'll be shown how to fill it out,' said the superintendent. 'Start on Monday. And Elsie. . . .'

'Yes, ma'am?'

'Don't wear those cosmetics when you come to work. We'd rather see your face.'

'Yes, miss.' Elsie's expression was sulky as she came towards Daisy, clutching her blue slip of paper. Behind her, at the table, the superintendent was making notes on a pad in front of her. Elsie seized the opportunity to pause by Daisy.

'Where d'you live?' she hissed.

'Nowhere yet. We've got lodgings in Bethnal Green, just for a few days.'

'Say you live in Silvertown, same as me. They won't take you on if they think it'll take you too long to get here. You can always move and make it true, if you're bothered,' said Elsie, noticing Daisy's doubtful expression.

'I thought you weren't going in the Danger Buildings.'

'Well, I changed my mind. A job's a job. Anyhow I live right next to the chemical works, where they purify the trotyl. You can't get much more dangerous than that. Might as well get the extra pay for it.'

'Do they pay more in the Danger Buildings?'

'Not 'alf.'

'Next,' called the superintendent.

Daisy walked up to the desk.

'Name?'

'Daisy Colindale.'

'Where do you live, Daisy?'

'Silvertown.' She wasn't even sure where it was. But the lie passed without question.

'Work experience?'

'I was in service until last spring.'

'And then?'

'I had a baby, miss,' said Daisy. The superintendent looked at her sharply.

'Unmarried?' But she had lowered her voice to keep it from the ears of the girls on the benches and it was sympathy, not condemnation, which Daisy recognized in those intent eyes.

'Yes, miss,' she said. 'My fiancé was killed in the first lot of fighting at Ypres.'

'I'm sorry,' said Lilian Barker quietly, and it was not just a stock response. 'Have you arrangements for your child to be taken care of, if you are taken on here?'

'Yes, miss. My sister-in-law'll look after her.'

'Are you prepared to work with trotyl?'

'Yes, miss,' said Daisy, thinking of extra pay.

'Good girl. Take this blue paper outside and you'll be shown how to fill it in.'

Elsie Parrish had waited for Daisy outside the building.

'Did she take you on?'

'Yes.'

'Doing what?'

Daisy realized that she didn't have any idea what, except that it involved something called trotyl, which Elsie had seemed to think was potentially hazardous, but which Miss Barker said was safe if you treated it with respect. 'With that yellow powder, like you.'

'Good-oh.'

'What's next?'

'Medical. To make sure we're up to the work.'

In a neighbouring building they joined a further queue and with a sinking heart Daisy anticipated another long wait. But if the interviews had been short, the medical was shorter. As each girl stepped forward to seat herself at the small square table, a female clerk took her name and the male doctor instructed her to stick out her tongue, even as he examined her hands and fingernails. If the tongue passed muster he glanced rapidly into the throat, pulled down the lower eyelids to inspect the whites of her eyes, then passed her on to the man at the other side of the table who would take a blood sample. That, too, was over in seconds.

Daisy had a feeling, as she went through this routine, that she was a minute particle in some vast, ongoing process, barely distinguishable as a human. From what she had seen of the Arsenal so far, the sheer numbers employed there made it impossible to add any personal element. But then she remembered the moment of sympathetic understanding in Lilian Barker's eyes as she'd confessed to her 'war baby'. It had been such a small thing, but it made her feel better.

Later, as they emerged through the main gate into Beresford Square, Elsie clutched at her forehead under the wide brim of her straw hat.

'I must be out of my mind! And you too! We'll be a right couple of canaries! Why did we do it?'

'I don't know,' said Daisy. 'You said yes, so I said yes.'

'Proper innocent, aren't you?' said Elsie, shaking her head. 'Come on, let's get a cuppa tea in the Services canteen in the Square and get acquainted, seeing as we're going to risk life and limb together.'

'I thought you wanted to work with your sister,' remembered Daisy.

'Not that much. Can't stand her,' said Elsie cheerfully.

'Where have you been?' Louella demanded, confronting Daisy in the doorway of the small front room at Mrs Jenkins' house. A flushed and wailing Harriet clung to her neck, the reduced volume of the small girl's howls indicating that she had cried herself almost to the point of exhaustion.

At the end of the quarry-tiled passage, the brown-painted kitchen door opened and their landlady looked out.

'Can't you keep that child quiet?'

'Sorry, Mrs Jenkins,' called Louella. She hustled Daisy into the room. 'Harriet's been crying all day. I was at my wit's end. I thought you'd had an accident or something.'

'I'm sorry.' Daisy was guiltily aware that she was even later than she might have been, having squandered almost an hour with Elsie Parrish over their cup of tea. After the months of worry and grief and grim endurance she'd shared with Louella, it had been such a relief and a pleasure just to chatter, the way she had with Joan and Mrs Driver in the servants' hall at the Grange, and the minutes had flown by. She'd had to drag herself away. She scooped the damply despairing Harriet out of Louella's arms.

'Shhh, all right, darling, Mummy's here.'

Harriet's wails shut off like a tap and she subsided with a shiver and a hiccup against Daisy's shoulder.

'Well?' demanded Louella. 'Any luck?'

'I start at the Arsenal on Monday.' Daisy wondered, as she spoke, how long it would take Harriet to grow accustomed to her extended absences. The shift in the Danger Buildings, she had learned, was twelve hours – seven in the morning till seven at night, or the reverse for those on night duty. The girls were expected to do thirteen days, followed by a day off, then thirteen days on nights, in turn. At least if she was at home sometimes during the day, her daughter wouldn't forget what she looked like.

'What work will you be doing?' Louella asked.

'I don't know,' said Daisy. 'Something with trotyl.'

'*Trotyl?* Do you know what that is?' said Louella.

'Not really.'

'It's TNT, you idiot. High Explosives. Like gunpowder.'

Daisy defended herself by pointing out that at least her encounter with Elsie Parrish had provided the Colindales with somewhere more permanent to live than Mrs Jenkins' establishment in Bethnal Green. Elsie had said her mam would be glad to have them as lodgers, there was a nice front room going begging and she and Daisy could go to work together, which would be cheery. Daisy had taken the room, sight unseen.

Louella was offended that she hadn't been consulted; but she was as intolerant of the bed bugs at Mrs Jenkins' house as the landlady was of Harriet's crying, and the rent had been ridiculous – a pound a week, extra for board, and the meals, by Louella's standards, were disgusting.

'Anyway, it's hard to find lodgings anywhere near the Arsenal, there's so many workers coming in from all over, looking for a place to live. I reckon we're lucky to get a room,' said Daisy.

'I saw James Allingham in the lane,' said Jessie to her niece on Laura's mid-August rest-day. 'On leave or something, I suppose, and going to visit Margaret at Jasmine Cottage.'

Laura didn't reply. It occurred to her, and she wished it hadn't, that she ought to go to see James and apologize for the white feather.

She had been trying to forget the incident, but it had a habit of resurfacing in her mind at inopportune moments, causing her to shudder with embarrassment. At least if she spoke to James, she told herself, it would end that particular source of embarrassment, though her other more important worries, like the safety of the young men she cared for, and the state of her marriage, and the unending influx of maimed and shattered soldiers into the wards at the hospital, had to be lived with because there was no help for it.

When she walked up the lane, still in her cotton nursing dress with the stiff white apron, James and Margaret were sitting on kitchen chairs in the garden to one side of the cottage, shaded from the sun by the branches of an apple tree. James wore the tunic of the Flying Corps, with the medal ribbon of his DFC sewn below the wings over his breast pocket. A forage cap was perched at an angle on his forehead. Like every other young man that Laura had seen in uniform, he seemed to have aged ten years in putting it on.

'Hullo,' said Margaret, sounding friendly enough. James stood up, unsmiling.

'I'll fetch you another chair from the house,' he said.

'There's no need to bother,' Laura said hurriedly. 'I don't expect I'll be staying long. I only wanted to have a quick word with you, James, about . . . the last time we met.' She realized that she had probably sounded rude, and tried again. 'And to say hullo to you, of course, Margaret. It seems ages since we met.'

Margaret looked from Laura's flushed face to James' carefully noncommittal expression.

'I'll fetch us all a jug of elderflower champagne, shall I?'

she suggested. 'Joan brought some over from the big house this morning and left it in the dairy.'

Margaret's tactful departure was followed by a silence. Then Laura said, on a deep breath, 'I expect you realize that I want to say I'm sorry for the idiotic thing I did in Guildford last year, when I gave you the feather.'

'Oh, that,' said James. 'It didn't matter.'

'Yes, it did. I've been remembering it with shame ever since. What I don't understand is why you weren't wearing your uniform that day, and why you didn't simply tell me at the time how wrong I was?'

'I suppose,' said James, 'I wasn't wearing uniform because I felt uncomfortable about the way the fighting men were everybody's golden boys and I didn't want to be congratulated by total strangers on my behaviour. And I didn't correct your assumption that I was a shirker because in a way you were right, and I deserved it.'

'How can you say that, when you'd come home to collect a medal?'

'The medal which I won by shooting down a few planes, because the pilots were less experienced than me, or less quick than me, or in machines inferior to the one I happened to be flying? That didn't seem to me to be a particularly heroic action. I joined the Royal Flying Corps because I hadn't the nerve to stand back and wait till I was summoned and I hadn't the stomach to fight on the ground,' James said frankly. 'In the air war is a matter of technique and timing and out-thinking the other fellow; you can bring it all down to the level of a game of chess, played somewhat faster and at a distance. If you win, your enemy falls out of the sky, trailing a nice ribbon of smoke and flame, and you don't have to pick up the pieces afterwards and shovel them into the ground. Someone else takes care of that. I took the softest option I could find. If I'd had any real courage I should have been a conscientious objector, white feathers notwithstanding.'

His stance and the look in his eyes challenged Laura to disagree with him. She frowned, unable to understand why he should rate the daredevil exploits of an airman so low and the stubborn resistance of a conscientious objector so high. With half her attention, she glimpsed a boy on a bicycle riding along the lane, his head and shoulders visible above the rose hedging. He braked to a halt and dismounted, leaning the machine into the hedge, and appeared at the gate.

Suddenly Laura realized what it meant. She clutched at her companion's arm.

'James. . . .'

'What is it?' he said.

'Telegram boy,' said Laura.

The colour drained from James' face. He began to run towards the front of the house. Behind him, Laura gathered her skirts and ran too.

As they reached the door, the delivery boy was coming away. He gave them a sombre nod as he passed. These days telegram boys never smiled. Behind him in the hall, Margaret was standing with the buff paper held between her fingers. She looked up at the sound of their footsteps.

'I'm all right,' she said. 'I'm all right.'

James was reminded of men he had seen, mortally wounded, who reiterated for their own consolation that all was well.

'I already knew,' said Margaret. She held out the paper and James took it, staring down as if the intensity of his gaze could change the words.

'Missing, believed killed,' he said. 'It isn't certain. He may turn up in a prison camp, or a hospital.'

'No. I know he's dead. I can't explain, but I've known for more than a week.'

James went to her and held her clumsily. After a moment's hesitation, Laura joined them and the three stood there together, arms across one anothers' shoulders, foreheads touching. Margaret was breathing in slow gasps. She raised her head and the lines of her face changed as her control evaporated. Slowly, the tears came.

'Oh, my dears,' she said. 'He was worth crying for, wasn't he?'

19

Now Laura was made to understand the meaning of personal grief and loss. He'd gone. He had never been hers and never would be, and the knowledge came home to her in a way that it had not done even with the news of his marriage.

Throat aching, cheeks stiff with dried tears, she walked back from Jasmine Cottage to the Grange where she found Jessie in the morning room and told her the news. In the way that Laura had once helped Mrs Emery, Jessie now helped Laura. She listened and cried with her niece, and afterwards she went down to Margaret at the cottage and cried again.

Early the next morning, Laura returned to Clandon.

'What's happened?' said Claire, seeing her face.

'Edward Allingham.'

'Oh, lord,' said Claire, understanding at once the meaning behind the two bare words. 'And Victoria Duffus' brother. I met her in Guildford yesterday. And her cousin's badly wounded. And that new VAD, Vera, went home. Her fiancé. There was another convoy of wounded in last night,' she added, after a pause.

'Better get on, then,' said Laura. Together, they disinfected the bed and the locker of a man who had died in the small hours of the morning, and prepared it for a new patient.

At half past six on a Monday morning in mid-August, a tram deposited Daisy Colindale and Elsie Parrish among a hurrying army of other workers outside the high boundary wall of the Arsenal. A light rain had begun to fall as they crossed the river on the Free Ferry and there had been a smell of damp rubber and of hot, crowded humanity on the trams which had brought them, first to the main gatehouse in Beresford Square, then to the No. 4 Gate at the Plumstead end where they had been told to report for work.

The guards at the gate, having inspected their passes, waved them on. Once inside the vast, sprawling complex of the Arsenal, they were directed by a guide towards a waiting train with open-sided carriages. Here, too, the transport was crammed, but by dint of energetic elbowing Elsie managed to secure them a couple of places on the hard bench-seats.

'Why a train?' Daisy wondered aloud.

'Because it's three or four miles across the marshes to the Danger Buildings,' said another girl facing them across the carriage. 'Not that anyone'd care if we had to walk it, I dare say, only they want us to have our energy when we get there, so we can work faster.'

Daisy stared at the speaker. The girl was about her own age or a little older, with a snub nose and a cheerful grin; but what Daisy chiefly noticed was the colour of her skin. It was tinged a dark yellow, as if badly jaundiced, and the brown hair that showed under the brim of her hat had a yellow-orange tinge at the ends.

'What's up with you?' the girl asked. 'Oh. My face, is it? Ain't you ever seen a canary before?'

The word rang bells in Daisy's head. *We'll be a right couple of canaries*, Elsie had said last week after the interviews. Now Elsie nudged her.

'Told you. It's the powder.'

'Doesn't it wash off?'

'No such luck,' said the yellow-skinned girl. 'It seeps into your skin and gets down your throat and comes out from inside you. There's some lotion called Hypo that they give you to rub in, but it isn't much good. Don't worry, they reckon it wears off after you stop working with the trotyl. Eventually. And it has its advantages. Free milk-ration for one thing. Also, I come a long way to work and sometimes it gets me a seat on the tram.'

Daisy slumped for a moment. She hadn't even started and already she had learned of a serious drawback to the type of work she'd be doing. Then she pulled herself together. With Harriet to feed, and Louella too, and Louella's baby due shortly, she had to earn as much as possible, as fast as possible. If the price to pay was to turn a funny colour, so be it.

The train toiled across the Plumstead marshes to an area of land inside a wide bend of the river, where a collection of huts and buildings stood isolated. Even though it was summer, on this rainy day a fine mist hung over the marshland. Climbing out of the carriage, Daisy glanced about her, noticing the long banks of grassed earthworks like ancient burial mounds which lay between the buildings, and the timber walkways on stilts a few feet above the ground, which connected them.

'Come on,' said Elsie, shepherding her towards a ramp leading up to one of the raised platforms.

'Oh!' Daisy uttered a stifled scream and clutched at her companion as a rat darted out from under the walkway and streaked past them, followed a second later by a ginger cat. The yellow-skinned girl from the train paused for a moment to watch the outcome of the chase.

'Got 'im!' she pronounced with satisfaction. 'Those cats were a good idea. They were brought in to keep the rats down and they're doing it a treat. Mind you,' she added, 'at the rate they're breeding, one day they'll 'ave to bring something in to keep down the cats.' She led the way along the boards. ''Ere we are. Shifting house.'

The interior of the shifting house was partitioned into two halves by a timber wall down the middle. In one half, a crowd of girls were stripping to their underwear. Most of them showed the same curiously tinged skin as the girl from the train.

'New, are you? Right,' said an elderly woman, approaching the latest arrivals with clean garments laid over one arm. 'Overalls. Write your work number on them.' She produced a box of rubber overshoes from beneath a bench. 'Put these on over your shoes. Your clothes can be hung on those pegs over there. Corsets, hairpins, rings, anything metal has to stay here, and no cigarettes, matches or sweets must go beyond that board into the "clean" area.' She gestured towards a footboard set across the floor of the room where the partition ended. 'Matter of fact, nothing goes in the clean area except you. I'm Auntie Norris, by the way.'

'Auntie', Daisy learned later, was the standard nickname for all the shifting-house attendants whose job it was to look after the girls, distribute overalls and guard possessions while their owners were at work. She began to remove her clothes under a notice headed 'Thoughts for Munition Workers', which informed her among other things that the motive for her work was patriotism, that she was as important as a soldier in the trenches and that on her his life depended. Daisy thought of Arthur, for whom her contribution to the war had come too late, and of Robert who had been killed by patriots, and she turned away from the notice to get dressed for the more prosaic purpose of earning a living.

Beside her, grumbling, Elsie unpinned her blonde hair and stuffed it into a cap with a drawstring rim.

'I'll look like a blooming pudding,' she complained, 'stuck on top of a sack of potatoes.' It had to be admitted that there was nothing flattering about the khaki trousers of coarse cotton and the shapeless tunic, buttoned tightly at the neck and wrists and fastened around the waist with a tie belt, though Daisy noticed that some of the girls had managed to vary the angle of their caps so that they looked like snoods and showed a fringe of hair. She tugged her own cap backwards.

'If you do that,' warned Auntie Norris, arriving beside her with a pale-green veil like an eastern woman's yashmak to complete the outfit, 'you'll probably end up with a carroty fringe.' She regarded Daisy wryly for a moment. 'Why should you care? You've already *got* a carroty fringe.'

Daisy pulled her cap forward again so that it covered every strand of hair and donned the veil. But she felt uncomfortable and claustrophobic with the fabric clinging around her mouth and many of the girls, she saw, soon pulled theirs off and tucked them into their belts.

Daisy rapidly discovered that one feature of work for women at the Arsenal was its monotony. A few of the girls in the tool shops were trained and experienced enough to do more advanced work, but in the main, each worker had a task, and it was that task alone which she was expected to carry out as fast as possible for the twelve hours of her shift. To encourage speed most of the jobs were paid at piecework rates.

For Daisy, the task was the filling of shells with TNT. All day she carried a leather bucket to a table in a bare shed of a workshop, collected a measure of the yellow powder, which another worker had weighed out from a wooden box on to a pair of large brass scales, carried it to a shell case standing ready on the concrete floor, and shovelled the explosive into the case with a brass scoop, tamping it down firmly with a long-handled plunger in between each addition of powder. When the shell had been filled she added a screw-in cap and one of the transport girls then wheeled it away on a trolley to another building to acquire a fuse. It was work that required a minimum of skill. It was well paid because it was dangerous.

'Why are the buckets leather?' Daisy asked her workmate Annie on the first day. Annie, the yellow-skinned girl of the train, was engaged in weighing out the powder.

'To avoid sparks.' Annie went on working as she talked. Nobody ever stopped and stood still at the Arsenal, with a war to win and an insatiable demand from the Front for the wherewithal to do it. 'And that's why the scoop is brass. Nothing steel allowed near high explosives. Even the firemen use leather buckets if they come out to the Danger Buildings. And that's why we walk around on platforms off the ground when we're outside, to keep our shoes from picking up grit that might raise a spark. Sparks,' said Annie grimly, 'are apt to cause a nasty explosion, as you'll know when you've been here a while.'

'Have you had one in here?'

'No. And we don't intend to.'

At least the shell-filling involved several separate

378

movements. In other parts of the factory, a worker might spend the entire day simply scooping up cartridge cases from a tray-topped table and loading them into a frame ready for filling, or swivelling the lever of a machine repeatedly from right to left and back again to stamp numbers on to an unending succession of shell cases.

At twelve o'clock they broke for dinner and the girls, having washed themselves and donned an extra layer of all-enveloping overall to keep any trotyl powder from contaminating their food, streamed along the wooden walkways to a vast canteen which must, Daisy reckoned, hold over a thousand workers. Here the level of animated conversation seemed deafening after the comparative quiet of the shell-filling buildings, where there were seldom more than half a dozen girls in any room at a time and it was generally considered inadvisable to chat because the trotyl might get into the crevices of your teeth and rot them if you opened your mouth too often.

The cooked meal was paid for by a ticket because no money was allowed beyond the shifting house. Daisy ate the meat and vegetables on her plate eagerly – she couldn't remember when she'd last had such a good meal, and wished that Louella and Harriet could share it. She took no part in the conversation around her because the chief topic was boyfriends, stirring uncomfortable memories of Arthur Bright in the hay barn, and of Will Griffin who hadn't answered her letter, a fact which still caused her a pang of distress whenever she thought about it.

Everyone's 'best boy' seemed to be in the armed services apart from Annie's, who was in a 'reserved occupation' because he was a skilled worker in the foundry at the other end of the Arsenal, casting gun barrels, and could not be spared to fight.

Elsie did not have a boyfriend, though she claimed to have had plenty and 'given them the push'.

'I thought that when I came here things'd look up,' she said. 'Thirty-five thousand men they've got working here.

Mind you, a lot of them are old, or disabled, but there's a few nice ones. Like Annie's must be,' she added, giving her workmate a sly glance which caused the girl to resolve to keep her Jim and Elsie Parrish strictly apart. 'But I 'ave to get stuck in the Danger Buildings, which is worse than a nunnery if you ask me.'

Other factories in the Arsenal were crammed with workers, perhaps hundreds to a vast room, but the girls in the Danger Buildings worked in small groups; presumably, Elsie said matter-of-factly, because it kept the casualties down in the event of an explosion.

'I wish everyone wouldn't keep on about explosions,' Daisy said as they made their way back towards their workplace at the end of the afternoon teabreak.

'Why not? We're on the brink, every minute,' said Elsie with relish. 'Just one little spark. . . . All it would take would be for you to slip off this platform and land on a bit of gravel on the ground and *Boom*! You'd be an angel.'

She shoved playfully at her companion. Caught unawares, Daisy lurched backwards, her feet in the rubber overshoes slipping on the drizzle-damp planking. She snatched at the handrail but it only bruised her wrist as, landing awkwardly, half-on and half-off the walkway, she tumbled backwards to the ground below.

It had been a drop of three feet and Daisy was not seriously hurt, but she had known a moment of absolute terror as she fell, anticipating the blast predicted by Elsie.

'Very funny!' She picked herself up, rubbed at her bruises and grasped at one of the wooden posts that supported the handrail which had failed to save her, intending to clamber back on to the platform.

'No. You'll have to wait there, now, until they bring you new shoes and another overall from the shifting house,' said Annie, her face pale. 'It's safety regulations. I'll go and tell Auntie.'

'Oh, Daisy. I'm ever so sorry,' said Elsie contritely.

'You will be,' said Daisy, 'if you ever, ever do that again!'

'How was it?' said Louella, when the breadwinner returned exhausted after her first day.

'Not too bad.' Daisy tried to sound positive. She would have liked to cheer herself up by cuddling Harriet, but her daughter was already asleep in the rickety double bed, thumb in mouth, her breathing peaceful.

'How did you get on with Harriet?'

'She cried for a bit this morning and asked for you. But I took her out for a long walk and she got over it and seemed quite happy.'

Daisy told herself that she was glad Harriet had proved so easily consolable. But for some reason, the knowledge hurt.

There had been a number of Zeppelin raids on London since April. In response, the searchlight and gun defences were becoming formidable and the organization for dealing with the intruders had been established. Now, whenever an enemy airship was spotted crossing the coast, the news would be relayed to the capital and work at the Woolwich Arsenal, considered a prime target, would be closed down until the 'all clear' signal.

Four hours into the start of Daisy's second week on night shifts, at the beginning of September, the maroon sounded.

'Air raid,' said Annie Higgs resignedly, flipping over the lid on her box of TNT.

The Arsenal workers were becoming used to interrupted shifts, but Daisy found it hard to match Annie's calmness, though this was not the first raid since her arrival in London. In general the Zeppelins had been more effective at spreading terror than in causing widespread damage; the risk of being hit by a descending fragment of anti-aircraft shell was higher than that of falling prey to the efforts of a Baby Killer, and she had learned to be philosophical about the chances of a bomb finding her. But this would be the first air attack that she had experienced in a factory full of high explosive, at which the enemy could be assumed to be aiming. It was not a comfortable thought.

'Come on,' said Elsie as the lights went out. 'Let's go down to the canteen. Maybe there'll be a concert or a sing-song.'

Hastily washed and in their coveralls, the canaries felt their way along the walkways to the canteen. As Elsie had hoped, there was a sing-song. Somebody was at the piano, playing by ear, and at the tables in the dark, a thousand voices were singing with determined cheerfulness a new popular song about roses blooming in Picardy. It would be like that all over the Arsenal as the raid went on. It kept people's minds off the noise of the raiders' engines and the thought of the bombs falling.

Just as the song came to an end, the sound of concentrated gunfire could be heard outside. Someone by the window said, 'Zeppelin coming over,' and there was a concerted rush for the door.

Daisy, hating the stampede, tried to hold out against the tide, but in the end she was swept forward. The girls ranged themselves along the handrail of the walkway, eyes fixed eagerly on the sky, where the stroking beams of many searchlights had caught and held the Zeppelin. The thrumming noise seemed deafening, though in fact the airship was some distance away. Anti-aircraft fire arched up through the darkness, buffeting the target but never quite hitting it. Then a new sound was added to the hubbub as through the bursting shells and streams of tracer flew an aeroplane, diving hard at the Zeppelin, slewing up under its tail and raking the hull with bullets.

Abruptly the searchlights were extinguished and the gunfire from the ground stopped. Now it was a duel between the plane and the raider; though as the vast silver airship powered steadily on, the aircraft flying alongside seemed more like a small, irritating dog yapping at its heels than an equal adversary. Then gradually a pink glow began to spread through the Zeppelin lighting it from within as if it were an enormous Chinese lantern. A tongue of fire poked from the bodywork, and the flame licked along its tilting length. With a roar like a blast furnace, it plunged stern-first towards the ground somewhere to the North.

All around Daisy, the spectators were cheering hysterically as the enemy burned alive. But Daisy didn't cheer. She knew that the Zeppelin crew had come to London with the intention of inflicting as much death and damage as possible, that they had probably dropped bombs on civilians in similar raids in the past and could have killed her or taken Harriet from her. But that was the war. She supposed they might have mothers and wives and small children at home, like any English airman, and she felt sick and sad for the waste of it all.

'It wasn't a Zeppelin, anyway,' reported Elsie, next day. 'Papers say it was a Schutte-Lanz, whatever that means. Came down near Cuffley in the end, though I thought it'd be closer. It seemed like it was all happening right overhead, didn't it? They're going to give the pilot who shot it down a Victoria Cross.'

The authorities, maximizing the propaganda value of Second Lieutenant Leefe Robinson's achievement, claimed that the fact that the airship's hull was made out of wood was an indication that the Germans were short of steel. They knew, though most of the munition workers and civilians they heartened by this suggestion did not, that the Schutte-Lanz was an old model and that wood was its normal construction material. The important thing in the war of propaganda, they had discovered, was not the truth, but what you could make people believe was the truth.

At any rate the British public was duly exultant. 'Falling like Lucifer, flaming through the skies,' trumpeted the *War Illustrated*, over a photograph of the burned-out skeleton of the airship. The new incendiary bullets that Leefe Robinson had used to bring down his prey had proved that the perpetrators of 'Teutonic Frightfulness' were not invincible.

At the end of September, as the Somme offensive dragged on, Charles McKay came on leave. His telegram announcing this fact was delivered to his wife at Clandon, causing Laura an anxious few moments as she opened it. She also took leave from Clandon and went home to Maple Grange.

Charles had not yet arrived when she reached the house, late in the afternoon, though Walker had been despatched to the station earlier in the day with instructions to collect the captain – Charles had been promoted a few months earlier – whenever he appeared.

Laura had time to change out of her nursing uniform into something less likely to remind the returning hero of the war he had left behind. An article in *Vogue* had advised ladies that above all, they should remember to be *feminine* when their loved ones came home and in her muslin blouse and high-waisted skirt, wearing Charles' Christmas diamond-and-pearl earrings in her lobes, Laura thought that she fulfilled *Vogue*'s requirement. She realized as she lifted the earrings from their embossed leather case that she had never worn them . . . and that Charles had left the dressing gown which she had given him hanging on the back of the door in the dressing room that led out of the guest bedroom.

She heard the sound of car wheels on the drive and went slowly down the stairs to meet her husband. She had been rather dreading the moment of seeing him again. So much time had passed since their marriage, so little of it had been spent together, and that little had been strained and un-satisfying. He had written letters, but mostly they had been dry and unexpansive, in contrast to the warm confiding of his pre-marriage correspondence. Not that Laura had cared, while the raw wound of Edward's death still seared her, and she had to admit that she had sometimes let an inexcusably long time elapse before replying. But it seemed to her now that it was time to start rebuilding her life, and since she had promised on oath to be a wife to Charles, she should start to live up to that promise.

In the hall, Charles was handing his cap and gloves to Ferry while Walker carried in his valise. The sight of him was a shock. He had become so gaunt and strange. She reached up and kissed him on the cheek. There was a constant nervous tremor about him, so fine as to be barely noticeable. More noticeable was the fact that his trousers and the elbows of his jacket were covered in mud.

'Charles, whatever has happened to your uniform?'

'I had a slight fall outside the station,' he responded, unsmiling.

'But you're not hurt?'

'No.'

Laura waited for an explanation. When none came, she took him off to the drawing room for some tea. Already her best intentions seemed to be foundering on the rock of his passionless manner.

'He's tired,' she told himself. 'He'll be better soon.'

'Fall be blowed,' Walker told Ferry later in the kitchen. 'We were walking towards the motor outside the station – and I had a devil of a job recognizing him, I can tell you, he's so much thinner than last winter. Anyway, just as we reached the motor, another car that was coming down the road backfired. The captain went barmy. He yelled "Get down!" and the next thing I knew, he was flat on his face in the dirt on the verge, with his hands over the back of his head. Got up a bit sheepish-looking afterwards. I suppose it was instinct, from being out at the Front. But he was shaking like a leaf all the way home – I saw him in the mirror.'

'If you ask me,' said Ferry, 'he's cracking up.'

Charles' commanding officer in France had been of the same opinion – which was why, with the army still locked in the throes of a major offensive, Captain McKay was home on leave. Charles knew it, and was shamed by it.

In the drawing room, Laura prepared to pour the tea.

'Do you have any whisky?' In the long hours of front-line duty, Charles had found a panacea for shame.

'At this time of day?' said Laura in surprise. Then she remembered that she was supposed to be making his leave a relaxed and happy event, and that querying his requests, even for alcohol at four in the afternoon, would not assist her in her aim. She walked to the tantalus on the table between the two long windows which overlooked the terrace, and poured him a small measure of whisky from one of the cut-glass decanters.

Charles downed it in one gulp, and held out his glass for a refill. Laura felt a shiver of alarm.

Her returned warrior continued to drink steadily through that evening. By the time that she judged it proper to retire for the night, he was glassy-eyed and speaking with the exaggerated care that betrays a state of inebriation; though in fact he had mostly kept silent through supper. Rupert compensated by talking a lot about the shell factory, its profits, the headaches of a female workforce, the various irritating food and commodity shortages . . . and the state of the war, as understood by him from his readings of *The Times* and the *War Illustrated*.

Both Laura and Jessie became uncomfortably aware that what Rupert said and what Charles thought about the war were poles apart. But Rupert, holding forth about the likely impact of the tanks which had made their debut on the Somme, did not notice his son-in-law's failure to concur with him about the new weapon's potential for wreaking total havoc on the Hun.

In the guest bedroom Laura donned her nightgown and brushed out her long hair, while Charles removed his clothes in the dressing room next door. 'I've become quite accustomed to doing without a maid,' she realized, and wondered in passing how her former maid was now. She had received a short note a week ago, with an enclosure of five pounds and the news that Daisy had become a munitions worker at the Woolwich Arsenal.

Laura had never expected the money to be repaid. She thought as she climbed into bed that she really must make an effort to find out more about Daisy's situation. She would postpone it until Charles' leave was over; there were more pressing concerns to attend to now.

After the first repugnance of her post-wedding connubial

experiences had faded, she had begun to see possibilities in sex. If Charles would only slow down and give her time to respond, she had decided, they might achieve something at least vaguely comparable to the excitement of Elinor Glyn's passionate lovers.

She climbed into the four-poster, arranged herself prettily, plumped up the pillows, and waited.

. . . And waited, with mounting indignation, for her husband to make his appearance. At last she slipped out of the high bed and knocked on the dressing-room door. When there was no answer, she turned the porcelain handle and entered.

The dressing room was mahogany-panelled, with a Bokhara rug spread on the floor. It contained a chest of drawers, a cheval mirror, a washstand, a trouser press and a cushioned Carolean daybed with caned back and seat. Upon this piece of furniture Charles lay sprawled. The electric light burned overhead, but to this he was quite impervious. Eyes closed, mouth open, breathing noisily, he was quite clearly dead to the world.

Even the slamming of the door did not wake him as Laura stalked back to her bed, her cheeks flaming. She had wanted to make this leave a proper start to her marriage. The plan was in ruins.

Half an hour later, her better nature struggled reluctantly to the surface. He would get cold. She returned to the dressing room and spread a blanket from the linen press and her husband's army greatcoat over his sleeping form. Then she switched off the light.

In the morning a contrite Charles appeared at the foot of the four-poster. 'Darling, I'm so sorry. I just couldn't stay awake.'

His jaw was faintly blurred with stubble, his eyes apprehensive. Laura sat up and pushed her hair behind her shoulders. She considered whether to remain angry, and decided that it was counter-productive.

'Of course you were tired out. It doesn't matter.'

'Honestly?'

'Honestly,' said Laura. 'Provided you come here now and make it up to me.' She lifted the covers and Charles climbed into the high bed beside her. He slid his hands up over her shoulders and touched his lips hesitantly against hers. Laura placed her hands experimentally on his back and stroked.

A little later she remembered that she'd meant to suggest he should take things a bit slower. There wasn't much point in making suggestions now. Within a few hectic seconds Charles had changed from a diffident and reserved lover into a man whose hunger almost frightened her. His mouth pressed avidly against hers, his hands gripped her so tightly that she was sure she would be bruised. Again, as she had felt in the days after her wedding, Laura felt invaded.

But this time a part of her mind and body enjoyed the experience.

On Charles' last night of leave, Rupert had ordered a special dinner regardless of food shortages and for once suspending his dislike of upheaval, he invited a few guests. Claire Lawrence and her parents, Rupert's sister Caroline and her husband Eric Delamere were gathered with the Brownlowes around the long table with all its formal trappings of silver and china, candles and flowers.

Through the soup, the turbot and the pheasant, Rupert held forth steadily on his favourite subject: the war, the cowardly deceitful and ineffective performance of the Hun, the general superiority of the British forces as described by his magazine and the likelihood that it would all be over by Christmas, even if the triumphant outcome had unfortunately been delayed by two years from the original estimate.

'. . . Though the end of the war will be bad news for me in a sense,' he added unwisely, 'because it will also mean the end of what has proved to be a very profitable business.'

There was a short silence while his entire audience tried to ignore the bad taste of this comment. It was with a sense of desperation that Claire, who always found Oliver's father hard to take in anything but the smallest doses, turned to Charles

'You are the expert among us. How much longer do you think it will last?'

Charles had been absorbing his wine with more attention than he had paid to the food, which sat almost untouched on his plate. He leaned back and took a long gulp from his glass before replying.

'God alone knows. Or maybe God's lost interest. *I* don't know. I've been crawling around in the mud for far too long to be capable of having a coherent opinion about anything.'

Another silence followed this pronouncement. Rupert cleared his throat, aware that the dinner-table conversation had taken a mordant twist. He motioned a hovering Ferry forward with the wine decanter and Charles' empty glass was refilled.

'Come now,' said Rupert heartily. 'Don't let's get depressed. At least now the cavalry has been in operation again, there's hope of you seeing some decent action.'

'What do you call decent action?' asked Charles, his eyes narrowed. Even Rupert caught a hint of danger.

'High Wood,' he said, a little less heartily. 'And Delville Wood. July the fourteenth. We read all about it at home, the first time they've used the cavalry since 1914. A triumph.'

'Was it?' said Charles.

'Yes, of course. Naturally. Our cavalry are of a so much higher standard than the Uhlans. I've read that the enemy cavalry hardly bother to hold their lances in the correct position these days, they rely on their guns instead, which is a clear indication of their shoddy and demoralized state.'

'For Christ's sake, you don't know what you're talking about!' Charles slammed his glass down on the table, with such force that it broke the stem. Wine spilled across the snowy tablecloth. Ferry darted forward and applied a napkin to limit the damage, but a moment later the wine stain was followed by drops of blood. Charles had cut his hand.

'Damn,' he said, wrapping his linen napkin clumsily around the gash in the gap between the thumb and the forefinger. Beside him Laura, rather pale, turned to help.

'I'm sorry you feel that way,' said Rupert, with dignity. He eyed his son-in-law with annoyance mixed with concern. 'We're all under rather a strain, aren't we? His last night,' he added in explanation to the assembled company. Charles closed his eyes.

The rest of the evening reflected the strain to which Rupert had referred. It was with some relief that the Lawrences and the Delameres took their leave as soon as it was polite to do so. The excuse, at least partly genuine, was that it took a long time to drive home with the severely dimmed headlamps which were all that the lighting regulations permitted.

'Play the piano for us, Laura,' said Rupert in the drawing room after the guests had gone.

'Not tonight, Pa. Please. I don't feel in the mood.'

Rupert was about to insist, but thought better of it. 'Very well, my dear. As you wish. I think I shall take a last cigar in my study and then go to bed. An old man like me needs his sleep.'

'You're not old, Pa,' said Laura automatically. She was watching Charles, who was helping himself to whisky from the tantalus. She came and stood beside him as he drank it.

'I wish you wouldn't,' she said, after Rupert had left the room. In one of the armchairs, Jessie stitched away quietly at the pieces of one of her eternal knitted baby-jackets for the Soldiers' and Sailors' Wives offspring.

'Wouldn't what?' Charles demanded, sounding belligerent.

'Drink so much.'

He looked down at her, his eyes bleak. 'What else am I to do?'

Laura's mouth tightened. 'I'm going to bed,' she announced. She laid a hand on her husband's arm. 'Will you be up soon?'

'Yes, I'll be along.'

But as Laura closed the drawing room door behind her, he was already moving again towards the whisky decanter.

Jessie watched him with troubled eyes. At first she wasn't sure if he realized that she was still in the room. Then she concluded that he didn't care. Finally he began to talk to her.

'You're not like Laura's father, are you? Not like our patriotic Rupert. I've seen it in your eyes, when he's boring on about our glorious exploits. You know it's not like that.'

'Yes. I know,' said Jessie gently, the woollen jacket held poised in one hand, the needle in the other.

'I'll tell you about the charge on High Wood – the triumphant charge. I saw it. They'd ordered in two squadrons of Deccan Horse and two squadrons of the Seventh Dragoons. The rest of us were green with envy. All those months of waiting, wallowing about in the mud of the trenches, and then someone else gets the moment of glory. That's what we thought. Moment of glory,' he repeated, staring down into his empty glass. He shivered.

'They passed us, clattering along the road. Oh, I'll tell you, the troops were cheering – some of them had never seen a cavalry unit going into action. The riders formed up, line abreast, several ranks deep, and then they rode up out of the cornfields towards the wood. A nice, gentle slope. The horses seemed to flow across it like a wave on a beach. It was beautiful to watch, just beautiful, a scene from a pageant – the golden corn, the horses galloping, the men tilted forward in their saddles, the sunlight glittering on the lances. . . .

'And then,' he said brutally, 'the machine guns in the wood opened up and cut them down like so many stalks of ripe corn.'

He stood up unsteadily, and swayed rather than walked towards the library table. Rupert's magazine lay open on the table and Charles stabbed a forefinger at the printed words. 'We carry our lances *properly*,' he quoted with savage sarcasm. 'Not like the Germans. They use their revolvers instead. It isn't pukka, is it, chaps? We die *properly*. Like they did at High Wood.'

His unfocused eyes wandered past Jessie to the door. 'I'm scared,' Charles announced quietly to no one in particular. 'I'm scared stupid. That isn't pukka either, is it?'

Jessie sat frozen in her chair. Suddenly Charles swung round to face her.

'Don't tell Laura,' he said clearly, and walked out of the room.

Laura was hovering on the edge of sleep when he came into the bedroom. She was just conscious enough to be irritated by the jolting of the bedsprings and the intrusive hand and arm sliding clumsily across her body.

'Darling . . .' said Charles, beside her ear. Whisky fumes assailed her nostrils. She screwed up her face in protest. The activities of her husband's hand, intended to arouse her, had the opposite effect.

'Oh, go away,' she said drowsily. Obediently he turned on his back and lay still. *My last night*, he was thinking, *and my wife doesn't want me.*

Laura woke and Charles was already washed and dressed. He was standing in front of the cheval mirror, buttoning his tunic as she sat up in bed, her golden-brown hair loose on her shoulders and her blue eyes still clouded with sleep.

'Good morning,' Laura said, stretching lazily.

Charles returned the greeting civilly but without warmth, eyes still fixed on the mirror as he adjusted his tie. Laura had a distinct impression that he was hurt or resentful about something. She sighed. Charles was always getting upset. What was it this time?

All that she could remember of the night before was that she'd gone to bed early and that her husband had chosen not to come with her. She'd been perfectly prepared for love-making, she'd even found herself anticipating it with a small thrill of pleasure. And then he hadn't shown the slightest interest, staying up instead to talk to Aunt Jessie, and probably to drink too much again. It wasn't her fault, Laura told herself, that Charles' leave had turned out to be such a cheerless event. It wasn't she who had created this bad feeling between them. So why did she have to feel guilty?

But there was something about the look in his eyes as he

turned away from the mirror that stung her conscience, a hurt, enduring expression, like a dog that's been kicked.

'Charles. . . .'

'Yes?' he said, fastening the leather belt round his waist.

'Aren't you going to kiss me good morning?' All that Laura had learned of seduction in her short married life went into the question. Charles hesitated, his expression half-tempted, half-wary. He took a step towards her and Laura discovered that her body was tingling with anticipation.

Downstairs, the long-case clock chimed the first of eight bells and Ferry struck the gong to announce breakfast.

'No time,' said Charles. 'I want a word with your father before he goes to the factory.'

Laura scowled at the door as it closed behind him. *Well, I tried*, she told herself, with a shrug of the shoulders.

'Shall I come to see you off?' she said later, when she had joined him at the breakfast table after Rupert's departure.

'I shouldn't bother,' said Charles. Laura was relieved. She hated public goodbyes. But another part of her was wishing that things could be different between her and Charles.

Next time, she told herself. *Next time he comes home I'll make it different*.

20

By the middle of October, Louella was still waiting to go into labour.

'It's late,' she said. 'Daisy, I think something's wrong.'

'I've heard lots of first babies come late.'

'Yours didn't.'

'My mother said babies come when they're ready,' said Daisy, wanting to reassure. But she, too, was worried. 'Perhaps we should ask Mrs Parrish. She's had plenty.'

Elsie's mother said comfortably that the baby was probably just a lazy little thing that didn't want to leave its mother. She advised jumping off a chair to speed things up a bit.

'I don't think that's a good idea,' Daisy told Lou before leaving for work. She felt bad about leaving Harriet with wan, listless Louella. Mrs Parrish had promised to take over the child-minding – at a price – for as long as need be until Louella was 'herself' again, but Daisy hadn't much faith in Mrs Parrish's capacity in that respect. It was true that Elsie and her sisters were healthy, happy individuals . . . but Daisy had gathered, from odd scraps of detail dropped into conversations with her friend on the journeys to and from the Arsenal, that they had been the survivors of a larger brood and that in the Parrish household the weakest went to the wall.

She debated whether to put Harriet into the creche at the Arsenal. But it was a long way to drag the small girl in the mornings and evenings, and another upheaval for Harriet, so she kept postponing it.

'Are you sure you'll be all right?' she asked Louella as she was putting on her coat. 'I could take some time off . . . but money'd be short.'

'No. You go. I'll be fine.'

'Don't go jumping off any chairs,' said Daisy.

'Don't be silly.'

All that day, scooping yellow powder into tall, brass shell-cases, Daisy told herself that Louella was young and strong and having a baby wasn't that terrible an experience. Any day now she'd come home and find her sister-in-law proudly nursing a new arrival. That very evening, as she walked along the street towards her lodgings, Mrs Parrish came out to meet her with a red-faced and indignant Harriet struggling in her arms.

'Lou's started the baby.'

'Oh, that's wonderful!' Daisy said with relief.

But it wasn't wonderful. Louella's son was born, after twenty-four hours of struggle, at ten the following morning. He lived for an hour.

Late in October of 1916, a cable was delivered to Maple Grange, addressed to Mrs Charles McKay. In Laura's absence at Clandon, Rupert took it on himself to read the cable.

From an upstairs window, Jessie had seen the delivery boy cycling up the drive and had hurried down the stairs. She hovered on the bottom step as her brother ripped open the envelope.

'Oliver?' she said.

'No. Charles.' Rupert was still scanning the few lines of the cable. Jessie groped for the square newel post beside her and hung on to it to steady herself as she waited for the lurching sensation inside her to subside. 'Oh. . . . Poor, poor Laura,' she whispered.

'Hang on. He isn't dead, just wounded. At some hospital in France. I'd better go and see him, I suppose.'

'Laura must be told immediately. I'll go to Clandon.'

'I think,' said Rupert firmly, 'that it might be better if I looked into this first. It says *seriously wounded*. Better if someone knows the facts and can break them to Laura gently.'

'But we have no right to delay the news,' protested Jessie worriedly.

'I,' said Rupert, heavily emphasizing the word, 'have every right to protect my daughter from unnecessary stress. The delay will be minimal, I'll go today. Then, as soon as I know what's what, I'll tell Laura.'

'Shall I come with you?' Jessie offered. She had an instinctive feeling that Rupert was not the ideal person to send on such a mission. But then, was she?

'No need.'

'Are you sure?'

'For heaven's sake, Jessica, I am capable of catching a boat by myself.'

Later, Jessie would blame herself for the submissiveness with which she accepted that decision.

Charles's first war wound had been picturesque. His current injuries were not. Because of this, the ward sister felt it necessary to have a quiet word with Captain McKay's visitor beforehand.

'He was very poorly indeed when he came in, but he's stabilized now.' She looked doubtfully at Rupert, fidgeting impatiently on the other side of the screened-off section of the tent that contained her desk. He was disgusted by the makeshift accommodation of the hospital, the long lines of cold, leaky tents among the trampled grass, and as he glowered at her across the desk, he reminded her of a fretful bull. It seemed unwise to let this big, healthy, abrasive male loose on someone so very fragile as the patient they were discussing. But the man *was* a relation, at least by marriage.

'We have him in a separate cubicle for now,' she said. 'The ones with facial injuries are very sensitive.'

'How badly hurt is he? Exactly?' Rupert demanded.

'Well, the thigh wound is bad. We almost had to amputate. But that should heal eventually, if there's no further haemorrhaging.'

'You said facial injuries?'

The sister hesitated, summoning the right tone of matter-offactness with which to minimize the shock effect of what she had to convey.

'He's lost his nose, his right ear and most of his lower jaw.'

'You mean, he can't talk, eat or hear?'

'His hearing's impaired, obviously, but the left ear is all right. Eating, well, he'll need a liquid diet. Talking, at the moment, no. But the surgeons can do wonders nowadays with replacement parts. And I've heard that a sculptor called Derwent Wood has started work at one of the London hospitals now, making painted masks of silver based on the patient's original bone structure. I expect we'll try to transfer Captain McKay there when he's a bit better.'

'A mask?' Rupert echoed. 'What's the good of that?'

'It means they can be looked at,' said Sister Dunlop quietly.

'But. . . .' Rupert struggled to assimilate the scale of the damage to his handsome young son-in-law. 'The man's *married*,' he said. 'To my girl Laura.'

'A lot of them are married.'

'Let me get this straight,' Rupert pronounced grimly. 'Are you telling me that he faces a future in which he will have to wear a tin mask for the rest of his life to be anything less than hideous?'

'Silver,' said the sister. 'Mr Brownlowe, perhaps you aren't ready to see Captain McKay just yet. Perhaps when you've had time to digest the situation?'

'No,' said Rupert. 'I'll see him. That's why I came.'

'My patient shouldn't be upset.'

'For God's sake,' said Rupert. 'He's lost half his face. What could I possibly say to make him *more* upset?' Then he took in the gist of the sister's comments and realized that she was on the verge of denying him access to Charles. After he'd come all this way.

'All right,' he said. 'I'll be tactful.'

Sister Dunlop wanted to say, 'I don't believe you know how to be tactful.' But Rupert Brownlowe was a forceful man and she could see that it would take a considerable amount of authority to keep him away from the soldier in the cubicle at the far end of the tent. Matron had that authority, but Matron was away for the afternoon and Sister Dunlop wasn't sure she was up to it. Besides, she had to take into account the fact that ever since Charles McKay's arrival, so far as he was able to communicate, he had been asking desperately whether he had a visitor yet. And at least a father-in-law was likely to be less emotionally unsettling than a hysterical wife.

'Wait here,' she said. 'I'll see if he's up to seeing you.'

Rupert drummed his fingers on the desk. It was several minutes before she returned.

'All right, come with me. But I can't let you stay long. He hasn't much stamina at the moment.'

She led him along the narrow pathway between two lines of beds, mostly containing comatose men. Those who were conscious watched him apathetically as he passed by.

'In here.'

The cubicle was formed by canvas screens tied together. Rupert brushed past her and Sister Dunlop returned to her cluttered desk. She felt tired and sad. Captain McKay, on being told that someone was here to see him, had brightened visibly and had made a noise which, now that she knew the name of his wife, she had been able to interpret as 'Laura?'. And she had had to disappoint him. But when she'd explained that it was his father-in-law who was waiting, and had asked whether he wanted to see the man, he had nodded. She had told him to use the bell beside his bed to call her if he was getting tired. She hoped she had done the right thing.

The screens made the interior of the cubicle even darker than the rest of the tent, into which the sullen daylight had filtered inadequately through the canvas. Rupert peered in the direction of the bed. Above the severely tucked sheets, Charles's forehead was swathed in bandaging. From the bridge of his nose downwards, further dressings masked his features. Only his worried, pain-clouded eyes looked out from the gap between. Rupert plonked himself down on the rickety wooden chair beside the bed, thinking irritably in passing that he wouldn't have given it house room in his scullery.

'Well,' he said. 'I've had a word with the nurse. This is too bad, my boy. Couldn't be much worse, could it?'

Charles's eyes swivelled towards him.

'Bad for Laura, too. I haven't told her yet. She's a sensitive girl. This is going to be very difficult for her. Not much of a life left for either of you, is there? Fortunes of war, I know.'

There was a long sigh from the bed.

'Let's face it,' Rupert said reflectively, 'she'll have to know the situation sooner or later.' He twitched his gold hunter watch out of his waistcoat pocket and consulted it. He'd been here in the tent for about two minutes. It felt like longer. Damnit, it was dashed difficult, conducting a conversation with a man who couldn't answer back.

'I feel for you, of course. But I feel for my daughter, too. You can understand that, can't you? Of course you can. You're a decent chap. Probably feel, as I know I would if I was in your position, that you'd have been better off—'

Charles uttered a groan and closed his eyes. Rupert stopped abruptly as he remembered that he had more-or-less promised that nurse woman that he'd be tactful. Telling the wounded man that he'd have been better off dead probably didn't qualify. But what the hell could you say in the circumstances?

'They say they can make you a mask. I suppose that's something.'

He had not noticed any movement but Charles, having surreptitiously groped for the hand bell at his side, was now ringing it vigorously. For a moment it crossed Rupert's mind that perhaps Charles' injuries had affected his sanity. He was half-irritated and half-relieved when Sister reappeared, a little out of breath, almost as if she'd run all the way from her cluttered travesty of an office, and told him briskly that the patient was tired now and must be left in peace. He thought of arguing the point – it was annoying to be chivvied out like this after so short an interview. But to be honest, what was the good of staying? Charles was hardly convivial company.

'Very well. You know best, Sister. I'll be at my hotel if I'm needed – here's their card with the address. I'll come back tomorrow to see how he's progressing.'

The next morning a messenger arrived at the hotel to say that Charles had taken a turn for the worse. By the time Rupert had got himself washed, clothed and shaved – he had no intention of going out in public unshaven, under any circumstances – and had reached the hospital, it was mid-morning and Charles was dead.

'I was told yesterday that he was mending,' Rupert said to the sister in charge. She was a different girl from yesterday's, another chit too young for the job, he thought critically.

'We hoped he was. But he suffered a further haemorrhage of the thigh wound shortly after five a.m.,' said the sister. 'There's always a slight risk of that, when the damage is so severe. Especially if they're restless. Will you stay for the funeral?'

'No. I have a business to see to. Oh, I suppose I'd better. It's a blessing, really, that he died,' said Rupert.

It was a judgement that he repeated to Jessie when he reached home two days later, with Laura in tow. En route from Folkestone, he'd collected her from Clandon and broken the news. On arriving at Maple Grange, Laura had gone straight to her room with a stone hot-water bottle and a glass of warm milk, well-laced with brandy by a shocked and sympathetic Mrs Driver. But even given her absence from the room, Jessie felt that Rupert's comment was jarringly heartless.

'How can you say that?'

'Because it's the truth.' Rupert justified his opinion with an unsparing list of Charles' injuries. 'I always knew he was a sound chap,' he added. 'Once he'd realized the decent thing to do, he did it. I dare say all it took was a bit of thrashing around, considering the state he was in.'

Jessie looked at her brother's satisfied expression and her skin crawled. 'Rupert, what did you say when you saw him?'

'Nothing he couldn't have worked out for himself.' It was not a denial of what the question had implied. 'He was no use to Laura in his condition. She couldn't have coped with such disfigurement. As I said, he did the decent thing.'

I should have known . . . I should have stopped him, Jessie told herself. But like Sister Dunlop, she had, at the crucial moment, doubted her ability to stop Rupert doing what he wanted. He had such a dense, unshakeable conviction of the rightness of his attitudes. He knew what was best. That it was best for himself, and not necessarily for those whom he controlled by his actions, had never impinged on his consciousness.

Jessie became aware of a draught. She turned her head. The door to the drawing room was open and Laura stood in the doorway, still in her nurse's uniform, her wide, appalled eyes fixed on her father's face.

The normal leave allowance for a bereaved VAD was two days. But when Laura's two days had elapsed, it was obvious to Rupert that she was in no fit state to go back. She moved in a daze, seemed not to hear what people said to her, and sat silently for hours at a time, staring into space. He had Walker drive him over to the hospital and after a brisk interview with the commandant, returned with the news that he had secured Laura's release. She could always reapply later he said, if she wanted to. Meanwhile her health was the most important thing.

The Brownlowes arranged a memorial service for Charles. Attendance was predictably thin – such services were commonplace with the Somme casualties and Rupert's less intimate acquaintances sent polite regrets without compunction. Claire Lawrence came, and most of the Delameres. Alice was still nursing in France. A message was sent to Charles' parents in Scotland but they answered that at present the journey was a little too much for them. Reading the reply aloud to an apathetic Laura, Jessie imagined them sitting silently in the grey, stone manor house in the Highlands that her niece had described to her, with their son's photograph on the mantelpiece shrouded in black ribbon, their lives empty. A scene that repeated itself in homes all over Europe.

James Allingham arrived at the church on a Flying Corps motor cycle just as the organ was striking up the first hymn. He took up a position in one of the back pews, behind the assembled staff from the Grange and a discreet distance from the chief mourners. He was currently stationed at Hainault Farm with a BE squadron to fend off the Zeppelins, Laura said dully, when her father commented on James' presence.

'I didn't really expect him to come,' she said. But she found that she was comforted by the fact that he had. Charles had so few people here to mourn him.

'Fear no more the heat o' the sun, Nor the furious winter's rages.' The vicar read aloud from a copy of *The Dramatic Works of William Shakespeare*. Charles' old housemaster had suggested the quotation in a letter of condolence to Laura that he'd written on spotting the 'Died of wounds' announcement among the long obituary columns in *The Times*. It had become a sad daily task, the scanning of those columns to learn the fate of his brightest and best former pupils. After the composing of many letters he had evolved a formula that included some small example of the lasting memory each departed boy had left with him. He thought the families appreciated that.

'I remember Charles made a splendid Guiderius in the school's performance of *Cymbeline* in 1910,' wrote the housemaster. 'He had a beautiful voice, even after it broke, and scored a resounding success with his rendering of this particular song.'

The vicar's voice could not be described as beautiful, but his tone was suitably sonorous with the solemnity of the occasion. 'Thou thy worldly task hast done, Home art gone and ta'en thy wages: Golden lads and girls all must As chimney-sweepers, come to dust.'

Rupert's sharp eyes had spotted the strip of medal ribbon stitched above James' breast pocket. At least there was one young fellow, Rupert muttered approvingly to Jessie at his side, who'd seen the error of his ways and abandoned all that pacifist claptrap he'd spouted at the outbreak of the war. Jessie did not reply. In her mind's eye she was seeing the shadowy figures of Laura and Charles standing at the head of the aisle, as they had been at their wedding in this church almost a year ago. The stained glass, filtering the winter sunshine outside, had tinted the pure white of Laura's wedding dress with colour as now it was patterning the altar cloth, and the sight of the two fair heads bent together under the vicar's extended hand as he'd blessed their union, had calmed Jessie's misgivings and given her hope for their happiness. *Golden lads and girls*.

Gulping hard, Jessie held on grimly to her control because it was improper for an Englishwoman to cry in public and beside her, Laura, who had more right than anyone to cry, was behaving with absolute propriety.

But in her own room, at night, it was a different matter. Laura's grief was deepened by a savage and lonely guilt. She was terribly afraid that her father had been right in what she'd heard him say to Aunt Jessie that she couldn't have coped with Charles' devastated features. So he'd had to die, because his wife was a coward. The guilt was compounded by the knowledge that in their brief time together, she hadn't loved him enough. And now it was too late.

She couldn't bear the sight of Rupert, who had pronounced the sentence of death on Charles for her sake. She wanted to get away from Maple Grange and her father's influence. She cast her mind about feverishly for somewhere to go, and remembered Mr Quiller of the YMCA.

'By all means,' he wrote in answer to her letter. 'We should be glad of another volunteer helper at the hostel.'

Laura packed her bags and announced that she was going to France.

Daisy was in a hurry. If she didn't get out of the house in two minutes she'd be late for work. Outside the window, the sky was already streaked with the pale fingers of dawn and Elsie had given up waiting for her and gone on ahead.

It would probably be freezing cold outside, especially on

the ferry with the wind blowing along the river. As Daisy lifted her coat down from the rack in the hall, Harriet whimpered sleepily in the room behind her. Louella propped herself up on one elbow in bed and put out a comforting hand.

'Shhh, darling, it's all right. Shhh.'

Eyes still tightly closed, Harriet rolled over and humped up on all fours. The snuffling broke into a wail. Louella scooped her up and sat with the covers pulled up over them both, cradling the small girl against her. 'Shhh . . . shhh . . . it's all right. . . .'

Harriet's flushed face nestled against Louella's cotton nightgown. With her dark hair hanging loose around her face, Louella looked like a madonna as she rocked the child in her arms. Daisy tiptoed back into the bedroom and found her handbag, checking through the contents for the identity pass which had to be shown to the guards on the gates at the Arsenal. Once she'd forgotten the pass. She'd only been saved from having to trail disconsolately home, deprived of a day's work and a day's pay, by the generosity of Elsie – who had torn a corner off her own pass for Daisy to show. Tucked mock-carelessly into Elsie's penny novelette for dinner-time reading, it had fooled the gate attendant as the workers streamed past him, but she didn't reckon her chances of being so lucky again.

The blue card safely in place in her bag, she turned to go. Louella was laying Harriet back on her pillow. The transfer from her warm arms to the cooler bedding disturbed the small girl and again she whimpered fretfully.

'Shh, darling. I'm here. Mummy's here.'

Daisy stood transfixed.

'Lou . . . you're not her mother.'

'Do you think I've forgotten that?' Louella's voice stayed at the same quiet level, but suddenly her eyes were blazing at Daisy in the lamplight. 'I remember it very well. Oh, just for a moment, now and then, I pretend . . . but I remember all right. She's not my little girl. She's yours. Yours and Arthur's. Your little bastard. My baby died.'

'Lou . . .' The venom in the other girl's words had shocked Daisy. She spread her hands uncertainly. 'Lou, I'm sorry. I didn't mean to hurt you.'

'It's all right,' said Louella. She managed a wavering smile with no humour in it. 'I know you didn't. And I didn't either. Let's forget it. You'll be late for work.'

'Oh, lord, so I will.'

There were no excuses for latecomers at the Arsenal. Late was late, and late too often was grounds for dismissal. Daisy ran.

But as the ferry crossed the water, she was haunted by the memory of Louella and Harriet. She'd been worried for a long time about Lou, about how she was coping with losing first Robert and then her baby. Now there was no evading the facts, Louella was becoming a bit strange. Her expression as she cuddled Harriet had been brooding, possessive; as if she were taking over Daisy's daughter.

When Daisy boarded the tram, it was crowded as usual. She resigned herself to standing. But a soldier on the end of a bench seat noticed her triangular badge that said 'On War Work' and, with narrowed eyes in the dim light, the yellow tinge of her skin.

'Hullo, it's a canary,' he said. Those passengers nearest to her stared and grinned. The woman seated beside the soldier looked down at her gloved hands, clasped in her lap. Suddenly he elbowed her sharply.

'Give the canary your seat, she's doing her bit, you aren't.'

'Oh, no,' said Daisy, because the woman was older, and thin, and looked very tired. But already she was standing up, humble and biddable. Clearly she was used to this kind of treatment.

'Here you are, girlie, sit down,' said the soldier, patting the vacant seat. Daisy glanced again at the woman whose place she was taking, but the woman didn't meet her eyes. She hesitated, then sat down, surrounded by beams of approval.

Annie Higgs had been right. Working with the trotyl did

sometimes get you privileged treatment on the tram. She almost wished it wouldn't.

Louella had never liked the Parrishes' front room, which faced the straggle of blackened streets overlooked by the Chemical Works in Silvertown. Built more than thirty years ago for the lower-status workers of the area, the cheap little house had a yellow-grey brick façade with an overcoating of soot. The rooms were dingy and there was no garden, only a small, square yard choked with washing lines. Every street was crammed to the limit with humanity, the normally over-crowded accommodation being squeezed even further by the demand for lodgings from the workers who flooded in from all around London to work at the Arsenal.

With Fred Parrish's two oldest sons in the army, the crush at the Parrish home should theoretically have been eased. But Elsie had moved back on quitting her job in service, and since Elsie and her sister had vacated the downstairs front room for rent-paying Daisy, Louella and Harriet, Fred and his wife still shared the front bedroom with the smallest boy and girl.

The construction of the house being shoddy, the Colindales were unwilling party to every argument and every conjugal moment between the Parrishes overhead. Fred, long inured to lack of privacy in his teeming family life, would cheerfully send the toddlers 'next door to your sisters for a bit' whenever he wanted to be alone with his wife. Louella had come to dread the phrase, audible through the paper-thin walls and invariably followed by an hour of bed-creakings and bouncings, gasps and giggles – which were a sickening parody of something she had shared with Robert and would never have again.

In the daytime she escaped with Harriet, taking the old perambulator for long walks through London.

She knew that her body had recovered from the physical strain of pregnancy and that one day soon she'd have to exchange places with Daisy as the breadwinner. Daisy was too nice to insist on it, but she made frequent wistful references to the fact that she missed being with Harriet, that she felt her daughter was growing up without her.

Louella didn't know how to bear losing the daily contact with Harriet. She thought sometimes that it was all that kept her sane.

The dilemma was on her mind as she wheeled the perambulator along a street in Blackheath, bounded on one side by a high brick wall. Ahead of her at the end of the street was the open green of the common. Set into the wall was a wooden door. It lolled on one hinge, the other being rusty and broken.

Through the gap, she saw a garden.

After the brick yards, the festoons of washing, the sparse patches of dog-sick grass by the river which were her daily lot in Silvertown, the sight of a garden was a tonic to Louella. She had been brought up in a farm cottage before the move to Bethnal Green. Her mother had loved plants and herbs, until Bert Wilkins knocked every capacity for love out of her, and had taught her daughter how to make them flourish. Part of the attraction of Robert, when he'd made his first self-conscious approaches in the lane outside the hop fields, had been that he came from a country town where the open farmland was never far away; and ever since leaving Guildford, Louella's grief over Robert – and now her baby – had had its echoes in the loss of the small plot which she'd tended since her marriage.

Cautiously she tried the latch on the wooden door. It wasn't locked. Viewed properly through an open doorway, the garden was utterly neglected, gone to ruin. Beneath the apple trees there was fruit lying rotting in the long grass among the blackening heaps of fallen leaves that no one had bothered to sweep up. A few shrivelled apples still clung to the bare branches of the trees, unharvested, when they should have been jam and crumbles for hungry stomachs long ago. And all this long grass between weed-choked flowerbeds could have been a vegetable garden, thought Louella. There was even room for a chicken-run, or a pig. It hurt her to see such waste.

She looked up at the back of the house to which the sad garden belonged. That, too, had a neglected appearance, with blistered, peeling paintwork and dirty windows. At some, the blinds were still drawn. At others, the curtains were pulled back unevenly. It was a biggish town house, three storeys and a basement, and she would have expected servants, but no servant would ever draw a curtain like that – without straightening the folds.

The property looked empty. She wheeled Harriet's perambulator through the arched opening in the wall and closed the door.

Harriet stared around her with interest and demanded to get down. Louella lifted her out and she set off with determination towards the steps that led down to the basement. For a few restful days just after her first birthday, when she had launched herself forward on her sturdy legs, Harriet had been slower walking than crawling, but all that was in the past. Nowadays, unless confined to the perambulator and kept there by a home-made harness of string, she had to be watched like a hawk. She had an immense capacity for getting into mischief.

Louella caught up with her on the third step down. She was about to retreat up the stairs again, with the outraged child kicking at her hips, when she happened to catch a glance of a stone-flagged kitchen and curiosity prompted her to carry the protesting Harriet down to peer in through the smeared glass.

A pine table with drawers underneath occupied the centre of the empty room. In the alcoves on either side of the kitchen range were cupboards, with fielded doors which had originally been painted white. Now the paint was yellow with age. Further cupboards ranged along one wall were glass-fronted to display the china they held, and there was a small, square oak dresser, appealing because of its simplicity, which displayed pewter mugs and plates. Whether empty of humans or not, the house still had its furniture.

'What are you doing?'

Guiltily, Louella spun round. A man was standing at the

408

top of the steps, watching her. To judge by his clothes, old but good, and his educated voice, he was the owner of the house. Oddly, his voice had expressed surprise but not anger.

'I was just having a look. I thought the place was empty.'

'It isn't.' The man was at least fifty years old, with a clean-shaven, fair skin and hair that was entirely grey. His eyebrows were remarkable, thick and tufty, giving him a permanently quizzical look. But if it were not for the eyebrows, Louella thought, the impression given by the lines on his face and around his grey-blue eyes would have been one of intense sadness. Still holding Harriet in her arms, she started to climb the steps again.

'I'm sorry,' she said. 'I really did think so. Looking through the gate. And it's been so long since I saw a proper garden.'

A reluctant smile touched the corners of the man's mouth, though not his eyes.

'Hardly "proper" any more. I'm afraid it has gone to ruin. I have had other things on my mind . . . and of course staff are difficult to find nowadays.'

Louella wondered belatedly if she ought to have addressed him as 'sir'. He was far above her social station. She carried Harriet towards the pram and found that he had followed her.

'Are you local? Would you like a cup of tea?' he said. 'And a glass of lemonade for your little girl?'

Louella was taken aback by the offer. Gentlemen didn't give cups of tea to the hoi polloi, especially when they caught them trespassing in their gardens. Not unless they had ulterior motives . . . perhaps he was going to leap on her once he'd got her inside his house, and make improper suggestions? But it was hard to envisage dark, illicit passions lurking beneath the very civilized exterior of this melancholy man. And a cup of tea would be very welcome on such a cold November day. She'd brought out cold food for herself and Harriet in a basket, as she always did on such expeditions, but that had been finished hours ago, and it was a long way home from Blackheath to Silvertown.

'Why are you asking?' she said bluntly. 'You don't

know me, I could be anybody. I could be out to steal something.'

'I can tell you're not. Why did I ask you? Because it's been a grey day and I would like someone to talk to for a little while. I don't see many people nowadays.'

It had been such a frank admission of loneliness that Louella felt touched.

'All right. Some tea would be very nice,' she accepted. 'But I mustn't stay long, I have to get back to Silvertown before dusk.'

'Silvertown? Is that where you live?'

'Just at the moment. In lodgings.'

'I've never been to Silvertown. Is it nice there?' he said politely, opening the kitchen door and standing aside to let her in.

'No,' said Louella frankly. 'It's terrible.'

The kitchen was almost as cold as it was out of doors. The fire in the range had gone out, or had never been lit. But just inside the door, not visible from the window, was a newish gas stove.

'Now let me see if I can remember how to light this,' said the man, finding a box of Vestas on the shelf above the stove. He made a couple of abortive attempts, turning the wrong tap or failing to get the match to ignite in time and having to fumble for another.

'Let me,' offered Louella. She lit the stove and looked around for a kettle. It wasn't very clean, she noticed as she filled it at the sink, and then realized how many months it was since she'd carried out the familiar action of making tea. A sharply poignant memory of Guildford, the kitchen there, and Robert in it, washed over her.

'Cups and saucers.' The man began absent-mindedly to open cupboards. *He doesn't know where the crockery is kept*, Louella thought. She supposed most gentlemen wouldn't. But if he normally left such things to servants, as was to be expected, where were they?

'You don't look after yourself, do you?' she asked, as he

410

finally located a cupboard containing what was clearly kitchen pottery and not 'best' china.

'I have a woman who comes in and does a bit of cooking and tidying. But this is her day off.'

'Whatever do you do for meals, when she isn't here?' Louella took over and spooned two teaspoonfuls of leaves and one for the pot into a chipped teapot.

'Oh, she leaves me something cold.'

'That's a bit depressing, isn't it?'

'It doesn't really matter.' He had found a tin of biscuits and, unwisely, put the entire tin in front of Harriet, who dived in with alacrity.

Looking around her, Louella thought that the solitary servant he had mentioned was taking advantage of this attitude. The sink was stained, the stove could do with a good blacking and there was unswept dust in the corners of the kitchen. That and the neglected garden. . . .

An idea began to form in her mind.

21

The name of Louella's new acquaintance, owner of the run-down garden in Blackheath, was Hector Ramsay. He was a widower who, until the fighting at Loos, had had a dearly loved son. Like so many soldiers who fell in the mud of Flanders or the Somme, John Ramsay had been reported 'Missing, Believed Killed', and the news had shattered his father's small, private world.

For a while after the telegram arrived, Hector could find no will or energy to care for the details of his orderly background. His friends, many of whom were dealing with their own bereavements in a thoroughly stiff-upper-lipped British manner, had lost patience with his grief. And the servants, discouraged by his listless refusal to make decisions, had drifted away for better-paid work in the war effort, or had been called up for the armed services. Now he lived alone, day following day in boredom and emptiness.

After the first offer of tea, Louella had called again, careful to make the day of her visit the same as the rest day of the slovenly servant. She was half expecting to be turned away with polite coldness, but the odd gentleman was glad to see her.

'And your little girl. I hope I have lemonade. Or would she prefer milk?'

'Either,' said Louella. Harriet was as likely to upend her cup as to drink its contents. 'But she's not my little girl. She's my niece.'

Installed once more in the kitchen, she made sounds of sympathy when the conversation turned to the presumed death of John Ramsay.

'It's so hard, you see,' Hector told her, 'to accept that he's really gone. There's no grave. Nobody in his unit saw him die. I keep hoping that perhaps he's still alive somewhere, though I suppose the more that time passes, the less likely that becomes.' It was a hope that he could not have voiced to his old acquaintances without incurring their well-meaning attempts to bring home the realities, but the stranger who sat at his kitchen table – this dark-haired young woman with the unhappy eyes – had an aura of understanding about her.

'My husband was at Loos,' Louella said quietly.

'Oh. Was he . . . ?'

'Not there. Afterwards,' she said. 'But he was gassed at Loos.'

'I'm sorry.'

'I haven't got used to losing him yet, either.'

The social gap between them was wide, but a shared grief bridged it. In time, she even told him about the way that Robert had died.

At five o'clock on the evening of Friday, 19 January, 1917, Daisy was at work on the day shift in the Danger Buildings and beginning to think about gathering her flagging energy for the journey home. There would be the usual scrimmage to board the tram, she anticipated wearily. Elsie always dealt with it so much more ruthlessly than she did, swarming up the side of the tram over the balustrade to the top deck while less athletic mortals tried to push their way up the stairs. Even when she was feeling well, Daisy couldn't keep up with Elsie, and today she was not feeling well.

She bent to dip a scoopful of yellow powder from her bucket and to dribble it into the neck of the shell. As she stooped again to repeat the operation, she felt dizzy. The scoop fell from her hand and clattered to the ground.

'What's up?' said Elsie, working a few feet away. 'Taken bad again?'

Daisy was sitting on the floor by now, forehead down on her drawn-up knees in an attempt to fight off the waves of nausea. She made an indistinct sound of assent. They were becoming a regular occurrence, these bilious attacks, but this was the worst so far. Her throat was sore and burning, with a sharp acid taste in her mouth. The room seemed to swim around her.

The principal overlooker in charge of operations in that building was hurrying towards them as Elsie squatted in concern beside her friend.

'Show me your tongue. Your teeth. When did you last have a break from trotyl?' The girls who worked with the powder were switched periodically for a few days' 'rest', performing inspection duties in other departments in order to cut down on exposure to the poisonous substance. But the precaution was not working with Daisy. Her latest 'rest' had been last week and already the symptoms had returned.

'See the medical officer tomorrow morning. And meantime you'd better go home and lie down,' said the PO.

'I'll take her home, shall I?' Elsie said.

'No, you'll lose pay,' Daisy protested. But the protest was only half-hearted and easily overcome. In her present state, the prospect of making her way home alone was too daunting for her to refuse Elsie's offer.

It was a relief not to have to contend with the usual rush-hour stream of workers disgorged from the Arsenal, and the tram journey from Beresford Square to the Free Ferry pier took a mere three minutes that evening instead of the twenty it could sometimes occupy. By a quarter to seven they were on the ferry, crossing the water, and the cold night air blowing on her face was dispelling Daisy's sickness, when they heard the distant boom of an explosion.

With one accord, Elsie and Daisy turned their heads towards the Arsenal.

Out in the butts on the marshes, the newly completed big guns from the foundry were often test-fired. The Danger Building girls were used to the sound. This had been chillingly different.

'I don't think it was from the Arsenal,' Elsie said.

'Look at the sky,' whispered Daisy.

414

The night sky above Silvertown had become suffused with a dull blood-red glow, which as they watched, paled to scarlet and then to orange-pink against which the buildings on the approaching north shore were sharply silhouetted. The pink became yellow, glaring bright, turning night into unnatural day. Then came a monumental thud, an earthquake shock of sound followed by a great gale of wind that rocked the ferry and sent passengers sprawling. Daisy, clinging to the handrail, managed somehow to stay on her feet. The sky was black with debris, raining down on the river. As the boat righted itself in the calm that followed the passing of the gale, Elsie shielded her eyes with her right hand and stared to the North-west.

'Oh, my God,' she said. 'It's Brunner Mond.'

I live right next to the chemical works where they purify the trotyl, Elsie had told Daisy when they first met at the interview for work at the Arsenal. *You can't get much more dangerous than that.*

The Brunner Mond Chemical Works, a factory for the manufacture of caustic soda until 1912, had been empty and disused when the war broke out, and with its river frontage and its proximity to the Arsenal, officials from the office of the Director General of Explosives Supply decided that it would make an excellent site for the purification of TNT. When they proposed that the owners should undertake this work, the suggestion was not received with enthusiasm – the factory was in the middle of a densely populated area and besides, the work seemed likely to be unprofitable at the proposed rate of payment. But Messrs Brunner and Mond had German antecedents and as such had to be seen to behave with unquestionable British patriotism, so they reluctantly accepted the contract and the plant began to operate in September of 1915.

By 1917 the people of Silvertown were used to living with the fact of the gigantic powder keg in their midst. They speculated sometimes about the chances of a stray bomb from a Zeppelin landing on the works, but with the human tendency to be philosophical about what you cannot change, they shrugged their shoulders and accepted the risk . . . until January the 19th, when a small fire broke out in the room at the top of the factory, where the TNT was loaded into a 'melt pot' as the first stage of the purification process. Spreading rapidly through the building, the blaze ignited the entire store of powder.

Five tons of TNT swept away a square mile of buildings, including most of the neighbourhood where the Parrishes lived.

Forever afterwards, the events of the ensuing hours were a nightmare blur in Daisy's memory. Everything that moved in the night, it seemed, was racing desperately towards Silvertown. On the north shore all was chaos. Within a two-mile radius of the source of the explosion, scraps from the demolished buildings had rained down out of the sky littering the ground with planks of wood, twisted chunks of metal and blocks of masonry. An entire boiler had been hurled intact through the roof of a house. Closer to the heart of the explosion, where burning material had been scattered, new fires were blazing. Even on the edges of the blast area, windows were shattered, roof tiles ripped away and dumped into the street.

Police vehicles, fire engines and ambulances swept by stridently. Daisy was jostled and bumped by near-hysterical workers returning to homes that no longer existed, or by rescuers shepherding shocked and tattered survivors to safety. A cordon had been set up across the west-bound road and a grim knot of policemen were trying to keep order.

'No, you can't pass this point. The army's in there digging, and the emergency services. You'd only add to their problems. Yes, the chemical works went up. No, I don't have casualty details. You'll have to go down to the church hall, they are setting up a centre to collect information and names there.'

Daisy and Elsie stumbled towards the church hall, hands linked to stop the surging crowds from separating them. No definite news about the Parrishes' home was yet available they were told by a Salvation Army worker struggling to maintain an air of calm in the face of universal panic. 'But I think that road's gone,' said a whey-faced, dishevelled woman holding a baby, with frightened children clinging to her skirts. 'I'm from the next road and it took the top half of the house off, straight.'

All around them voices contributed scraps of information and glimpses of horror.

'They can't get near those streets, the fire's too hot.'

'The gasometer's gone up. And the flour mills.'

'There must be hundreds, thousands, killed or buried alive.'

'I was running down the road and something came flying and hit me in the chest. I looked and it was a man's head. After that I didn't run no more. . . .'

'She was holding the baby so tight as she ran . . . when she fell down, we had to prise it away from her. And it was dead. Dead of suffocation. . . .'

The scale of the catastrophe was beyond comprehension. Daisy closed her eyes and prayed.

Please, God, not Harriet; please, God, not Harriet. . . .

On Saturday morning the national newspapers carried a government announcement of two lines which had been issued at 11.40 p.m. the previous evening: '*The Ministry of Munitions regrets to announce that an explosion occurred this evening at a munitions factory in the neighbourhood of London.*

'*It is feared that the explosion was attended by a considerable loss of life and damage to property.*'

By then, in the cold daylight, Daisy and Elsie were among those digging in the ruins. The walls of Elsie's house had collapsed inwards and until the rubble had been cleared, it was not possible to know how many of its occupants had been inside. Certainly they had not been accounted for, so far, by the lists of casualties going up at the various hospitals and shelters around the district which the two girls had toured all night long, in vain.

Daisy's fingertips were bleeding from scrabbling among the rubble. Climbing over a heap of brickwork she had fallen and cut open her ankle. Blood was still trickling over her dusty shoes. Somehow her exhausted body continued to obey the dictates of her mind and she dug on steadily.

At the next house, workers had unearthed a body and they came to fetch a door from the Parrish house on which to transport it to the morgue. Daisy had found the door too heavy to lift but once it was removed, in the dust and debris beneath it, she turned up a rag doll.

Mrs Colindale had made the doll in the summer that Harriet was born, in the short time that was left before the pain overcame her. The smiling face was stitched on to the flat cotton surface of the head. The woollen plaits came from an old yellow cardigan, unravelled, and the dress of striped cotton had once been a blouse of Daisy's. Now the face was torn open and the shredded rag stuffing spilled out.

Beside Daisy, Elsie was shifting and hauling great lumps of fractured brickwork, calculating aloud. 'Dora'll still have been at work, that's one thing. And Dad was on double shift. Mam and Lucy and Gordon, with luck, they could have gone down to the ferry to take him his dinner.'

Louella would not have been at work, Daisy was thinking, eyes closed, pressing the torn doll to her cheek. *Louella had no reason to take Harriet down to the ferry.*

'Daisy! Over here!'

At the foot of the heap of rubble that was all that remained of what had been home for six months, Louella stood with Harriet in her arms. Stumbling and slipping on the shifting debris, Daisy ran down to her daughter. In a few moments Harriet was in her arms and she was crying with relief while Harriet was crying about the ruined doll.

'But where were you?'

'In Blackheath. It's a long story.'

Louella hadn't told her sister-in-law about the house at Blackheath and Hector Ramsay. She wanted her plan to work first.

On Friday it had worked. She had persuaded Hector that his current servant was inadequate and lazy, she had confronted the woman and dismissed her on Hector's behalf, and she had established herself as his replacement housekeeper. She had begun to attack the neglected housework and had cooked the new employer a good, nutritious evening meal to celebrate her new status. It would mean travelling back to Silvertown in the dark, but she had decided that the occasion warranted the hiring of a cab. To prevent Daisy from worrying when she came home from work, she had despatched a message to the Parrish house to explain that she would be back later.

In Blackheath, as she set the table in the kitchen for the meal which Hector insisted that she and Harriet should share, they had heard the explosion. It had been heard, indeed, in Guildford and even in Norfolk people had felt the shock wave. They had gone out on to the heath and seen the glare of the fires and at first Louella had been afraid it was the Arsenal that had suffered the explosion.

Hector had come with her in search of a cab, and when one was finally found with a driver prepared to go towards Woolwich, he had climbed in beside her.

'There's no need to come,' Louella had said.

'I want to be sure you're safe.'

There was something in his voice as he said it . . . the first inkling that she'd had from him, that she might be more than a housekeeper.

The cab had been unable to get through to the scene of the disaster since for more than two miles in every direction the roads were jammed with rescuers or the rescued, or the vehicles of would-be sightseers. So they had gone forward on foot, with Louella carrying Harriet. Now, as Louella explained the situation in rapid undertones to Daisy, Hector could be seen waiting diffidently at the corner of what remained of the street.

'I think he's sweet on me,' Louella added at the end of her sparely worded narrative.

'Oh, Lou . . . you wouldn't . . . ?'

'I might,' said Louella.

'Oh, Lou . . .' Daisy said again. 'How could you?'

She means, how could I after Robert? thought Louella. But Hector wasn't 'after Robert'. She couldn't have entertained the idea of lovemaking with another man who was young and virile like her husband had been. To give comfort to an older, gentle, and above all generous man in the way that he just happened to need, that was a different matter. Aloud, she said, 'Why not? Anyway, whatever happens, for the time being we'll have a roof over our heads. And considering all this . . .' she made a sweeping gesture over her ravaged surroundings, 'it's a good thing we will, isn't it?'

In the days that followed, Daisy had to adapt at speed to changes. First, she had to get used to the idea that Louella, as a housekeeper or as a kept woman, had secured them a very comfortable home in the pretty Regency house at Blackheath.

Once she had met Hector Ramsay, she understood Louella's behaviour better and when she saw the night nursery on the top floor of the house, which was available for Harriet, she had to suspend her qualms.

The room was bright and sunny, at the front of the house with two dormer windows set in the slope of the roof, overlooking the green of the heath. The small fireplace with its bow-fronted grate had smiling cupids climbing either side of the surround, and the wallpaper was of tiny bluebirds on a cream ground. There was a bookshelf full of well-thumbed old picture books and a trunkful of toys. The child's bed of white-painted wrought-ironwork was covered by a pretty patchwork quilt which was almost as finely made as her mother's quilt that Daisy had been forced to sell in the desperate times after Robert's death. On the roundel at the centre of the bedhead was impressed a unicorn, lying in a forest glade with its legs tucked under it, and on the footboard in a smaller roundel, a pair of doves. In one corner on the painted boards stood the rocking horse that Hector's son John Ramsay had ridden as a small boy.

Harriet headed straight for the horse and could not be detached for more than an hour.

By Monday the details of the scope of the Silvertown explosion were emerging. The Brunner Mond building had simply vanished as if it had never been, leaving a crater in the ground a hundred yards across and twenty or thirty feet deep. The official figures were that sixty-nine people had been killed on the spot; ninety-eight seriously hurt, of whom some more were likely to die because of the severity of their injuries; three hundred and twenty-eight slightly injured and a further five or six hundred had received minor damage from flying glass or debris. The chief reaction beyond horror was of stunned relief that in view of the scale of damage to the buildings around the works, the casualty rate hadn't been worse. So many people had had lucky escapes, missing death by inches as lethal debris hurtled past them. In one yard by the river, the local paper reported, a horse was killed a few feet from a nesting chicken whose eggs were undamaged.

Though five tons of TNT had been ignited, by purest chance a further thirty-seven tons had been removed from the site on the previous day.

'If that's what happened with five,' said Elsie on Monday morning in the Danger Buildings, 'forty-two would have blown up the whole of London.'

Elsie was amazingly resilient about the loss of her home. Her family, mercifully, had escaped unscathed because, as she had hoped, at the time of the explosion her mother and the smaller siblings had been waiting at the ferry to give their father his dinner before he returned for the second half of his double shift. The community had 'chipped in' with clothing and temporary accommodation for the homeless while the government set up its scheme for the speedy replacement of their lost possessions and the repair or rebuilding of their homes.

'I didn't lose much except my clothes, and I was sick of those anyway,' said Elsie, and began to hum as she worked. She had a new 'best boy', one of the soldiers who'd helped in the search for survivors, and she considered that every cloud had a silver lining.

Other residents of the street had not been so lucky. One neighbour who had been ill in hospital at the time of the explosion had discharged himself to go in search of his family and had eventually found his mother, wife and two small daughters in three separate mortuaries. Daisy knew the little girls; they had sometimes stood on tiptoe to peer into Harriet's perambulator when the Colindales first arrived in Silvertown. She had thought herself used to grief, but she couldn't imagine such suffering as this man must now be enduring.

Daisy had almost forgotten the bilious attack which had caused her to leave the Arsenal early on the fateful Friday. The principal overlooker remembered it however, and she was sent for a thorough medical examination, at the end of which she was pronounced no longer fit to work with TNT. Subsequently transferred to filling bullets with lead shot instead, in a factory far from the Danger Buildings, she wasn't sure whether to be relieved or to worry about the drop in pay. There was no danger money available for working with lead shot.

Filling shells had involved standing and walking about all day. To fill bullets, Daisy sat with seven other women at a tray table, continuously scooping up handfuls of grey, greasy lead pellets to drop them into a frameful of upended bullet cases. Once filled, the cases would be shifted elsewhere to have the ends stamped on to them.

'Been a canary?' said one of the women, noticing her complexion as she took her place shyly on the first morning. Daisy nodded.

'So was I, till it messed up me insides. Then I was on the cordite bagging for a bit, only my husband come home on leave and said he wouldn't have me being in the Danger

Buildings. Pity, the money was good. Anyway, you'll like it here, won't she, girls? There's your locker. You can bring in your own teapot and crockery from home and have a brew up in the day.'

The work was the most boring and repetitive that Daisy had ever undertaken in her life. If only she could be at home with Harriet in the nursery, she thought wistfully. But Louella, finder of the accommodation, controlled those who benefited from it, and Louella said that Hector couldn't be expected to feed and house three people for nothing. A working wage would still be needed. Daisy tried to stifle the suspicion that it was an excuse to keep her apart from her own daughter.

In the spring of 1917, Rupert Brownlowe was able to look with optimism on the progress of the war. Though the year had begun badly, with the torpedoing of the transport ship *Ivernia* in the Mediterranean and the admission that German submarines had accounted for three million tons of Allied shipping, much of it British, the shortages arising from this blockading of imported supplies could be counterbalanced by advances on the Western Front.

On 9 April, the Canadians had succeeded in taking Vimy Ridge. Previous French and British attempts to wrest from the Germans the vantage point which overlooked all the industrial plains towards Douai had been costly failures. Now a combination of mining, tunnelling and raw courage had won the Ridge and the Allies were surging forward to liberate Arras five miles to the North-east. The guns and the cavalry were on the move again. And the United States had joined the war.

On 2 April, President Woodrow Wilson had persuaded Congress to declare war against Germany and the decision was made official on 6 April. Rupert opened a jeroboam of champagne for the occasion and called the staff at the Grange together to celebrate. That the American forces were not yet ready to take any practical part in the fighting did not reduce the morale-boosting impact of the news for Rupert.

He needed cheering up. He was sometimes bewildered by the way the world was treating him. In a sense he was having a good war. As he had commented during the dinner party at which his now-deceased son-in-law had been so regrettably emotional, the making of shells for the Ministry of Munitions had proved a rewarding experience, both financially and in terms of personal satisfaction. As a consequence of doing such valuable war work, he had been invited to attend committees, which in turn bred further invitations to join other committees, so that he felt his social standing in the district had improved considerably in the last two years.

But he had paid a price. His well-run household had lost a number of its employees, his domestic peace had been disrupted. His stables, a source of pride for two decades, had been broken up . . . and the blow that really hurt, his daughter had gone gadding off to France in the aftermath of her widowhood, behaving as though she blamed him for her husband's death when he had only acted in her best interests. When he had tried to prevent her ill-considered departure by the only means he knew, the curtailment of her allowance, she had told him coldly that as a widow she now had access to her husband's funds and that if Rupert wished to discontinue the allowance, that was his privilege.

It had been a shock. He had always thought Laura was fond of him. Leaving, she had looked through and beyond him with the eyes of a stranger. Her letters were few and sparsely worded and she had declined his invitation to come home for Christmas, saying that she was needed at work. Her absence left him feeling bereft to a degree which surprised him.

He did not express his loneliness to anyone. Instead, he took his bruised feelings out on his work, which now included taking part in the Local Tribunals to hear appeals against conscription into the armed services.

At the outset of the war, there had been more volunteers than the army could cope with, but as the months dragged on and the casualties mounted, it became a problem to supply adequate numbers of soldiers to man the trenches along the extended line of the Western Front. Those who had not stepped forward eagerly in the opening months were now hanging back, with some justification at the sight of what lay in store for them. Increasingly severe moral pressure on the laggards having failed to remedy the problem, there had been first the Derby Scheme of the autumn of 1915 which 'encouraged' men to testify their willingness to fight if need be; then the Military Service Act of January 1915 which had called up all unmarried men between the ages of 18 and 41. In May of 1916 the act had been extended to include married men as well. But many of those now being sucked unwillingly into the conflict were quick to lodge appeals against their conscription.

The Local Tribunals system had been set up to judge the rights or wrongs of these appeals and Rupert, an enthusiastic official canvasser for the Derby Scheme whose attentions had induced many a reluctant hero to put forward his name, had been asked to take part. He rapidly acquired a reputation as a harsh repudiator of claims for exemption on compassionate grounds. The needs of King and Country, in Rupert's opinion, came first. Family a poor second.

When the newly promoted First Lieutenant Oliver Brownlowe came home on leave in June, having seen some severe fighting round Arras, Rupert had to concede that Oliver, who as a child had given his father cause for concern over his lack of independent spirit, had become an adult; the problem being that, with Oliver, maturity seemed to have taken the form of a quite unwarranted critical attitude towards his father.

Their first clash was over Rupert's attitude towards the Tribunals.

'I've had men before me today,' he complained at supper after a particularly exasperating session, 'who bring new, undreamed-of interpretations to the phrase "essential occupation". A tripe-scraper claimed this morning that he had to carry on with his work because no woman would have the stomach for it.'

Jessie uttered a smothered sound and Rupert looked at her sharply.

'Did you wish to comment, Jessica?'

'I thought,' said Jessie, 'that there spoke a man who had no idea of the kind of work regularly undertaken by nurses in our hospitals at the present time.'

'Quite,' said Rupert. 'So I told him. And a strong, healthy man who should have gone at the outbreak of the war said that his wife had died and his five young children would be destitute without him. I pointed out that the Separation Allowance would pay for perfectly adequate child care in his absence. He said but what if he died, and I said, then there'd be a pension. He said but a pension can't replace a father's loving care. I said what nonsense!'

'Yes,' said Oliver, thoughtfully. 'Fatherly loving care *is* a bit of a nonsense in your book, isn't it?'

Rupert was not sure how to interpret this remark so he left it alone.

'One man tried to excuse himself by saying his business would collapse without him because his brother, who was his partner in the venture, had already been taken for the King's Rifles. I told him that a business can be started again and his country's need should be his first priority. . . . And so many of the men in factory work could be combed out now that it's been found their jobs can be done adequately by women, but they all ask for exemptions nonetheless. And their employers aid and abet them, saying they can't do without a dairyman, or they can't teach a woman the same level of skill in a month as the man they'd lose had acquired over the years. "*That's as may be,*" I tell them. "We all have to make sacrifices." Do you know one of them had the unmitigated cheek to ask me what sacrifices I had made!'

'Did he?' Oliver looked up quickly. 'And what did you reply?'

'I told him, *I have given my son,*' Rupert said.

'Poppycock!' said Oliver, with a sudden, startling vehemence. 'You didn't give me, Pa, I gave myself. And if you *could* be said to have "given" me, it is entirely in keeping with your general conduct, which is never to part with anything that you value.'

He left the room abruptly, leaving his father staring, open-mouthed, at the place where he had been.

To Jessie, Oliver was less truculent and more forthcoming. He told her about the awful mud of the Western Front, which could swallow a horse or a man in the space of a few minutes if he slipped off the duckboard causeways that were the only means of crossing the morass. And about the flooded trenches in which the infantry passed their days and which were sometimes the lot of a gunnery officer as well when he was on Observation Post duty.

'They've given us leather jerkins and waterproof capes now, because the greatcoats were too long and dragged in the mud or the water, and at last someone whose contribution to the war is the ordering of supplies has twigged this basic fact. The cape comes in useful as a groundsheet, though there's been so much rain that getting soaked is inevitable whatever we wear. And the men have thigh-length gum boots, new issue for this last winter, which are some help except that they get wet through inside with condensation so they just replace one form of damp with another. They stuff the legs with jute sandbags but their feet still get soaked. By the way, Aunt Jessie, Laura mentioned in one of her letters that you've been sewing sandbags. Sterling work! You can't imagine how badly they are needed.'

Jessie, blushing, thought that his comment made worthwhile the long hours that hurt her eyes and made her fingers sore with handling the rough jute.

'They had so many cases of trench feet last winter that this year it's been made a court-martial offence to have it. I wonder,' said Oliver, sarcastically, 'how long it will take some Red Tab to work out that a wonderful way to keep the casualties down would be to issue a directive saying that it's a court-martial offence to get killed or wounded . . . ? As if the poor devils could help it! If they're standing around in water for days at a time, the outcome is pretty predictable.

'So now there's an official drill: every morning, between nine and ten ack emma, every man in turn in each section has to haul his boots off and rub his feet with a vile sort of whale-oil concoction supplied handily in a tin for that purpose by central stores. It makes his feet even chillier and whiffier than before, and his poor junior officer has to inspect him to make sure he's done it. Ugh!' He wrinkled his nose. 'I heard of a trooper the other day who came out of the line and reported sick with trench foot, which by the way could lose him his toes so he doesn't contract it for fun, and some puce major started shouting about how it was a potential court martial, and he'd obviously neglected his drill. The man said he'd been waist-deep in water for the last four days and the only way he could get his feet high enough to apply the whale oil would be to lie on his back and stick them in the air, which would have been counter-productive because he'd have drowned! The major couldn't admit he'd been in the wrong so he just woffled for a bit about taking more care in future.'

Jessie, watching her nephew's face, saw to her relief that though his comments betrayed a disquieting disrespect for some of his commanding officers, there was none of the dazed air of endurance that had so frightened her in Charles McKay's expression. Somehow, fingers crossed, this new, hardened, pipe-smoking Oliver was coping with the war. Sometimes he even managed to make it sound funny.

But there were further clashes between Rupert and his son during the course of the next few days. Oliver spent most of his time with his fiancée and her family, but when he was at Maple Grange every dinner-table conversation, however amicably begun, dissolved into an argument.

Rupert was at a loss. If Oliver had been still a schoolboy, he would have known how to deal with the situation – with a good thrashing. But a son who was taller than he was, with nearly two years of active service behind him . . . ?

Jessie tried to act as peacemaker. It seemed to her that it

was not so much Rupert's comments as Oliver's scathing responses to them that caused the trouble. Mealtimes at the Grange had always been subject to the imparting of wisdom by Rupert at the head of the table. It was only now that Oliver had openly begun to take issue with his father's opinions that they had become such difficult occasions. She talked the problem over with Claire.

'I agree it's a pity for them to be at each other's throats all the time. But I don't know what to do about it,' said Claire, 'short of keeping him away from his father, which I have been trying to do as much as possible. To be honest, I have to bite my tongue myself sometimes to stop arguing with Rupert when he's giving us all the benefit of his experience. And I'm not out there, doing the real thing like Oliver is. It must be much harder for him. The only thing I can think of is that at lunch today, you and I keep Oliver talking and simply don't give Rupert a chance to make any provocative statements.'

At first the tactic seemed to be working. Oliver was happily launched on an account of some complicated exploit on the Somme last November, involving a gun to be moved, a team of panic-stricken horses, an oncoming platoon of enemy infantrymen and the untimely arrival of a trench mortar-bomb.

'The darned thing went up right under one of the horses. Scooped it up, clean as a whistle, dropped it down in a tree: forelegs dangling, hind legs draped over a branch – the only remaining branch, as it happens, the rest having been lopped by previous accidents. Nasty sight,' said Oliver wryly. 'It certainly bothered Griffin – you remember Griffin, Aunt Jessie, the under-groom here before the war? Decent chap. I saw tears in his eyes as he picked himself up from the floor and looked at that horse. Then things got a bit hot because the Huns were almost on us and the horses that weren't hit had scarpered and there we were, stuck. But then Griffin stopped blubbing over the horse and organized the drivers to put in some brute force and we got the gun slewed round. No gunners, they'd gone down in the general mêlée, but Griffin helped me on the aiming side and we managed to fire off a couple of rounds, one of which put paid to the opposition luckily, and that gave us time to get another team out to bring in the gun. I'd never realized that Griffin knew how to fire the darned thing. So when we got back I slapped in a recommendation for a medal and a suggestion that he should be switched to being a bombardier, as the pay's better. But the powers-that-be turned the bombardier bit down, silly asses.'

'Quite right,' said Rupert waspishly. 'I imagine that it's a position requiring a responsible attitude.'

'They don't come much more responsible than Griffin.'

'I'm afraid I have to differ with you there.' Rupert launched on an acerbic account of the groom's unmannerly behaviour at the Grange during Laura's wedding and added that he had heard the man had ended the day by being arrested for brawling in a public house and he'd had to be kept locked up for the rest of his leave.

'Oh dear,' said Jessie. 'I didn't know about that. I suppose he never saw Daisy, then.'

'But I think you must agree, hardly an indication of responsible behaviour,' Rupert said.

'I'm not surprised the poor blighter was upset,' said Oliver. 'I knew he was sweet on Daisy, but I never realized you'd thrown her out of here, Pa.' Claire, he realized, was kicking his ankle under the table, but he ignored her. 'When I asked about Daisy, that time when I had a letter to give her, you didn't tell me that you'd sacked her – you just said she'd left your employment.'

'I didn't see the need,' said Rupert, 'to go into detail on a distasteful subject.'

'Distasteful is the word. What did you have against the poor girl anyway?'

'Her illegitimate child,' began Rupert. Oliver snorted.

'War baby. A mistake. A misfortune, not a crime. Haven't you ever done anything rash along those lines, Pa?'

'Certainly not,' said Rupert, his annoyance at the question being partly influenced by a tremor of discomfort at the

430

memories it reared in his mind, memories that he had put down very resolutely over the years. Once, as a callow adolescent, he'd had an unfortunate peccadillo with a pretty servant girl at the house of a friend with whom he was staying in the school holidays. She'd been a sunny little thing, a bit like Daisy, he supposed, and he'd lost his head. In retrospect he'd decided that the girl had been a brazen hussy who'd seduced him knowing perfectly well what she was doing, but the fact remained that the deed had come out, the girl had been dismissed in tears; he'd been threatened with a horse-whipping by his friend's outraged father and the whole thing had been pretty unpleasant. Now he remembered the girl's reproachful eyes – she'd tried to tell him, in a most embarrassing scene, that she loved him – and the suppressed guilt made his mood ugly.

'Am I to assume, then, from what you say, that Miss Lawrence will shortly be announcing her forthcoming confinement?'

There was a short, dangerous pause. Oliver pushed back his chair and for the third time in a year, Rupert seemed in imminent danger of assault in his own home.

'Let it go, Oliver,' said Claire quietly. Oliver went on staring at his father for a long moment.

'What a bounder you are,' he said at last, breathing deeply. 'And what a pity that we can't choose our parents.'

It was not a happy note on which to end his leave.

Father and son said their goodbyes, without warmth, in Rupert's study an hour later. It was Jessie who waited with Oliver and Claire on the front doorstep for Walker to bring the motor round.

'If you see Griffin, Oliver,' she said, 'he might like to know, if he has not yet made contact with her, that Daisy Colindale is living in London now and working at the Woolwich Arsenal. She wrote to Laura, but unfortunately gave no address. If I learn of one, I'll send it to him via you, if I may?'

Oliver didn't answer immediately. Although he had been prepared to argue with his father over the merits of the driver, he was not sure that he wanted to be turned into a go-between for the purpose of furthering Griffin's romance. But then, remembering the incident with the gun that had been recounted at lunchtime, he thought it was the least he could do.

Claire went with him in the Landaulette to Guildford, holding his hand under the travelling rug, with Magnus lying across their feet on the floor of the motor. For Claire, the agony of public goodbyes was a lesser evil than the loss of an extra hour of Oliver's company.

'Oh, I've just remembered something,' Oliver said as Walker drove down the hill towards the station. 'I thought I'd rather like to take Magnus back with me this time.'

'You can't be serious,' said Claire.

'Why not? Some of the officers have their dogs with them. It keeps the rats at bay and helps to keep you warm at night,' said Oliver.

'I'd never forgive you if you took him,' Claire said with sudden intensity. Oliver looked at her, surprised.

'Why not?'

'Because he's all I've got of you.' Her voice trembled. In the long months between Oliver's leaves, Claire remained endlessly braced for the buff envelope that would bring bad news, and the exuberant welcome of his dog was a safety tap for her emotions after a stressful day at Clandon. Claire had a tough exterior, but without the relief of being able to cuddle Magnus and cry sometimes into his rough coat, she would be lonely indeed. But Oliver wouldn't understand. Much as she loved him, she was learning to live with the fact that he kept his emotions handily contained in locked compartments and when she was out of sight, she was largely out of mind.

'I won't take him if it upsets you,' said Oliver with unusual gentleness. 'It probably wasn't such a good idea.' As he spoke, he was recalling last month's advance towards San Quentin. Riding forward to reconnoitre a new position for the guns, he'd entered the remains of a village lately evacuated by the

Germans and seen a little rough-haired dog running among the ruined buildings, eager and worried, looking for its lost master. He'd tossed it a biscuit from his rations and it had followed his horse for a mile. He wondered what had become of that dog. Magnus was better off at home.

22

'Daisy Colindale? You're wanted in Lady B's office.'

Daisy paused with a handful of pellets poised above the frame of bullet cases. The boy messenger had gone before she could ask him any questions.

'What've you been up to, then?' said one of the other women working at the table.

'Nothing, as far as I know.'

'Got anybody at the Front?'

'No. Nobody close.' Sometimes, Daisy knew, bad news was relayed to a worker by the lady superintendent. Her thoughts flew to Harriet, whom she had left seven hours ago at Blackheath, still asleep in the pretty white-painted bed in the night nursery at the top of the house. Daisy's imagination conjured images of a red-headed toddler tumbling down the stairs, or lying sick and feverish with some rapidly developed illness. She dropped the lead shot back into its tray and climbed off her stool, her heart thumping with fear.

'Bet she comes back with a wipe.'

A gale of laughter rose from Daisy's fellow workers. Lilian Barker, it was said, had the capacity to reduce errant female munition workers to floods of tears, but the sympathetic side to her nature prompted her to keep a copious supply of handkerchiefs in her desk for them to weep into. Girls summoned to an interview with Lady B were generally expected to return clutching a hankie.

The lady superintendent's office was in a building that the workers called 'Rose Cottage', close to the Beresford Square gate. It was small and functional, simply furnished with a desk, a leather-covered armchair and a bookcase. On the mantelpiece above the fireplace stood a jar filled with sprays of jasmine. On the wall were framed photographs of groups of munitionettes and a map of the Arsenal. The lady superintendent looked up from a mass of papers on her desk as Daisy came timidly into the room.

'You sent for me, miss?'

'Yes. Don't worry,' said Miss Barker kindly, seeing her apprehensive face. 'It isn't bad news. At least I don't think so. There's a man at the main gate, asking for you. You can take time off to see him, if you want to, though I'm afraid it would mean losing your pay for however long you take.'

Daisy hesitated, trying to think who the waiting man might be. In any case, could she afford to lose any wages?

'Do you know who it is, miss?'

'I believe he said his name was Will Griffin. Driver Griffin of the Royal Artillery.'

No need to extract a handkerchief from her desk on this occasion, Miss Barker decided with relief. The girl's face was positively glowing.

Griffin had been experimenting with one of the new gas respirators for horses, murmuring reassuringly as he attached it by its straps behind Diamond's frantically twitching ears, when First Lieutenant Brownlowe appeared in the horse lines, fresh back from his sojourn in England.

'Hullo, Griffin.'

'Hullo, sir. Did you have a good leave?'

'So-so. I found it a bit difficult to deal with the gap between Guildford's view of the war and mine. What in heaven's name is that contraption?'

'Gas mask for the horse, sir.'

'Looks more like a nosebag. Does it work?'

'No, sir.' Griffin explained that every horse on which he had fitted a respirator so far had not unreasonably assumed that there would be oats or barley at the bottom of it and had consequently chewed and worried at the mask until it had worn its way through the material, a process that took approximately three minutes' wearing time.

'Oh well. Back to the drawing board . . . I've a message for you, Griffin, from my Aunt Jessie.'

'Oh yes, sir?' Griffin looked wary. He had had no communication from the Grange after the altercation with Rupert Brownlowe at Miss Laura's wedding. He supposed that Mrs Driver had decided it wasn't advisable or loyal to carry on a correspondence with someone whom her employer had ordered off the premises and he wondered now whether Oliver Brownlowe was aware of that little spat with Mr Rupert.

'She says, re Daisy Colindale, Daisy's working at the Woolwich Arsenal nowadays. No address as yet, but if she gets to hear of one, she'll let you know.'

'Thank you, sir,' said Griffin, going a dull red from his forehead to the point where his neck disappeared inside the scratchy collar of his khaki tunic. Suddenly the straps of Diamond's respirator seemed to need every scrap of his attention. When Oliver had gone, he removed the ineffective accessory, giving a soothing tug to the mare's ears and a consolatory pat on her rough-coated shoulder, wondering as he did so whether he was grateful or otherwise for Miss Jessie's well-intentioned message. He hadn't seen Daisy for nearly three years and since the day in Guildford, seventeen months ago, when he'd knocked at her door only to find her gone away, he hadn't entertained any realistic hope of seeing her again. He'd thought he was past caring. Now, a few words of her whereabouts, which weren't even sufficiently specific for him to be able to write to her, had churned up all those supposedly dead emotions.

He groped inside the flap of his breast pocket and brought out his paybook. Inside it, the scrap of photograph was still there . . . and when he looked at the blurred sepia features he knew that he still loved her.

But what the hell could he do about it?

The question remained unanswered for two weeks. Then he learned that he had been awarded a Distinguished Conduct Medal for his contribution to last winter's exploit of the rescued gun. With the award came a fortnight's leave.

436

Captain Forsythe handed him a travel warrant, effective immediately.

He stood outside the main gate of the Arsenal in Beresford Square. The gate was set in a tall red building flanked by wall, with a clockface in the brickwork high above the arch of the gateway. Five o'clock. He'd arrived at four, not knowing how to go about his search and had found, predictably, that the guards on the gate would not let him by without a security pass. Eventually one of them, worn down by his stubborn insistence that he simply had to find this girl, had agreed to relay his inquiry to someone they called Lady B. She'd come out to the gate to see him, a dumpy middle-aged woman with shrewd, kind eyes behind the round lenses of her spectacles.

'I understand that you want to contact one of our women workers?' she said.

'Yes, ma'am.'

'But you don't know which factory she works in?'

'No, ma'am.'

'That is a little tricky. We have thirty-five thousand girls here.'

Griffin's heart sank. He thought that if this turned out to be another wild-goose chase, he probably couldn't bear the disappointment.

'What is this girl's name?'

'Daisy Colindale, ma'am.'

It was said of Lilian Barker, with awe, that she never forgot a face or a name. She frowned with concentration for a moment, then said, 'Would she be a red-haired girl? In her early twenties? Pale face and freckles?'

'That's right,' Griffin said eagerly.

'She started in the Danger Buildings, filling shells, but I believe she's making bullets now. I'll see if I can find her for you. If you wait here, I'll get her to come out. Assuming she wants to see you, of course.'

That had been almost an hour ago. He considered the possibility that Daisy might not want to see him. She might be married by now. Even if she wasn't, it was hopelessly optimistic to imagine that she had anything other than the vaguest memory of him as a man who'd once worked at the same establishment, nothing more . . . but all the same, he couldn't imagine her leaving an old acquaintance standing disappointed in the street. Not his Daisy. Griffin would have laughed at the suggestion that he was superstitious . . . but unconsciously, inside his trouser pockets his fingers were crossed.

Behind him in the crowded square, preparations for the evening's trade of Beresford Market were gathering pace. Saturday night was a festive time in the Square. The daytime market took on a second lease of life when the Arsenal workers, released from their factories and energized by the prospect of a day's rest tomorrow, flocked towards the stalls and entertainments. Already the flower vendors had banked their stands with fresh blooms; the street traders had restocked the displays of clothing, gimcrack jewellery and brightly coloured shawls; the conjurors and escapologists had set up their pitches and the Salvation Army band was running through a selection of tunes.

An elderly man in a shabby jacket with frayed cuffs had found a clear space on the extreme edge of the market area, where the traffic of the road ran round the square, and was opening up a very battered suitcase full of small brown glass bottles. Inside the lid of the case was a square of cardboard written over in straggly black lettering. Griffin narrowed his eyes and deciphered the announcement that Simpson's Elixir of Love would steal you a heart for the price of a bag of fish and chips.

He grinned wryly at the claim and the man, catching his eye, snatched a bottle from the case and darted across the road towards the soldier, weaving skilfully in and out of the passing motor vehicles.

'Sir!' Arriving panting at Griffin's side, he did not let shortness of breath impede the flow of his sales pitch. 'I can see you are a man of discernment and enterprise. The very

438

man, indeed, to profit from the purchase of my elixir of love! Only sixpence and guaranteed to bring you bliss beyond your wildest dreams.' As Griffin had not yet walked away, he took another breath and launched on a further round of patter.

'Water gathered by me personally from the fountain at Versailles where the King of France courted Madame de Pompadour. Infused in a long and delicate process with herbs that have been recognized over the centuries for their aphrodisiac properties. One drop of this in her porter, sir, and your lady friend will be putty in your hands.'

'No thanks.' Griffin was half-amused, half-repelled by the old man's suggestive leer.

'Oh, sir! How can you afford to pass up this opportunity? Don't you trust me, is that it? Why, I can show you a sheaf of letters, grateful letters of thanks from satisfied customers whose lives have been transformed by my potion. Take it, sir. I urge you to take it.' And he thrust the bottle into the soldier's resisting hand.

'Hullo, Griffin.'

When he turned round, Daisy stood behind him in the gateway, smiling uncertainly, a raincoat folded over her arm.

Under the straw hat, her copper-coloured hair still strayed from its chignon in the old way, but her face was a little thinner and firmer than the young girl's face that he remembered. Her pale, freckle-dusted skin had a faint tinge of yellow to it – he'd heard about canaries and his heart lurched at the thought of her doing such dangerous work. He transferred the glass bottle and shook her outstretched hand formally. The hand was warm and dry, her fingers thin and delicate. The first time, he realized, that he'd ever touched her. His palm burned at the contact.

The potion-seller seized his opportunity. 'Sixpence, sir,' he reminded Griffin. 'You owe me sixpence.'

Distractedly, Griffin fumbled for, and handed over a coin. Anything to get rid of this unwanted spectator. The man pocketed it in triumph.

'Thank you, sir. Good luck, sir. Guaranteed bliss!' He hurried back to his suitcase across the road.

Daisy and Griffin stood together in awkward silence. Griffin flogged his brain for something to say.

'I hope you don't mind me looking you up at work. I heard you worked here, Miss Jessie at the Grange mentioned it, and seeing as I was in London. . . .'

'Of course I didn't mind. It's nice to see you after all this while.' But Daisy remembered the letter she'd sent and the reply she'd waited for in vain, so there was a touch of reserve in her manner. 'What's that you just bought?'

Griffin glanced down at the bottle and shoved it into his pocket. 'Nothing,' he said.

Daisy turned her head towards the medicine man's open case. There was nothing wrong with her eyesight. Having read the card, she blushed. It started from somewhere below the cotton dress that buttoned at her throat and spread up over her features to her smooth forehead and on to the tips of her ears. In the old days at the Grange, he'd loved to watch Daisy blush.

'Have you got time to take a walk around the square? Or do you have to go back?' he asked, with an effort at control. His instincts kept urging him to grab her and kiss that sweet mouth, while his cautious mind instructed him to stay cool.

'No, I don't have to,' Daisy said. 'I can have some time off, Miss Barker said.'

They strolled among the stalls. Daisy had never lingered in the square like this before, she'd always been hurrying from one tram to another to get back home to Harriet; even more so now that the journey to Blackheath took an hour and a half. She was half-enchanted by the colour and the bustle, half-tense at the closeness of Griffin beside her.

'I'm a bit surprised to see you,' she said. 'I wrote to you once but you never replied.'

Griffin stopped dead. 'You wrote? When? I never got any letter.'

440

'Oh. It was after that time you came to Guildford and I was away.'

Suddenly Daisy's heart was pounding at the look in his dark eyes, a mixture of delight and consternation.

'I wish I'd known,' he said.

'Well, you know now. I didn't hear and I was afraid – I thought,' she corrected herself hastily, 'that you might have been a casualty, or that maybe you didn't want to be bothered to reply.'

'No fear of that.'

After that, the tension was eased in a way . . . though it was replaced by an electric awareness of what lay in the air between them: a confession, restrained but undeniable, of caring for one another. A dangerous and delicious time. They went to the canteen in the square where Daisy had talked with Elsie Parrish on the day they were taken on at the Arsenal. At a corner table they ordered tea and sat facing one another across the stained tablecloth.

'I wanted to write when I heard about your Arthur,' said Griffin, 'but I never knew what to say. Then I sent a note with Mr Oliver when he came back on leave, but by then you'd left the Grange.'

'Yes. You know why, don't you?'

'They said you had a little girl.'

Daisy let out an almost imperceptible sigh of relief. He knew about Harriet and he was still here, seeking her out.

'Does she look like you?' he asked.

'A bit. A lot, I suppose. Red hair and green eyes. But she's a bossy little thing.'

Griffin grinned, teeth white against his brown skin. 'You're not,' he said.

'No. How much leave have you got?'

'A fortnight. This is the third day. The first I was travelling, yesterday I had to collect a medal.'

'You aren't wearing any medal ribbon.'

'No, I haven't had time to sew it on yet,' said Griffin.

'I could do that,' offered Daisy, and blushed again. Outside

441

in the square, the Salvation Army band was playing *Tipperary*. She felt enormously, deliriously happy.

There was so much to talk about: Griffin's years of the war, Daisy's life in Guildford and London. She told him about Robert and he said gently that he was sorry to hear it, wanting to take her hand and not yet daring to do so, postponing the physical contact because he was afraid it would shatter him. By the time they emerged from the canteen, an hour later, the sunshine of the afternoon had been replaced by grey rain clouds and the hot, heavy airlessness of thunderstorm weather.

'Quick, there's the bus!'

They had arranged that Griffin should come back to Blackheath with Daisy; she was almost sure that Mr Hector would be prepared to give a soldier on leave a bed for the night. As the bus wound its way through the streets, the sky grew steadily darker and when at last they stepped down at the bus stop beside the heath, the heavens opened. In moments Griffin's black hair was plastered to his forehead as the rain streamed down his face and clung to his lashes. Daisy under her straw hat was more protected, but her thin coat did not keep out the rain. A flash of lightning lit the sky, to be followed in a bare second by a clap of thunder.

'Shall we go into the church until it stops?' gasped Griffin.

Close by, at the edge of the green, stood a large yellow-grey brick church with a tall spire. Heads down, they ran towards shelter and let themselves in through the heavy oak door to the still, echoing silence of the nave.

'That's better.' Griffin ran his hand back through his wet hair, pushing it off his forehead. Daisy hugged her arms around herself, shivering at the contact of soaked cotton against the skin of her shoulders and back. As the thunder rolled outside, they walked down the aisle together, elbows almost, but not quite, touching, looking up at the gothic-arched, stained-glass windows, the brass memorial plates let into the white walls, the pulpit with its spiral staircase and the carved lectern.

The lectern, instead of the usual eagle, was a griffin, wings spread to carry the Bible. Daisy stood on tiptoe to stroke her finger against the carving.

'Your namesake.'

'Yes. Literally,' Griffin said. 'That's how I got my name. I was a foundling, you see.'

'A foundling? Do you mean, you don't know who your parents are?'

'No. I'm told I was discovered one dark November day in a basket in a church in Guildford, aged about two weeks – and hungry. There'd been a party of gypsies camping in the area and it was thought they'd had a small baby with them, and one day they were gone and there I was in the church with no explanation, wailing lustily.'

'Oh, you poor thing,' Daisy said softly. Unconsciously she made a cradling gesture with her arms. Griffin knew that it related to the abandoned baby he'd been and not the tough young man he was now, but the movement gave him a warm, cared-for feeling that left him weak inside.

'So what happened to you after that?'

'Barnardo's home.'

'Oh. . . .' Daisy's eyes were eloquent with sympathy as she imagined Griffin growing up outside the consolations of family life.

'It wasn't so bad,' he said, something he had made himself believe during his stoical and lonely adolescence. 'Anyway the first priority was to give me a name. So the vicar who found me called me Will, partly after his father William and partly because I was such an obstreperous little thing, and as the basket had been dumped under a griffin carving, probably a bit like this one, that was my surname.'

Daisy considered. 'Could have been worse,' she said, the corners of her mouth lifting. 'Could have been a gargoyle.'

Griffin threw back his head and laughed. 'Will Gargoyle.' He tried it. 'Doesn't have the same ring, does it?' And then gradually, as they faced one another, the smile faded from his face to be replaced by a look of something that was almost pain.

443

'Oh, Daisy. . . .'

He lifted his hands to her shoulders and hesitantly brought his face close to hers. Her breathing suspended, Daisy managed to keep still, waiting, until he understood that what he wanted was what she wanted too. His lips touched against hers and retreated, and returned. Then he was kissing her properly, his arms crushing her to his chest.

The Reverend Nicholas Grey emerged unnoticed from the vestry to change the candles on the altar. He saw the young couple embracing beside the pulpit and he was about to tell them that God's house was not a proper place for such activities. But as they drew apart for a moment before coming together again, he saw the young soldier's dazed, absorbed expression and that of the girl, and it occurred to him that if this was not a proper place for the discovery of love, where on God's earth was? So he retreated quietly and left them to it.

Four days later, Griffin and Daisy were married by special licence in the church on the heath.

'That bottle of stuff you bought in Beresford Market,' said Daisy by lamplight in the small bedroom on the top floor of Medlar House in Blackheath. 'What did you do with it?'

'Threw it away,' said Griffin, sitting on the edge of the bed, his eyes resting on Daisy as she unfastened all the small pearly buttons of her blouse, one by one, with a care that was at once maddening and delightful.

'Seems a shame,' said Daisy, looking at him sideways under her lashes, a dimple appearing in one cheek. 'Bang goes sixpence. And that man promised you such bliss, didn't he, with the elixir of love?'

Griffin stood up and took over the unbuttoning procedure. His hands shook slightly, but even so, he was faster than Daisy. She seemed to lean towards him a little, her lips parted, her green eyes clouded with love and longing. When, with her blouse opened, he suspended the disrobing of his wife

444

while he kissed her, her hands crept up to unbutton his shirt in turn, and then to slide inside and around to his back. The muscles under her exploring fingers were firm, the skin smooth and warm. She brought her soft body against his bare chest and heard him gasp and felt dizzy with the power of his love.

'We don't need any potions,' said Griffin.

On the first day Daisy had been afraid of the moment when Will met Harriet. What if they didn't get on? But in the way that horses trusted Griffin, Harriet had trusted him, going quietly to his side with her wide eyes fixed on his face and leaning against his knee. Within a few minutes he was playing 'This is the way the Lady rides' with her and Harriet was giggling ecstatically as he bounced her into the air and dropped her backwards to the ground.

'Hobbledee, hobbledee, hobbledee . . . and *down* into the ditch!'

''Gain,' she demanded insistently. 'Do it 'gain.'

'You don't mind,' said Daisy anxiously when Will asked her to marry him, 'that Harriet isn't yours? Promise you'll be kind to her?'

'I promise. She's yours. I'd love her for your sake,' Griffin told Daisy, and then, 'No. That's wrong. Harriet is entirely lovable for her own sake.'

When he went back to France it felt like dying. Now Daisy could understand the agony of Louella when Robert returned to the Front. The thought of him was always there in everything she did. Walking through Blackheath, past the street-corner shrines that carried lists of the local war-dead, decked with the flowers of the bereaved, she prayed that Will would come back to her.

He had made it possible for her to leave the Arsenal and be with Harriet. The army now paid a Separation Allowance to the wives of men who got married on leave. Daisy worried about giving up her war work; bullets were still needed as much as ever. But she and her daughter had been parted for so long. Surely it was someone else's turn, now, to produce ammunition?

Louella's face grew sharp and ugly when she learned of Daisy's decision.

'I'll pay you fair rent. Well, I'll pay Hector I suppose,' said Daisy. 'Now I've got the Allowance. It isn't that much less than I was getting on the bullets.'

'Why should you stop work now? Use your sense. The Allowance would be extra. You could save up for when the war's over and he comes back, then you'd have something put aside to make a start with.'

'But I want to look after Harriet.'

'Don't you think I look after her properly?' demanded Louella, her voice rising.

'It isn't that. Of course it isn't. Lou, I'm so grateful to you for all you've done for her. But I'm her mother.'

Daisy steeled herself to withstand her sister-in-law's desperate, angry eyes. In a way, she felt like a criminal, stealing Harriet back. But it had to be done.

In France, at the YMCA in the smoke-filled atmosphere of the hut with the distinctive red triangle over the door, Laura was working her way through grief. All day she served thousands of cuppas to the thousands of soldiers passing through. She fried and dished up endless platefuls of fish and chips, uncaring in her sleep-walking state about the greasy smell that lingered in her hair. She stirred vast, bubbling vats of custard to ladle over acres of apple pie and played the piano for the concerts and the church services. Sometimes, though Mr Quiller spared her this duty as much as possible, she even met the relatives of the wounded off the ferry at Boulogne and drove them to the hospitals in the area. And thought, *if I had gone to Charles, instead of Pa, would he be alive now?*

'When are you coming home?' wrote Rupert from The Grange. She left the letter unanswered.

Despite her energetic and apparently thick-skinned manner,

Claire Lawrence was capable of moments of sensitivity and in one of these, she realized that Jessie Brownlowe was missing her niece.

Laura's departure had hurt her father; and deservedly so, in Claire's opinion. Not only had Rupert kept the news of Charles McKay's injuries from his daughter for a vital two days, but he had been at best unkind and tactless to Charles when he'd visited him in hospital . . . and at worst, Claire had understood from the brief discussion she'd had with Laura after the memorial service, Pa might have driven Charles to his death.

Claire held no brief at all for Rupert. But poor Jessie, too, had been cut out of Laura's life when she went to France; and Jessie, who had offered consolation in the past when Laura needed it, making herself vulnerable by this closeness, did not deserve such treatment. Claire tried to fill the gap by spending as much as she could spare of her time off from Clandon in the older woman's company.

On one of her free afternoons, in July of 1917, Jessie met Claire for lunch in Guildford. Jessie's numerous volunteer activities now included helping at the War Hospital Supplies Depot, which a group of Guildford ladies had established in the rooms above Simpson's in the High Street. There, on several days a week, she cut and rolled bandages to be despatched to the London distribution headquarters in Cavendish Square.

'It's an absolute hive of activity,' she told Claire. 'They make all sorts of things for the hospitals – splints and surgical appliances out of papier-mâché, pyjamas and slippers, and there's a men's section which turns out wooden bed-rests and crutches. Sometimes there's a hundred of us volunteers working there at the same time.'

'You obviously enjoy it,' said Claire, smiling.

'Oh, yes. I'm ashamed to say,' Jessie admitted, 'that there are times when I do rather *enjoy* the war – my little bit of it. Life used to be so dull. Now I'm busy, people think I'm useful, and I do love it when I play the paino at the sing-songs and the soldiers show that they're having a good time. If it wasn't for the war, I'd still be checking laundry lists and approving menus at home. Is it awful of me?'

'No, it isn't. I think everyone involved must feel the same, to some extent. I enjoy working with the other girls at Clandon. And it feels good when I've finished a roomful of dressings and I know that my efforts have helped the patients to feel better, more comfortable, that because of me they'll get well again. The ones that do,' Claire qualified sombrely. That morning one of the Abdominal Wounds in the main-hall ward had died and she was still feeling low because of it. There would be a funeral tomorrow in the little church on the edge of the park . . . every death still affected her, though she ought by now to be hardened to it.

The dining room was crowded and busy. At the next table a small group of soldiers, who wore the distinctive blue pyjama-style suits which were standard issue for convalescents, were trying to catch the waitresses' attention. Jessie and Claire watched as their frustration mounted. The worst of it was that when a second group of soldiers entered, also blue-suited, but bandaged and with crutches, the waitresses hurried to take their orders, abandoning any attempt to work in rotation.

'It isn't fair, is it?' said Jessie in an undertone. 'I know those boys near us. They're from one of the Canadian corps, they come to my sing-songs. Not that they can sing now, poor souls! They are gas cases, which in its way is as disabling as losing an arm or a leg, or having a head wound. But it doesn't show, so they don't get the sympathy.'

An elderly lady, on her way out after having consumed her meal and paid her bill, paused by the new arrivals with the visible wounds and dispensed sixpences all round.

'Treat yourselves to a drink from me, boys. This country is proud of you.'

The gas cases, unregarded at their table in their corner, watched with jaundiced expressions.

'What they need,' said Claire thoughtfully, 'is a few well-placed bandages.'

Her voice carried and one of the soldiers flashed her a rueful grin. 'Too right, miss,' he said in the hoarse, effortful whisper of a man with abraded lungs. 'You're a nurse. How'd you like to fix us up with some decent dressings and slings, so we can get our share of the sympathy?'

Claire considered for a moment. 'I would,' she said, 'if I had any bandages about me. It would be rather a good joke, wouldn't it? But sadly, they're all back at the hospital.'

'I could lay my hands on some bandages. . . .' said Jessie.

It was a practical joke, an idea born in a moment. But between Jessie's filched rolls of bandage from the Hospital Supplies Depot, the crutches from the carpenters' workshop and Claire's skill – exercised in a quiet corner of the park at the bottom of Castle Hill, in due course the half-dozen gas cases had been transformed into men with truly daunting injuries but with courageous smiles that could not fail to melt the hearts of local residents.

'Right, boys. Let's see if we can't get ourselves invited out to tea,' said the ringleader who had first made the suggestion to Claire.

They hobbled away. It was purest bad luck that at the end of a highly successful afternoon they should encounter Rupert Brownlowe in Quarry Street. Rupert did not often attend his sister's sing-songs but he had been present at the last, and he recognized the gas cases.

At first their new accoutrements puzzled him. Then he understood, and was horrified by a blatant attempt to defraud the citizens of Guildford of their sympathy sixpences.

'Rest assured,' he told the dismayed soldiers, 'that I shall be reporting your disgusting behaviour to your senior officer!'

When Walker collected Jessie from outside the Depot at five o'clock that afternoon, Rupert was in the back of the landaulette. Jessie was surprised and more surprised when instead of heading for Seale, the motor continued up the High Street.

'Rupert, where are we going?'

'I have some business at Clandon,' he said brusquely. Since

her brother was clearly in one of his blacker moods, Jessie did not question him further.

Arriving at the hospital, he held out his hand to help her get down from the car.

'I need your assistance, Jessica. Come inside with me.'

In the commandant's office he demanded to see the senior Canadian officer. The commandant raised her eyebrows at the rudeness of her visitor, but rang a bell to summon one of the nurses.

'Ask Major Mackenzie to come in here, will you?'

In due course a tall soldier with greying hair and faded blue-grey eyes levered himself into the room with the aid of two crutches. He listened silently while Rupert made his complaint.

'It was an arrant fraud committed for pecuniary advancement. I demand that these men be punished,' said Rupert.

'But Rupert—' began Jessie from behind him.

'Be quiet, Jessica.' Rupert flapped a silencing hand backwards, too irate to be careful of his manners in front of strangers. Jessie winced, and both the major and the commandant looked uncomfortable.

'Who were the soldiers concerned?' asked the major, after a pause.

'I don't have their names. They refused to give them,' said Rupert indignantly. 'But Jessica here can identify them if you order a parade. They have been guests at my house unfortunately. Get the men turned out and she can look them over.'

'This is a hospital,' said the major. 'Some of our people can't turn out.'

'I meant the mobile ones, obviously!'

'Rupert . . .' said Jessie again. He ignored her.

'And they must have had help,' he told the commandant. 'Some of your nurses must be involved. Those bandages were professionally applied. An investigation is called for.'

'Rupert. . . .'

'Oh, shut *up*, Jessica.'

450

'This is ridiculous!' said Jessie with a sudden force that took everyone by surprise. All eyes focused on the meek little brown-haired woman with the distressed eyes, half-hidden by the bulk of the fulminating civilian.

'Rupert, if you had only told me why we were coming here, I could have saved you the bother. Those men. It was a joke. A game. At my suggestion. They did it to oblige me, it wasn't any fraud. I made them a wager,' Jessie improvised, 'that they couldn't pass muster as disabled cases. I said the citizens of Guildford weren't that green. You proved me right. That's all there was to it.'

Her voice tailed away. Rupert was gazing at her in horror. On his shiny forehead, a vein bulged.

'A joke,' she repeated. 'I do hope they won't be punished simply because they were kind enough to indulge my silly sense of humour.'

'Jessica,' said Rupert, 'you do not have access to slings and crutches. You could not have tied those bandages. You do not have the skill. At the very least you must have had an accomplice. A nurse.'

'No,' said Jessie bravely, wondering how much trouble this could mean for Claire and determined not to find out if she could help it. 'I did not. I got the things from the Hospital Supplies Depot. You may not have registered the ways in which I spend my time, but I am now an expert in bandages.'

'Well, sir,' said the major, 'in view of what your wife has told us. . . .'

'She is not my wife!' exclaimed Rupert. 'She is my sister. She lives in my house and she is dependent on my charity!'

In the silence that followed, Jessie faced her brother.

'I will wait in the car, Rupert, while you continue your discussion.' Chin high, she walked towards the door. For a man on crutches, the major moved quickly to open it and with a brief nod of acknowledgement, she swept past him out of the room.

'She couldn't have tied those bandages to save her life,' said Rupert contemptuously.

451

'But since she says that she did, sir,' said the major, 'propose that as gentlemen we should take her word for it.'

'I agree,' said the commandant.

Rupert was about to argue but thought better of it. He realized, to his chagrin, that Jessie's behaviour had made him look silly. The major was right: to insist on an investigation would be to insist that his sister was a liar.

'I bow to your judgement,' he said with suppressed rage and followed Jessie out of the room.

'What a nasty man,' said the commandant when Rupert had gone.

'Quite,' said the major.

'All the same it was rather naughty of your boys . . . any idea which ones were involved?'

'I've got some names in mind. They slunk in from Guildford a few minutes before he arrived, looking very worried. I'll have a quiet word and keep 'em in line, shall I?'

'If you will,' said the commandant, and closed the subject.

The presence of Walker in the front seat, theoretically shut off by a glass screen but potentially capable of overhearing anything said by the passengers, kept Rupert from expressing his feelings in the motor, but once they reached Maple Grange it was a different matter.

'Jessica. My study, if you please.'

Jessie found to her surprise that his words did not have their usual effect. She was pumped up with excitement over what had happened in the commandant's office. She'd taken on Rupert – and she'd won. After years of doing what he said, holding her tongue, squirming at his meannesses, suffering his interference – she'd spoken up. And he hadn't been able to do a thing about it! After all, what power did he have over her unless she gave it to him? As she followed her brother into his study, her heart was thumping but her head was high.

'As regards your conduct this afternoon Jessica, words fail me.'

'That makes a pleasant change,' said Jessie, which left Rupert, for a moment, genuinely bereft of words.

'Surely,' he said at last, 'on mature reflection you must see that you have behaved in an irresponsible manner?'

'No,' said Jessie. 'I'm sorry, but I don't. I was involved in a joke. A bit of fun. We weren't doing any harm. Everybody was enjoying themselves until you interfered. I thought your reaction was narrow-minded and, frankly, ridiculous.'

'Jessica. . . .'

'Yes, Rupert?'

'I would remind you that you do owe me some degree of loyalty.'

'Why?'

'Because . . .' he floundered, and recovered. 'Because I provide the roof over your head.' *And that*, he thought, *should bring her to her senses*. It didn't.

'If you consider that I don't earn my keep, Rupert, tell me now, and I will leave. My income from Mother's jewellery is small, but I believe I could survive on it, living frugally in a little cottage somewhere. Somewhere *local*,' she added reflectively.

This rejoinder took Rupert so much by surprise that he actually sagged. In the time it took him to recover his breath a few glimmers of caution began to temper his anger. At this moment Jessica was being very irritating indeed and her attitude left much to be desired, but. . . . He had always taken the duties she performed for granted and he allowed her so little autonomy in carrying them out that it was often possible to forget that she did anything at all, but in general, he conceded reluctantly, she did earn her keep. In fact, she came very cheap, far cheaper than the housekeeper he would have to employ if she were not there. And if this quarrel were allowed to go on and she did leave Maple Grange, while she would undoubtedly rue her stupidity, she would also cause a great deal of embarrassment to Rupert. What would the community think of Miss Brownlowe living 'frugally' in some squalid little cottage within a stone's throw of her brother's house?

453

'Let us not overreact,' he said.

'No. Let's not. Am I to pack my bags, or ring for some tea?'

With an effort, Rupert managed a smile.

'Don't be silly, Jessica. Tea, of course.'

Jessie tugged at the bell-pull beside the door and Joan appeared.

'Tea in the drawing room in five minutes please, Joan. The Darjeeling, I think,' said Rupert.

'Earl Grey for me,' said Jessie. Her third gesture of independence that day.

23

Jessie had had a tiring day at the War Hospital Supplies Depot, not just doing her usual work, but also consoling a fellow bandage-roller whose son in the Queen's, seriously injured in last April's fighting around the Hindenburg Line, had finally succumbed to his wounds two days ago. The bereaved woman came to work as usual, stoical to the last, but mid-way through the day her stoicism had dissolved.

'I suppose it's better for him . . . he was so terribly hurt. But I shall miss him so,' the poor mother said distractedly, the tears dripping off her chin. Jessie found her a handkerchief and patted her hand and wished dismally that she knew the right thing to say in such circumstances. Not that there was a right thing to say . . . but this did not prevent her from feeling that every banal phrase she conjured up was decidedly inadequate.

When she left, late in the afternoon, Walker had not arrived to collect her from the Depot. He was often late these days, as Rupert's erratic requirements took priority, and she suspected sometimes that her brother kept her waiting deliberately as part of a silent campaign to re-establish his supremacy after the incident of the bandaged soldiers. Jessie shifted her weight wearily from one foot to the other and decided that she needed a reviving cup of tea which, if taken at a table near the window of the café a short way up the High Street, would enable her to watch out for the Landaulette in comparative comfort.

The café was crowded with convalescent soldiers, bringing unwelcome memories of the event which had precipitated her defiance of Rupert. But a cluster of them had just vacated a table by the window, and she sank gratefully down into a chair. The tea, when it came, was too strong and the tiny portion of milk in the jug proved entirely inadequate to combat this fact.

'We're short of milk,' said the waitress flatly.

'No sugar?' Jessie inquired, not very hopefully.

'No sugar.'

Jessie sipped. She was spoiled, she told herself, by milk from the Home Farm. It was high time she accustomed herself to the shortages that most of the townspeople had to cope with nowadays. Food prices were more than double what they had been at the start of the war, thanks to scarcity of some commodities, and that had brought real hardship to some families that she knew of. In December of last year a Food Controller had been appointed by the Ministry of Food 'to promote economy and to maintain the food supply of the country', but some of his edicts seemed to Jessie to display a lack of awareness of the lives of the poor. It was all very well to suggest that the well-off should cut down on their consumption of bread, in the light of the wheat shortages. They could switch to other foodstuffs, but for someone from a poorer family bread was often the mainstay of the diet and its bulk could not easily be replaced. Mrs Dale from the Depot, for instance, whom Jessie had attempted to console today . . . her thinness wasn't entirely due to worry and grief over her son. She brought in her own dinner because she couldn't afford the canteen, and if you took away the bread from her midday bread and cheese, there wasn't much left.

'Excuse me, ma'am.'

Jessie looked up, startled. A uniformed figure was standing by her table. In the midst of the youthful soldiers, scarcely more than boys, who were the other occupants of the café, the man who had spoken to her seemed out of place. Although he was leaning on a stick, his tall figure was as fit and spare as that of any of the younger men, but his lined forehead and the greying streaks in his brown hair betrayed his middle age.

'Miss Brownlowe, isn't it? I'm Major Mackenzie. Michael

Mackenzie. We met a few days ago. Do you mind if I share your table?'

He was, Jessie realized, the officer who had been standing in the background when she had contradicted Rupert in the matron's room at Clandon hospital. Then, distracted by the occasion, she had mostly noticed the crutches, which he had now discarded for the stick. She nodded in response to his request, her stomach fluttering with embarrassment.

'I hope your brother wasn't too angry,' said the major, pulling out a chair and lowering himself carefully on to it with a grimace that showed he was only just up to abandoning crutches.

'Mmm,' Jessie said ambiguously. She stirred her tea to calm herself down. Rupert had hardly spoken a word to her since she had challenged him to evict her from his home, but his manner was eloquent of unforgiving fury. She knew that his silence was intended as a punishment, but she was hanging on to her own anger and she had told herself that Rupert silent was a considerable improvement on Rupert hectoring on in his usual manner.

'Must've taken a bit of nerve, owning up the way you did,' said the Canadian quietly. 'I sure did admire you for it.'

Jessie gave him a startled glance, which he met steadily. He had blue eyes with laugh lines spreading out from the corners, she noticed, and the flutter of nerves in her stomach returned, but for another reason that was at once strange and oddly familiar.

'The men say you play the piano,' he said.

'Oh, yes. The sing-songs.'

'That's right. I'd like to hear that. Would it be all right if I come along to the next?'

Jessie gave him the details of the next At Home For Soldiers to be held at the Grange, and wondered where she was getting the ridiculous impression that an assignation was being made. At her age!

*

457

'Getting a gong on Saturday,' wrote James to Laura, in the September of 1917. 'Embarrassing process. Can you come and help me bear it?'

The investiture was in Paris, the occasion alfresco in a park near the *Ecole Militaire*, with a military band. The French, it seemed, were handing James a Legion of Honour to add to his English medals. Laura asked him how he had earned it and he said laconically that it was a long story. Clearly the relaying of tales of heroism was not to his taste.

Laura had been put out to find when she arrived that Margaret Allingham née Churchill was also James' guest for the ceremony. It was to be expected, she supposed, since Margaret was James' sister-in-law and nowadays working again at Camiers. But if she'd known, perhaps she wouldn't have come. She and Margaret had disliked one another before they'd accidentally shared a moment of grief more than a year ago. Mourning for Edward had dissolved their differences at the time, but now Laura wasn't sure on what footing they stood.

They waited side by side on the grass in a crowd of proud relations and interested spectators. The general who hooked on the medals was assisted by a pretty young lady, apparently some well-known singer, who followed up each congratulatory handshake with a kiss on both cheeks for each of the heroes. The general and the singer had reached James, standing wooden-faced in a row of uniformed men. The kisses obviously discomfited him. Laura wondered idly if James had been kissed by many girls. The man next in the line, in a French air-force uniform, was less inhibited. He gathered the young lady into his arms and soundly kissed her on the mouth.

The general looked taken aback, but the girl seemed pleased as she straightened her hat. The audience whistled and cheered and the airman grinned unconcernedly. The general's lips twitched beneath his moustache as he moved on down the line.

'What an appalling man that flier is,' muttered Laura.

'It's just a bit of fun,' said Margaret. 'Very French, don't you think?'

'But he's so full of himself.'

Later, after the general and his companion had been driven away in a black military limousine, the decorated soldiers and their guests drank champagne from tall, fluted glasses and made decorous conversation on the grass while the band played popular tunes. Margaret met an old patient of hers from Camiers whom she remembered as a 'Head Case' rather than by name, but who had obviously made an excellent recovery judging by his recent acceptance of a *médaille militaire*. They talked together a short distance away while James and Laura listened to the band.

'James. May I be introduced to your beautiful companion?'

The French airman whom Laura had considered appalling stood beside them. He smiled at Laura and she gave him a cold, discouraging stare in response. He needn't think that he could charm every girl he met, simply on the basis of his good looks and his hero-airman status; though he *was* good-looking, she conceded, with his dark eyes and quizzically arched brows in a finely structured face. A bit like Edward. . . .

To her consternation, she felt that old flare of sexual attraction which she thought she'd extinguished for good.

'Oh. Yes. Laura, this is Gérard.' For some reason, James seemed unenthusiastic about complying with the newcomer's request. He wasn't returning the Frenchman's smile. 'Lieutenant Gérard de Montrémy. His escadrille hangs out near Amiens, flying the new Spad XIIIs. He's a lunatic. Gérard, may I introduce you to Madame Laura McKay who works with the YMCA hostel at Calais.'

The Frenchman captured Laura's right hand and raised it to his lips. It was a clichéd theatrical gesture which should have made her laugh, or irritated her. Instead, because the mischief in his eyes made it clear that the cliché was deliberate, it left Laura oddly breathless.

'Madame . . . ?' He made a question of it. 'Your husband is with the armed forces?'

'He was. He died of wounds last year,' said Laura, wishing that her heartbeat would behave itself. It was ludicrous, she told herself crossly, that this Gallic Romeo could have such an immediate effect on her and with so little effort.

'I am sorry.' Suddenly the laughter had died from his eyes. There was a pause. Laura wanted to look away, and found she couldn't.

'Life goes on,' she said.

'Yes. Life goes on. But it takes courage. . . . *Eh bien*, am, as our friend James told you, a lunatic,' said Gérard de Montrémy, with a deliberate switching of the subject and an infusion of lightness into his voice. 'And he is a ver-ry cautious man who does not so much outfly the Hun as out-calculate him. What did you think of the investiture?'

'I thought it was a solemn and touching occasion,' said Laura waspishly, 'until your performance.'

The young man laughed, seeming delighted rather than offended by her asperity. 'You disapprove? I assure you, if I had seen you at that time, I would not have wasted my time with that young lady.'

'Oh, do tone down the charm, Gérard, it's making my ears hurt,' said James. He tilted his champagne glass and let the clear, bubbling liquid pour on to the grass. 'It's too early in the day for this stuff. Shall we go and find ourselves some coffee instead?'

Margaret had finished her conversation with her former patient and the four of them – since the Frenchman seemed to have attached himself to the group – went in search of refreshment. They went in Gérard's car which, disconcertingly, had a number of bullet holes in the sides.

'How did you get hold of the car?' Margaret asked. 'It looks like a German Staff Corps motor.'

'Ah, it's a long story. . . .' But unlike James, Gérard was not averse to recounting his exploits. 'I came by it at the beginning of the war during the Marne retreat. At that stage I was still in the Hussars and my squadron of men were

460

penned in by advancing German units, so I went out on a reconnaissance to try to find a way for us to escape. I was walking along a road when I heard a motor coming towards me beyond the next bend of the road. Of course it must be Germans! So I ran back, hurled myself into the ditch and waited. Soon the car came into sight, the driver stopped to open the gate securing the road . . . at which point I rose from the ditch and . . . *despatched* its occupants.'

'That was the easy bit,' put in James dryly. 'He then drove it back to the French lines, under heavy fire from the Germans because of his French uniform and from the French because of the enemy's Staff pennant on the car. His commanding officers were so impressed he was still alive that they gave him the car along with a medal. The first of many wasn't it, Gérard?'

'And more importantly, they accepted my request for a transfer to the *aviation militaire*,' said Gérard. He flashed a smile at Laura which somehow contrived to give the impression that he was sharing a private joke with her. 'And that, Madame Laura of the sad eyes, is how I became an airman.'

In 1914 Laura had been in Paris as a schoolgirl. She could remember the Sunday walks, the girls parading in their crocodiles, very conscious of the appraising eyes of the young men in the streets; but conscious also of the chaperonage of Madame, the proprietress of the school, whose livelihood depended on the restoration of her charges to their parents, finished, polished and virgo intacta. Flirtation in those learning days had been restricted, exciting . . . and safe.

Sitting beside Gérard de Montrémy at a table in a pavement café, Laura was aware that he was flirting with her determinedly, that he was not in the least safe . . . and that she didn't care.

An hour later, after too many cups of coffee, she reminded herself that there was work to do at the YMCA in Calais. She pushed back her chair.

'I must be getting back, I suppose.'

'I will take you,' said Gérard, immediately rising to his feet.

'To the station? That would be kind.'

'No. To Calais.'

'But it's a long way,' Laura said foolishly.

He shrugged. 'I am going to Amiens. It's the same direction. Besides, for your company I would go to Berlin.'

James watched them morosely as they walked away together, and Margaret watched James.

'Have you ever told Laura how you feel about her?' she asked gently.

'If I ever work out how I do feel about her,' he said with a snatch of anger, 'I probably will.'

Margaret sighed. Men were such obtuse idiots sometimes. The situation was as plain as daylight to her.

Gérard drove fast and skilfully. The unusual car attracted stares along the route and Laura could tell that he enjoyed being the centre of attention. He was like a little boy, she thought with exasperation. But the charm . . . that was undeniable.

'Is James important to you?' he asked suddenly.

'He's a friend,' Laura said.

'Only a friend?'

'Yes. Why do you ask?'

'Because I wish to be more than a friend. But it would not be honourable to poach on the territory of my fellow aviator,' said Gérard with a directness that made Laura gasp. Englishmen waited for months, or years, before they made such intentions so plain.

In the days that followed, she alternated between delight, bewilderment, frustration and fear. The French airman's concentrated wooing made her dizzy. Flowers arrived daily at the YMCA, great opulent bunches of them, causing an embarrassing shortage of vases. Ingenuous little messages tucked among the stems announced that he was thinking of her, that he longed to see her again. . . . The flowers would be followed hours or days later, unpredictably, by Gérard himself – ready to sweep her off in his eye-catching car to some restaurant or club, where they would spend half the night talking about any and every topic under the sun. He would deliver her back to the YMCA in the small hours, sleepy, drunk with happiness and also with more wine than was sensible, and he would tell her that she was lovely. But so far, apart from the kissing of her hand, which he infused with a sensuality that almost drowned her, he had not touched her. She ached for him to do so.

She began to understand the erratic nature of his appearances. In between the flowers and the wine, the restaurants and the evenings with Laura, Gérard flew his plane across the lines, engaged in mortal combat with the enemy . . . and won. At any time he might not come back. Already it was an unbearable thought. How could she let go of caution so utterly? she berated herself.

How could she help it? After the long darkness of her grieving for Edward and her guilt over Charles, it was irresistibly tempting to bask in this burst of sunshine.

On the ninth day after their meeting, he drove her to Paris again. Laura by now was shameless in manipulating her duties at the hostel. She had found that one of the other helpers, a shy mouse of a girl called Constance, could be persuaded to cover for her. Constance, having seen Gérard, derived a vicarious satisfaction from assisting Laura's romance with the heroic airman to whom she could never aspire herself. All she asked in return was scraps of information about the evenings they spent together: the menu, the décor of the restaurant, what Laura had worn. . . .

Driving through the outskirts of the city, in the sunlight of a late September afternoon, Laura remembered that Constance would at this moment be washing the dishes on which she had served up a hundred stodgy meals on Laura's behalf. She promised herself that someday, somehow, she would make it up to her friend. Poor little Constance, had she ever had a man to love her? The soldiers could reduce her to a stammering jelly by their teasing, and frequently did. It must have taken considerable nerve, Laura recognized, for the girl to wrench herself away from home and offer herself for overseas service.

'This is my home.'

Gérard had stopped the car in a street near the Parc Monceau. The road was lined with houses in the ubiquitous, pale grey stone of Paris. The studded double doors were more like fortress gates, set between the shuttered and grilled windows. Gérard tugged at a blackened iron ring recessed in the wall beside the nearest gate and somewhere, distantly, a bell rang. Shortly, one of the twin doors was opened inwards, and an elderly man stood in the aperture, clothed in a dusty black suit. His expression was mainly of dismay as Gérard addressed him.

'*Bonjour, Victoire. Monsieur et Madame, sont-ils chez eux?*'

'*Mais non, Monsieur Gérard. Ils sont à la campagne.*'

Gérard frowned. 'My parents are away at their other house in Brittany,' he explained to Laura. 'It's a pity. I wanted you to meet them. *Tant pis*, since we are here you may as well come in and see the house.'

He took hold of her hand as she stepped over the low footboard of the gateway into a stone-paved passage. The gesture had seemed casual but beyond the footboard, where there was no need for steadying, he still retained her hand in his own. Heart thumping, Laura left it there, and wondered whether she was wise to do so.

At the end of the passage, another door opened into a courtyard garden. At sight of the garden, Laura gasped. She had not expected anything so beautiful and so deliciously scented to lie hidden behind the grim, dusty façades of the houses in the street. But it seemed that they had only been servants' quarters. The fourth wall of the court-yard, facing them, proved to be the front of another, grander house.

Here there were no bars over the long windows in the creamy façade, divided by carved pilasters and topped by a stone balustrade. Twin flights of steps flanked by delicate ironwork led from left and right to meet outside the elevated front door.

The servant, Victoire, scurried round in front of Gérard, groping in his pocket for keys. He had unlocked the door by the time they climbed the steps. Inside, the hall was dark, smelling of polish. Underfoot, the floor was of white marble, inset with lozenges of black. A stone staircase with another of those lightly intricate wrought-iron balustrades curved upwards in the shadows.

'Ouvrez les volets, Victoire,' commanded Gérard. *'C'est comme une tombe ici.'*

'Partout?' the man said, hesitating.

'Oui, partout. Je veux montrer la maison à Madame.'

The caretaker darted up to the window on the half-landing of the soaring staircase and began to unbolt the wooden shutters and fold them back. Sunlight streamed into the hall and glanced off the glass droplets of the chandelier overhead, momentarily dazzling Laura as Gérard led her towards the stairs. Under the polished handrail, the ironwork was a complex entwining of acanthus leaves and stems, the lace-like frailty of the pattern belying the strength of the material from which it was made.

Victoire ran on ahead and could be heard drawing further bolts back into their sockets in the upstairs rooms as his master and the master's lady friend ascended the broad staircase.

'The salon,' Gérard said simply, opening great double doors, panelled and gilded, and ushering her into the room beyond.

Laura was used to comfortable, well-furnished homes. Sylvia Brownlowe had bought antiques for Maple Grange and Grandmother Cathcart's house was full of Chippendale and Hepplewhite. But she was not familiar with the opulence and grandeur of French antique furniture. This room was like the palaces of kings, if on a smaller scale. Under her feet a vast Savonnerie carpet stretched away to the far wall. The walls were hung with blue-and-brown tapestries of hunting scenes. A huge mirror topped the marble fireplace, along the mantelpiece of which were ranged an ornate ormolu clock, its enamel face wreathed with bluebirds, and china figurines that even she, no expert, could guess were extremely valuable. The furniture consisted of grand armchairs and damask-upholstered sofas, inlaid marquetry tables shining with a century of devoted polishing and, against the walls, glass-fronted cabinets crowded with further priceless porcelain. It became clear that Gérard's family was very, very rich.

'It's beautiful . . .' she said inadequately. He shrugged, bored by familiarity with the treasure house.

'My parents are collectors. It is their whole lives.'

He led her to an armchair before striding away to relocate the lugubrious Victoire. From another room she heard him demanding tea, immediately, for Madame Laura. She twisted in her deeply cushioned chair to look at the photographs in their silver frames clustered on the lacquered table beside her. A formal and rather daunting couple she guessed to be Gérard's parents. A smaller picture in an oval frame beside them was not a photograph at all, but a miniature of Gérard in his aviator's uniform. The painter had exactly caught his mischievous smile.

She leaned forward to examine the portrait more closely. The artist's name, scrawled in the lower left-hand corner, was that of a woman, and Laura found herself wondering whether she had been a friend or a commissioned artist and also how well, by the time the painting was finished, she had known the subject.

Gérard reappeared and sank into the twin of her chair, a few feet away.

'We shall have tea, and then I shall show you the other rooms. It is such a pity that my parents are away. They would have been delighted to meet you.'

Laura glanced involuntarily at the stiff couple staring from their silver frames. It was hard to imagine them being delighted by anything.

'They look rather grand,' she said.

'I suppose they are on the whole. But true connoisseurs of beauty. And warm towards anything that makes me happy. On both counts they would adore you . . . as I am afraid,' he admitted cheerfully, 'they adore me.'

The silent Victoire brought the tea, to be poured into porcelain cups decorated with birds and flowers, so fragile that Laura was almost afraid to lift hers. Gérard said nonchalantly that the service was from Sèvres and thought to have connections with Madame de Pompadour. Afterwards, he took her on the promised tour of the house, a dizzying succession of rooms crowded with treasures.

'And this bed, I am told, was slept in by Napoleon.'

Laura looked at the bed set in a curtained alcove. It was more like a gigantic sofa with its three raised and upholstered sides covered in rose satin damask. On the wall behind it were hung renaissance paintings of nude ladies in languorous poses, which made Laura feel uncomfortable. She supposed it was gauche to have a reaction to what, after all, was supposed to be high art, and to cover her embarrassment she asked Gérard if it were true about Napoleon and the bed. He shrugged.

'It's perfectly possible. The great man did a lot of travelling. He had to sleep somewhere. Myself, I have never slept in this bed. I wonder if it is comfortable?' He tested the springing with his hand. Laura had a sudden, vivid mental image of Gérard stretched out naked on the rose satin damask, smiling his wicked smile. She moved hastily away.

'It's a lovely, lovely house. What a shame it's all closed up,' she said.

'It is the war. But one day,' said Gérard, 'the war will be over and the house will be opened up again and there will be a celebration. Music and laughter and dancing. Perhaps you and I will be the cause of it?'

Laura laughed wryly. 'You and I? Or you and one of the many other girls that you must have danced and laughed with this year?'

'You and I,' he repeated. 'You don't believe me, do you?' he added ruefully. 'You think I am only flirting with you. It is not surprising, I suppose. I should not have kissed the singer with the medals. Because I did that, and you saw it, you think that I have no deeper feelings.'

'Do you blame me?' Laura tried to sound light-hearted despite the turmoil in her mind. She couldn't drag her eyes away from his lean, expressive features. He spread his hands.

'How can I convince you otherwise? It is true that I like women, I have always liked women. For me, it is natural when I see a pretty lady to flatter her, to pay her attention. But with you. . . .' He took a step forward, and now he was only inches away. Laura knew she should retreat. Instead, she stayed rooted to the Aubusson carpet.

'With you,' he told her simply, 'it is more than liking, and it is not flattery.'

'Don't be silly.' Her voice shook. 'We hardly know each other,' said Laura, and thought how very inane, how very English that sounded. And that what Gérard was saying was probably equally French and not in the least sincere, so that she would be the biggest fool in Christendom if she believed a shred of what he was saying.

'But there is something between us,' he said quietly. 'Isn't there? A spark. Admit to me, to yourself, that you feel it too? It is not common, it deserves recognition. You and I, we meet and there is a lifting of the spirits. I will tell you something, Laura.' He took her hand. Now she could not retreat. 'I am a romantic. Sensible men like your friend James, Englishmen, they find it amusing. But I want to love. It has been my ambition. Since I was a boy I have wanted to fall madly in love, to meet someone who can set me on fire, take away my breath, tumble me out of reality and into enchantment. And I have waited, and sometimes I have thought for a moment, Is she the one? and it has *almost* happened. But never quite. Until you. I mean that. Please believe me. Life is short. And we do not have the time to learn to trust each other.'

Slowly, very slowly, his hands travelled up her arms and to her shoulders, drawing her towards him. He tasted her mouth at length, prolonging the moment, building a fire in her that sent her senses spinning. The voices in her mind kept on telling her to beware, but she was past caution. All her life, it seemed, had been directed towards this union. Nothing mattered but this moment. Unwise, unsafe, ridiculous, loving Gérard had to happen.

In the bed that had possibly been the resting place of Napoleon, Gérard de Montrémy made love to Laura and she thought recklessly that she would pay any price for such an hour of happiness.

Later, Victoire watched them without comment as they left by the gates across the courtyard. His scrutiny made Laura shiver.

'Come to the aerodrome with me? I want to show you my plane.'

Gérard was in a reckless, silly mood, drunk with love, and Laura indulged him. She loved the light in his eyes and the sensation of riding on clouds. She was long past caring about propriety and common sense. He drove her to the airfield near Amiens and his mechanics wheeled out the Spad, a sleek silver bird with broad tricolour bands on the wings and an eagle in flight, his personal insignia, painted on each side behind the cockpit. A single seater, or she would have begged a flight. Smiling, he kissed her hand and her mouth.

'Watch me, Laura. This is for you.'

He switched on the engine. His mechanic swung the propeller and, bending low, pulled the chocks away from the wheels. The plane trundled forward across the grass, gathering speed. The magical moment of lift occurred. It soared into the sky and in her heart Laura, standing at the edge of the airfield, lifted with it.

'Hullo, Laura.'

She turned, coming back to earth with an effort. James

Allingham stood at her shoulder, giving her his usual diffident smile.

'What are you doing here?' she asked.

'I came over an hour ago to talk shop with the CO here. Then someone mentioned you were on the airfield.' His head was tilted back, his eyes on the silver plane. 'Gérard's about to give you an aerobatics display, I take it?'

'I don't know. He just told me to watch him.'

'He's brilliant at it. But a bit prone to overstressing his machine,' James said quietly. 'The Spad's a great plane but tricky at low speeds.' The biplane was climbing almost vertically heavenwards. It seemed to hang in the air, the engine screaming, before the continuing of the circle turned it on its back.

'Climbing loop. Not many planes have enough power,' said James with professional interest as the machine completed the circle and righted itself. It climbed again, seeming to slow in the sky till it hung almost motionless. The noise of the engine cut out. Laura's heart lurched.

'It's all right. It's part of the manoeuvre,' said James. 'Standard spin. He can do these with his eyes closed.'

Laura longed to close her own eyes as the Spad spun in a series of circles towards the ground. Seemingly feet above the aerodrome it pulled out and raced away with a burst of engine speed. Again it climbed the sky, then tilted its wings in a series of rocking movements which brought it swooping earthwards.

'Falling leaf,' supplied James helpfully. The undercarriage of the silver plane skimmed the hangars. By now all the mechanics had downed tools and other pilots had emerged from the huts dotted round the airfield to watch the display.

The Spad was small in the distance by this point. With a sudden, startling movement the nose reared up and the machine flipped over sideways, spinning one complete circle before resuming its course.

'Flick roll. Good one.'

470

The plane turned back towards the aerodrome. Over their heads, it dipped forward into a steep dive until it was racing vertically towards the ground. Laura's hands flew to her mouth to suppress the scream that rose inside her.

'Bunt,' said James grimly. 'The idiot. It's too dangerous.'

The Spad had gone over into an inverted dive. It levelled out upside down and roared across the airfield, then suddenly seemed to lurch in the air. Unbelievably, the leather-clad body of the pilot swung loose, dangled, upside down, for a heart-stopping moment, then lurched again. And broke away.

'Safety harness gone . . .' said James. 'Oh God!'

The body had turned, arms spread, and was plummeting downwards. What Laura chiefly remembered afterwards was the way that Gérard's legs trod the air as he fell.

She turned away, stumbling against the figure of James standing close behind her. His arms scooped her against his woollen uniform. She closed her eyes, feeling sick. Something pressed into her cheek – the embroidered wings sewn to the breast pocket flap of his tunic.

Time passed at a crawl. She had no need to watch. She could tell from the final gasp of the watching mechanics, which sent an answering jolt through her body, the exact moment when Gérard hit the ground. Seconds later, unregarded, the empty Spad slewed into a tree at the edge of the airfield and exploded in a ball of fire.

The arms around her tightened, then relaxed.

Astonishingly, Gérard wasn't dead when the ambulance reached him. His body, though fractured in many places, clung doggedly to life. James annexed someone's car and followed the ambulance to hospital, with Laura at his side. White-faced and frozen, she didn't speak during the journey.

'It's a matter of time,' said the surgeon, shrugging his shoulders.

All that night, Laura sat by Gérard's bedside, holding his dry, cold hand and straining for the faint sound of his breathing. She was remembering the photographs of his stiff, formal parents who adored him and the beautiful town house, closed and shuttered, in which there would now be no joyous celebration. Just before dawn he died without recovering consciousness, and James, a hovering shadow in the background, drove Laura back to the YMCA hostel.

'James, how can we stand it?' Laura said in the car. 'How can we stand it, time after time, when everyone we care about is killed?'

'I suppose,' James answered, remembering squadrons of dead men, 'the answer is not to let yourself care about anyone too much.'

'But how do we stop ourselves?' Laura cried on a note of despair.

'That,' said James soberly, 'is the bit I haven't worked out yet.'

Two days after Gérard's death, Laura came to the hospital at Camiers to speak to Margaret Allingham.

'I need a job.'

Margaret had heard from James about the flying accident. Now, looking at Laura's white, haggard face, she felt unspeakably sorry. But her first duty was to her patients.

'What kind of a job?' she said carefully.

'I have been a nurse,' said Laura. 'A VAD. I want to be a nurse again. I want to be doing something for every minute. Something desperate.'

Margaret studied the distraught girl.

'Wounded men are not there for your therapy, Laura. They need more than that.'

'I'll give them more than that. I'll give them everything. Please. If you talk to your matron, she'll take me on. I have to do something. I can't just sit and think, I'll go crazy. I'll break into pieces. Margaret, you know what it's like.' The words spilled out, urgent, pleading. Tears sprang in Laura's eyes.

Margaret put her hands to her forehead. Yes, she knew what it was like. In the weeks after Edward died, she too had needed

472

something to occupy her, something exhausting and vital, to fend off reality. Nursing had saved her.

'You aren't old enough for an overseas posting.'

'I am. Nearly. She won't care, if you say you know me. Margaret, *please*.'

'You'll do whatever is needed? Promise you won't let me down?'

'I promise,' said Laura shakily.

'All right. I'll talk to Matron.'

And Laura joined the staff at Camiers.

It was Margaret who wrote to let Jessie know of Laura's latest tragedy. Jessie, helpless, could only pray that her niece would be strong enough to survive it. Tragedies were all around Jessie now.

At Maple Grange, as the autumn rain turned the Flanders farmland into a morass, Mrs Driver's nephew was reported missing in the mud of Passchendaele and Mr Ferry's cousin's son died of the new and even more lethal mustard gas that the Germans were using for the first time to repel the doomed Allied offensive of Third Ypres. News came of Billy Marshall, the gardener's boy, now a prisoner of war.

'He was lucky,' said Mrs Driver to Joan. 'Shot six times. Lay out in No Man's Land three days, his mum says, and then the German stretcher-bearers took him to one of their casualty clearing stations. They took out five bullets but the sixth was too close to his spine, so they've left it in. We'd better send him a food parcel through the Red Cross.'

Joan nodded listlessly. Her 'best boy', of the territorials who had been billeted at the Grange in the opening weeks of the war, was long gone, a casualty on the Somme. There had been a succession of 'best boys' since then, local men home on leave or convalescents from the hospitals in the area. Each one lasted for the length of his leave. When she waved them goodbye, she consigned them to history. She no longer let herself get attached to anyone.

Jessie worried about Laura, about everyone. She even

473

worried about Rupert, whose morbid interest in the losses to Allied shipping, and the consequent rises in the prices of his shares, was making him highly unpopular in the area. Once he had come home, speechless with anger, with a clod of mud spattered across his back by someone who had called him a 'war profiteer'.

24

Even before she had been forced to relinquish the care of Harriet to Daisy, Louella had turned some of her energies on the neglected garden of Medlar House. A large part of the lawn had been dug over, Hector had paid for plants and the result was a crop of vegetables which not only fed the household, but also produced a large surplus to be sold to a nearby greengrocer. At first Louella kept the money earned in this way in a small jar on the kitchen mantelpiece. By the autumn of 1917 the jar had been replaced by a bigger biscuit tin, stuffed with notes and coins.

'If it wasn't for the flour shortage,' Louella lamented, carrying a large basket crammed with newly gathered potatoes, cauliflowers, parsnips and tomatoes into the kitchen where Daisy was preparing the midday meal, 'I could be making a fortune. Pasties and pies and ready-cooked meals for the workers who've got no time to cook for themselves. The jam from the orchard sold very well.'

This year the plums and apples had not withered on the trees or blackened in the grass as they had the year before. Louella had gathered them, peeled and sliced and simmered them into jam for sale. The troops might be sick of plum-and-apple jam, but the civilian population had snapped it up. The biscuit tin that contained Louella's earnings grew almost too heavy to lift.

'I thought you couldn't get enough sugar for jam-making,' Daisy said, adding the rinsings of last night's bacon-boiling pot to the assortment of leftovers that were the staple ingredients of the Ministry of Food's recipe for wartime soup. There seemed to be shortages of everything these days, but sugar had been the first – ever since the outbreak of the war had cut off the normal source, sugar beet from Germany and Austria. This summer the would-be jam-makers who had filled in application forms for an extra ration, to be doled out according to the quantities of fruit they had available, had been disappointed by a late announcement that the allocation scheme had been scrapped. It was rumoured that German submarine attacks on supply ships were to blame.

'I put in salt,' Louella said. 'It cuts down on the need for sugar. If you keep the jam for a couple of months before you eat it, apparently you don't taste the salt.' She dumped the basket of vegetables on the table, stepping neatly over Harriet who was seated on the floor slotting carved animals into a wooden Noah's Ark in a haphazard way which did no good to their paintwork. Like all Harriet's toys now, they came from the trunk in the nursery and had been bought long ago for John Ramsay, but she was as happy with model farms and lead soldiers as she might have been with dolls.

'Can I have some of those vegetables for the meal?' Daisy said hopefully, eyeing the glistening tomatoes that were now being packed into boxes by her sister-in-law for delivery to the greengrocer.

'No, all these are promised already. Oh, all right,' Louella said, pushing a grudging handful of parsnips towards Daisy in response to her reproachful gaze.

'Doesn't Mister Hector mind you selling everything from his garden instead of putting it into his dinner?' Daisy said.

'He doesn't mind whatever I do.' And it was true. Louella could twist Hector Ramsay round her little finger. He was devoted to her, that much was apparent in his every look.

'You shouldn't take so much advantage, Lou.'

'Why not?' Louella lifted her shoulders. 'He'd give me anything. He's asked me to marry him.'

Daisy had been about to slice into the first of the parsnips to add to the soup. At Louella's revelation, she dropped her knife and the vegetable rolled away across the table and bounced on to the floor. Harriet, distracted from twin giraffes

476

and zebras, scrambled after it as her mother stared open-mouthed at her aunt.

'Lou!' said Daisy.

'He asked me two weeks ago. And in case you're wondering, I told him I'd think about it. I'm still thinking about it,' said Louella airily. 'So he's being particularly obliging about anything I happen to want at the moment.'

Daisy felt a pang of sympathy for Hector Ramsay.

Laura had hoped, when she made her appeal to Margaret Allingham for a nursing job at Camiers, that she could blank out thought by filling each day with a remorseless workload until the pain she suppressed had seeped away, and one morning she would wake to find that she was almost whole again.

On the whole the scheme worked. She arrived in the middle of the campaign of Third Ypres, and as the hospital coped with the massive casualty lists, there was simply no time to dwell on the loss of Gérard. She stumbled at night to her camp bed in a cold bell tent, too tired to care about anything.

Even the news that the Germans were now bombing the hospitals around the Ypres battle zone barely penetrated her stupor of exhaustion. If the bombers came to Camiers she told herself with a shrug, they would end her misery. If they did not, there was work to do.

But in November when the Ypres campaign drew to a close in the face of winter, there was a comparative lull in the arrival of the convoys of wounded. It left her open to the onslaught of memories. Sometimes she was racked by the idea that she was responsible for Gérard's death. A small, hateful voice whispered in her mind that the display that killed him had been done for her sake, in the aftermath of their lovemaking. If she had said 'No,' beside the Napoleon bed, if she had kept her head, might he still be alive? At other times she felt savagely angry that he had taken such a risk so needlessly. *Gérard's about to give you an aerobatics display, I take it*, she remembered James saying at the airfield, as the silver plane climbed the sky. *He's brilliant at it. But a bit prone to overstressing his machine. . . .*

'Oh, Gérard . . . it wasn't my fault.' But what did it matter whose fault the accident had been? The result was the same. And the living person who was paying the price for it now, in the agony of loss, was Laura.

It was then that she discovered in the apparently reserved Sister Allingham an unexpected, steady source of comfort. In an unobtrusive way, Margaret was somehow there at the moments when Laura was most ready to give way to despair, and she found herself confiding in her old enemy to a degree that astonished her. The compulsive need to go over and over the circumstances of her meeting with Gérard and their short, intense love affair, to reiterate her sorrow, began to fade. Margaret too revealed some of her own deeper feelings over Edward's death and tentatively a friendship was built.

'Did you know,' Laura said as they took a walk together during a rest period one December day, 'that I was in love with Edward?'

'Yes. I knew,' said Margaret. Laura watched her apprehensively.

'Don't you hate me for it?' she asked.

'How could I hate anyone for loving Edward?' Margaret gave her companion a wry sideways smile. 'It was impossible not to love him so far as I was concerned. I'll admit that when I first realized how you felt about him, I found it threatening. I couldn't understand why he would prefer me.'

'He did though,' said Laura, remembering the day in the bluebell wood, Edward's defence of his fiancée and the flat statement that he was not interested in anyone else. 'He really loved you.'

'Yes,' said Margaret quietly. 'He really did.' She had never told anyone, and she did not tell Laura now, of her experience on the night she dreamed of his death: the fleeting presence and the hand that had touched her cheek. But it had finally dispelled her doubts about the depth of Edward's love, even as she lost him for ever.

478

'I was so jealous of you,' Laura said. 'I thought the world had come to an end and I would never love anyone else. I only married Charles as a reaction to the news of your wedding. Poor Charles, he really deserved better than that. And then by the time I'd started to love him a little instead, it was too late . . . and that seemed like the end of the world, too, until I met Gérard.'

' "This too shall pass . . ." ' said Margaret.

'Is that a quotation? I suppose that's one of the things that made you and Edward close. Knowing the same poetry.'

'I think that particular line is biblical. But yes, poetry was something we both loved, it made a tie between us.'

'I wonder what ties I could have found with Gérard? Perhaps there weren't any. Perhaps I was just a passing whim. I'll never know, now. But for the time we were together, it was perfect.'

'I suppose we could be said to be lucky then, you and I,' Margaret said gently. 'We are two women who have known perfect times.'

'Auntie Lou, Auntie Lou. . . .'

Harriet was eating her tea when Louella came into the kitchen. Her eyes aglow with welcome, she dropped her slice of bread and jam and slid off her chair to run across the kitchen towards Louella.

'Don't touch, Harriet, you're all jammy,' said her aunt sharply, putting out a hand to fend her off. Clearly, Harriet's affectionate but sticky fingers were not fit to be allowed anywhere near the clothes of the new, smart Louella. 'Daisy, a man will be coming shortly with a couple of rabbits to sell. I met him this morning at the greengrocer's. Will you call me when he arrives? I'll be in the garden.'

At the end of her outstretched arm and detaining hand, Harriet looked up at her in hurt bewilderment. Life was very confusing. She'd learned now that this woman wasn't to be called 'Mummy' but 'Auntie Lou', or her other 'Mummy' would correct her and look upset. But why didn't Auntie Lou ever cuddle her any more? She felt a hollow sense of loss and rejection that showed on her small face and Daisy felt a sudden longing to smack Louella, hard. Controlling the impulse she bent to gather up her daughter and plant a reassuring kiss on Harriet's round cheek, but Harriet, unconsoled, wriggled impatiently. She didn't want any old cuddle. At this moment she wanted Auntie Lou.

At Christmas Louella had married Hector Ramsay. For Daisy, the outcome was uncomfortable . . . or perhaps it wasn't just the marriage that had changed her relationship with Louella. Once they had been friends as well as sisters-in-law but after Daisy had stopped working at the Arsenal, Louella had become hard and brusque. It was only to be expected after she'd had the care of Harriet for so long that she should mind when she found herself supplanted, but Daisy's efforts to mitigate the blow had been snubbed. And yet Daisy had a feeling that Louella's hardness was a shell and that inside she was hurting herself.

Louella worked at her vegetable gardening business, and when she could come by the ingredients she also cooked meals to sell to the busy workers of Blackheath or Woolwich. With Louella immersed in commerce, somehow Daisy became, by default, cook-housemaid to the household as well as a payer of rent. Patiently she told herself that Louella's behaviour arose from the unhappiness of the previous three years. When she had known security for a while, perhaps she would mellow again.

The rabbits, when they arrived, were not the dead animals for the cooking pot that Daisy had assumed, but alive, eyes peering and noses twitching inquisitively through the slatted bars of a crate. Daisy fetched Louella as instructed, and the man was taken away to the end of the garden to construct a rabbit run. Louella was planning to add the breeding of a source of meat to her enterprises.

Since Will Griffin's return to the Front, he had managed to send Daisy some kind of communication every week for her reassurance, though sometimes it was only a buff field-service postcard devoid of details, and not a letter. She knew that in the gap between the sending of the mail and its arrival, something might have happened to Will, but even so she was happy on the letter days. At Christmas she had sent him a pudding, properly made from carefully hoarded ingredients, not the ersatz concoction of the Ministry of Food recipes, together with a cake, toffees and a tin of cocoa. She'd packed the parcel with care, thinking of his face as he opened it, thinking of the small pleasures that its contents could bring him in the midst of his hard life. She added a card and the same message she'd sent him in the first Christmas of the war, from Maple Grange, *Keep safe*.

In return he'd sent a toy whistle for Harriet and for Daisy a lace handkerchief with apologies that it wasn't something better, and with all his love.

It was enough.

There was a possibility, Hector told Louella in February of 1918, that she might eventually be entitled to a pension as a result of Robert's death. For some months now Members of Parliament, and in particular a Labour MP called Philip Snowden, had been raising persistent questions in the House about the fitness of the Field General Courts Martial to impose death sentences on men who had often undergone considerable hardship prior to their offences. There was further disquiet about the attitudes of the Poor Law Guardians towards the families of the executed men. So far Snowden's questions had been fielded blandly by the Under-Secretary for War – along the lines that in the current situation very little could be revealed and it must be assumed that everything that was being done was being done for the best by the commanders in the field. But after the bloodbath of Third Ypres, this argument was less convincing than it might have been in the earlier days of the war. Attitudes were changing. It was becoming recognized that generals were fallible and indeed the Prime Minister had just sacked one of General Haig's chief supporters of the war-of-attrition theory, Sir William Robertson, from his position as adviser to the Cabinet.

Louella didn't care about politics. She was far more concerned about the introduction of the official rationing of meat, butter and margarine which had just been introduced. The meat rationing would be good for business when the rabbits had multiplied, but the other controls were a nuisance. She had become an expert at bartering and wheedling supplies out of the local shopkeepers, but rationing, with coupons to be produced for everything, tying you to one shop only as your supplier, would put paid to that. She fidgeted impatiently as Hector told her about Philip Snowden's campaign.

'This Snowden sounds like a decent chap,' he said. 'Would you like me to write to him on your behalf, get him to take up your case?'

'What for?' said Louella.

'To try to get you a pension. The matter is supposed to be under consideration.'

'You knew I had no money when I married you,' said Louella. It wasn't strictly true, the money in the biscuit tin was accumulating fast. But Hector needn't know of such details. Having money that she'd acquired by her own efforts made Louella feel safe in a way that money dispensed through a man, even a generous man like her husband, could not.

'I don't suggest it for myself,' Hector said, hurt. 'Of course it would be yours, if a pension could be obtained for you. I only thought—'

Abruptly Louella's apparent calm snapped. Nearly two years after learning of Robert's death, she was snatched back to that shocked, trembling state to which she'd been reduced by the cold, official letter.

'No,' she said. 'I don't want money for Robert. Blood money. *Here's a pound or two, m'dear, for your man that's gone*. And their consciences washed clean. No. Let them keep their money.'

She was trembling. Hector put his arms around her and held

er until the shaking of her body had stopped. He thought
adly that it would be better if she cried, but she stayed
ry-eyed and bitter. She had helped him to recover from
he death of his son and he'd thought at the time that the
elp was mutual; but now he was beginning to realize
ow deep were her wounds. And she wouldn't let him comfort
er.

n February, Germany and Russia signed the treaty of
Brest-Litovsk, ending hostilities on the Eastern Front. The
lmost immediate impact of this was to free German troops
nd resources to concentrate on the Western Front. The
mpending threat of intervention from American forces added
rgency to the calculations of General von Ludendorff,
ontroller of German strategy on the Western Front,
nd in March of 1918 he launched a new offensive on the
omme.

Along fifty miles of the front south of Arras, twenty-six
livisions of the British army were confronted by sixty-three
livisions of the enemy, with inevitable results. The line
rumbled. Within four days the British troops were in full
etreat.

The southern sector of the German advance surged towards
he railway junction at Amiens, after an advance of forty miles
n a few days. Ahead of the advance streamed the ambulances
carrying the wounded to the hospitals along the coast.

Wake up.' Margaret was shaking Laura by the shoulder.
Another convoy.'

Laura groaned. It seemed like only a few minutes since,
aving been on duty all day, she had fallen on to her bed,
ully clothed. She groped for her watch and found that it *was*
nly a few minutes. Somewhere outside she could hear the
oar of ambulance engines. She struggled into a sitting
osition, blinking at the light of Margaret's torch shining in
er eyes.

'I'm off duty,' she protested. 'Can't someone else . . . ?'

'Everyone's turning out. Come on.' Margaret was alread on her way out of the tent, leaving the torch lying on th bedclothes.

As Laura ducked under the tent flap she bumped in another figure in nursing uniform: a uniform, she saw by th wavering light of the torch, that was crumpled and dirty, th apron bloodstained. The pale, weary face was unfamiliar.

'Do you mind awfully if I use your bed?' said the nev comer faintly. 'They said just find somewhere empt and flop.'

'Who are you?' Laura said dubiously, recoiling in distas from the thought of this unclean stranger in her bed.

'Nurse Barnet, from a casualty clearing station near Arra We were evacuated from the line of the advance. We've ju brought a convoy in. May I?'

'Well . . . all right . . .' said Laura. The consent wa superfluous. The girl had already crashed on to her bed an appeared dead to the world.

'Several hundred "walking wounded",' said Margare when Laura joined her in the 'D' lines. She was lighting lantern as she spoke, to add to the one that was alread swinging from the ridge of the tent. 'Though most of the should be stretcher cases if there'd been enough stretchers t go round! Matron says there's more serious cases due in an minute and we're to deal with this lot.'

The 'we' to whom the walking wounded had been allocate were three nurses including Laura and Margaret, an orderl and a grim-faced medical officer.

'We can't possibly cope with several hundred,' Laur protested.

'We'll have to. There's no one else available.' Margare was already hurrying to organize a table and chair for th medical officer, together with a pile of equipment to appl fresh dressings.

'You get their dressings off ready for the MO to look a them,' she told Laura briskly. 'Phyllis and I will do the rest.

She handed Laura a pair of scissors and pushed her toward

484

he doorway of the tent. Already a line of men awaiting reatment had formed outside. They were filthy, exhausted, lank-eyed with pain. Along the path behind them the queue engthened as a series of blind men filtered forward in a chain, ach man's hand on the preceding man's shoulder. Gas cases, hrapnel cases? Laura swallowed.

'Come in,' she said, clutching her scissors.

The first man who limped in had a thigh wound. The ressing applied at some field station was stiff with dried lood. It would need patient soaking to remove it with the ninimum of pain. She sat him down on a chair and looked round for a source of warm water.

'What's the problem?' Margaret hissed, hurrying to her ide.

'It'll need soaking off.'

'No time for that. Not with hundreds waiting. You'll just ave to tear it off. We'll deal with the bleeding afterwards vhen the MO's seen it.'

Laura looked at the man, who must have overheard what vas in store for him. His eyes met hers. She saw his mouth ighten with apprehension.

'Margaret, I can't . . .' she whispered. She was too tired, it vas too much.

'You must.'

'I just *can't* . . .' quavered Laura. Margaret gripped her arm. n the lamplight her eyes blazed. Laura had never seen her ooking so fierce.

'Laura,' she said, very softly and coldly, 'you promised me vhen I persuaded the matron here to take you on that you vouldn't let me down. You promised me you'd do the job. Now live up to that.'

Laura walked back to the waiting patient. She gripped the cissors. 'It'll be quick,' she said. Her voice wobbled. She cut he dressing down the middle, gripped both halves in her ands, and wrenched sharply. The man cried out with the pain. But the dressing was off. The orderly steadied him as he tumbled towards the MO's table.

485

'Next,' said Laura faintly, to the second man in the silently advancing queue.

Half an hour later, Margaret snatched a moment from the constant stream of dry dressings, wet dressings, boric-ointment dressings and splints that passed under her hands, to look at Laura on the far side of the tent. She was ripping the bandages from wounds with a methodical series of movements, like an automaton. Cut . . . grip . . . pull. . . . She was crying steadily, the tears running unregarded down her face. But she was doing the job.

Somehow, with the aid of French reinforcements and strong air support, the rot was stopped north of the Somme. An all-out German attack on the ravaged town of Arras failed, and by April, Ludendorff's troops, undernourished, exhausted and with transport and supply problems brought on by the speed of their progress, abandoned the advance on Amiens.

At Maple Grange, Rupert was beside himself with excitement as the news of the Allied forces' rallying filtered through. 'Heroes Who Kept The German Hordes At Bay', sang the *War Illustrated*, and 'Staying The Avalanche of Massed German Might'. Photographs of cheerful, triumphant troops crowded the pages.

Jessie, though relieved that the war was not lost, as had seemed an awful possibility for two weeks, was less inclined to crow. She was thinking of Laura and Margaret, coping with the after-effects at Camiers, and of Claire at Clandon when the tide of the casualties rolled on . . . and she was dizzy with thankfulness that Michael Mackenzie had failed his medical. If he hadn't, she told herself, he might have been in action with his brigade in this terrible fighting, instead of fretting impatiently in an administrative job in the Canadian camp at Wisley.

She kept her reflections to herself. There was no point in worrying Rupert with any reference to Laura. Nobody mentioned his daughter to Rupert these days. And he didn't know about Jessie and Major Mackenzie. Nobody except Jessie new about her and Major Mackenzie. Not that there'd been much to know, until lately. Just his steady attendance at the ing-songs, followed by invitations to tea in Guildford; long conversations in which Jessie lost her shyness and found herself talking happily about all sorts of subjects she'd never discussed with anyone else.

... But on the most recent of those occasions, he had taken her hand at the moment of parting.

'Jessie,' he'd said quietly. 'There's something I'd like you to think over. It's a big step so I don't expect an immediate answer, but ... I guess you know I think you're a damned fine woman. Some time, when the war ends, and it has to end some day soon, I'll have to go back home. I'd like to ask you to consider coming with me. As my wife.'

'We've got our old guns back out of store,' wrote Oliver Brownlowe to Claire Lawrence in September of 1918. 'We're hunting the Hun again in support of the cavalry.'

Through that spring and summer the fortunes of war had shifted to and fro as the Germans launched further desperate offensives, in Flanders and on the Marne, that were as desperately repulsed. Near Amiens in August it had been the Allies who went on the offensive and the demoralized, exhausted German army who gave way. For them it was the beginning of the end. Now the eagerly awaited American forces were streaming into the war zone and they had nothing left to give in return. The chase was on to the Hindenburg Line.

Oliver held his pen poised above the page for a moment, wondering how to finish his letter. In a few minutes he'd ride on ahead to reconnoitre the lie of the land for the guns to follow. With a clear picture of Claire's smiling face in his mind, he scrawled a final line. 'At this rate it really will be over by Christmas. Can't wait to see you.'

His groom brought up his horse to the farm building that was today's billet. Before mounting, he handed the man the letter, addressed to Claire at Clandon.

'Can you see this gets in the post, Stephens?'

'Yes, sir.'

Oliver swung himself into the saddle and rode away. He returned the salute of Driver Griffin as he cantered through the horse lines. By nightfall he had not returned.

'It looks as though we have lost Captain Brownlowe . . . wrote Griffin to Daisy by the light of a lantern in the remains of a barn somewhere near the Messines Ridge. The barn was being shared with a dozen other drivers and two dozen horses but at least it wasn't booby-trapped like the abandoned German dugouts which the battery had earlier investigated and rejected. Perhaps a booby trap had caught Oliver Brownlowe? Griffin supposed he would never know.

'It's a very odd feeling, knowing he's gone. I am rather low about it tonight, darling. I never rated him highly at the start of all this, but he turned out a good man and a good officer after all.'

Daisy, reading the letter at Medlar House, mentioned the likelihood of Oliver Brownlowe's death to Louella – sadly because she remembered Mr Oliver as a gangling schoolboy and because Will had liked him. To her surprise, Louella laughed.

'So Rupert Brownlowe's lost his son! Now let him feel something – if he can!'

Daisy had forgotten the scene at Maple Grange after Robert died. Louella, clearly, had not.

In October Laura came home on leave for the first time in two years.

She had not wanted to take the leave, but Margaret had told her firmly not to be a fool, and in the end she had discovered that she did, after all, want to see her Aunt Jessie again. As for her father, she supposed he would have to be faced sooner or later.

Walker collected her from the station in response to the telegram she had sent announcing her arrival. It was from him that she learned that hers had been the second telegram delivered at the Grange that day. The first had conveyed the news that Captain Oliver Brownlowe was Missing, Presumed Killed in Action.

Laura sat in the back of the Landaulette and her numbed mind tried to take it in. Oliver. Exasperating, clumsy, affectionate, all her life the other half of herself. And now she'd lost him. And it was too much for her. Was there never to be an end to this losing of all the men who mattered to her?

At the Grange, an older, thinner Ferry welcomed her with his usual dignity but with a catch in his voice.

'What a sad day it is, Miss Laura.'

In the background, Mrs Driver and Joan bobbed curtsies and tried to smile despite their woebegone faces. Then she was being hugged, without any attempt at dignity or noblesse oblige, by Aunt Jessie.

'Your father's in his study. Will you go in to him?' Jessie said, releasing her niece eventually. Tears glittered in the hollows beneath her eyes.

'In a minute. Has anyone told Claire?'

'I sent a message as soon as we had the telegram. But Oliver had probably arranged for her to be informed as well, in the event of. . . .' Jessie's voice faltered and she groped for a handkerchief. Sick at heart, Laura went slowly into the study.

Her father was seated at his desk, with his back to her. He was writing something on a pad in front of him. He turned his head as she closed the door behind her and crossed the room. Just for a moment, something, some flicker or emotion, showed on his face. Then it was shut away.

'Ah, Laura,' he said, as if she'd been gone for five minutes and not two years. 'Come and give me your opinion on this.'

With a feeling of anticlimax that she noted even in the midst of her grief, Laura crossed to his side. Pa had never been demonstrative. And it was a terrible day to come home . . . but couldn't he have shown some pleasure or relief at seeing her again? Or some need for her in his sadness, some willingness to comfort her in hers, rather than this matter-of-fact reception? But it wasn't his style. It had never been his style. In the old days all the gestures of affection had come from her, and now she had lost the inclination. She realized, as she reached the desk, that in the hour since he had learned of the loss of his son, he had been prosaically penning a letter to the local paper to announce the fact.

'Do you think it will do? Have I phrased it properly?' he asked.

'Yes, Pa.' Laura felt a wave of revulsion. The man wasn't human. 'I think it will do,' she said dully.

'Well, I'll just address the envelope. Run along and get your aunt to give you some tea.'

Claire arrived late in the afternoon in Doctor Lawrence's little red Austin. Magnus flowed out of the passenger door, barking, as Laura and Jessie came out of the house to meet the grief-stricken fiancée, dreading the moment. But Claire's eyes were shining.

'It's all right! Didn't you get a second telegram? One arrived for me this afternoon from a nurse in a hospital in France. He isn't dead. He was brought into a casualty clearing station. Wounded, but alive.'

'How badly injured?' Jessie asked in the reaction that followed her first flood of thankfulness.

'I don't know. A head wound and a leg injury. But his life's not in danger, that's the main thing. They are transferring him to a hospital in England very soon.'

'Which hospital in France is he at?' said Laura.

'I don't remember. Camiers, I think.'

'Oh. I'd have been there,' said Laura slowly, 'if I hadn't come home.'

When they told Rupert, he fussed about recalling his letter to the local paper.

At a hospital near Southampton, Oliver lay in an invalid carrier at the end of the terrace which overlooked the lawns. He was waiting for the nurses to come back and take him in.

'A breath of fresh air will do you good,' they'd said, but

490

he must have been out here for hours. Perhaps they had forgotten him?

The carrier was an oblong tray made of open wicker work, with sides about a foot high. He had explored the structure with his hands in the time he'd lain there with nothing else to do. The sides curved up at the head to hold in the pillows. There were two large wheels at the head, two smaller ones at the foot, a handle behind. He felt like a baby in a pram – and that, Oliver thought savagely, was how they treated him! As if his injuries had affected his brain.

They hadn't. He was as sane now as he'd ever been. Saner. In the past four years he'd learned a lot about survival and the things that mattered. And just lately he'd begun to think that perhaps he might survive this war and actually put all that new-found sense to some good use. A few seconds in a field near Neuve Eglise had changed all that.

He'd finished his reconnaissance and was riding back to the battery when he'd spotted a water trough at the edge of the field and, dismounting, had led his horse towards it. The animal, scenting the water, had pulled forward eagerly and Oliver had released the reins and strolled after her, knowing that when she'd drunk her fill she would stand there patiently waiting for him. So he was some distance away when the bomb concealed in the long grass under the trough exploded.

'You're a lucky man,' the medics had said. He supposed they meant 'lucky' because unlike his mare he hadn't died, 'lucky' because a detachment of infantry had found him shortly afterwards and taken him to a casualty clearing station. The blast had sent a chunk of the trough's metal tearing past his legs, shearing the flesh from one calf. That, they told him, wasn't too serious, though he could say goodbye to tennis matches on summer lawns. More problematic was the fact that some part of the explosion had damaged his eyes.

'Bilateral retinal detachment', they called it. Or to put it more bluntly, Oliver was blind. He wasn't sure they were right about the luck.

He could tell that the sun had gone in, because it was getting colder. What if it rained? He gripped the sides of the carrier and wondered whether to call for attention, but he didn't know if he had the energy and besides it was too humiliating a prospect.

And then, to his relief, he heard footsteps approaching along the gravel of the path.

'Nurse?' he said. 'Is it time to go in yet?'

'It's not the nurse,' said a familiar voice. Caught off guard, weak with shock, Oliver let his hand drop from the side of the carrier. Something alive and cold pushed inquisitively at his dangling fingers. It was replaced by a warmer sensation, a damp and rough caressing of the palm of his hand.

'I've brought Magnus to see you,' said Claire.

'We're getting married,' Claire told Laura afterwards. 'You can be the first to congratulate me.'

'Was it good news, then, about his eyes?' Laura asked on an upsurge of hope.

'No. Bad news. It's very rare for someone with his condition to recover their sight. They said I should face up to the likelihood that he'll always be blind.'

'Oh,' said Laura. She pictured Oliver in the years ahead, groping and tapping his way through life, with Claire hovering perpetually at his elbow, sharing her eyes with him. It was a chilling thought.

'At least he'll always see you as young,' said Laura lamely. One corner of Claire's mouth lifted in derision.

'That's what my mother said. That's what everyone says. *He'll always see you as young.* Do you know,' she said leaning forward, 'when I went to see him at the hospital today and we agreed to get married anyway, he touched my face all over with his hands, very carefully. Stroked me, as if he was defining the boundaries. As if he was *learning* me. He'll know every line, every wrinkle, every bulge,' said Claire, 'better than I'll know it myself.'

There was a pause.

'Claire, why are you doing it?' said Laura at last.

492

'Marrying Oliver? What else can I do? Blind or not, he's still the man I love. Besides, do you remember that Bruce Bainsfather cartoon? The two soldiers in a shell hole? *If you know of a better 'ole, go to it.* I don't know of a better hole. I *have* to have someone to care about, someone to look after and make a home for, it's in my nature. Silly, isn't it?' She forced a smile. 'Me, the suffragette, admitting that my life doesn't have a meaning unless it's dedicated to some man. I know so clearly what flawed creatures they are, but somehow that doesn't stop me needing one . . . and there's never been anyone but Oliver for me. Whenever I've thought of marriage it's been with him. When he went to the Front I prayed to heathen gods, Laura, I made a bargain with whatever fierce and pitiless thing it is that controls our destinies and I said, I'll pay anything, do anything, for the rest of my days, only please send him home to me alive. Fool that I was, I forgot to say alive and well. But perhaps if I had, there would have been no bargain. The gods like their little joke, don't they?'

'The Great War ended today at 11 a.m.' wrote Rupert Brownlowe in his diary on Monday, 11 November, 1918. Sitting in his office at the factory, he underlined the entry neatly, twice, then he went out into the building to lay off the workforce.

Jessie heard the news in the upstairs rooms of the War Hospital Supplies Depot in Guildford High Street. It had been expected for some time. British troops had breached the Hindenburg Line on 5 October and on the following day, Germany had requested an armistice. While the rival statesmen argued over the details men had gone on fighting and dying, but at last, following the abdication of the Kaiser and his flight into neutral Holland, there was no further resistance to the terms laid down by the Allied powers.

At eleven o'clock, the appointed time for the ceasefire, the supervisor of the Depot rang a bell to call for silence.

'The war is over.'

The entire building erupted into a pandemonium of delight, a reaction that was echoed all over the country.

Jessie's first thought was, *Thank God!* Her second thought was, *Now Michael will go back to Canada.*

He would want his answer.

25

On a day in mid-November, a letter came for Daisy from Mrs
Driver at Maple Grange.

'Oh!' exclaimed Daisy, scanning the cook's untidy sprawl
of handwriting for news of the various members of staff she'd
known. Louella looked up, frowning, from the task of laying
a breakfast tray for Hector, who was feeling unwell.

'What is it?'

'Mr Oliver. He isn't dead after all, just wounded. But
blinded,' she discovered, reading on, and the delight died out
of her voice.

'It isn't enough,' said Louella obscurely, and carried the
tray upstairs.

An hour later, Hector appeared at the foot of the stairs,
clinging dizzily to the newel post, and asked for his wife. But
Louella could not be found in the house or the garden. She
had simply disappeared.

Worried by Hector's greenish pallor, Daisy helped him back
up the stairs to his bed, filled him a hot-water bottle, made
him tea and laid a cool hand on his burning forehead.

'I'll get a doctor. May I?' she asked. Hector nodded
speechlessly. But when Daisy, with Harriet in tow, had found
the nearest doctor's premises, it was only to be told by his
weary wife that he was out, that there was a flu epidemic
raging and that there was really nothing to be done except
keep the patient as comfortable as possible and hope for the
best.

By nightfall Hector was obviously seriously ill and there
was still no sign of Louella. Daisy was torn between keeping
infection away from Harriet and concern for the gentle man
who provided her home. Crossing her fingers that her daughter

would come to no harm because of it, she did what she could for him, wondering between fury and anxiety what had become of her sister-in-law.

It was almost midnight when Louella returned. Daisy came downstairs at the sound of the front door closing and found her in the hall, removing her coat and gloves. Under the gloves her hands were filthy and scratched and as she hung up the coat, Daisy thought it smelled faintly of smoke. There was a dark smear of ash on her cheek.

'Where have you been?' Daisy demanded.

'Keeping a promise,' said Louella. There was an oddly peaceful look about her. 'Settling a debt.'

'Hector's really ill.' Daisy had no time for cryptic answers. 'I've been worried sick about him.'

Louella's peaceful expression faded. She pushed past Daisy and ran up the stairs. When Daisy followed her up a little later, the door to Hector's bedroom was closed but from behind it she heard the murmuring of Louella's voice, gentle and soothing.

Hector's dose of influenza was comparatively mild but even so he was ill for nearly a month, during which time his wife nursed him with dedication. When he was on his feet again, it became apparent that the near-loss of her husband had penetrated Louella's hard, protective shell. It was with real affection that she spoke to him, and her manner towards Daisy and Harriet had softened too.

Daisy found it a relief, seemingly the only relief in an otherwise grey existence. Mercifully Harriet had escaped the flu, but her mother was worn down with worrying in case she didn't, and with supporting Louella's efforts to care for Hector.

The end of the war, so long awaited, had proved such a disappointment. It was true that there were no longer the fresh casualty figures to dread, but there were still sad lists in the papers under the heading 'Died Of Wounds'. Now, too, people were dying of this new, virulent flu. The food shortages went on, unemployment soared as the munitions workers were thrown out of work, and there was no sign of the troops coming home.

The demobilization of an army takes time, and there was the reclaiming of Belgium and occupied France to be seen to first. The armistice was officially only a cessation of hostilities, with neither side admitting defeat, but as the Allied forces marched through the liberated territories to an ecstatic welcome, and into Germany to sullen stares from the population on the far side of the Rhine, the distinction was academic.

It was not until February of 1919 that Griffin wrote to Daisy saying that he had finally been released from his contract of 'three years or the duration', and giving the date and the approximate time of his arrival in London.

She met him at the station. As the train drew in, the carriage windows were pulled down and an eager mass of soldiers craned out to scan the waiting crowd for the first sight of a familiar face. Daisy strained on tiptoe and there was Griffin: thin to the point of gauntness, his dark eyes hollow, but whole and well and home at last.

'Will!' Daisy waved and beside her Harriet mimicked the action, though from her level she could see nothing but the backs of people's legs.

'Aren't you lucky!' said an elderly woman next to her, bending down to smile at the small girl. 'Your daddy's come home safe and sound.'

Harriet was collecting new words. 'Daddy?' she repeated, puzzled.

'Bless her,' said the woman to Daisy. 'Of course she wouldn't know, he's been gone so long, I dare say.'

Daisy was too happy and too distracted by the imminence of the reunion to contradict a well-meaning stranger. Anyway what did it matter what the woman thought? In another moment she was in her husband's arms and kissing any part of him that was immediately accessible, and he was doing the same to her. Harriet watched with interest. She recognized the man who was hugging her mother, he'd played 'This is the way the lady rides' with her; a long time ago, but she didn't forget the people she liked. She tugged at the material of his tunic.

'Daddy,' she said experimentally, when they finally disentangled a little. 'Daddy.'

Daisy, disconcerted, flicked a glance at Will's face and found he was smiling.

'It's all right,' he said. 'I like it. It sounds right.'

Daisy picked up Harriet, and this time it was round both of them that he wrapped his arms.

Oliver hated blindness. When he first recovered consciousness and realized what had happened to him, he couldn't, simply couldn't cope with the fact that the sight he had taken for granted was gone for good. When the stark reality was no longer avoidable, he raged to exhaustion-point over his loss.

Even the fact that Claire said she loved him and still wanted to marry him in spite of his disability had barely skimmed the surface of his despair. In a way, it deepened it. The whole balance of their relationship had changed. From now on he would be the dependent one, the one in need of care, and although he loved Claire, he found the prospect of such a rôle humiliating. Often he thought that he would rather die.

Gradually the shock and the anger faded. He began to get used to the dark. Claire, endlessly patient, spent long hours with him once he came home to Maple Grange, talking and reading to him to fend off the boredom and frustration of his situation. When Claire was unavailable, Laura – newly back from Camiers – took over the task.

Laura didn't just read his books to him, she commented, discussed, argued . . . and gradually it dawned on Oliver that his sister, who had never achieved anything spectacular in the way of academic success at her unambitious girls' school, had a mind at least as sharp as his.

'It's so silly,' he said. 'You can run rings round me when it comes to analysing literature and I'm the one who was going

498

to Oxford and you're the one who's supposed to stay at home and look decorative. It's a pity we can't swop places. Looking decorative is about all I'm good for, now.'

'Things will get better,' Laura said, trying to sound encouraging.

'The worst of it is, I've nothing to do.' He chewed his lip discontentedly, his right hand clenched on the knobbed top of the stick he used to find his way safely round the house without bumping into things.

'You'll find something . . .' Laura began.

'Quiet!' He flapped his stick in her direction. He had become distinctly peremptory since his injuries. Laura waited, wondering if her brother was always going to be this difficult to live with, or whether he would rediscover the sunny side of his nature eventually.

'Why don't we?' he said suddenly.

'Why don't we what?'

'Swap places? I mean you *could* go to Oxford.'

For a moment Laura thought he was suggesting that she should dress up in his clothes, apply a false moustache and enter the portals of Balliol under his name.

Then he went on, 'I know about the entrance exams. I could give you some coaching. I've got all the books here. And we can get you extra tuition if need be. You could try for Somerville in the summer.'

'No, I couldn't possibly . . .' Laura began.

'Why not. You've nothing better to do, have you? I've nothing better to do. It would give us both a goal.'

Laura considered. It was true that she had nothing to do. After the hectic life at the hospital, the leisurely pace at Maple Grange drove her to screaming point. Life was a slow, repetitive cycle of dressing, eating, sleeping and making polite conversation: all activities which she had once found quite satisfying but which now lacked appeal. The high spot of a day might be a dinner party or a walk, or a shopping trip with her cousin Alice, also newly returned from nursing in France. At least Alice had a point to her shopping. She had become attached to one of her patients, a cavalry officer who had lost both legs, and planned to marry him in the autumn.

'He isn't Hugh,' she had told Laura, fending off her cousin's congratulations with bleak honesty. 'No one could replace Hugh. But he needs someone, and I need someone. And he's a man I can be fond of.'

Laura was attached to no one, though there had been plenty of opportunities in France despite the stringency of the regulations which attempted to control contact between the nurses and their patients or the soldiers who passed through the area on their way to and from the Front. There was always a young officer eager to buy a pretty nurse a meal or a drink and many of the girls had been happy to indulge this inclination, though usually in decorous twosomes with a colleague and always with a weather eye out for Matron.

It wasn't respect for the old standards of behaviour that had kept Laura aloof from the flirtations that went on around her. It was simply that after Gérard any other man seemed utterly colourless. In fact nothing had stirred her interest or given her pleasure until she began to read to Oliver and discovered that she *liked* Shakespeare and Chaucer and Wordsworth. She thought she would like to know more.

'Let's try it anyway,' Oliver said into the silence.

'All right.'

A few days later he had a better idea. James Allingham had recently returned to Hindhead and was at a loose end until he took up his place at Oxford in the autumn. He too could participate in the tuition of Laura.

She had last seen James on the night that Gérard died. She wasn't sure what painful memories might be stirred by another meeting. But when he came, she found that she was glad to see him again.

His hair still flopped untidily, he still had his freckles, but his diffident manner that she remembered in the schoolboy, that air of not quite knowing where to put himself, was long gone. James, though quiet, was now competent, confident and she recognized with a small shock of surprise, rather attractive as a man. He smiled and held out his hand, his brown eyes meeting her gaze directly.

'Hullo, Laura.'

'Hullo, James. When did you get back?'

'A few days ago. It's good to see you,' he said with unmistakable sincerity, and Laura had a curious feeling that she was on the brink of some new and happy discovery.

Like an ill-maintained house that collapses when its occupants move out, Margaret's health gave way when the pressure was removed. She had come back to England on a hospital ship, like one of her own patients, at which point her numb fingers and leaden legs were finally diagnosed.

'It's disseminated sclerosis, isn't it?' she said to the doctor who tapped with his rubber hammer at her knees and ran a file over the soles of her feet to test her reflexes. He was an old friend of her father and she knew him well enough to expect frankness from him.

'It may be,' he admitted cautiously.

'It is. I've suspected it for a long time. This is the second recognizable attack, and the most serious, but I've had all sorts of little symptoms that support the diagnosis. Don't worry,' she added. 'I can cope with it.'

Yes, she could cope with it, the doctor thought, as she had coped with everything else. Four years of wartime nursing and the loss of her husband. It was so often these enduring women who developed this particular condition, as if they turned their sorrow on themselves instead of letting it show to the world, or as if fate punished them for pretending to be uncrushable.

'The course that it takes . . .' he began.

'. . . Is unpredictable. I know. At its worst, a wheelchair, speech difficulties, perhaps blindness. If I'm lucky, the occasional attack and long remissions. I'm assuming I'll be lucky.'

'You're a brave girl.' Doctor Morris had seen Margaret grow up. He'd applauded her decision to become a nurse. The

501

illness she had now would finish that side of her life, and he felt it was tragic.

'Doctor,' she said quietly, 'I have nursed wounded men over the past few years against whose injuries my current problems seem positively paltry. I have a lot to be thankful for.'

In May of 1919, Laura, visiting Margaret at her parents' home at Iffley, was shocked by the lines on her face and the streaks of grey in her dark hair. Perhaps they had been there in France but she'd been too wrapped up in the work to notice. Now she realized that Margaret, still under thirty, looked and sounded twenty years older.

Mrs Churchill's 'general' brought tea on a tray, and the soothing ceremonial of pouring it out tided them over the first awkward minutes.

'You are looking very well,' Margaret said.

It was true. Divested of her stark nurse's uniform, elegantly dressed in a cornflower-blue suit of fine wool, Laura seemed to glow. The spoilt golden girl that Margaret could still remember from 1914 had matured into a beautiful young woman, self-assured but no longer proud. The war which had ruined and degraded so many people had refined Laura.

Margaret sipped her tea, though she didn't really want it. If not occupied, her hands were apt to twist themselves unconsciously together, automatically massaging her numb, stiffened fingers.

'I gather you are seeing something of James,' she said.

'Yes, I am. How did you know?' Laura asked, colouring.

'He came to visit me yesterday, being a dutiful brother-in-law. Actually I am maligning James by saying that. He came to visit me, being a friend. He mentioned that you hope to study at Somerville.'

'If I get in,' Laura said. 'Do you think I'm up to it?'

'Of course you are. Why do you ask?'

'I used to think that you saw me as a silly young girl, good for not very much.'

'I did,' said Margaret, frankly. 'I hope I'm a better judge of character nowadays. Now I think you are an intelligent and brave young woman with a bright future ahead of you, if you have the nerve to take it. James will help you.'

'Yes, he will . . .' Laura smiled, remembering her recent encounters with James. 'He's been so good for me. When I'm with him, I believe in myself.'

'I'm glad you have someone,' said Margaret. There had been no hint of reproach in her voice but, conscience-stricken, Laura realized that the woman who faced her did not have anyone, that she had lost her love and might never find another.

'I'm sorry,' she said helplessly.

'Why sorry?'

'Because I'm happy and I have no right to be. So many other people are suffering so much and I've been rescued, and I probably deserve it least of all.'

'There's no virtue in suffering if you don't have to,' said Margaret. 'The war's over. The sooner the damage is mended, the better. Love is a good way to mend damage. *Do* you love James?'

'Oh, yes,' said Laura. She thought for a moment, then went on hesitantly. 'I really do. Not in the same way I loved Gérard. I don't know if you could feel that degree of intensity or anguish more than once in a lifetime. Maybe it wasn't love at all, just the burning of my wings in a candle flame, and if he hadn't died I'd have fallen to earth. . . .' The words conjured an image, unforgettable, of Gérard plummeting as his limbs trod the air, and she shuddered. 'But with James it's as if I've come home. He knows all the bad things about me, he's been there in so many of the bad times in my life, and he still wants me. It makes me feel so *safe*. I must have been stupid before, not to see how well we meshed together. Or perhaps it's that he fits the person I've become.'

'In any case you're happy, and I'm glad,' said Margaret. 'Enjoy it. What's the use of being a survivor, if you don't make the best of it?'

It was true, she thought, with a tinge of bitterness. Laura was a survivor. She seemed to have the knack of picking up the pieces of a broken heart and fitting them back together into an acceptable gift for the next man. There would always be a lover for Laura.

. . . But for Margaret, never again. Her own heart was not to be mended, it had gone out whole to Edward and lay with him in an unmarked grave in Belgium.

But we had our time together. I was so happy then. It will last me a lifetime.

It will have to.

She saw Laura's expression and realized what her own face must be showing. Out of habit she pulled herself together.

'What other news have you? How is Oliver? And Jessie?'

'Oliver and Claire are married. And the most wonderful thing has happened. Did you know he was blinded and the surgeons said there was nothing to be done? Claire wanted to marry him anyway. I thought that was heroic of her. But a couple of months after the injury, his sight came back! Not entirely, one eye is very blurred still, and he has headaches at times and the vision isn't perfect even in the good eye. But it's so much better than blindness! He didn't tell anyone at first, he couldn't believe it would last. But one morning when Claire had just arrived and we were talking, he wandered in with his stick and told her quite casually that he'd never much liked that red dress she was wearing, it clashed with her hair . . . and waited for the penny to drop. You should have seen her face!

'As for Aunt Jessie – oh, Jessie stunned us all by announcing that she was going to marry a Canadian major and go back with him to Montreal! Sly Aunt Jessie, we had no idea. I miss her terribly. . . . But Pa was pole-axed. He thought she was part of the furniture. All he could bleat when she told him was, "But who's going to look after me?" '

'And what did Jessie say to that?' asked Margaret, with a genuine smile breaking out across her face.

'She looked him up and down and said, "You could get married. There are plenty of desperate widows in need of an establishment. Or you could hire somebody, you made enough money out of the war." And that's true,' added Laura soberly. 'He did – though he lost a lot of it when his factory burned down. Did you hear about that? Luckily all the shell-making equipment had been cleared out, or it would have meant an awful explosion. As it was, the damage to the building was total. The police say it was arson but they haven't found out who did it. Someone said they saw a woman hanging about in the area on the night of the fire, but they didn't recognize her. The police asked if there was anyone who would wish to do Pa harm. But I'm afraid he's very unpopular in the district because of profiting from the war, they say, with his share dealings, and especially over the way he sacked workers as soon as the shell orders declined. We wouldn't know where to begin to make a list of people who wish him ill! Oliver treats him with contempt and I'm going to Oxford in the autumn if I get through the exams, so I think he's rather afraid now of being lonely. But of course he won't show it. And I have to say he deserves it.'

When Laura had gone, Margaret picked up the letter that she had been reading when the visitor was announced. A former patient of hers had sent her a handwritten copy of a poem by his friend and fellow-officer Siegfried Sassoon. It was to be published officially as part of a collection of his poems, later in the year. Margaret turned again to 'Aftermath', with its bitter recognition of the speed with which the world was putting away the memories of a four-year nightmare, and she re-read the closing lines.

> 'Have you forgotten yet?
> Look up, and swear by the green of the spring
>   that you'll never forget.'

Margaret had been wishing, earlier, that she could have shared the poem with Edward, with whom she had shared so much poetry in the past. Now she found that she could imagine his voice, reading the lines, and it was like having him in the room with her.

At the Menin gate in Ypres, in the summer of 1930, a crowd began to gather in the evening sunlight.

The remnants of the walls flanking the Menin road under which soldiers had sheltered from the artillery barrages were still in place, but the old gateway with its flanking stone lions had been replaced by an imposing edifice with a wide arch spanning the road. One of the lions still topped the monument, its face turned towards the battlefields. On all the white stone slabs of the gate's uprights, line upon line, were engraved the names of those British soldiers who had died in the Ypres salient and who had no known grave. Already it was a place of pilgrimage for the people who mourned their loss.

A policeman stopped the traffic and two men of the Ypres Fire Service, holding trumpets, walked to the centre of the road. A hush fell on the assembled crowd.

A woman with streaks of grey in her dark hair and a small, golden-headed boy watched, hand-in-hand, while the trumpeters sounded the Last Post. As the echoing notes faded away, there was a self-conscious spattering of applause from those who had come for the spectacle. Others with a more personal interest in the engraved names were crying unashamedly.

When the trumpeters had gone and the spectators were dispersing, the woman approached one of the stone uprights, taking a withered posy out of her bag, very carefully because it was fragile and her hands were clumsy. The satin ribbon which tied the stems together had once been crimson but was faded almost to brown and the colours of the crumbling flowers were barely identifiable.

'I haven't forgotten, Edward. By the green of the spring,' she said softly. She stooped to lay her offering among the fresh wreaths and sheaves of flowers clustered at the foot of the wall, under one of the slabs which recorded the fallen of the Queen's Royal West Surrey Regiment.

'What are those, Aunt Margaret?' said the boy, aware of a solemn atmosphere but too young to understand the significance of the occasion.

'Only a few dried flowers,' said Margaret Allingham to James and Laura's son Edward. 'But precious to me, and that is why I gave them.'

She turned away from her bridal bouquet.

THE END

THE VILLAGE
by Sarah Shears

Part one of the Fairfields Chronicles

Set in the heart of the Kent countryside and spanning the
period from the turn of the century to the end of the Great
War, THE VILLAGE introduces us to the inhabitants of
Fairfields Village, whose lives and loves become irrevocably
entwined over the years. Richly evocative of Edwardian
village life – from the brutal poverty of the slum dwellings
of Richmond Row, to the grand splendour of Marston Park –
this superb saga, with its wonderful cast of characters, depicts
the changing pattern of English country life, portrayed by one
of our best-loved novelists.

0 553 40161 7

SOLO
by Jill Mansell

The day Tessa sat down and ate four banana sandwiches was the day she realized she was pregnant. For twenty-seven years she had hated bananas with a vengeance.

When Tessa Duvall, a struggling artist, reluctantly agreed to accompany her best friend Holly to a party at the elegant Charrington Grange Hotel, she had every intention of sneaking off early. For parties full of strangers bored the knickers off Tessa and this one proved to be no exception – until she encountered Ross Monahan, whose wicked reputation was as high profile as the hotel he owned and ran with such panache. But whilst Holly set about ensnaring his reluctant brother Max, Tessa simply accepted Ross for what he was, a sensational one-night stand . . . until she realized, weeks later, that one-night stands can have far-reaching consequences. Spirited and independent, Tessa determined to cope with her pregnancy – by going solo. But Ross, unaccustomed to being rejected, had other plans.

0 553 40360 5

A SPARROW DOESN'T FALL
by June Francis

For young Flora Cooke the misery of the Second World War and the hardship it brings is both real and unrelenting. When her husband Tom is reported missing, presumed dead, Flora is left to raise her family alone amidst the ruins of war-torn Liverpool.

As she struggles to come to terms with the tragic news, Flora attracts the attention of two very different men. One offers security whilst the other offers the prospect of a new life in California. Both promise her love.

But it takes another great tragedy before Flora finally listens to the promptings of her heart and seizes a second chance at the happiness that has for so long eluded her.

0 553 40364 8

TO HEAR A NIGHTINGALE
by Charlotte Bingham

'A delightful novel . . . pulsating with vitality and deeply felt emotions. I found myself with tears in my eyes on one page and laughing out loud on another'

Sunday Express

Brought up in smalltown America by a grandmother who despises her, Cassie McGann's childhood is one of misery and rejection. Fleeing to New York she falls in love with handsome Irish racehorse trainer, Tyrone Rosse, and when he marries her and takes her back to Claremore, his tumbledown mansion in Ireland, it looks as if she has found happiness at last.

Passionately in love as she is, Cassie finds the all-male world of horses and racing rather lonely. There is much for her to learn, not least about the man she has married. Tyrone's success depends heavily on the whims of the rich owners, men – and women – who can be very demanding. And Cassie must learn to endure the enmity of one in particular, who comes out of her buried past determined to destroy her.

When tragedy strikes, it seems that Cassie must once again face rejection and lose her hard-won security. But although the chances of success are slim and the cost in personal happiness considerable, she will not give in, and fights against all odds to survive in a world closed against her.

0 553 17635 8

BELGRAVIA

by Charlotte Bingham

'The story takes place during a London Season. Georgiana is poor, posh and very beautiful. Jennifer is rich, middle-class and very fat. They are both, as are all their contemporaries, in search of a marriage that will enrich or ennoble them. But *Belgravia* is much more than a romantic comedy. It's a kind of cross between *Vile Bodies* and *Love in a Cold Climate* – a very funny book, full of eccentric characters'

Books and Bookmen

'Marvellous . . . a very accomplished novel'

Jilly Cooper

'You'll love it'

Sunday Times

0 553 40427 X